Her desire for vengeance was an unwavering flame

But even if Krysty had known beyond doubt her bullet would split that dark-haired skull, she wouldn't have taken the shot. Yes, the captain had to die. She had to kill him, or at least be the cause of his death even if her finger didn't pull the trigger or her hand plunge the blade.

But he was just one among many. A significant one, but merely one. To claim his life would risk throwing her life away—with her friends still unrescued and the bulk of her blood debt unpaid.

Krysty wouldn't do that.

So she watched them drive off out of sight, unmolested. Intuition told her they were heading back to the massacre site, to the rim above Ryan's unmarked resting place a mile toward the center of the earth. Why they might be bound there she couldn't say. It didn't matter, and speculation was no part of her nature in any event. She let all thought of whys and wherefores slip from her mind.

There could be only her quest. Worry, fear, anticipation—these could only weaken the resolve Krysty needed to keep her weary legs driving her relentlessly on.

JAMES AXLER

DEATH LANDS®

Vengeance Trail

A GOLD EAGLE BOOK FROM

W☉RLDWIDE®

TORONTO • NEW YORK • LONDON
AMSTERDAM • PARIS • SYDNEY • HAMBURG
STOCKHOLM • ATHENS • TOKYO • MILAN
MADRID • WARSAW • BUDAPEST • AUCKLAND

First edition June 2005

ISBN 0-373-62580-4

VENGEANCE TRAIL

Printed in U.S.A.

Like to the Pontick sea,
Whose icy current and compulsive course
Ne'er feels retiring ebb, but keeps due on
To the Propontic and the Hellspont,
Even so my bloody thoughts, with violent pace,
Shall ne'er look back, ne'er ebb to humble love,
Till that a capable and wide revenge
Swallow them up.

—William Shakespeare,
Othello, III, iv, 454

THE DEATHLANDS SAGA

This world is their legacy, a world born in the violent nuclear spasm of 2001 that was the bitter outcome of a struggle for global dominance.

There is no real escape from this shockscape where life always hangs in the balance, vulnerable to newly demonic nature, barbarism, lawlessness.

But they are the warrior survivalists, and they endure—in the way of the lion, the hawk and the tiger, true to nature's heart despite its ruination.

Ryan Cawdor: The privileged son of an East Coast baron. Acquainted with betrayal from a tender age, he is a master of the hard realities.

Krysty Wroth: Harmony ville's own Titian-haired beauty, a woman with the strength of tempered steel. Her premonitions and Gaia powers have been fostered by her Mother Sonja.

J. B. Dix, the Armorer: Weapons master and Ryan's close ally, he, too, honed his skills traversing the Deathlands with the legendary Trader.

Doctor Theophilus Tanner: Torn from his family and a gentler life in 1896, Doc has been thrown into a future he couldn't have imagined.

Dr. Mildred Wyeth: Her father was killed by the Ku Klux Klan, but her fate is not much lighter. Restored from predark cryogenic suspension, she brings twentieth-century healing skills to a nightmare.

Jak Lauren: A true child of the wastelands, reared on adversity, loss and danger, the albino teenager is a fierce fighter and loyal friend.

Dean Cawdor: Ryan's young son by Sharona accepts the only world he knows, and yet he is the seedling bearing the promise of tomorrow.

In a world where all was lost, they are humanity's last hope....

Chapter One

J. B. Dix chewed a dust-dry blade of buffalo grass and leaned back against the wag, its sun-heated metal pinging as it cooled in the breeze. Beneath the low-tipped brim of his fedora, he watched a little girl named Sallee, scabbed legs splayed in the dust by the track, as she played with a flop-eared, vaguely humanoid bundle of rags.

"What do you reckon that thing is, anyway, Jak?" he asked his companion, who perched on the wag's hood walking a short leaf-bladed throwing knife along the backs of his bone-white fingers. "Rabbit or mutie?"

Jak Lauren flicked his keen ruby toward the rags and laughed. He was scarcely more than a child himself, despite a veteran's scars. His skin was chalk white, and his long hair, wind-whipped around his shoulders, was the color of fresh-fallen snow.

"Mutie," he said.

The sky's blue skin was bare of clouds. The layers of earth defining the walls and pinnacles of the Big Ditch, the old Grand Canyon, glowed as though lit from within the Earth itself in bands of colors—yellow, red, burnt-orange—muted but so rich they seemed to vibrate. The sun that brought out all that glory shone down on the desert above the great canyon like a laser beam, and struck those below with the impact of heat of molten steel. But the tall, statuesque redheaded woman in the jumpsuit and blue cowboy boots didn't mind. It was the sort of day that Krysty Wroth loved most. The kind of day where you didn't have to be an initiate of Gaia, as she was, to find the beauty hidden in the devastation that was the Deathlands.

She let her green eyes slide from her two friends, to the caravan of a dozen battered wags parked by the edge of the Big Ditch with their engines cooling, while several people labored to change a flat tire, on to Doc Tanner, standing by offering unsolicited advice to Mildred Wyeth as she checked the dressings on the stump of a woman's shin. A diamondback had bitten her on the ankle three days before, just outside the ville of Ten Mile, and her own husband had chopped off her leg with an ax to keep the venom from spreading.

Nothing was dampening the travelers' spirits, though. They were bound from the fringes of the Deathlands proper, away to the east across the Rocks, to the fledgling ville of New Tulsa, where some of their kin had already begun to carve a living out of the land. The land wasn't much less desolate than what surrounded them, although better watered by rain. But that very land, sere tan land dotted with cactus and hardly less unfriendly scrub, looked like Paradise to a folk accustomed to rains of acid and skies of murk.

And that sky of pure, open blue, with only a few clouds as white and innocent as baby lambs, affected them like some kind of happy drug: jolt without the edge. They laughed and chattered like kids and even sang. Some just wandered aimlessly, gazing around themselves in wonder.

"I'm going into the bushes for a bit," Krysty called to her friends, "to answer the call."

Ryan Cawdor, her lover, acknowledged her with a wave of his hand. He stood with his back to her on the rim of the precipice, the wind ruffling his shaggy black curls and gazed out and down into the giant cut in the earth's flesh with his lone eye. A single dark shape wheeled out over that emptiness and the strange land forms striped with muted colors— ochre, orange, buff—at the level of the small party of humans and their machines perched perilously on the rim. From the fingerlike tips on the wings, Krysty was satisfied it was an eagle, not a screamwing.

No threat. Having duly notified her companions, she went off into the scrub to tend to her affairs. For all the utter naturalness of such functions, Krysty had been raised to be modest.

She didn't hear the raiders until they were right upon them. No one did. The wind's unceasing whistle and mutter masked the sound of engines coming fast from the east until the wags they propelled were braking to a stop alongside the halted caravan in a swirl of dust.

Suddenly men were leaping off half a dozen wags, longblasters in their hands. Krysty caught a flashing impression they all wore olive or camouflage, military-style.

Several travelers cried out in fear. Kids squealed and ran to parents frozen by shock. By reflex, Ryan spun, bringing his Steyr sniper rifle to his cheek.

Two of the intruders' wags were pickups with M-249 machine guns mounted on welded-together pintles behind the cabs. One MG snarled a burst. Krysty saw dust spout off Ryan's coat.

He fell from sight, straight into the Big Ditch.

A woman broke shrieking toward the brush with a toddler in her arms. Several longblasters cracked, including at least one on full-auto. Mother and child fell kicking in a whirl of dust and bloodied rags. Their cries subsided into bubbling sobs. Another burst stilled them.

Hidden behind scrub and a rise in the earth around the roots of a mesquite bush, Krysty felt as if she had been frozen into a block of amber like a mosquito Ryan had once shown her in some half-destroyed museum. Her hair, possessed of its own mobility and nerve-endings, flattened to her skull and neck.

Her companions still in the open—J.B., Mildred, Jak and Doc—stood just as still, hands raised. She felt a flash of rage that they hadn't fought as Ryan had tried to do, but she stifled the thought in the sure knowledge that had they done so they, too, would be staring at the sky right now.

A coldheart stepped down from the cab of wag whose gunner had downed Ryan. Though he wore no insignia he was clearly the man in charge. He was tall, broad-shouldered, long-limbed, slim waisted. His clean-shaved face was as beautiful as a statue's, smooth and unscarred, the rich warm brown of a light-skinned black man's. His hair, curly bronzed brown, was cut short on top, though not buzzed. In back it was caught into a long braid at the nape and thrown forward over the right shoulder of the steel breastplate he wore over his camouflage blouse. A well-maintained 9 mm Heckler & Koch blaster rode in a combat holster at his right hip. Command presence radiated from his face and posture, the way the light and heat of the sun radiated from his mirror-polished armor.

He shook his head and sighed. "All right. Let's get this done. Line them up for inspection."

The surviving travelers, Krysty's companions among them, had their hands on their heads, except for mothers with children too small to know what was going on. These kept one hand on the head while the other clasped the youngsters to their skirts. The coldhearts herded them into a line at the edge of the clearing in the scrub near the rim, well away from the canyon itself. It seemed the raiders wanted no part of that long drop.

Other raiders had clambered onto a couple of the travelers' wags and began pitching out their possessions. These were few and mostly valuable. Some of the travelers had taken a piece or two of furniture with them, but these were the exception. There was plenty of nonperishable stuff left over from the megacull, lots more than there were people to use it. Bulky items like chairs and chests of drawers weren't worth dragging across the Deathlands unless they had powerful sentimental value. Otherwise the travelers' wags contained tools, clothes, meds, food, water, even some weapons. All stuff needed for survival in their new homes and, for that matter, on the long and perilous journey to get there. All, with the possible exception of clothing, commanding good value in trade.

The coldhearts didn't seem to care. They just pitched whatever was on the wags they selected into the dust.

"Some guards you turned out to be," spit Kurtiz, a young man with shaggy light brown hair and beard prematurely shot with gray, whose front two incisors were missing. It gave his voice a sort of lisp. He was straw boss of the travelers' train, the man who actually got things done. He was able at his job and generally quiet—until now.

J. B. shrugged. A sec man had already relieved him of his M-4000 shotgun and was searching him for weapons.

"Friend," the Armorer said, "you can't argue with a leveled blaster."

"*Can* argue," Jak said with a bitter snarl as a coldheart took his .357 Magnum Colt Python and a collection of throwing knives. "Not win."

J.B. had sounded casual, but Krysty saw the way a muscle

twitched at the hinge of his jaw. She knew then as if she felt it herself the terrible void he had to be feeling, and what it was costing him not to so much as look at the place from which his friend had dropped off the earth. He had been best friend and comrade in arms to Ryan Cawdor for years before either man ever met Krysty Wroth. And even though Krysty was Ryan's mate and soulbond, it was only because she herself had shared mortal danger and hardship with him that their own kindredship was as close as that between the two blood brothers.

Beside him, Jak vibrated with fury, lips skinned back from his teeth. But he kept his hands knotted in the snow-colored hair at his nape. Doc gazed into nothingness. Mildred was as impassive as a stone statue, but her eyes were bloodshot. Krysty knew that meant she was in the grip of fury every scrap as hard to control as Jak's.

"The next one who gets chilled," rasped a short, wide white man wearing a Kevlar coals coop helmet with sergeant's chevrons painted on the front. His face looked as if it had been cut out of granite with a none-too-deftly wielded geologist's pick.

The tall handsome sec chief stalked along the line of quaking backs. As he passed some he tapped lightly on shoulders. Those so indicated were yanked from the line by the coldhearts and ramrodded toward a stakebed truck that had earlier been full of raiders. When Kurtiz was chosen, he suddenly shook off the soldiers holding his arms, as if the awful implication of the process had suddenly struck home.

"Nukeblast it, you can't—" he began.

The crack of a longblaster put a premature period to his exclamation. He dropped as if the long shabby coat he wore were suddenly untenanted. The hole the 5.56 mm bullet had made in his homespun shirt on its way to drill clean through the heart wasn't visible from where Krysty crouched.

The short sergeant kept his M-16 leveled from his waist. "Next one gives any shit gets bursted in the belly," he said. His voice was as rough as lava rock, and as hard and cutting.

When he came to the companions, the sec chief selected J. B. and Jak without hesitation, paused at Doc, then passed him by to select Mildred. Mildred seemed to hang back as soldiers grabbed her arms. J.B. caught her eye and shook his head all but imperceptibly.

She bowed her head and went where they took her. In the Deathlands, survival wasn't optional. The time to go down fighting had passed. There was no fool like a dead one, as Trader used to say.

The ones chosen were fit-looking men and women without children, a few teenaged boys and girls, twenty-two or -three in all. Many still stood shivering despite the warmth of the sun, waiting with their hands on their heads.

As the implication of their being left unselected sank in, they began to cry and plead despite the example made of their trail boss. Then again, it now made little difference, and they knew it.

A stout figure whose repetitively chinned face was flanked by great winging gray side-whiskers stepped forward from the ranks of those not chosen. Sweat poured down in streams from the brim of his battered leather top hat. This was Elliot, called Hizzoner, by himself anyway, self-proclaimed mayor of the travelers' settlement-to-be. As to what his precise contribution was to the welfare of the train to justify his claims of leadership, his two knuckle-dragging bodyguards, Amos and Bub, discouraged the others from asking impertinent questions.

"Now, just a minute here, boys," he said, "let's not be too hasty here. Happens I'm the leader of this here little procession across the wasteland."

Banner, the sergeant, who happened to be nearby, backhanded him across the face with casually brutal force. The plump self-proclaimed mayor measured his none-too-considerable length in the dust.

"Triple-stupe," a sec man muttered, prodding the selected captives into the bed of a wag. "Ain't figgered out what he *was* don't mean shit to a tree, now."

With surprising agility, Elliot rolled to his knees, clasped his hands prayerfully and commenced to plead. "No, you can't do this! I can help your baron. I'm a man who unnerstands the way of the world!"

The raiders wordlessly began to line up behind the weeping, imploring rejects.

Elliot reached back and grabbed a nine-year-old girl by a bony grubby wrist, dragging her forward. She was clad in a torn smock that was all over stains in shades of yellow and brown.

"Take my little girl—do with her what you will," he blubbered. "She'll please you up right. Trained her proper, myself!"

One of the mothers of the other children spoke up. "They're gonna take what they want anyway, Elliot, you damn fool," she said bitterly. "They got the blasters. Now stop your sniveling and die like a man!"

"Wait! Amos, Bub! Help me! Ya gotta!"

His two heavyweight henchmen evaded his eyes as they took their places in the wags. Banner cuffed the politician on the side of his head. "Back in line, asshole. Make this messy for us, we shoot you in the belly and just leave you."

"'Twas brillig, and the slithy toves…'" Doc began to recite loudly as the weeping would-be mayor crawled back into line. His eyes, aged beyond his years as much by the horrors of being snatched from his family and hurled through time as by the desperate sights they had witnessed in the Deathlands, had lost all hint of focus.

The commanding coldheart halted with one boot up in the cab of his wag. His men had already secured the travelers' wags and begun firing up their engines. He turned his head and stared at Doc.

"What did you say?"

"'All mimsy were the borogroves—'"

"'And the mome raths outgrabe,'" the coldheart officer finished, striding back to him. "You know something of the classics, then, old man. Can you read?"

"Read, yes," Doc responded, as though replaying to a voice from beyond the moon. "Read, breed, if you prick me do I not bleed?"

"Nuke-sucking oldie's mad as Fire Day," the sergeant said. "Do him with the others."

"No, Sergeant Banner," the sec chief said. "The General will want this one."

The sergeant scowled. "It's strong hands and backs we need to fix the track—"

The sec chief tossed him a single look. His eyes were pale brown and as clear as new glass.

"Yes, Captain Helton, sir," the blocky sec man said briskly. He seized Doc's arm and yanked him out of line. "Come on, then, you crazy old shit. General's got his little hobbies."

For a moment no one breathed. The coldhearts were clearly not used to anything but instant obedience to their commands, nor slow to let their blasters enforce them. Surely if Doc continued raving; the youthful captain would lose patience and allow Banner to ice him with the others who'd been deemed useless.

But since it no longer required the shelter of lunacy from the imminence of certain death, Doc's rational mind reasserted itself. He lowered his hands—Banner's finger never so much as twitched on the trigger—and shot his frayed cuffs. "Lead on, my good fellow," he said to the sergeant.

As the old man was dragged toward the wags, Krysty felt tension flow out of her muscles. The future was a void a million times greater than all the Big Ditch and then some. But on some level below thought she wouldn't watch another of her companions—the only family she had left to her—die before her eyes. Even if it meant her own death.

Of course, her future was empty without Ryan. But she had duties: as a friend, as mate to the companion's fallen leader, she couldn't allow herself to die.

Yet.

The children wailed and sobbed and clutched their mothers' skirts. The mothers, Deathlands women, tousled their children's hair, bit back their own tears and murmured reassurances they knew were lies. One little girl was trying to break from the line, screaming and crying and tugging at her mother's hand. The sec chief frowned. He followed the direction her free hand was stretching in. He walked to where the small rag rabbit—or mutie—lay at the bash of a clump of saltbush; picked it up, brought it to the little girl, knelt and handed it gravely to her. She took it, suddenly quiet, her grimy cheeks scoured by her tears. He smoothed the dark hair on her head, stood, pivoted on his heel and walked back to his wag.

As he passed Banner, he nodded once.

The sergeant barked a command. The machine gun that

had killed Ryan and its mate on a second raider wag snarled. The bullets raked the line of rejects carefully between two and three feet off the ground, to take adults in legs or bellies and kids in heads and chests, anchoring all neatly in place. Most screaming and thrashing in agony, a fortunate few lifeless-limp, the unarmed travelers went down in the dust.

The firing stopped. Arcs of flying brass empties flashed in the sunlight to fall with an almost musical tinkle to the hard-pan. The moaning of the wind was joined by the shrieks of the injured.

Banner spoke again. Again the machine guns ripped the bodies, those that stirred and those that didn't. It seemed the marauders had bullets to burn. Finally the sergeant walked along the line of now-motionless travelers, firing a handful of single shots from his longblaster. Then he turned and joined his comrades in the wags.

One of the raiders who had come in the stakebed truck that now contained the caravan's survivors took a frag gren from his web gear, pulled the pin and let the safety lever fly free, then tossed the bomb under the broken-down wag that had caused the caravan to halt. He turned and walked away without waiting to watch the result. The gren went off with a crack muffled by the wag's bulk.

The sec man who'd thrown the gren joined his comrades who were crammed into the two travelers' wags they had emptied. Engines growled. The convoy rolled off along the bare-earth track, to the west, raising roostertails of khaki dust.

The derelict wag's gasoline tank, ruptured by the blast, caught fire with a whump and billow of yellow flames. The vehicle began to burn ferociously, puking black smoke into a sky that was already beginning to mask its clean blue face with clouds.

Krysty emerged from her hiding place. Her joints ached from maintaining the unnatural position she'd been forced to endure. Red ants had crawled up her legs inside her jumpsuit and bitten her shin and thigh. Their venom made the tiny wounds pang like stabs. She ignored all.

She walked with the deliberation of a drunk to the edge of the precipice, where Ryan had stood, where last she had seen her lover. Her beautiful high-cheekboned face was set like stone. She looked down, half fearing what she would see.

There was nothing. The slope angled sharply down for perhaps forty yards, pitched over a cluster of granite boulders, which resisted erosion better than the prevalent sandstone, and straight down in a sheer fall to the floor a mile below. Ryan's body wasn't in sight. Presumably it was way down at the bottom, hidden by sheer height.

She turned away, looking over the bodies of their former traveling companions: Kurtiz, Elane, Natty and the rest. The little girl Sallee lay facedown, with her toy inches from her outflung fingers, its grime glistening with her blood.

Moving as if through water and all her limbs were lead, Krysty picked through the items the coldhearts had so contemptuously pitched into heaps on the ground. She needed what supplies she could carry: food, water, meds. Even something extra for barter.

She wouldn't just lie down and die. She would follow the men who had murdered Ryan and the travelers and kidnapped her friends. She would kill them all, and free her friends.

Of course, she was but one woman, alone in the wasteland, afoot in pursuit of wags. And all the supplies she could lift, as strong as she was, would be quickly exhausted in this waste. Particularly water.

It meant nothing to her. Nothing at all. She would follow her vengeance trail to the end, whatever it would take.

She set out along the track the wags had taken. She had no hope, but hate was enough. Concern for herself was no part of the picture.

She was dead already. Inside.

SOMEWHERE AT THE BOTTOM of a deep well of darkness and misery, Ryan stirred.

It felt to him as if the skin of his chest was a big bag wrapped around forty pounds of busted glass. With every laboring breath he drew, it felt as if a thousand jagged points stabbed and rasped at his raw nerve endings.

Worse, as he became aware again, was that he could hear his breathing. Not just the ragged in and out of exhalation that was always with you whether you paid it mind or not, but a nasty wet slurping noise combined with a hiss. And it was hard to breathe—bastard hard.

Sucking chest wound, he realized. So-called, one of his father's healers had told him back home in Front Royal long ago, because it really sucked if you got one.

And unless you got pretty quick attention, so did your chances of living.

Krysty! The name went off like ten pounds of smokeless powder off a blasting cap in his mind. She and the companions hadn't come to his aid, which meant they weren't able to.

For a moment, in the damp, dark misery of his mind and body, he fought the clammy jaws of panic. He was hurt bad and alone.

He tried one of the deep-breathing exercises Krysty had taught him to calm himself and banish the terror that threat-

ened to rob him of the last remnants of his selfhood, his man-
hood, and whatever he might laughingly call hope, sucking
the air way down with his abdominal muscles.

It worked, too. Not because supercharging his system with
oxygen had its usual soothing effect on the system. But because it felt as if some giant mutie bastard had plunged a
twenty-inch saw into his flat belly and was sawing for all he
was worth.

Whatever else you could say about it, it took his mind off
feeling sorry for himself.

His eye opened. It was resisted by some kind of thick
gumminess, but the jolt of white-hot agony that racked his
being, as he breathed in, did the trick.

The first thing he saw was lots of nothing much: blue dimness as far as his eye could see. After a moment he noticed it
deepened in the direction the not-so-gentle pull of gravity was
telling him was downward, was banded in various shades
and hues, was molded into cone and curtain shapes.

He was lying on the very lip of the Big Ditch itself, with
his outflung right hand, fingers tingling as though with crawling fire as circulation restored by some unnoticed movement
returned feeling to them, hanging over a mile of space.

He rolled his eye down. The right side of his face was
pressed to a rough rock surface. The tarry looking pool spread
around it tended to confirm his suspicion that what had glued
his eyelid shut was his own blood, spilled in a copious quantity.

He rolled the eye up. A granite outcrop, almost black in
the dusk, hunched over him like a leering gargoyle. He could
only guess that after being shot—a remembered flash of pain
in his chest, of spinning dizzily into blackness vaster by far
than the Grand Canyon—he had tumbled down the steep, but

not sheer, slope and bounced over that last humpback boulder to come flopping to a stop on a hard ledge of rock.

Needless to say, it had busted hell out of him. Needless to say, it was nothing compared to what would have happened had he actually gone over.

But it wasn't going to matter a bent, spent shell case if he couldn't do something for himself and fast. He'd suffocate if the wound wasn't tended to. He knew what had to be done: apply what Mildred called an "occlusive dressing," a sort of valve that would flap shut and seal the hole when he inhaled, but relax and expel air when he breathed out. It wasn't all that complex an operation, and anything reasonably airtight would do for a patch. Nuke it, he even had the proper material for the job tucked away in one of his pockets.

The problem was, could he even get to it, or use it if he could?

Then he heard, above the mocking whistle of the wind and the thin shrill cry of a redtailed hawk on the hunt, the tiniest scrape of something moving on stone. And he realized that the injuries he already had might turn out to be the least of his problems.

He wasn't alone.

Having another living being find you helpless in the Deathlands was an almost automatic death sentence. Even if that being walked on two legs like a human being. Mebbe worst if it *was* a human being. Ryan had known plenty humans, no few of them barons or their sec men, who gave away nothing to stickies when it came to rapacious cruelty.

He took stock of his resources. He still had all the weapons he could want. He could feel the familiar weight of the Steyr lying across his left leg, the big broad-bladed panga in its sheath on his hip. Even his SIG-Sauer with the built-in suppresser—he reckoned that was the hard object prodding a busted-end rib around in him every time he fought down a breath. He had feeling back in his right hand, even if it *was* feeling like it was being held in a fire, and could move his fingers.

But his left wasn't responding. A node of unusually savage ache in the giant throb of pain that was his being suggested he might have a busted clavicle on that side. Which meant he could count that arm completely out. No force of his will would get the limb to so much as move. It just mechanically couldn't happen, any more than the toughest man could walk with a broken pelvis.

He looked around, hoping his stalker would miss the motion of his eyeball in the gloom. *Stalkers.* That was the first thing he saw. Shapes, strangely hunched, gathered around him. He could make out no detail in the gloom. They were small, no more than three feet high, max. Not that it mattered. A three-legged coyote pup could put him on the last train west in his current condition.

A shape loomed over him. He could make out the glint of moisture on big staring nightmare eyes, big teeth gleaming pale behind animal lips. He tried to roll away. His body refused to obey. He tried to bring his right arm up to ward off the monster. It didn't work. All he could do was turn his head frantically from side to side on his neck and make animal sounds, half-panic, half-defiant fury, deep in this throat.

A small paw stretched out over him.

Blackness took him.

Chapter Two

"Robbed!" howled the tall man with the painted ax-blade face. "*Cheated!* All our days of scouting and waiting gone for nothing."

Red Wolf paused dramatically, glaring out from below the wolf's head he wore like a cap over his own, with the rest of the pelt hanging down his broad bronze back. He was a one-time war leader of the Cheyenne from the Medicine Bow country. Or so he said. The multimegaton pasting that had taken out the Warren missile complex had left that very part of southern Wyoming and northern Colorado a howling wasteland as virulent as anything the Midwest boasted.

Not that anyone was going to go up there and check. He had proved time and again that his heart was as cold as the coldest, his case as hard as the hardest, and justified his role, not just as a member of Chato's outlaw horde, but one of its leaders. If he wanted to dress in dead animal parts and various colors of paint, nobody was going to challenge him—who wasn't ready to chill or be chilled on the spot, anyway. Chato himself was an Indian, though much smaller and with quieter tastes.

The problem with Red Wolf wasn't what he claimed to be. The problem was that he *was* a bone outlaw, a seething vessel of barely repressed murder at the best of times, and he was taking the loss of the travelers even harder than the rest of what passed for Chato's command council.

The other eight stared at him from the circle, where they squatted in the flickering feeble light from a fire of dried brush scraped together in the center of the cave. They looked lean, predatory and expectant. They also looked as if they were trying desperately not to bust down and cough their lights out. The cave etched into the sandstone bluff by wind and water and maybe, just maybe, improved by the hands of similar bands of desperados of ages past, was cool even in the heat of summer, which this wasn't. But there was no smoke-hole, much less a chimney. Consequently a fogbank of nasty sage-colored smoke that went up the nostrils and down the throat like prickleburrs hung from a height of two feet off the floor to somewhere near the irregular arch of ceiling above.

"Not much we can do about it, *pinche*," muttered El Gancho, a bandit from northern Mex. He was a squat, leering man with a bad eye and a worse mustache.

"But we know who to blame," the tall Indian chiller said, eyes glittering like obsidian chips. Chato felt what had seemed like a fluttering of butterflies in his belly turn into a minor temblor.

"Easy now, friend," said ginger-bearded Ironhead Johnson. He was a woods-running coldheart originally from up on the Musselshell, and more recently from Taos and parts south, who had headed west and hooked up with Chato's growing band when the upper Grandee valley got too hot for him. He had been shot in the head on at least four occasions, with no more effect than minor deteriorations of personality and impulse control, neither of which had been notable before. One bullet scar was a white pucker over the inside end of his right eyebrow, like an off-center third eye. "Spilled blood can't go back in the body."

"No?" Red Wolf smiled like his namesake. "At least we

can spill the blood of the one who is responsible. The one who brought us together, the one who held us back from raiding ranches and villes. The one who said there was no point alerting potential targets before we'd got at least one fat score."

He was glaring straight at Chato now. Chato felt sweat run down his face. The yellow headband that restrained his own heavy black hair was already soaked.

"Who?" Red Wolf demanded, voice rising, with a crazy edge to it. "Who? I know who. I'll *tell* you who. I'll—"

The crash of a shotgun blast in the close confines seemed to implode Chato's head even as the flash from a cutdown muzzle dazzled his eyes. Red Wolf staggered back as a buck-and-ball load—four chunks of double-ought buck and a .72-caliber lead ball—took him about the short ribs on the right side. Blood, flesh and chunks of yellow-gleaming bone were blasted free.

Red Wolf was a strong man all the way through. He staggered back only two steps, doubling over, grabbing at his ruined midsection. He raised his head for the charge from the second barrel to shatter his face like a clay shitpot. He measured his length backward on the sandstone, arms outflung, the last reflex spasms of his heart pumping out great gushes of blood that was black in the firelight and steamed like lava.

Chato became aware that he had screamed. Thankfully no one had heard him. No one was hearing anything at all but a loud ringing and echoes of the enormous roars.

Len Hogan allowed his Izhmash scattergun to tip forward from where recoil had sent it pointing toward the low ceiling. Smoke seeped from the muzzle, and then from the breech as he cracked it open to eject two red plastic-hulled empties and feed in a couple more from a pocket of his colors, the grime-blackened sleeveless denim jacket he wore as a vest.

Shave-headed, taller even than Red Wolf had been even before partial decapitation, and as lean as a gallows pole with an incisor missing from a mostly lipless mouth framed by a black handlebar mustache, he had been thrown out of the Satan's Slaves biker gang for unpredictable violence and brutality. Actually, his erstwhile buds had been intent on lynching him, but he proved to be better than they were at tracking.

He was one of the cooler heads on Chato's executive council.

"Enough of that owl-screech shit." The ringing had subsided enough for Chato to hear him speak. He snapped the shotgun action closed with the flick of a massive wrist enclosed in a studded leather bracer. The rest of the group was busy surreptitiously trying to sidle even farther away from him than they'd been sitting before. Owing to certain peculiar rituals of the northwest bike gangs, the giant coldheart smelled like a chop-shop shitter with backed-up plumbing. "Who, your ass. Talk don't load no mags."

Chato made himself relax. At least a little. Otherwise he was going to lose it here and now, and that would put him in a world of hurt. Hogan had not, he knew, killed Red Wolf, because Red Wolf was stirring up rebellion against Chato. Hogan did it because he liked to kill people, and this was the first handy excuse he'd been presented for some time.

And that, in a spent casing, was pretty much the problem staring him in the face.

A White Mountain Apache by birth and upbringing, Chato was in many ways an actual genius. For example, taking best advantage of the coldhearts' natural propensities for speed and sneakiness, he'd crafted the scouting system that had passed the word of the caravan's capture back to headquarters, by means of a relay of flashing mirrors, within hours of it going down.

He could talk a snake into paying in advance for a year's tap dancing lessons. He was a triple-wizard organizer. He could spin grand schemes all day long, and all night, too, if the Taos Lightning held out.

And there, unfortunately, his military ability screeched to a brake-burning halt. Right on the edge of the Big Ditch.

He was first off a coward. It wasn't just physical cowardice, but really physical cowardice, physiological reactions to threat over which he had utterly no control. The very prospect of physical danger would induce a terrible quaking that started in his belly and moved outward till the shaking threatened to jar loose one molecule from another. An immediate threat simply launched him in uncontrolled flight, assisted by explosive voiding of the bowels.

Red Wolf's fury had already set Chato to shaking. It was only a stroke of bastard luck that Hogan chilled him before his threat-level reached Chato's voiding stage.

That was manageable. Lots of great war leaders have been more than a little nervous in the service.

The other problem was more serious. He had no clue how to actually fight.

All his life, it seemed, he had been adept at talking his way out of trouble. As an orphaned runt, small even by Apache standards, he'd had ample opportunity to acquire the gift growing up. When exiled by vengeful tribal fellows on totally false charges of witchcraft, and totally true charges of misappropriation of tribal resources, he had stumbled into the midst of a band of mostly white-eyes coldhearts whose natural first impulse was to kill him in some picturesque and protracted way and he would let his well-tried tongue spin its silver web just to have something to do.

Unfortunately, sometimes that tongue moved faster than

his brain. He talked himself into positions not even his cunning and insight could then see any way out of.

So it was with that fast-talk extravaganza out beneath a swollen desert moon. Not only had the outlaws spared him. They had become the nucleus of a whole coldheart army. Bad men had flocked to him, until he had a force of between one and two hundred of the best of worst of the region's outlaws: the scum de la scum. Men so bad even average, everyday coldhearts had got a bellyful of them.

And he had no clue what to do with them.

The approach of the caravan had been a godsend. As Red Wolf complained, Chato had been reluctant to allow his men to attack any of the villes in the surrounding area, nor even try to pick off any isolated ranches. He did know enough to understand a very little of that would raise the country against them, but his more immediate motivation had been simple fear. Leave aside the fact he had no remote intention of exposing his own hide to puncturing by irate sec men or sharpshooting ranchers. What if something went wrong? He was operating on zero tolerance here. One serious setback and all the smoke he'd spun would evaporate and all his mirrors would shatter—and his boys were just the ones to know how to give him a proper send-off with the sharp-edged shards.

It was a classic politician's cleft stick. He couldn't afford to fail, but he couldn't afford to put off action much longer. So the word his intelligence system brought him of a caravan moving through his territory came as a godsend. Even the report that they'd hooked up with a half-dozen hard-core fighters to enhance their security didn't bother him unduly, once he'd got a description of those "fighters." Their leader was a one-eyed mystery man who, granted, anybody in the whole Deathlands above the age of three would make for a stone chiller and no mistake. But the others: an albino boy, a sawed-off runt with glasses, a gaunt old crazie who carried a cane and a couple of bitches. What could they bring to the dance?

So the caravan looked like easy pickings. And because the travelers simply couldn't afford to carry much that wasn't extremely valuable, it was rich—relatively. Split among a hundred and a half marauders, though, with the subchiefs naturally taking extra-large bites of the pie, it wouldn't seem rich for long. Chato, however, hadn't thought past that point, not because he lacked the mental ability, but because he didn't dare. Something would come up. Or else.

Unfortunately the train had been such easy pickings that a bunch of damned paramilitary interlopers had gone right ahead and picked them. And "or else" had arrived ahead of schedule.

"So now," said the dapper outlaw, perhaps the most feared of all, known only as El Abogado, in the mildest of tones, "what do we do? Like any creature, we must feed."

Trust a coldheart named El Abogado never to lose sight of the son of a bitching bottom line, Chato thought bitterly.

There was only one thing to do.

Chato sucked down a deep breath. By a miracle, he managed not to choke on the smoke.

"I have a plan…" he said.

"WHOA!" J.B. EXCLAIMED, grabbing at his fedora to hold it clamped firmly on his head as the splintery wood floor of the wag whacked him hard in the tailbone and bounced him a good four inches in the air. The wag was jolting along at a good fifty clicks an hour—or not so good, on a road that wasn't much more than a couple tire tracks in the hardpan, already starting to deepen and widen into arroyos from the

erosive force of infrequent but fierce rains. Way too fast for
the suspension, one way or another.

Almost all the chosen from the wag caravan had been
herded together in the coldhearts' stakebed wag, including
three of the captive companions. Doc was riding in the cab
of the lead wag, second in line behind a Baja-buggy scout
with its own rollbar-mounted machine gun, squeezed between the captain and his driver. It couldn't have been too
comfortable for him, all crammed up against that unyielding
body armor, even leaving aside the company, J.B. reckoned.

At the outset the pair of guards keeping watch on the prisoners in the bigger wag had ordered them to keep their heads
bowed and their fingers interlaced behind their necks. That
hadn't lasted. Even free to grab on to what handholds the wag
offered and one another when it didn't it was all the prisoners could do from getting tossed in a big snake-mating-ball
of butts and elbows. Their captors, while coldhearted enough,
were more than *just* coldhearts, it was painfully apparent.
They were sec men, probably calling themselves soldiers,
from the way they dressed in odds and ends of uniforms and
gave one another salutes and titles, military-fashion.

And if there was one thing sec men hated it was disorder.
It made their jobs harder. So the order about clasping hands
went by the dusty way.

The captives rode mostly in shocky silence. Overhead, the
glorious blue that had so fatally intoxicated them was being
blotted as clouds came racing in, lead-gray. The Armorer saw
Mildred looking up at them. To her, their speed was unnatural and still alarming for all the time she'd spent unfrozen and
in the present day. To the others, it was the fact that the sky
had been almost clear that was disconcerting.

The late Hizzoner's bodyguards, Amos and Bub, had left

women behind, bleeding out in the dust. Lanky rawboned Bub had two kids, a boy and a girl, who now had flies crawling on their eyeballs. He was blubbering about it with his huge slab of ham hands covering his face. At least J.B. reckoned he was mourning his woman and children. It stood to reason not even a would-be sec man would be wasting tears on the once and never mayor of New Tulsa.

Stacked right next to J.B., Bub, the burlier and relatively smarter half of the team, was glaring at the companions with little pig eyes which, if bloodshot, were as dry as the goat track beneath them.

"That bastard Kurtiz was right about one thing," he said in a voice like a rusty old oil drum rolling down a rocky slope. "You nuke-suckers weren't shit when it came to being guards."

Jak, sitting on the Armorer's left, stiffened and snarled. J.B. touched him lightly on the arm.

"You got one thing right, friend," J.B. said. "We *aren't* shit."

"Don't crack wise with me, you sawed-off little—"

The first two fingers of J.B.'s right hand lashed out and snapped the backs of the tips against Bub's blond-stubbled jowl, as quick as a diamondback strike. They did no damage, but stung. Bub shook his head once and blinked, totally off balance.

Which meant that when J.B. brought his left hand whipping around in a hooking palm-heel strike that mashed Bub's already generally shapeless nose across his face, the blow slammed the back of the goon's skull into one of the heavy uprights rising from the periphery of the truckbed. Bub's moaning subsided, he clutched his face as blood trickled between his fingers and down his spine. It began to diffuse in thin, red spiderweb nets through the sweat coating his thick neck.

"Hey!" the younger of the two guards yelled from the rear of the truck. "Hey! Stop that! I'm warning you!"

He raised his M-16. J.B. smiled placatingly and held up his hands, palms forward, to show that he was unarmed and innocent of ill intent. The other guard, older and obviously case-hardened, just rolled his eyes and gave the Armorer a tough look.

"Man's got a point," Mildred said bitterly. She sat across from J.B. with her knees up and her arms around them. "Some defenders we turned out to be."

"No talking!" the young guard exclaimed, jabbing the air with his weapon.

J.B. ignored him. Notwithstanding the initial fuckup about ordering the prisoners to keep hands behind heads, the raiders had obviously run this drill before. As if to emphasize the fact, the older guard was toting a 12-gauge Browning A-5 autoloading shotgun sawed-off to the gas check, a pretty serious crowd-control implement. If the prisoners got seriously frisky, and particularly if they showed signs of trying to make a break for it, the guards were ready, willing and able to commence some serious blasting.

But it was also obvious the raiders needed bodies and they needed lots of them—warm, fully functional, and not leaking from extra orifices. So the captives enjoyed a certain amount of leeway.

"We just got caught flat, Millie," J.B. said. "The wind, the sun, the bright blue sky—we got loose and careless, and now here we are."

"Be quiet!" the younger guard shrilled, flourishing his longblaster wildly. "I told you! I'll shoot! I will!"

"Cody," the older man growled, "knock off that shit before I lay this mare's leg up alongside your empty damn head, won't you? Who gives a rat's red ass if the bastards talk?"

Cody sank into sullen silence. The older man held on to the upright at the front-right corner of the bed with his left hand. The other held his sawed-off across his drawn-up knees. He stared back at the captives from a face as hard and flat as a cast iron pan.

Mildred's eyes caught J.B.'s. He tried to give her a reassuring smile, but he realized it just looked like somebody was turning a nut at the back of his head and tightening the skin around his mouth. He knew he couldn't piss down her leg and tell her it was raining—her of all people. But she and he were paired, and he felt he owed it to at least try to do what he could to keep her spirits up.

He thought of Ryan and had to look away. He took off his glasses and polished them with a handkerchief he removed very gingerly from his pocket. After a few moments he put the specs back on and faced the black woman again.

Mildred was still gazing at him with curious fixity. Once she had his eyes back she let her own run meaningfully down toward his scuffed boots.

He nodded, slow and slight, a motion that would be lost to anybody not studying him a lot more closely than anybody but Mildred Wyeth seemed to be in the general jouncing and jostling induced by the truck banging along across the desert. The frisking he and the others had gotten had been professional but cursory. The sec men were looking for weapons. It didn't occur to them that J.B. might have a full lock pick kit concealed on his person, much less a couple of odds and ends, including more picks and mebbe a weapon or two; and never in a thousand years would they suspect what might be hidden in, say, a hollowed-out boot heel.

Then J.B. shrugged. "Don't see we got much choice but to take the cards as we're dealt them," he said, "than play them as they lay."

She frowned.

"With Ryan dead—"

"Ryan not dead," Jak said firmly.

J.B. looked at him sharply. The albino youth patted himself on the solar plexus. "Feel here if was."

"Don't talk nonsense, Jak," J.B. said with quiet determination.

Jak's eyes lit up in anger. "Listen—"

"Take it easy, you two," Mildred said. "We got to stick together right now."

The traveler sitting to Mildred's right cocked his head. "What about that bitch of Cawdor's?"

Mildred's elbow jabbed hard into the traveler's ribs. Air oofed out of him. "Oh, sorry, Seymour. You just take it easy now. And remember it's not good to speak ill of the dead."

He glared at her and rubbed his side. He said no more, though.

A woman toward the front of the wag had gotten agitated. "So that's just it?" she demanded. "We just let them shoot down our friends and loved ones and scarf us up as slaves, and that's it? End of story?"

"You got a better idea, Maisy?" asked a heavy black-bearded man in coveralls patched in variety of colors.

The woman gazed wildly around at her fellow captives.

"They got the drop on us," J.B. said, loudly but very controlled. "And that's all there is to it. Spilled blood can't go back in the body."

The woman at Maisy's side took her arm and whispered urgently in her ear. The hard-bitten guard tipped up his scattergun until its foreshortened muzzle pointed at the now-overcast skies. He didn't say anything, didn't even change expression. But the implication was clear.

There would be no more conversation out of the captives. Not because of any silly rules, but because they were getting themselves all stirred up, talking. If they got too stirred up, it would make more work for him.

That wouldn't happen. And even though the shot-column didn't spread out any too quick even from a barrel that short, the odds were pretty good that whoever the coldheart picked as designated troublemaker wouldn't be the only one to cop some .33-caliber double-aught balls.

The captives clammed up. But J.B. thought he heard Jak mutter, deep down in his throat, "Ryan not dead."

HEAD DOWN, back bowed beneath the weight of the pack she carried, Krysty trudged toward the lowering sun.

She had begun to feel, not hope—never hope, never again—but a kind of lessened futility. Lessened immediate futility anyway.

It wasn't her nature to analyze. Her conscious mind had been nothing but a bright blur for the past several hours. But she was far from stupe, and her subconscious kept working.

The raiders were well organized and even smart by sec men standards, let alone coldheart ones. The massacre hadn't been sadistic butchery. It hadn't even been casual. It had been businesslike. Whoever the murderers were, they were professional about it.

Their behavior was at the other end of the world from the wild irrationality most coldhearts displayed. Calculating.

They had been happy enough to take what loot the caravan wags offered, but they dumped the contents of the two wags they needed to transport their own people in without hesitation or question, including provisions they themselves used every day—food, water and ammo. It wasn't so much that they spurned those items as that they didn't even trouble to look for them, even though all were present and all reasonably expected to be. The only cargo they kept was spare fuel stored in the vehicles, and that the wags themselves obviously required.

Far from worrying about their own resupply, they had taken on two dozen extra mouths. Krysty knew why even without the sergeant having grumbled to his superior: the raiders needed slave workers. To do what, she wasn't sure—something about a track—and didn't particularly care. What was potentially useful to know was that the raiders hadn't been concerned even though those same consumables were necessary to keep the captives alive so they could do the work the raiders needed done. Gaia, even ammo, if some of the captives needed extra persuading. And it was through neither inexperience nor the shit-for-brains slavery to the impulse of the moment that controlled most coldhearts, and mutie marauders too, for that matter.

This bunch knew exactly what they were doing. Every step along the path.

If they didn't need to worry about food and water, they weren't far from replenishing the same. It followed as inevitably as night was about to follow the desert day.

Granted, a wag could cover ground a shitload faster than a woman afoot, even one as strong and driven as Krysty Wroth. But another thing her subconscious worked out, and allowed to seep osmotically into the white void of her conscious mind, was that a job that took a lot of hands generally took a fair stretch of time to do as well. Wherever the marauders delivered their captives, they probably wouldn't be moving on for a spell.

The knowledge, slowly assimilated, added energy to her step. It might take a few hours or many days, but she had at least some solid ground of reason on which to base a belief that she *would* find her friends and Ryan's killers.

A scrub jay yammered abuse at Krysty from a bush. The sound brought the woman back to the here-and-now with a jolt of alarm. She had been in zombie mode, total whiteout.

She was lucky. In the Deathlands, if you zoned that far out, you usually came out of it about the time a stickie was pulling your face off.

She raised her head and took stock of her surroundings. The sun was falling toward a shoal of mesas with wind-scooped faces, tawny and rose. There was no sign of the raiders, and the marks their tires had left in sand were lost to the eternally restless wind. But there was something, a squat blockiness ahead at the bottom of a broad valley. Buildings. Studying her surroundings, Krysty could make out patches of dark pavement showing through drifted sand, the remnants of a flanking ditch. There had been a hard-top road here. Mebbe even a highway.

Bad news, in that if the raiders turned off along it, they'd make at least somewhat better time than along the unimproved dirt track they, like the caravan, had been following. It remained unlikely the raiders were going farther than she could walk in a matter of days.

Meantime, the buildings offered possible shelter for the night. This wasn't the seething gut of the Deathlands, with monstrous beasts, humanoid muties and acid rain storms ready to destroy the traveler caught in the open. But there were still plenty of nasty things that came out at night. To hunt.

She began walking toward the structures.

J.B. WAS ROUSED from sleep when the stakebed wag began to slow. Despite scowls from the guards the other captives were scrambling to their feet to peer forward toward whatever awaited them.

A brown hand, strong but altogether feminine, appeared before his eyes. The Armorer grinned at Mildred as she helped him up. She gave him a taut smile back.

He couldn't see much over the cab, so he leaned his head over the wood side of the bed and peered forward. What seemed like a couple hundred people were laboring away in the middle of the desert. And parked next to them, gleaming like polished silver in the sun's slanting rays—

"Well, I'll be dipped in shit and fried for a hush-puppy," J.B. said in admiring amazement. "It's a train!"

Chapter Three

The screen door of the derelict diner banged open. Two men were suddenly among the cracked-vinyl booths and the peeling Formica tables, longblasters in their hands.

Both aimed square at Krysty Wroth.

"Freeze, bitch!" the younger, taller intruder shouted. Blond bangs hung in his sunburned face from beneath a turned-around ball cap. His partner, who was darker and whose dark-brown hair was beating a hasty retreat from his own forehead, just grinned a nasty grin.

After only the briefest hitch in her motions, and her breathing, Krysty calmly went back to doing what she was doing—cooking corned-beef hash made from the supplies she'd brought from the massacre site over a fire built of brush and driftwood in what had been the little kitchen's deep-fat fryer, once upon a time. The pot was one she'd found hanging behind the counter. A handful of the fine sand that had drifted against the diner's east wall served to scrub out the accreted dust and gunk of the past century.

"Hey," the blond intruder shouted. "Din't I tell you to freeze, bitch?"

"Easy, Matt, easy," his pal soothed. "They're so much more fun when they're warm."

He sidled around the periphery of booths, holding his re-made M-16 with one hand. In the light of the kerosene lanterns she was working by, she could tell that both men wore retread U.S. Army blouses, both OD green, both with unfamiliar round patches on the breast. Just like the men who had killed Ryan and hijacked the caravan.

The man came right up beside her. She smelled his stinking breath, felt it defile her cheek. His dirty-nailed fingertip followed it, unwinding a scarlet lock down to the line of her set jaw.

"Well, well, well," he murmured, "what have we here?"

She didn't shy away from the touch, just kept stirring and tossing.

"Bitch-slap the skag, Ben," Matt said, shifting weight from left boot to right with poorly checked eagerness. "Show her who's boss."

"Naw, naw, gently now. She's a cool one, aren't you, honey? I like that. I bet a girl like you could show us a good time. Big nasty redhead like you."

He grabbed her, lowered his face to nuzzle her neck. She fended him with the back of his hands. He yanked his head back, anger flaring in his dark eyes.

"Now, now, don't be in too much of a hurry, boys," she said in her throatiest voice. It was a voice guaranteed to raise wood on a week-old stiff. "Why don't you'll just relax and make yourselves comfortable while I fix you a nice big dinner?"

The rage drained from Ben's eyes. He smiled. Nodded. Laughed a little laugh.

"You know, hon, you're right. Been a long, hard day, getting shut of that asshole General and his merry men. I'll feel a lot stronger once I get around a good old home-cooked meal."

He let her go and went back around the counter. Matt was

almost vibrating with outraged horniness. "What are you doing? What? Why are we waiting?"

"Relax, kid," Ben said, hoisting a cheek onto one of the round pedestal stools at the counter. There had been three; one was missing entirely, the other had been uprooted and lay against the foot of the counter.

"And quit waving that damned blaster around. You make me nervous. Our little redheaded bedwarmer is a smart one. You can tell just by looking at her. She knows better than to try to run on us. Don't you?" He propped his own blaster next to his stool.

Krysty gave him a zipper-busting smile. "Now, why would I want to run anywhere, sugar?"

"But, but—" Matt sputtered.

"Sit your ass down," Ben commanded.

Matt complied. He sat at a table in the middle of the little room. He didn't put his longblaster down, although he did aim it at the ceiling. "What are we waiting for?" he asked peevishly.

Ben chuckled indulgently. "Didn't you ever hear the story of the old bull and the young bull, boy?"

"No."

"This old bull and this young bull came upon a fence. And on th' other side of that fence, what should they see but a whole herd of fine young heifers swishing their tails over their nice firm fannies."

"This one's got a nice ass," Matt said, staring at Krysty and almost drooling. "I can tell."

"She surely does. Now, pay attention to my story. This young bull sees them heifers, and he says, 'I got an idea! Let's jump the fence and fuck us one a' them heifers.' And this old bull just shakes his head and says, 'No. What we gonna do, we're gonna walk down to that gate, walk through it nice and peaceful, and fuck *all* them heifers.'"

He laughed, grandly amused at his own joke. His gales of laughter died slowly away as he realized his younger companion wasn't laughing with him.

"Go ahead," Matt demanded. "Git to the punchline."

"That *was* the punchline, you triple-stupe nuke head!"

"Weren't funny."

"Well, did you at least get the point of the story?"

"There's a point?"

Ben dropped an elbow to the bar and sank his face in his hand.

"Well, now, don't go being unreasonable, Ben," Matt whined. "You said it was a joke. You told me so. And a joke got no point. It's supposed to be funny." A light dawned dimly. "Except that joke weren't funny."

He looked questioningly at Ben. The older man just waved a world-weary hand.

"Lookit, the bitch is all done cooking. Can we do her now? Can we?" He licked his lips. "I wonder if she got red fur on her pussy. Do redheads have that? Red hair on their pussies?"

"We ain't et yet, you damn fool."

"I was going to make up a batch of nice biscuits," Krysty said, "if you big, strong men can just hold on to your appetites a little longer. And wouldn't you like something to drink while you're waiting?" She nodded her head back toward a canteen sitting on the counter.

Ben nodded, picked it up, began to unscrew the top. Then he stopped. A cagey look came into his eye.

"You wouldn't be trying to pull one on us, now would you, honey? Here. You take a drink first. Then we'll know it's safe."

He tossed the canteen at her. Holding his eye, smiling seductively the while, she undid the lid and took a long draft. Then she put the lid back on and tossed the canteen back. He drank greedily and pitched it to Matt in turn.

"So what are two such handsome men doing way out here in the middle of nowhere?"

Water ran down the side of Matt's chin. He lowered the canteen and wiped his mouth with his sleeve. "We're. Uh, that is—"

"We're deserters," Ben said cheerfully.

"Deserters?" Krysty said. In her mouth the word sounded like a marvelous thing. Like a baron combined with an old-time movie star. But better. "Does that mean, like from an army?"

"Sure does," Matt said proudly. "The Provisional United States Army!"

"Well, that's what they call themselves," Ben said. "They're really just a bunch of coldhearts under command of the General. But they like to play like they're an army."

"That's why we run," Matt said. "Got tired of all the bullshit. Get out of bed when somebody else says. Haul our asses all over this sorry-ass desert rounding up limp-dick civilians to work on the line."

"The line?" Krysty asked.

"Railroad line. Same one runs out back of this shithole."

"See," Ben said, "the General ain't just any old asshole like one of your bug-heap barons. He's got himself a train."

"A train?" Krysty asked.

"A train. But not just any old rail wag. It's an armored train."

"MAGOG," Matt said. "That's what he calls it."

"What's that mean?" Krysty asked.

Ben shook his head. "Don't mean nothin'. It's just what the General calls it."

"He found it," Matt said, with something like pride. "Scavvied it out of some big ol' underground bunker somewhere. All fulla weps and food and everything. It's only the biggest, most powerful rail wag ever built. The General, he says it was built for something called the War on Drugs. Gonna be sent down to someplace called Columbus—"

"*Colombia,* nuke breath!"

"Colombia. Except the world blew up. Everybody knew about it got iced. But it was all protected and everything. In perfect shape when the General found it. And it runs off fusion batteries so it don't never need to refuel. Got all the power a body'd ever want."

"Sounds...impressive," Krysty purred. "What's this General doing with this train of his?"

"Says he's trying to put America back together," Ben said. "Don't put much stock in that myself. I think he wants to be just another baron, but mebbe carve himself out a bigger empire."

"Sounds like a pretty big job."

Ben shrugged. "That's another reason we run," Matt said. "He been at it years, conquered himself a mess of little villes along the line, keep him supplied and shit. Still just like taking a piss in the ocean." He had another drink. "I saw a ocean once."

"Weren't no ocean, stupe," Ben said. "It was the Gu'f of Mex."

"That's a ocean. I couln't see acrost it, anyway."

"You mean this General can travel anywhere he wants in this armored rail wag?"

"Not exactly," Ben said. "Lotta breaks in the line."

"That's why we was stuck out here in nowhere," his partner said. "'Nother washout in the fucking line. Had to go round up a mess of dead-ass civilian stupes to fix it. Buncha bullshit."

"Our scout wag busted an axle a few miles down the road from here," Ben said. "We was basically out on our own at that point. So we decided what the hey, threw away our talkies and took off. Heard us a rumor from some of the workers there was a big old buncha coldhearts gathered out in the scrub somewheres 'round here. Fixin' to hook up with 'em, give that a roll."

"Man got to start to think about settlin' down, puttin' down some roots, build him a future," Matt said. "Can't spend your whole danged life rollin' aimlessly along a old steel rail to nowhere."

Ben nodded sagely. "General says he's looking for something called the Great Redoubt. Supposed to be where the old guys stored up everything needed to put the whole country back together after the war. Even before the war, this was. Communications, supplies, weps—the works."

"Crazy old nukesucker."

"No shit. Like the boy says, man gets tired chasing after phantoms. Needs somethin' more substantial. Something with meat on the bones."

He cocked his head and looked at Krysty. "Speaking of meat on the bones, why'n't you hurry up there, little mama? I'm getting a real appetite worked up myself now, and not just for that chow that's smelling so good."

"Well," Krysty said slowly, "since you've been such good boys, and told me what I needed to know, it's time you got what's coming to you."

She turned quickly, her right hand filled with her .38-caliber Smith & Wesson blaster. She was already squeezing the double-action trigger, timing the lengthy pull so that the hammer released just as the short barrel came to bear on Matt's bangs. The gun roared, making a shocking racket for such a small weapon.

Automatically, Krysty stepped sideways left, away from Ben, in case he made a grab for her. He didn't. But he was sharp and fairly quick; he was leaning forward and trying to reel up his longblaster by the strap.

She swung her right hand around, arm still straight, bringing her left hand up to wrap the fingers and brace her grip on the piece. She fired two shots, blinding fast, into his torso at a downward angle. His leaning motion carried him off the stool and hard onto the ancient cracked linoleum.

Krysty swung her blaster back toward Matt, in case he needed another dose of what he had coming. Then she noticed the old sign by the door, a square frame on a skinny metal post, its message Please Wait to Be Seated barely visible for the years of fading—and also Matt's blood and brains, the color of the half-baked biscuits rising unattended in the pan, dripping down the front of it.

Almost at her feet, Ben groaned and stirred. She aimed her blaster down at him.

But he was no threat. One of her bullets had smashed through his lower jaw on its way down into his chest. It was still about half-attached, his breath bubbling like a well of gore from somewhere within the mess.

Ben's lower jaw seemed to be working with a purpose, and his half-moored tongue moving as if trying to shape a word.

"Mercy." That's what she thought he was trying to say.

"Of course," she said, and shot him between the eyes.

Krysty reloaded her blaster. It would've been more frugal

to cut the coldheart's throat, but she had scavvied plenty of .38 Special ammo from the luggage left behind by Ben and Matt's former comrades. No point in making things harder on herself than they already were.

She walked to where Matt lay. He was spread-eagled on the filthy, cracked, sand-gritty linoleum with his longblaster fallen across his thighs. Instead of the sky, he was staring at the diner's cracked, discolored plaster ceiling. His cap had been flipped clean off his head, possibly by the impact of the bullet that had evacuated his skull. She knelt and picked it up. It looked new, crisp and scarcely faded by sun or sweat, meaning it had to have been salvaged from storage fairly recently. It was black. The front bore a picture of the face of a man wearing an odd cap or hood with a black stripe down the center. Curvy-blade machetes or short swords with nonstudded knucklebow guards were crossed behind his head. Above it was the word "Raiders." Around the whole was a sort of shield.

She stuck the cap on her head. She had miles of open desert to walk. It would be good to have something to keep the sun out of her eyes.

Her biscuits had burned on the bottom. Indifferently, she flipped them over. She finished cooking the biscuits and put them and the hash on the counter, still in their respective pans. What she was making looked as if it would have been enough for all three, in fact, but she had planned to eat it all herself and still did. She was a tall, muscular, extremely active woman who generally had a hearty appetite. And even if she didn't have much appetite this night—and doubted she ever would again, beyond sheer pangs of hunger—it had been a calculated decision to fix herself a large and proper meal. Her vengeance trail stretched long and hard before her. She would need every ounce of strength she could muster to see it through to the end.

She seated herself gingerly on the stool. The red-ant bites no longer throbbed with that weird, expansive intensity such acid-laden bites left in their wake, but the wounds still felt raw, and the muscles of her groin and thigh ached from the venom's aftereffects. Ben's cooling corpse was softer than the floor, so Krysty rested her boots on him while she ate.

As she ate, she thought about what she had learned and what it meant to her quest.

A train! she thought wonderingly. She'd seen the tracks her whole life without thinking much of them—just another artifact from the strange lost days before skydark. A track even ran right behind the abandoned diner and gas station and she had never even taken note of it, except as a terrain feature, and the fact that the endless miniature ridge on which it was laid offered potential cover and concealment. It was just part of the landscape. She had never really thought somebody might be able to use the rails to travel any particular distance. Sure, she'd heard the legends of wild tribes of folk who actually traveled the lines on marvelous wags, paying no mind to the world to either side of the narrow right of way, and of course discounted them as legend.

And here was this General with his giant train, armored and fusion-powered, trying to reconquer America—and killing her man and kidnapping her friends to do it.

She shook her head. Her locks writhed sympathetically around her shoulders. Matt and Ben were right about one thing: he was a crazy old nukesucker.

That datum was of limited use: pretty much all barons were crazy, and she also concurred he was no different from most. Just more mobile.

The real problem from her viewpoint was that mobility. She had been correct in her surmise that the wags of the raiders who had hit them—was it only that day?—were returning to a nearby base. But that base wouldn't stay put. And she couldn't hope to pace a train on foot.

But the train called MAGOG was stopped now, the deserters said. That was why they had scooped up the hapless travelers, and carefully picked only the ones who looked fit for physical labor. They couldn't go anywhere until they fixed a break in the line.

She wished she'd been able to string them along longer, pump even more information out of them. Oh, well. If wishes were wings, she'd be circling over the train right this instant, scoping things out like a falcon looking to stoop down and score.

There'd been no way. Young Matt had been just about to lose it and go for the cheese right then and there. And Krysty wouldn't submit to that, vengeance or no vengeance.

An owl hooted somewhere out in the night, beyond the busted-out front window. The wind had come up again, temporarily scouring out the stale death smell and replacing it, temporarily, with the astringent odors of dust and dry vegetation. She finished her meal without having tasted a scrap of it, and set down her fork.

She would find the train and do what she had to do. If the train was gone, mebbe the marauders would have left some wags behind. If not...

She shrugged. She could come up with possible bad outcomes from now until dawn, from now until she died of old age, for that matter. Not one of them would make her road any shorter or easier to walk.

She sighed, stood, wiped the soles of her boots carefully

on an unbloodied area of Ben's blouse to make sure the soles weren't wet and slick from blood. She was going to have to drag the corpses outside. They were going to draw scavengers from miles around. She couldn't lock the diner, with the windows gone and all, but there was no point inviting hungry predators inside.

If the chase went on long, she'd need all the barter goods she could find. Krysty knelt and began to rifle through Ben's effects for items of value.

Chapter Four

"Ah," the General said in satisfaction, leaning back in a red plush chair and sipping from a goblet of brandy. "It's definitely a rare treat to encounter a man of your culture out here in the wasteland, Doctor Tanner."

Doc started to reply around a mouthful of apple and cinnamon omelet and toast that he would have found ambrosial had it been served to him back in his very own long-lost house in nineteenth-century Vermont by the beloved and equally lost hand of his wife Emily. Instead it had been dished out by the hand of a solemn stone-faced servant from a brass chafing dish heated by a little cup of clear, odorless, smokeless burning fuel.

Realizing that standard Deathlands etiquette would hardly answer these circumstances, Doc hurriedly finished chewing and swallowed, not without regret for the unseemly haste. Covering his mouth, just for security's sake, by pretending to dab it clean with a spotless white-linen napkin, he nodded and replied. "I might say the same, General. I might well indeed."

They sat in oak-paneled and comfort-conditioned splendor, two men of knowledge at ease with one each other and their world, taking their breakfast and engaging in the art of conversation. Even for a man of Theophilus Tanner's unique experience, it was one of the most—what was that eminently useful modern word?—*surreal* moments of them all.

The General—that was how he had been introduced and
the only way Doc had heard him spoken of—was a short burly
man with buzzed grizzled hair and features that might have
been carved from granite by a skilled but hasty sculptor. Even
taking his ease with an apparent act of will, the enormous
vigor that animated him was evident. He was a man made for
action. Right now he wore a maroon robe over white paja-
mas with blue pinstripes. On the right breast of the robe was
sewn a patch showing a fierce eagle clutching lightning bolts
and weapons, with a stars-and-stripes shield over its own
breast. Above it arced the legend Mobile Anti-Guerrilla Operations Group. Below it was embossed the acronym
MAGOG.

"I trust you find your accommodations to your liking, Professor," the General said, allowing his steward, a tall, olive-
skinned man in black trousers, white shirt with stand-up collar
and bow tie, to replenish his coffee.

"Quite, General."

He had, in fact. He'd been kept separate from his companions ever since leaving the massacre site by the Grand Canyon. Nor had he seen for sure where they were taken, although
he surmised they were bound for a barbed-wire stockade with
some tents pitched inside that had been erected near the work
site. He hoped they were well, and not terribly mistreated. He
wasn't overly concerned. Obviously their captors wanted
them alive rather than dead, and to judge by past performance, it would be but a matter of time before one of them,
most likely the ever-so-resourceful John Barrymore Dix, figured out a way to spring them all.

His captor had introduced himself as Marc Anthony Helton, Captain, Provisional U.S. Army. He was a very polite and
well-spoken young man, despite his regrettable propensity

for casual mass murder. He was fascinated by Doc, and grilled him about who he was, where he'd come from, and what experiences he had had. Tanner had cloaked his responses in sufficient vagueness to avoid giving away any significant information without convincing the young officer that he was too far gone mentally speaking to be of real interest to the General.

At least, he hoped he had.

On arrival, young Captain Helton had taken cordial leave of him. Soldiers had hustled Doc onto the train straightaway. There, he was brusquely ordered to strip and sent into a bank of showerheads to cleanse himself under a guard's watchful eye. He would never believe a mere shower could equal the sybaritic luxury of a tub of steaming water, and candidly, he was the most inclined of their brave little band to be careless in matters hygienic, but the hot gushing water and the sense of cleanliness it produced were alike bliss-producing.

Once dried, he had been given a rough and rather itchy set of garments of the depressing greenish shade favored by the U.S. Army of the twentieth century. After he put them on he had been marched to another car and locked into a small passenger compartment. Ironically, he had been allowed to keep his cane, although naturally, his bulky LeMat cap-and-ball revolver had been appropriated.

Indeed, the General just upon the instant picked up the pistol and began to examine it with keen interest, turning it over and over in his hard, scarred hands.

In his compartment, which he had to himself, Doc had been served a better-than-adequate meal. Surprisingly, it had been a stew of game—rabbit and deer at the very least, with a possible hint of quail—along with carrots and potatoes and seasoned with sage. All seemed quite fresh, and the bread rolls that came with it were palpably hot from the oven. The butter tasted real. Doc hoped his friends were well fed and housed.

The bench unfolded into a bed, which was the most comfortable he'd known in many a moon. He slept soundly, and blessedly without dreaming, until a peremptory knock had awakened him, and his clothes—cleaned and pressed, by the gods—had been thrust upon him.

Now he sat in a kind of sitting room in the General's personal car, eating another splendid meal and drinking coffee—freeze-dried, regrettably—while the General peered down the LeMat's barrel, the long .44-caliber main barrel, and the auxiliary 12-gauge barrel in front of the cylinder. In tribute to Doc's vast storehouse of knowledge, the General addressed him as "Professor."

"A remarkable weapon, Professor," the General remarked, setting the big pistol down on a table beside his red-plush chair. "But isn't it kind of an eccentric choice?"

Doc gave a debonair wave of his coffee cup, pinky extended. "One who knows the proper formula, and, more important, the proper technique, it's all in the caking—for manufacturing black gunpowder, as I do, can produce it far more simply, from much more readily available materials, than any more modern smokeless propellants."

"Ah, but it still requires percussion caps to ignite the powder, doesn't it? My whitecoats tell me they need to be filled with high explosives that are unstable and fairly dangerous to handle—not to mention the chemistry's a bit more involved than mixing saltpeter, sulfur and charcoal."

Doc shrugged. "I see that I am caught out. Your Excellency is not the first to observe that I am, indeed, an eccentric."

The General held up a hand. "No need to call me anything

that fancy. I'm a pretty down-to-earth guy. 'General' or 'sir" will do just fine."

Doc nodded and sipped. My, what fine manners he had for a murderer, he thought.

Since joining Ryan and the rest, Doc had become a far different man from the one who had capered and spouted half-remembered snatches of poetry for the delectation of the unspeakable Jordan Teague and Strasser, his brute of a sec chief. His spine, for example, had recovered a remarkable degree of rigidity, although his grip on sanity was still not of the firmest, sadly. But he still knew how to show a pleasing face to power, and didn't scruple to do so at need. Besides, for all the shockingly direct evidence Doc had of at least some of the General's crimes, next to the likes of Teague he was an innocent babe.

As a matter of fact, the General's manners *were* pretty good for a Deathlands murderer.

"I must admit that coming upon a man of your obvious culture and erudition, in the midst of this barbaric waste, is lots like finding a pearl in a midden heap," the General remarked.

Doc tried to stifle a wince. Owing to a saw that was old when he was young, he associated pearls with swine, and swine… He shook himself delicately. The memories didn't bear touching upon, however lightly. Especially since Cort Strasser had already been called to mind.

"The General is too kind," he said. He pushed his plate away; his appetite had vanished. "And since you are a man who clearly appreciates quality when he encounters it, I feel it is incumbent upon me to point out a valuable resource that your subordinates are running a shocking risk of simply throwing away."

The General leaned forward with an eagerness that surprised Doc, and a hunger in his gray eyes that shocked the other man. Obviously he'd probed a nerve, he thought.

He nodded and forged ahead. "Certain of my associates, who were…detained along with myself, are men and women of remarkable attributes. To employ them as mere manual laborers constitutes a shocking waste of valuable resources, and a truly unforgivable oversight on the part of your subordinates, I fear."

Slowly the General leaned back. Doc watched the tautness in his face sag into disappointment, and anger flare in his eyes. He braced himself for doom.

The General looked aside for a moment, scowling. When he turned back to Doc his expression was returning to neutrality.

"Very well, Professor," he said, "tell me more."

"NUKEBLAST IT!" the guard howled as Jak sank sharp teeth into his wrist. He battered the youth's head and shoulders with his free hand. Jak hung on, as tenacious as a weasel. "Leggo, you rad-sucking son of a mutie gutter slut!"

Taking advantage of the distraction to lean on his shovel as he watched, J.B. shook his head.

Another guard came running up and swatted Jak in the head with the butt of his M-16. Whatever its merits as a long-blaster, the M-16 was reputed to have been made originally by a toy company. In any event it didn't weigh much, having been designed not to, and its butt was mostly nylon. It was a piss-poor piece to buttstroke a body with. Without so much as flinching, Jak back-kicked the guard in the balls. The man sat down hard on a red-ant hill, then rolled onto his side, moaning and clutching himself.

Guards converged. Along with the blasters, the soldiers

overseeing the work gang carried truncheons, some actual scavenged PR-25 side-handle batons, others simply sawed out of either table legs or baseball bats—J.B. couldn't tell which. They rained blows upon Jak's head and shoulders until he let go and fell to the ground, grinning at them with a mouth red with blood that wasn't his. Then they commenced to stomp him.

J.B. sighed. The boy clearly had some hard lessons to learn about when to kick back and when to just bow your head and take what was coming and bide your time. But he couldn't just stand by and watch his longtime comrade-in-arms get kicked to death. He was going to have to do something, which likely meant his getting stomped, as well.

He was just shifting his grip on his shovel when the situation escalated. A young and probably fresh-minted sec man ran up and shouldered his M-16. As serious as a multiple stomping was, it was nothing to being in the way of a sleet of nasty jacketed 5.56 mm bullets. And the new arrival seemed blissfully unaware that no matter what angle he chose there was no way to shoot the miscreant without ventilating three or four of his buddies as well.

"That's enough! Stand down there, you men." Banner's voice was like the roar of an enraged gravel crusher as he strode toward the altercation.

The guards fell back from the prostrate Jak. The boy with the M-16 stiffened like a dog pointing the grouse. His finger tightened on the trigger.

"Bledsoe! If you don't lower that piece right now, I'll ram it so far up your ass you'll be looking at the front sight cross-eyed. Do I make myself clear, you polyp on a mutant salamander's asshole?"

The newby hastily lowered the rifle and snapped to. J.B.

nodded in appreciation of the sec man's unexpected elo-
quence. An asshole Banner might be, but an asshole with
style.

The others fell back from Jak's well-trampled form. The
youth had been lying in a fetal curl, with his face hugged into
his knees, protecting himself as well as he could. He rolled
to his belly, got to hands and knees and shook his head.

The guard whose wrist he had bloodied pulled out a Beretta and aimed it at Jak's head.

"Moredock, what's wrong with you?" Banner shouted.
"Secure that weapon."

"But, Sarge, we gotta make an example—"

"*Now.*"

Moredock holstered his blaster. It took him only three
tries.

"What we 'gotta do,' skunk ape, is get the damned railbed
built up again so we can lay new rails before we all die of old
age. We can't go shooting our whole labor force just because
you're too fuckwitted to keep order. Unless you want to take
his place swinging a pick, Corporal?"

Moredock hit a brace. "Sir, no sir!"

"Pick him up."

A couple of the guards who had been thundering on Jak
now dragged him to his feet by his biceps. One red eye was
puffing shut, but aside from a thin trickle out of his left nos-
tril, the blood on his face still wasn't his own.

"Ah, the albino." Banner nodded. "You were with the
bunch I helped scoop up yesterday. You listen to me, boy. We
need you to do a job of work. But don't get the idea we can't
fix the track without you. Act up again and I'll stomp your
brains out your nose myself."

The sergeant glared around at the onlookers, guards and

captives alike. "Don't you all have things to do?" Everyone turned away, suddenly eager to be doing those things.

With dark looks, the guards let Jak go and backed away warily. He stood panting like a winded dog, still grinning defiance.

J.B. scooped up a shovelful of earth and walked over to Jak, to look as if he intended doing something useful with it. Then he dumped the dirt and grounded the tool again.

"That's no way to do it, Jak," he said. "That's way too hard a road to see to the end. Take an old man's word for it."

Jak shook his head so that his snowy mane flew wildly, then hawked and spit a blood loogie in the sand. "Kill sergeant."

"If you live long enough. Keep up the way you been, though, you'll be staring at the sky when the stars come out."

Anger flared like a lasing ruby in Jak's eyes.

"All right, party time's over!" a guard yelled at them. "Get back to work."

Jak turned away. J.B. moved on to join other laborers shoveling dirt into barrows.

Some time later Mildred approached. Across her shoulders she carried a pole with a water bucket at either end. She knelt and set down the buckets, then stood back as the thirsty laborers crowded around to ladle up water.

She looked angry. J.B. reckoned he knew why.

"Don't none of us like it, Millie," he said quietly, "but the one thing it ain't is personal."

She glared at him, then shook her head. "Yeah, I know. Slavery's an equal-employment opportunity these days. But that wasn't how I was raised."

She looked around. There was still water, and the workers were still jostling one another to drink.

"Bastards almost killed Jak," she said. "I wish I could look at him."

"Boy's tough. Knows how to handle himself, too. I don't reckon they hurt him much."

"We've got to get away from this madness."

He nodded. "Looks like they'll finish their repairs here in two, three more days. What do you think they'll do with all us civilian laborers then?"

"We can't leave Doc."

"That's the angle I haven't figured yet. Give me time—unless you got any ideas?"

She shook her head.

"Well, then we need to spring the Doc, blow out of here, and double back to find Krysty."

"That poor child. I can't imagine how she must be feeling—"

"Hey! You! Get back to work, you lazy bastards." Moredock was striding toward the knot gathered around the water buckets, a fresh white bandage on his wrist and blood in his eye.

Then he dropped to his knees. A wondering expression came over his face. He opened his mouth and burped blood. It ran down his chin in a torrent. He fell onto his face as a gunshot echoed off the railway embankment.

The desert bloomed with howling coldhearts.

Chapter Five

It wasn't a good plan.

Chato might not know anything about strategy and tactics, but he was glumly convinced his plan sucked anyway.

The plan was not to try creepy-crawling the giant rail wag in the dark. Oh, no. It was bristling with weapons: machine guns in turrets, gren launchers, rockets—who knew what? And it had sensors, sirens and searchlights.

Chato may have been clueless when it came to strategy and tactics, but he did know the basics of breaking and entering. He and all his coldhearts had zilch for a chance of sneaking in undetected and making off with any worthwhile loot.

What he had sold the others on, if not himself, was this: it was by night that the soldiers expected to be attacked. By night they hunkered down inside their giant invincible armored wail wag and just waited for somebody to be stupe enough to try them on. Even the captives in their compound—and whoever was stuck in the majority of the train's cars that weren't armor-plated—were protected by the monster's sensor envelope and its truly stupendous firepower. Chato's bandits could fire up the tents and the soft-skinned wags, but that wouldn't bring them jack. What would be the point?

No. The coldhearts were intent on stealing shit. Torture, murder, rape—who didn't like that? But it was merely sugar. Plunder *paid*.

And while the lost travelers' caravan had represented a pretty piddly haul, all things taken with all, the armored train held treasure beyond the coldhearts' wildest dreams.

So the coldhearts would attack by high, wide daylight. That was when the greatest number of sec men would be outside their protective metal shell, spread out and vulnerable. The heavy weapons mounted on the train would be reluctant to fire and risk killing their own, or even the slaves they needed to fix their steel highway. And mebbe the slaves would take the attackers for liberators, and rise up against their captors. Or at least bolt in panic, and one way or another cause a hell of a mess. Under cover of which the raiders could get in at the train, overpower the defenders, and give themselves over to the customary orgy of rape, slaughter and, of course, pillaging.

Chato's followers had bought it, anyway. Especially when it was presented with all the power of his magic gift for talking people into things. Which was what got him into this mess in the first place. But he had no choice now. It was go forward or die.

They'd catch him if he ran.

ONE OF IRONHEAD JOHNSON'S mountain men fired the opening round, the one that chilled Moredock, from a scoped and heavy barreled Remington 700. He lay on his belly on a low hogback five hundred yards south of the train, and used his possibles bag for a rest. Johnson's men were probably the most formidable fighters, man for man, of all the coldheart army. Johnson himself had disposed of the three-man observation post dug in on the rise, using his trademark foot-and-a-half-long, double-edged Arkansas toothpick.

At this point the track ran east and west straight as a laser beam. A road, its pavement still largely intact, but serving now mainly as a super-durable bed for layers of drifted sun-baked mud, ran along the south side of the embankment. The compound where the slave-laborers were sheltered under canvas was south of the road and the giant, gleaming, fusion-powered engine, to allow trucks to trundle back and forth carrying supplies from freight cars well back in the train.

From the east appeared a small fleet of dune buggies and wags, filled with young men waving longblasters. These were the Wild Boys, a local crew of coldhearts commanded by Wild Wess Wilhelm.

An arroyo cut from six to ten feet deep, with steep walls that had fallen in places because of rare but intensely savage downpours, ran at a diagonal south of the road, passing about two hundred yards from the slave stockade. From it now erupted most of the rest of Chato's misfit army: El Gancho's pistoleros from northern Mex, mounted on horseback.

Hogan's contingent of fifteen outlaw bikers on lowslung, snarling sleds. No dirt bikes, to say the least, the heavy motorcycles had been wheeled by hand along the soft sand of the arroyo bottom, to a place where a cave-in provided a natural ramp. Small in numbers, his band was unsurpassed in cruelty.

Most of Red Wolf's band of Plains Indian cutthroats had ridden off in a huff after their leader's demise. However, staunch individualists that they were, seven or eight had remained and now joined the charge on their painted ponies.

And finally, twenty or so random chillers, who had drifted into the army at large, but not yet into any kind of affinity group. These loose ends had been sent off with the main body under the command of Bug Eye Mueller, who was suspected by many of being a mutie because of his unfortunately protuberant eyeballs, but who was so mean nobody ever so much as mentioned it.

The throat and purse-slitters of El Abogado, snoop and poop specialists all, formed no part of the attack. They had their own assignment.

And finally, Chato himself sat nervously on his paint pony atop a hill well to the south, leading from the rear where he could keep a good eye on the proceedings as was appropriate to a coldheart warlord of his stature. Or so he'd told his faithful followers.

No, it wasn't a good plan. But it was shitloads better than admitting he'd drawn a blank, and having his coldheart followers decide to see what his insides looked like, preparatory to picking out a new leader.

"DOWN! Everybody get down!"

J.B. had already followed his own advice, and was speed-crawling toward the fallen corporal on leather-jacket clad elbows. Mildred, as seasoned a combat veteran as any, had also hit the dirt before the shot finished echoing.

Pretty much everybody else, guards and captives alike, was standing around, completely clueless to what was going down—even as two more guards were nailed by snipers.

However, not even the slowest or most stunned of wits could long mistake about 150 coldhearts, armed to the eyeballs and howling for blood, charging at them on horses, outlandishly modified motorcycles, and their own hind legs. The soldiers on guard, well-trained by Deathlands standards—meaning they had some—unslung their blasters, took up firing positions and started shooting.

So did the crews manning the heavy weapons mounted in casements and pop-up turrets on the armored wags of the train. MAGOG was like a weird monster millipede: its first ten or so segments were armor-plated, as were the very last two wags, a second engine and a gun-bristling caboose. Other armored wags were spaced at intervals among the more conventional freight and passenger wags. As he pulled Moredocks's Beretta from its flap-covered field holster, the Armorer heard the snarl of 5.56 mm machine guns, the throaty growl of 7.62 mm M-60s and, sweetest of all, the Thor's-hammer pounding of the .50-caliber Browning M-2. He could feel the muzzle-blasts, beating on the back of his jacket and stinging the exposed back of his neck.

Looking up, he saw the nearest attackers were still 150 yards off. He rifled the stiff for spare mags.

As PLANS WENT, Chato's wasn't really all that bad. Given the resources, it was about as good as might have been come up with.

Of course, it was doomed. He'd been right about that.

For one thing, MAGOG carried more dedicated fighters than Chato had, not to mention another hundred or so support types, cooks and clerks, who could fire a CAR-15 or submachine gun out windows and firing ports about as well as anybody. And neither Chato nor any of his followers had the remotest conception of how much sheer firepower MAGOG mounted.

Two could play the sharpshooting game, for instance. There were four dedicated antisniper turrets, each containing a shooter behind a Barrett Light Fifty sniper rifle and a separate spotter, each using mounted optics far superior to what Ironhead Johnson and his boys had. As Johnson realized, peering at the train through ancient but excellent Zeiss binocs for the few short heartbeats before his head turned into pink mist. Not even iron was proof against a 709-grain jacketed slug traveling about four times the speed of sound, it turned out.

Nor had the coldhearts grasped the fact the General had dozens of machine guns of various calibers at his command. And here came the first serious hitch in the plan: however reluctant the rail wag soldiers may have been about firing up their own buddies, much less the laborers, many of their machine guns were mounted on *top* of the train, where they could fire right over the heads of guards and prisoners alike.

Then there were the automatic grenade launchers, and the 82 mm mortars that quickly began to chug and cause big gouts of earth and assorted body parts to spout up out of the desert.

And Wild Wess Wilhelm received the surprise of his life—and death, as it happened—when a rack popped out the top of the train's engine. He didn't see it, because it was infrared and invisible to the unaided eye, the laser-designation spot painted right on the pearly third snap-button of his shirt as he rode standing up behind the roll bar of his Baja buggy. He did see the puff of white smoke as the Hellfire antitank guided missile came off the rack, however.

He had time to shout a hysterical command to his driver, who was already yanking the wheel hard right in a turn, which would have rolled the buggy and spilled them all out to their deaths or at least painful and crippling injury. The huge missile, however, struck the lower edge of the roll bar before the tires had even broken loose in a skid. A jet of copper from the shaped-charge warhead, so incandescent hot it was almost plasma, simply vaporized young Wilhelm's midsection and right shoulder and about half the head of the driver. Then the speeding wag began to roll broadside, but now as a ball of fire trailing blazing fuel and a giant caterpillar of black smoke. Another buggy lost it, veered from the road and took off end for end trying to avoid the blazing wreck, scattering its occupants in every direction. And then the machine guns began raking the wags that were attacking along the road.

The second serious problem with Chato's plan now appeared: the expectation that the slaves would either flee in panic, disrupting the defenders, or better still actually begin to fight with their guards. But few of the captives had grown up in what anybody would call sheltered circumstances; life really was tough all over. As for regarding the attackers as liberators, trust of scruffy wild-acting guys with blasters wasn't deeply engrained in the contemporary psyche. After all, however badly the soldiers had treated and were treating their slaves, it was the coldhearts who were shooting at them.

Of course, there are always a few who don't get the message. Ten or fifteen captives did try bolting and got ripped to wet red rags, some with fingertips scraped bloody from trying to claw their way up the steep railway embankment. Most of the slaves had too much sense to try to outrun the bullets cracking past their ears, and instead just dropped flat against the ground.

Doomed, but not entirely futile. The attackers boiling out of the arroyo had appeared suddenly and were fairly close at hand. A lot of the slower ones got minced and mulched by the horizontal lead storm. Others went to their bellies and opened vigorous, if not particularly accurate, fire.

The rest quickly got under the heavy weapons' arcs of fire, so close the blasters mounted atop the train couldn't depress any farther to track them. It was one of the few true cracks in mighty MAGOG's defenses. And eighty or ninety armed and angry coldhearts were pouring through it.

Crawling with less alacrity than J.B., Mildred had reached the body of a soldier downed in the first ragged volley of sniper fire. With MAGOG's blasters thundering overhead and shutting out the screams of the injured, she pulled free his M-16. She assumed a classic prone firing position, her body at forty-five degrees to the target, behind the stiff, using him as cover and a rest. She was a devoted pistol shooter—an Olympic competitor, in fact—but she could shoot a long-blaster with a high degree of accuracy.

Clicking the selector to single shot, she began to take out targets. She aimed at the coldhearts she deemed most threatening—the ones who seemed to be shooting most effectively themselves. At almost every shot, a bandit dropped.

J.B. had taken cover behind the late Corporal Moredock and was firing aimed singles from the Beretta with a two-handed grip. Thirty yards away from his friends, Jak had scooped up two M-16s from downed guards, one gazing sightlessly at the sky, the other rolling around shrieking and clutching a shattered shin, out of the fight. Not a great marksman, he was firing both at once.

From the hip.

Normally there was no craftier fighter than the albino youth from the bayou. Not now. All the fury that had been building within him since he had watched his friend and revered leader fall into the Grand Canyon the day before boiled up within him and out his mouth in an unending scream of fury, and out the muzzles of the M-16s in uninterrupted streams of lead.

One of Red Wolf's hawk-faced Plains chillers, riding a buckskin, charged Jak with a feathered lance. Jak stood his ground and blasted the mount with both rifles. The horse screamed in mortal agony as it reared, fountaining blood from a dozen holes, and fell over backward, trapping its ri-

der's leg and crushing his pelvis and the lowest three verte-
brae of his spine. As he howled in his own death agony, a second Plains rider charged, raising a war club with a cast-iron
ball for a head. He was already too close to take down with
the M-16s' lightweight bullets.

Having spent some time on his own ranch in New Mexico, Jak knew a thing or two about horses. Specifically, that
a horse wouldn't run over anything it thought could trip it.
He knelt and ducked his head, making an X of the two longblasters before his face. The horse, disregarding its rider's in-
tentions, launched himself and jumped clean over the
white-haired boy, who was dropping and rolling to his right
even as the great shadow passed over him. From his back he
emptied both magazines into the bare back of the rider. Un-
injured, the horse ran on, eyes rolling, foam flecks flying
from its nostrils.

A biker roared toward J.B., firing an Uzi over his T-bar
handlebars. He didn't hit anything, the way his ride was
jouncing all over the place. More concerned with the imprint
the front tire would make on his forehead, J.B. recoiled by
reflex to a sitting position, firing the Beretta as fast as it would
cycle. He wasn't just spraying and praying. The biker went
over the back of his postage-stamp-sized seat with the Uzi still
blazing.

For another heart-stopping instant the heavy bike charged on.
J.B.'s eyes got wide behind his glasses and he cocked himself
for a wild spring to the side. The outlaw sled wobbled, toppled
and slid toward him broadside, raising a big bow-wave of khaki
earth and dried weeds. J.B. held his hands up before his face.

The bike stopped with its tires spinning inches short of
Moredock's corpse.

J.B. heard a familiar voice cry out. Reflexively he looked toward it—to see Mildred, in a perfect kneeling position, aiming her M-16 right between his eyes.

Chapter Six

Leading four of his bros, Hogan rode his bike back along the road toward the rear of the train. He realized the machine guns couldn't reach them here. Laughing and shouting in triumph, he was firing away into the passenger cars, their metal skins too thin to stop the bullets from his Ruger Mini-14. He couldn't tell if he was actually hitting anybody, but it didn't matter. He was laying some hurt on the monster. It wasn't invincible after all.

But neither was MAGOG helpless.

The bikers came to an armored wag. Fearing shooters firing out blasters, Hogan stopped busting caps himself, leaned low between his high curved bars and accelerated rapidly.

As a result, he was past the killing zone when a strip of four Claymore mines mounted along the side of the armored car were initiated remotely from within. They went off with a rippling, ear-busting crack that spewed the roadway with about ten thousand steel marbles. The four riders behind Hogan simply disintegrated in shreds of flesh and steel, blood and gasoline, that all instantly began cooking in a hell-stew on the road as the gasoline lit off.

That was enough for Hogan. He was braver than most, man or mutie, but he knew when his match had been met. He kept the throttle cranked and went rocketing along the rest of the train, past the armored wags at its tail, relying on speed and surprise to keep him untouched by the sprays of bullets and 40 mm grenades that hosed out after him, until he vanished safely through the smoke from two downed wags, all blazing away on the road barbecuing their occupants who hadn't been lucky enough to bail, some of whom were still bitching about the fact with wild screams.

Of course, the bullets weren't stopped by the smoke. And MAGOG's gunners, who had a whole freight car full of them, didn't stop shooting them blind. But as soon as he was well within the smokescreen—steering around the furnace wrecks by sheer road-weasel instinct—he cranked the bike ride and lit out cross-country, passing quickly between a low rise and getting clean away.

J.B.'S EYES WIDENED again as flame blossomed in four yellow petals from the flash suppressor of Mildred's M-16. A vicious crack left his left ear hearing nothing but a loud ringing. Hot air stung his cheek like a red ant's bite.

He turned. A squat man in a filthy grayish sweatshirt and baggy sweat pants loomed over him with a fire ax raised over his head in both hands. He had a weird bowl-shaped haircut and was looking cross-eyed at a small, neat blue hole right through the bridge of his nose. He collapsed at the tip of the Armorer's boot, the back of his head missing.

J.B. blew out a long breath, then threw himself down behind Moredock again to take stock of the tactical situation.

Shots were still cracking in both directions. The heavy weapons still split the sky overhead. They mostly seemed to be working the far ridgeline, trying to hose off any snipers the Barrett gunners had missed. But nobody was charging.

J.B. grinned at Mildred and gave her the thumbs-up. She grinned and bobbed her head back. He dropped the empty mag out of the Beretta's well, stuffed in one of the extras he'd gotten from the corporal, then shoved the weapon down inside the back of his waistband. He scuttled around Moredock and the bike that had almost run him over, to snag the machine pistol its rider had no further use for. J.B. had a particularly soft spot for that particular piece of Israeli ironwork, overly heavy as it was and shit-for-blowback besides. It was reliable, and it got the job done; he frequently carried one. He was pleased to find three full—he hoped; no time to count rounds now—magazines stuffed in the pockets of the cold-heart's vest.

"Jak," he shouted, looking around through the smoke and dust that hung in the air. There was a breeze, as always, but the embankment and the train caused it to eddy right here and do a piss-poor job of clearing the air. "Jak, are you all right?"

"Fine." The Armorer saw the youth staggering toward him through the smoke, holding a trench knife with a spiked knuckle-duster handguard in one hand and a baseball bat studded with cut-off nails in the other. He looked as if he'd bathed in blood, then rolled around in the dust to dry it off. Which was probably about what happened. It made him look even more menacingly unearthly than usual.

"Find a blaster and follow me," J.B. called. "You, too, Millie."

"Got him covered, John. Catch, Jak." She tossed him a Marlin lever-action carbine with brass brads pounded decoratively into it, outlining the stock and foregrip. He dropped the bat and caught it deftly.

He led them up the railway embankment, which, while steep, was climbable. Bullets kicked up little spouts of dust near them, none near enough to pay attention to.

Once at the top he went to his belly and rolled right under

the train. Mildred and Jak goggled. They looked at each other, shrugged and followed his example.

ROCKING IN HIS PLUSH CHAIR out of fear for his friends he couldn't quite suppress, Doc watched the battle unfold on a bank of monitors mounted in the command center in the car just behind MAGOG's engine. Escorted by a pair of guards armed with MP-5 machine pistols in pristine condition, the General had led him forward through a flexible armored gangway that connected his personal car to the headquarters wag. They had then sat in climate-conditioned comfort, sipped sherry and watched the ultimate in reality TV.

Guilt panged him at sitting there in safety while his friends risked their lives. He wasn't the greatest asset in a fight, he knew, but he held his own and longed at least to share their peril. But there was nothing he could do.

As with the General's quarters, the soundproofing was almost perfect. He could hear nothing of the shooting outside, much less the shouts of rage and screams of mortal anguish. He could sense the vibrations of the heavy guns firing outward from the train, weird harmonics weaving subsonic melodies he felt in his bones rather than heard. One sound unnervingly not blocked out was the irregular *thunk, think-thunk,* like hail on a rooftop, of bullets striking the armored shell right by their heads and bodies.

"Don't worry," the General had said, when Doc's head had jerked away reflexively from the sound of an early impact. "Nothing'll get through this baby. And the walls won't spall, even from point-blank hits from a 30 mm chain gun." Doc wasn't sure what that meant, but it sounded duly impressive.

Doc had been far more impressed by the volcanic outpouring of fire from the train. He was also impressed by how surprisingly ineffective it was, comparatively speaking. To be sure, he could see scores of bodies, or sizable chunks of them, strewed across acres of desert. But that kind of outgoing firepower should've scoured the land, not just of all life, but everything, right down to bedrock. Or so it seemed to him.

Still, the carnage had been quite exemplary. He had to admit that. He hoped he hadn't turned too green.

Something beyond worry and incipient nausea began to bother him as the volume of fire began to diminish.

"If I may be so bold as to speak, General—"

"Go ahead."

"I notice that all our attention is being drawn to the south side of the train."

The General nodded crisply. "I was just noticing the same thing. You've an acute military eye along with your other accomplishments, Professor."

He uttered orders. His words broke off crisply and decisively without being barked or snapped, and men obeyed them, it seemed, because it never occurred to them that they might not. Whatever else one could say about the man, he had a gift of command, which Doc couldn't help but admire.

The techs pressed keys and the views on the monitors rearranged themselves, so that the largest ones showed what the hardpoint-mounted cameras on the train's north side showed. Even as they did so, the hailstorm thumping suddenly began to sound from that side of the train.

The monitors showed muzzle-flashes sparking from the brush hard by that side. Doc could make out forms prone or crouching in concealment. He realized they were too close for the train's mounted weapons to touch them.

The General grunted. "I should've ordered that brush cleared back at least two hundred yards," he said. "I'm getting lazy in my old age. Still, we can't clean up the whole Deathlands."

He smiled. "At least, not until we find the Great Redoubt. Then what won't we be able to accomplish? It'll be a great day, Professor, eh? What's that?"

Apparently some of the cameras were dirigible. An operator had swept one back to look along the side of the train, then panned back out again. He swung the remotely operated camera inward once more to reveal the heads and shoulders of three people, lying on their stomachs firing outward at the coldhearts attacking from north of the line.

"By the Three Kennedys!" Doc exclaimed. "Those are my friends!"

"ESCAPIN'?" Jak asked J.B. as they crouched beneath an armor-shelled wag.

"Not without Doc," Mildred said quickly.

"Like Millie said," J.B. agreed.

"Then what?"

"Fighting. Don't you think it's a little funny that all the excitement's been happening on one side of the train?"

Jak looked surprised, bobbed his head.

"What can the three of us do if they're sneaking up from that direction?" Mildred asked.

"Mebbe keep 'em from getting onto the rail wag. Mebbe get somebody's attention, draw us some help. At least keep from getting back-shot, sure."

"I'll buy that." For a moment it looked as if she might say more. After all, the Armorer was talking about helping the people who had murdered Ryan and a lot of helpless women and children, and carried them all off as slaves.

But the MAGOG soldiers held at least some constraints on

their behavior, some code of something at least a bit like decency, which was more than the attackers had.

She popped the mag from her M-16, made sure it was loaded, then drove it home with the heel of her hand. "Let's do it."

EL ABOGADO'S creepy-crawling artists had been sent, indeed, to creepy-crawl the train. With the major assault attracting everyone's attention everywhere except to the north, it was hoped that would give them some opening to slip inside the train proper. And once within that impregnable metal shell, who knew what they might be able to accomplish?

Fearing, correctly, that the great rail wag had automatic sensors that might detect their approach whether or not any human was looking for them, the would-be infiltrators had been ultracautious. It worked, in that they approached within sprinting distance of the train without detection. It didn't, because their approach had taken longer than planned. The main assault had already petered out, allowing defenders to think about something other than immediate survival.

J.B., Mildred and Jak had spread out and crawled forward on their bellies just far enough to bring their blasters to bear on the scrub north of the track. The Armorer and Mildred both had M-16s. J.B. had passed Jak the Uzi. Since Jak was an indifferent shot, it made sense for him to have the least accurate blaster.

Marksman or not, Jak's predator's eyes spotted movement behind a creosote bush. He splashed 9 mm bullets at it from the Uzi. He missed. The wiry little outlaw reared up and fired back with a decrepit bolt action .22 rifle. He didn't come any closer to his mark than Jak had, but Mildred planted a bullet unerringly between his eyes.

Detected, the infiltrators went to ground and opened a brisk but wild fire at the trio. The friends fired back, killing two and tagging at least three more.

Then shots cracked out to the left and right of them along the north side of the train. Soldiers were crawling beneath the train and shooting from inside the cars through windows and firing ports. Grens thrown from the top of the train began to burst in the scrub.

By this time, the shooting from the train had almost stopped for lack of targets. The attackers on that side were dead, fled, or hiding. El Abogado's posse weren't hang-and-bang fighters by skill or temperament. Sensing that all chance of success was blown, they melted back into the scrub.

A squad of sec men began a fire-and-movement advance into the scrub in pursuit. Several wounded coldhearts were dispatched with bullets behind the ear. The sec men kept moving forward by cover-to-cover rushes, but without much chance of catching any more.

A new voice began barking out orders in a voice not much softer than the crack of a .308. The soldiers at the train redeployed into a semicircle facing the three companions.

Pointing their longblasters at them.

ANOTHER PARTY profoundly impressed by the volume of fire laid down by MAGOG was Chato. The sudden stunning coruscation of really big muzzle-flashes had made his decision for him on a preconscious level. He turned and gave the boot to his pony, and was already below line of sight heading away when the thunderous roar rolled over the hill.

He hadn't gone half a mile before he rode into a broad shallow wash with a bottom of fine, almost-white sand. At the far side sat a solitary rider: El Abogado in his immaculate frock coat and Panama hat, astride his cream-colored mule with black-tipped ears.

"Where are you going in such a hurry, my friend?" the coldheart asked the fleeing warlord in Spanish.

His life suddenly become a misery, Chato answered truthfully, "Away from this fiasco."

"Indeed. I believe I shall accompany you."

"But what of your followers? Do you not seek to avenge them?"

"They're dicks."

"Well, do you...do you intend to drag me back in disgrace so that you can take my place?"

El Abogado laughed. "As what? Leader of an even bigger bunch of dicks? Ah, no, my friend. In all the Deathlands, there is no commodity so plentiful as violent fools. It's as well to be unburdened of this lot, don't you think?"

Dumbly, Chato found himself nodding.

"What do you want of me?" he asked, still incapable of believing anything but disaster—bloody, painful disaster—impended.

"You are an exemplary sociopath, Chato."

"What does that mean?"

"It means you have yourself a new partner. Such gifts as yours are useful. Shall we ride on? The brighter of our former followers will be fleeing the debacle behind us by now. It would hardly do for them to overtake us, now, would it?"

And so they rode away south together, Chato on his paint pony, El Abogado on his fine mule. As they did, it seemed the weight of the whole world dropped away from Chato's skinny shoulders.

Chato's coldheart army was a monster. Sooner or later it would devour him. He had known that from the start. But now—

Now he was free.
He began to smile.
It had been a good plan after all.

Chapter Seven

J.B. carefully laid his black longblaster on the cinders and rose, hands spread and raised. "All right, boys. Everything's easy. Just stay back off the trigger."

His two companions did likewise. It wasn't as if they had much choice.

"I hope we just did the right thing, John," Mildred murmured from the side of her mouth. Any chance they had of slipping away in the confusion had evaporated.

"All right, you three," Banner commanded. "Down the embankment. Hands behinds your heads."

Half crouching, Jak shot the Armorer a questioning glance, as did Mildred. He shrugged, then slowly complied. The other two followed.

"Walk over there by the brush," Banner said. "Don't turn around."

"Now, let's not get way ahead of ourselves, here, Banner," J.B. said over his shoulder. "We're on your side."

"Penalty for civilians carrying blasters is death."

"But we fought the coldhearts for you," Mildred said.

"No exceptions." The wind blew through an endless pause. "Sorry."

"Yeah, that makes everything just fine."

"Won't die this way," Jak snarled as they approached the scrub, barely bothering to keep his voice down.

"Me, neither," the Armorer said. "Slim chance is better'n none. When I count three, scatter like quail, children."

"Sergeant Banner!" It was another familiar voice. "What's going on here?"

"Firing party, Captain Helton, sir." The sergeant sounded disgusted. Whether with the handsome young officer, with himself, or with the situation, J.B. couldn't tell.

"What are you talking about? These people fought for us."

"That's what we're trying to tell the man," Mildred called. The three had stopped on the edge of the brush. The chance offered by the captain's intercession seemed better than that of bolting. And anyway, the Armorer counted fast.

"Regulations, sir," Banner said.

"That's absurd!"

"One," J.B. said under his breath.

"General order number twenty-three," Banner said. "Prisoners caught in possession of weapons are to be executed immediately. No appeal, no exceptions. General's a real stickler about that. You know that, sir."

"Two."

Helton's face fell. "Well, if that's the way it's got to be…"

J.B. flexed his legs slightly and opened his mouth to say "three."

Somebody new sang out, "Captain Helton, Sergeant Banner! Orders from the General."

"Don't leave us in suspense, Corporal McKie," Helton said.

"General wants to see these three prisoners in his office at once, sir."

RYAN CAWDOR OPENED his eye.

Blackness. Hintless of stars. Was he blind?

If he was, it would be the capstone misery of a mighty pyramid of them. His whole body was a pulse of pain timed to the pounding of his heart. His head hurt as if it had been recently used as an anvil. He felt the mixed sensations of clammy heat, nausea, and being somehow unmoored from the world that indicated a fever raged in his body. And beneath it all there lay a vast aching void, a sense—a knowledge—of loss.

He realized, then, that dim light was seeping into the lower edge of his field of vision. He expelled a long breath in relief and rolled his eye down. Dust-colored light, as if it were shining in through a tunnel mouth just out of sight around a curve. He lay on his back with his head propped on something yielding. His body was swaddled in what he guessed for blankets.

He suddenly remembered. Wags appearing out of nowhere. Uniformed coldhearts with blasters. A great flickering muzzle-flash, pale yellow in the sun. A blow like a sledgehammer to the upper chest.

Falling.

"Krysty," he croaked. His voice was like a gate that hadn't been opened in a hundred years.

A strange high-pitched chittering sounded in the darkness right by his head, causing him to start. After the fact he realized it had said, "What's the matter with his eye? He can't seem to see us."

"You forget, Light Sleeper," said a second voice, lower-pitched enough that Ryan understood it in real time. "Real humans don't see in the dark as we do. Their eyes are so small."

Real humans. That could mean only one thing—he'd been captured by muties. He remembered his previous brief flirtation with consciousness, as he lay broken on a rock, half-hanging over the maw of the Big Ditch. The small, furtive figures sidling toward him in the twilight, the misshapen hand reaching out for him...

Adrenaline thrilled in his nerves, the need to escape. He tried to spring to his feet. He couldn't move. The cloth wrapped around his arms and legs bound him as effectively as steel bands.

"Give us a light, Light Sleeper," the second mutie said.

Ryan's body heaved, arching off the cool ground beneath him, once, twice, three times. Then it fell back spent. He was helpless. His consciousness swam from sickness and exertion. Fighting back oblivion he lay, glaring into the dimness in which he could still see only the vaguest suggestion of movement. His chest heaved, far more with rage and frustration at his helplessness than fear. He heard a snap, then another.

What were they? he wondered wildly. Stickies? Scalies?

A third snap. The ancient lighter finally produced a sufficient spark to ignite the butane stream. Yellow light flared.

Ground squirrels?

He lay in a small cave, with an irregular dome of packed-dirt ceiling five feet high. Two creatures sat hunched over him, gazing at him with huge mild eyes. They were about the size of a small chubby child, roughly three feet tall, although they might possibly be closer to four standing erect, presuming they were bipedal. Which didn't seem a bad presumption, since one was holding the lighter in what seemed to be a furry three-fingered hand. They had little snub noses and round cheeks and round ears that came to black-tufted points. The fur on their bellies was buff colored.

They looked... Well, like a cross between humans and squirrels and something called an Ewok, which he'd seen in an old vid.

"Rest, human," said the one without the lighter. "You're feverish."

"Who—what are you?" he croaked. To his ears, his words were harder to understand than theirs; they came out in such a tormented croak.

"Ow! My thumb!" Light Sleeper exclaimed. He yanked the singed digit back from the hot friction wheel. Darkness reclaimed the cave.

The second voice said, quite distinctly, "We are the Little Ones."

Blackness claimed Ryan once more.

AFTER HE HAD DISMISSED his new conversational partner's associates to get squared away in their new quarters and assignments, the General shooed Helton and the other guards out of his office. When he was alone, he pressed a button hidden on the underside of the writing surface of his rolltop desk. A moment later a figure descended the spiral staircase from the overhead pass-through and battle deck.

A splendid touch, that, the General thought for the thousandth time. He hoisted his brandy goblet to the long-dead designers for so well combining space-efficiency and elegance.

The man who stepped off the brass-railed stair wore black knee-high boots, whipcord riding pants of a color somewhere between the olive drab worn by many of MAGOG's crew and gray, and a stiff tunic, just off-white, with a high square collar that suggested either a man of the cloth or an ancient Nehru jacket. The General, who loved little better than reading about powerful men of previous eras, had learned all about Nehru from the reference works stored in the database of MAGOG's unbelievably capacious living steel. Along with being stiff, the tunic had a bulky look to it, as if it concealed body armor. The General knew better.

That pleased him, too. He liked having things on people. Especially his own subordinates, and most particularly when they were as capable and unscrupulous as his head of intelligence.

The new arrival was small and spare, almost desiccated. The skin stretched over his narrow skull was oddly colorless, although more like a sun-bleached version of his jodhpurs than the albino captive who'd just been hustled off, snarling and struggling, with his wrists still secured behind him by nylon restraints. Except for thin arched eyebrows that might have been drawn on, his head was as bald as the globe of the pre-War Earth on its polished-brass stand in the corner of the General's sitting room-cum-office. The only discordant touch in this ensemble of shades of gray was the black Mad Dog eyeglasses he wore. He never showed himself without them.

The General saluted him with his goblet. "*Ave,* Hubertus! Hail and good morning."

Hubertus smiled thinly. The gesture appeared to hurt his narrow lips, as though they were cracked.

"So, do you think it's them?"

"Let me see," Hubertus said in a siccant voice. He raised a black-gloved hand and began to tick off points on the fingertips. "A short, middle-aged man, deadly in combat and a master gunsmith, who wears a fedora, a leather jacket and wire-rimmed spectacles. A long-haired albino youth. A sturdy black woman and a tall, erudite derelict whose mind had a tendency to wander great distances. A tall man with long, curly black hair and an eyepatch, who habitually carries a sniper's rifle. Finally, a tall woman of remarkable statuesque beauty who, if reports can be believed, has brilliant red hair that moves of its own accord, like Medusa's serpents."

He lowered his hands and shook his head. "I wish I had reviewed young Captain Helton's report of yesterday's raid earlier."

"Don't beat on yourself," the General said. "It was just another strong-back sweep. We do 'em all the time. Who knew anybody unusual would be lurking among a gaggle of sorry-ass travelers?"

"Just so. But it is my business to know, and it embarrasses me when I do not. I detest surprises. Counting the one-eyed man who attempted to resist our men and fell into the Big Ditch after having been shot, we have accounted for five of the six individuals who are most commonly and consistently reported as turning up, totally at random, in locations from north to the south."

"Except the woman."

"Except the woman. Unless there exists another band of five individuals precisely fitting descriptions repeated dozens of times—and even the names they gave us match up well with our information—then either the woman has left the party or she managed to elude Helton's men. Given that she figures prominently in practically all reports we have collected, she is an accomplished survivor. My wild-ass guess is that they simply missed her."

"Nobody's ever managed to bag the one-eyed man before."

Hubertus gave a curious one-shoulder shrug. "The trail ends for all of us, General, sooner or later. Few if any of the opponents Ryan Cawdor and friends have encountered in their past can have been as well-trained and equipped as our soldiers."

"I wouldn't be so sure of that, Hubertus. If a third of the stories are true, he was the toughest nut of the whole conspicuously hard-shelled bunch. I'd feel better if we at least had a body." He sipped. "Ah, well. Like you say, everybody's string plays out sometime. Yesterday must not have been a good day for him."

He rubbed his hands together. "Well, thank you, Hubertus. This is good news overall. Damned good news indeed."

The intel chief continued to stand stiffly, even for him. The General cocked a heavy eyebrow at him. "You still have something on your mind, S-2?"

"Sir, there's one thing I'm having trouble understanding."

The General raised both eyebrows. "*That* I find difficult to believe. Go ahead, Hubertus. I'm dying to hear."

"I fail to see why Your Excellency posted the new captive to billets as if they were common recruits, rather than remanding them to me for a thorough interrogation."

The General, normally a man of fanatical persistence, had long ago given up trying to break his intel chief from calling him "Your Excellency." Mebbe he hadn't tried quite as hard as he might have.

"The only explanation for their cropping up all over the continent and no doubt beyond—sometimes, our correlation of reports indicates, being spotted in one location mere hours after having been reliably observed a thousand miles away— the only possible explanation is that they possess the secret of the matter-transfer network."

"Mebbe so, mebbe so. Probably, I guess. But I'm after bigger fish, Hubertus. Much bigger."

"The Great Redoubt," Hubertus said tersely. His expression suggested someone had recently tracked fresh dogshit on the luxuriant rug.

"Of course! That's key, Hubertus. Absolutely key."

He tipped his head to one side and regarded his intel chief

quizzically. "You still think I'm chasing will-o'-the-wisps, don't you?"

"Certainly, Your Excellency has solid reasons for postulating the existence of this 'Great Redoubt,' so-called."

"'Postulating?' Postulating? My ass. It's in the damned *records,* Hubertus. In the database files in black-and-white."

"So are approximately eleven thousand pages of documents pertaining to Bigfoot and the Loch Ness Monster."

"But the Great Redoubt exists. The old guys knew the war was coming. They set up their Continuity of Government program far in advance. We could deduce the existence of the Great Redoubt from what we know of their thoughts and actions even if they didn't explicitly talk about it in the records!"

"Your Excellency is no doubt correct."

"Then wipe that skeptical smirk off your face. Look, the redoubt is real. It's key to everything. Don't you see? If—strike that, when—we find the Great Redoubt, we'll get the mat-trans system too. Where else would complete documentation on such a system be stored? Where else would its control center be? Mark my words, Hubertus. I am going to find the Great Redoubt, and find it soon. I'm already close enough to smell it. And when I do, you—we—will have your damned mat-trans as well!"

"As you say, sir. That being the case, why not let me probe for what they know?"

"Because, if they are who you believe they are, I don't think torture will break them. Not even your special brand of torture. Like I say, they're hard-core. Even the women. And I wouldn't be surprised at all if they all knew the secret of willed self-death."

Hubertus made a skeptical noise, somewhere in the depths of his tunic.

The General leaned forward in his chair, making emphatic motions with his large hard hands as if to break down his intel chief's resistance with karate chops. "Look. We're the good guys here. We're working to bring an end to the anarchy. Restore peace and prosperity. Reclaim the Deathlands for life. These are intelligent people, exceptional people—hell, they've shown that, even if by some chance they aren't who we think they are. If we give them half a chance, they'll probably come around to us on their own. And even a torture fan like you has to admit that freely given assistance, not to mention information, is a damned sight more reliable than the coerced kind."

"Perhaps," the intel chief said tartly.

The General sighed. "You're a tough nut yourself, Hubertus. I suppose I like it that way. A damned yes-man would make a sorry excuse for a chief intelligence officer. All right, then. They're human." If he noticed a slight additional stiffening on Hubertus's part he gave no sign. "They're not chilled titanium. If we just give them a little time, decent food and decent treatment—not coddling them, mind, just the same as what the rest of our heroic men and women get—they're going to soften. Let their guards down. Let something slip. If we can just get them to relax, eventually we'll learn whatever we need to know."

"I suppose anything is possible, General."

"Betcher ass. And finally, if they don't come across, we can always torture them," the General said. And laughed explosively at the look on Hubertus's pinched face.

As his master's mirth subsided, the intel chief turned to go. When he reached the stairs the General said his name. He turned back.

"Your Excellency?"

"Bring her to me."

"Sir?"

"The missing link. The one unaccounted for. Krysty Wroth, of the mobile hair and radiant beauty. Find her, Hubertus. Bring her to me."

"It shall be done."

Chapter Eight

Walking down the passageway through the rail wag car, J.B. studied the thick back of Banner's neck. The hair was cropped short there as everywhere on his head, petering out completely before it reached his collar. Just below the last of the hair, offset a bit to the right of the spine, was the red bump of an insect bite, possibly from an early-season deerfly. Staring at that neck, J.B. thought about wrapping his hands around that neck and squeezing.

The presence of the two sec men marching right behind him insured that such thoughts would remain in the realm of pleasant dreams.

That, and his friends. Their encounter with the General had been brief, but had conveyed the impression he was just a straightforward, no bullshit kind of guy. And J.B. didn't buy that for a minute.

Because without saying it, or a word that could be taken as menacing or even cross, the General had made it very clear that the prisoners—recruits, as they were to be regarded from here—were all very much hostage to one another's good behavior.

And that was fine. If he was far from free, he was at least out of the slave compound and out of any kind of shackles. Three squares a day and a dry, warm and reasonably safe place to bunk looked like a pretty good deal at this point. He could hack it for a while.

The General had to die. That went without saying; you didn't ice the best friend J. B. Dix ever had in his whole life and just go on picking and grinning and sitting in the sun. It was just a matter of time.

But there was no reason it shouldn't be the easiest possible time.

When they reached what J.B. judged to be roughly the midpoint of the train they came to a car with a locked steel door. Banner punched a three-digit code into the pad beside it, being sure to shield it with his body. J.B. made a show of looking elsewhere and taking off his glasses and polishing them. Of course he was watching like a hawk, but the sergeant was too careful. He yanked open the door.

"Who the fuck is it?" a sawtoothed voice demanded.

"Banner," the sec man growled. J.B. grinned. Banner wasn't a man who was used to being talked to like that. It was fun to be around when he had to take it.

"Got a new assistant for you, Leo," Banner said.

J.B. stood on tiptoe and craned, trying to see around the sergeant, who was taller than he was as well as wider. His pulse was already racing. The air that had puffed out when the door opened carried the unmistakable peppery tang of blaster oil.

"I hope he's not as dead from the neck up as that last sorry sack of shit you brought me," Leo said. "I've heard about people blowing their own heads off cleaning blasters. Never saw anybody triple stupe enough to actually do it before."

"Naw. This one's a real expert."

"Yeah. Everybody's an ex-spurt. Of Daddy's jizz. Even if the better part of you did run down your daddy's hind leg, Banner."

Banner made a noise deep in the barrel of his chest and

stepped aside. Past him, J.B. saw a man a little bit taller than the sergeant but considerably heavier. Indeed, he looked like a couple hundredweight of potatoes poured into a pair of greasy coveralls. He had graying ginger hair that stuck out in random clumps like bunch grass from all around a face that looked like a collection of fists. The pores on the big red tuber of his nose looked like the holes in a hornet's nest. He was cleaning his hands on a red rag.

"In," Banner said to J.B.

The Armorer brushed imaginary dust off the leather sleeves of his jacket and strolled past Banner without glancing at the man.

Leo jerked up his multiple chins in a peremptory gesture. "Don't let the door hit you in the ass on the way out, Banner."

"You two enjoy your dream date," the sergeant said. He backed out and shut the door with what J.B. thought was unnecessary force.

He looked around. He was in a well-lit and well-equipped armorer's shop.

It looked like heaven to him.

"Name's Dix," he said, "J. B. Dix."

From somewhere Leo whipped out a silvery handblaster and aimed it at J.B.'s forehead.

"Show me the secret of the M-9," he growled, "or I put some hair on the wall!"

MILDRED WAS INTRODUCED to Singh, the thin, harried dark woman who was MAGOG's chief medic, in the antechamber of what she was by now not surprised to discover was a small but immaculate and well-appointed surgery, all gleaming stainless steel.

"You're actually a doctor?" Singh asked, skeptical over her pulled-down mask. People these days were extraordinarily disease-resistant by Mildred's standards, but when it came to cutting open human bodies, only a fool took chances. "How is that possible?"

"I'm a healer," Mildred said cagily. "I was trained by a knowledgeable old man."

Singh nodded. "I guess I'm lucky to have you. After the raid, I need all the hands I can get."

Looking past the woman to where a group of people in pale green scrubs were prepping a patient, Mildred was startled to recognize an erstwhile member of the travelers' caravan on the steel table. "You're treating the laborers?"

Singh's expression hardened. "They're human beings, aren't they?"

Mildred was doubly startled; it was a reaction more out of her own time than this. "I watched them gun down two dozen men, women and children, just because they weren't fit to work on the track."

The medic nodded grimly. Then, glancing over her shoulder to make sure no one was in earshot, she leaned her head close to Mildred's and whispered, "Don't expect anything that happens on this train to make any kind of sense. That way you might keep some semblance of sanity."

"EASE UP THERE, friend," J.B. said. "I ain't got enough hair to have you going and doing that."

Leo's blue eyes were watery but determined behind the lenses of his safety glasses. He said nothing. The blaster didn't waver by a thousandth of an inch.

"Your M-9 Beretta," J.B. went on, "called the Model 92 for the civilian market—that's an *S* there, with the slide-mounted safety, and I'm rad-blasted if I know why they thought that was an improvement over mounting it on the frame—had one peculiar vulnerability."

Almost casually he reached up and laid a hand over the top of the blaster. His index finger punched the magazine release, spitting the magazine onto the floor. His thumb pressed the takedown-lever release on the right side of the frame, just in front of the trigger guard. His third finger pushed down the takedown lever itself. The three motions flowed one into the other with precise practiced speed.

Then he pulled the slide assembly, with barrel and recoil spring, forward right off the weapon, leaving Leo holding nothing but the frame.

"Which happened to be that you could take one apart while it was pointed at you. *If* you knew what you were doing." He tried not to sound smug.

Leo turned up his free hand and opened it. J.B. dropped the blaster parts into it. The chief armorer worked the muscles of his face. It looked like a giant trying to crack his own knuckles one-handed.

"You'll do for now, you smug son of a bitch," he said grudgingly. "I'll prob'ly kill you in the morning."

THE WIND STIRRED dry silver-gray tufts of buffalo grass. Though winter was near its end and the days were warm, the brief but furious spring rains hadn't brought the first hints of green to the land. Which were about all the green this land ever got.

The grass tickled Krysty's nose as she lay on the red sandstone caprock rim of a low mesa with her nose stuck in the clump. She was watching the rail line that lay below. She'd been following it for two days now. Rather, she was watching the now-dirt road that ran alongside it.

Four vehicles rolled east, two open scout wags and two pickups filled with sec men and their longblasters. In the passenger seat of the lead dune buggy rode the youthful captain who had overseen the massacre, metal breastplate gleaming, face shining like a young god's.

Krysty's muscles and belly squirmed with the desire to sight down one of the M-16 longblasters she had relieved the deserters of, draw bead on that fine young head, end that brief but oh-so-destructive life with a spinning needle-nosed bullet. She forced herself to lie still. The range was two hundred yards at least, not an easy shot. The M-16 was capable of accuracy over surprisingly long ranges, but this one had only iron sights, and its light bullets were susceptible to the treacherous desert wind over distance. And Krysty wasn't the marksman Ryan had been, to say the least.

Even if she had known beyond doubt her bullet would trephine that dark-haired skull, let air and sunlight in and life out, she wouldn't have taken the shot. Yes, the captain had to die. She had to kill him, or at least be the cause of his death even if her finger didn't pull the trigger or her hand plunge the blade.

But he was just one among many. A significant one; but a mere one. To claim his life would risk throwing her life away with her friends still unrescued and the bilk of her blood-debt unpaid. She wouldn't do that.

So she watched them drive out of sight, unmolested. Intuition told her they were heading back to the massacre site, to the rim above Ryan's unmarked resting place a mile toward the center of the earth. Why they might be bound there she couldn't say. It didn't matter, and speculation was no part of her nature in any event. She let all thought of whys and wherefores slip from her mind.

She did keep awareness of the fact that patrols from the rail wag were out and about, with at least one all but certain to be heading back along this road at any time. There were also the coldhearts the two deserters had been looking to join. She rose up from her hiding place, moved a little ways around the end of the mesa, then began to pick her way downslope where a finger of red stone would hide her from view from the road.

She had plenty of food, mostly jerky and MREs, and water. She'd be okay for a few more days. After that, if she hadn't accomplished her mission…

No. There could be only her quest. Worry, fear, anticipation—these could only weaken the resolve she needed to keep her weary legs driving her relentlessly on.

Forcing all conscious thought from her mind, forcing herself to concentrate solely on her footing and awareness of her surroundings, Krysty picked her way down the slope toward the desert floor.

Chapter Nine

"Still nothing?" the General asked. His voice was calm and level.

That could be deceiving, Hubertus knew. The General was normally a rational sort, but he had a temper, to say the least. And no one with any major share of his marbles intact enjoyed bearing bad news to a baron.

Especially when the bad news was that one had failed in a task entrusted by one's baron.

"No sign of the woman at the place where the civilian convoy was detained. The patrol has spent the last day searching outward in a widening spiral. The only thing of any note that Captain Helton has reported—"

A nice touch, that, Hubertus thought. Emphasizing that if there were any blame to be spewed about for the failure to fulfill the General's whim for the red-haired woman, his very own fair-haired boy Captain Marc Helton stood squarely to catch much of it. Which, of course, was why he insured the boy was put in charge of the expedition.

"—was the discovery en route to the site of the bodies of the two men who vanished a week ago. They seem to have deserted, as we surmised. They had been shot and looted and left behind the ruins of a gas station. A concentration of crows and vultures drew the scouts' attention to their corpses."

The General nodded. " Jackson and Price. A disappoint-

ment. They came from good families, those boys. I expected
more of them. Not as good as Marc's family, of course, but
plenty good for enlisted men. Not your usual delinquents
who turn into coldhearts. Mark my words, Hubertus. There's
nothing more important than family. That's what shapes a
man's character, gives it content."

Good thing the General didn't know his family, the intel
chief thought. Although, given the nature of the task Hubertus performed for the chief, he realized, that might not be
strictly so.

"Captain Helton speculates the coldheart horde caught
them and killed them." He hesitated. "I fear that is almost certainly the fate that has befallen the Wroth woman as well. I
must state as my considered opinion that she's dead."

The General sat in silence, scratching his chin. Hubertus
stood braced and tried not to quake. A drop of sweat tickled
his thin neck on is way down into his Nehru collar. He wasn't
a coward, but he knew the danger he was in.

"Bring them in," the General said.

"Your Excellency?"

The General waved an emphatic hand. "Bring them back.
Call in the patrol."

"Without the woman, sir?"

"They don't have her, do they? What kind of cockamamie
question— Oh."

He nodded abruptly. "I see. You're afraid I'm disappointed.
More to the point, you're afraid I'll blame you."

He leaned forward in his chair. "Listen here, old man. When
I was a child there was a man in our ville who had an old tele-
vision and DVD player, and slaves to ride fixed-bicycle gen-
erators to power 'em. He used to charge people to watch his
vid collection. That was where he got the money for the slaves.

"We watched all these videos from before the war—I guess I'm stupid, that goes with saying, doesn't it?—and the ones I liked best were the ones with lots of action. Blasters firing, explosions with bodies flying everywhere. Big surprise, right? But one thing always puzzled me. The villain in these old vids was always chilling his own henchmen. Sometimes just for the sheer spite of it. I know now it was to show the audience just what a bastard bad guy he was. But what I couldn't figure was why anybody would work for someone like that. Why didn't his goons run off the second they were out of his sight?"

If Hubertus were the boss in question, it would be because he'd hunt them down and chill them in various horrible protracted ways, and their families, too. But he kept his peace.

"Now, you know I've got no patience with incompetence, Hubertus, and a lot less with disloyalty. I know you think I've turned into a big old mush melon because I'm not letting you torture our star new recruits. But I've never been one to shrink from a good drumhead court-martial, nor standing the guilty up against a wall immediately afterward. And you know that for a fact.

"But hell, I know. Finding this redheaded she-devil was a pipe dream. It was never that important in the first place, nothing at all in comparison to grabbing the brass ring. You know what I'm talking about, Hubertus!"

The intel chief nodded. He knew.

"The track repairs are done. We're ready to roll. And I could have every soul aboard this train out searching until the sun burned out without turning up a missing party, even if she didn't jump in the Ditch or wind up playing R&R for about a hundred plaguer coldhearts. It goes without saying anything that could be done, you and Marc have done. I try never to blame a body for not doing the impossible. Dead or fled, we can't screw around with her any longer. Radio Helton and tell him to haul ass back here. We'll roll the moment his wags are secured."

"And the laborers, sir?" They weren't actually any of Hubertus's responsibility. But he felt he had to say something to keep from betraying how relieved he was.

The General frowned in momentary thought. "We'll leave them the water that's in the tower we built for the compound and some MREs."

"You're letting them go?"

"Yeah." The General had already turned away and had picked up a sheaf of hand-written reports.

"As Your Excellency wishes," Hubertus said.

WIND WHISTLED, veered and boomed. Head down, the ball cap she had taken off Matt crammed down on her own red hair, a pair of sunglasses she had taken from his pocket shading her eyes, Krysty clambered up another slope furred in gray bunch grass and dotted with low brush. The mad desert wind lashed her with grit and sticky bits of dried vegetation. To her left and below ran the rail line, and the road that paralleled it. The sun was high in the sky, but still short of the zenith. Despite the wind the morning was hot, although nothing to what it would be in a matter of weeks at this time of day.

She resented the cost in time and energy of keeping as much as possible to the high ground. The wisdom of it, however, had been reinforced an hour or so before when the patrol she had seen go out a couple of days earlier returned at speed. She had seen the wink of sunlight off the captain's burnished steel breastplate as the wags passed a quarter mile away. Intuition told her MAGOG was preparing to move on, that repairs on the track neared completion if they weren't finished already.

Inside she was whipsawed, now ablaze with the nearness of her quarry, now chilled through the guts with the dread that it would escape. Nearing the point of psychic thermal shock, the best she could do was to drive herself without rest, drinking on the move from her rapidly dwindling store of canteens and water bottles, and hope she made good enough time. To try to move along the track or road, exposed, would be begging to be caught—to fail.

Worse even than having MAGOG slip away was the prospect that she would die in a ditch like a dog, without liberating her friends or taking her revenge.

A few feet from the top, a loose rock slipped beneath her foot. Her ankle torqued dangerously. Only barely did she manage to avoid spraining.

Even so, the weight of her pack and the deserters' two longblasters strapped to it drove her face-first into the sand. She reared up her head, shook it and spit out dry dirt. Crying out in frustration, she pushed herself up on all fours.

Whether it was a rustle of sound, all but undetectable beneath the wind, or movement in her peripheral vision, she didn't know. Some sensation made her turn her head and look left.

It saved her vision and her sight.

Fluid struck her glasses like water from a squirt gun. She recoiled. Milky liquid half obscured both lenses of polarized glass. Then, some dripped onto her right cheek. It clung and burned like fire.

She screamed and rolled. One hand knocked the glasses from her face, the other grabbed up a palmful of sand, trying to scrub the burning fluid from her violated skin.

She was up on her knees and one arm. Her jade green eyes tracked frantically over the scrub to find the source of the attack.

It stood beneath a low chamisa fifteen feet away—a scorpion at least six inches long, its carapace yellow with branching black markings. Its pincers clacked before its nervously working mandibles. Its tail was raised over its back, aimed at Krysty like a blaster.

As she looked, the tail darted forward. Possibly pumped-out by the motion, a stream of greenish-blue liquid squirted toward her eyes. With strength born of terror she reared upright on her knees. The venom passed where her face had been half a heartbeat before and struck at the base of a clump of grama grass. It made a sizzling sound and a stomach-clenching reek. Silvery strands of the bunch grass blackened and shriveled from the poison.

There were neurotoxins in that hellbrew as well as acid or a fast-acting enzyme. Krysty felt her cheek twitching where the tiny poison drop had landed, and she was having trouble focusing that eye.

With a heave of her shoulders she shucked her pack. She threw herself to the side. Whether the creature had sprayed again she didn't know.

She hit, rolled and came up into a crouch. She couldn't see the mutie arthropod anymore. It was no comfort—the opposite, in fact. She didn't want the jointed horror lurking in ambush, or sniping her from cover.

She drew her handblaster. The solid weight of the revolver reassured her, even if she wasn't sure how much use a blaster would be.

A waving of tall tufts of grass in a manner contrary to the wind alerted her. She had the snubby pointed and was pulling through the long trigger action when the yellow-and-black creature scuttled into view. Its tail was cocking back for a shot of its own.

She fired three times, trying her best to aim using the notched backstrap and low front sight. Her second bullet neatly clipped the bulbous black stinger off the scorpion's tail.

It ran at her, claws clacking. She jumped up. The heel of her right boot flashed down right in the midst of the churn of segmented legs. Gasping in fury, pain and terror, she stomped the loathsome thing into the earth. Then she carefully dragged her heel through some sand drifted at the bottom of a bush to try to scour off the poison and keep it from eating through her boot.

Wheezing like an asthmatic, she staggered to her pack. Her right eye was watering so severely she could see nothing from that side but a blur. Given time, she might be able to find appropriate herbs to make a poultice and counteract the workings of the toxin. But time was a luxury she didn't have. She would have to rely upon the minute quantity of the poison she had been exposed to, and her own mutie powers of accelerated healing. And if she lost sight in that eye, well, it hadn't slowed down her beloved Ryan.

She knelt, hauled up the pack, pulled the straps over her shoulders, then struggled to her feet. The pack felt like lead, her legs like sandbags. Bent, she stumbled to the top of the hill.

There it was. A mile away, gleaming like a river yanked out straight in the sun.

MAGOG.

And then she saw that it was moving.

"No," she breathed. But, yes, the giant silver serpent was in motion, scarcely perceptible, but increasing as she watched in shocked horror. Without smoke or sound audible at this distance, it was pulling out toward the east and the Continental Divide.

She stood and watched as if held in some kind of suspended animation. When the train had almost passed the hill on which she stood transfixed, it was as if someone had thrown a switch and suddenly restored power to her systems. She began to run down the hill, heedless of the way her overloaded legs jarred the sockets of her hips at every step, heedless of obstacles, heedless of the need to remain unseen. She was empty of everything except the blind desperate need not to let her quarry escape.

She was too late. As if there were anything she could do to stop the fusion-powered behemoth, once it built up speed.

Stumbling, reeling, vision blacking around the edges, her lungs feeling as if they were being ripped in two each time she breathed, she reached the bottom of the hill. The last wag of the train was already over a quarter-mile distant and receding at a good clip.

Somehow she crossed the road and hauled herself up the steep embankment without even being aware of effort. She stood square between the endless narrow steel bands only to see the last of MAGOG disappear around the hip of a low distant mesa.

The wind was a wild howl now. A tumbleweed fetched up against her leg and clung like an amorous poodle. She let slip her pack again and went to her knees.

Stretched herself full length across the ties and sobbed in frustration.

Chapter Ten

On board MAGOG no one was paying particular attention to where the train had been, either the troops in the terminal blaster car or the techs in the General's command center just back of the front engine. Had a fresh horde of coldhearts swarmed onto the tracks behind them, somebody probably would have noticed. But a lone woman climbing onto the tracks a couple of hundred yards back attracted no one's attention. Even a tall, beautiful woman with red hair that moved of its own accord.

Of course, the hair was wound up under a ball cap and details like that were invisible at that distance anyway.

So not even the great man himself, who was in the command center gazing raptly at the tracks in front of his mighty rolling fortress, happened to observe that the woman he'd been hunting for was standing right out in the open, getting smaller and smaller with increasing distance.

Twenty-four hours later, MAGOG's massively parallel processors automatically deleted those particular digitized images captured by the rear-mounted video cameras from RAID storage to save space. And no one was the wiser.

THE FORMER SLAVE-LABORERS milling around their tented compound looked like refugees whose war had fled them, rather than the other way around. Marching down the road, fueled solely by her own indomitable will, Krysty was conscious enough to be amazed that they had been left alive.

She was still more amazed to see a handful of wags parked in a neat little pen of their own off the main compound, including the ones stolen from the travelers' caravan.

People raced toward the red-haired woman as she strode up to the barbed wire. As they saw the look in her eye and the very resolute way she moved, they stopped, then faded away from her. The fact she had a pair of longblasters slung in an X across her back might have had something to do with it.

A burly black-bearded man in overalls came out the open gate. "Krysty? Krysty Wroth?"

It was one of the travelers from the caravan. She couldn't for the life of her remember his name. It didn't seem important somehow.

"We thought you was dead," he said.

"Not yet."

He pulled his head back on his thick neck and blinked his brown eyes at that. He didn't seem to quite know what to say.

"Where are they going?" she demanded.

"What?"

She grabbed him by the straps of his overalls. "The train! Where's it headed?"

He shook his head. "I dunno. They didn't say."

"They didn't even tell us why they left us here alive," said a thin woman Krysty didn't remember seeing before. She turned her head aside and spit in the dust. "Not that we'll stay that way long once the food and water they left runs out."

Krysty let go the big man and walked on, around the main compound, toward the wag park. The vehicles were empty. She picked out the least battered of the lot, a red Chevy S10 faded pink by the sun. She walked up, looked inside. The key was in the ignition. Once they were through with the wags the General's gang had just walked away from them, serviceable or not. As they had from the captives.

She opened the door.

"You can't."

She stopped and turned. It was the woman who had spoken to her earlier, standing at the entrance to the wag corral. Thirty or so of the abandoned captives stood behind her. They didn't look threatening. Mainly confused.

"Those wags're our lifeline," the woman said. "Either to get us to provisions or provisions to us. Either way, we need all of 'em."

Krysty unslung one of the M-16s. The crowd gasped and melted back a few steps. The hatchet-faced spokeswoman swayed, swallowed, set her jaw and stood her ground.

Moving deliberately, Krysty laid the longblaster on the hardpacked earth at her feet. She set down a loaded mag as well.

"I'm taking the wag," she said. "Here's payment. Or I'll fight. Your call."

The released slaves said no more. Krysty threw her pack onto the seat on the passenger side, then climbed in behind the wheel.

The engine started the first try.

The crowd gave way slowly as she drove out of the wag corral and turned east onto the road. She drove off without so much as a backward glance.

A pair of riders were approaching the compound from the east. A scrubby little half-naked Indian-looking guy on a pinto pony and a mustached man in a dapper linen suit and Panama hat mounted a nearly white mule with black ear-tips. Krysty drove straight, without acknowledging their existence, forcing them to split to either side of the road to keep from being run down.

She kept on going, following MAGOG. Where it went, there her trail led.

"BITCH!" CHATO EXCLAIMED, waving a fist at the Chevy's rear bumper.

"Go easy, my friend," El Abogado advised. "There rides a remarkable young woman. She carries a load of doom with her, as weighty as the world. Best to let her go her way, out of our lives."

Chato gave him a narrow look.

"Trust me," he said.

Chato shrugged it off. He had important plans, far too important to be distracted by some off-the-wall white-eyes bitch. He steered his pony back onto the road and booted it toward the laborers' camp.

At its edge, he reined in. He was pleased to see a crowd of mebbe a hundred souls assembled outside the wire. It was as if they awaited him.

Clearly, here lay his Destiny.

Chato was back in his manic phase.

He sat as tall as he could—there were advantages to being on horseback—and announced, "My friends, my name is Chato, and I have come to save you from this anarchy!"

"YOU POOR BABY," Mildred murmured to the naked child who stood in the black rubber washtub. He was a boy about eight years old with light brown hair just beginning to cover his scalp in fuzz. The residents of the ville called Milan, just east of the Continental Divide, tended to shave their children's heads to prevent their catching lice. His scalp, like the rest of him, was covered with red weals and weeping blisters. "That's a good boy. Just keep still."

She was washing him all over with a rag soaked in cool, clean water from a stream running down from the nearby mountains. She was mostly wringing the cloth near his body to soak an area in water, then more dabbing or brushing than anything like scrubbing.

Although there was a nasty hot spot to the west where a one-megaton ground-burst had taken out the Fort Wingate ordnance storage area, this part of what had been western New Mexico like much of the Southwestern desert had been spared some of the nastier chem and rad-related aftereffects of the last war. When a freak chem storm had struck early that morning, just hours before MAGOG pulled in, they had been caught almost totally unprepared. They didn't know how to respond, although the natural reflex to get in out of the rain, amplified by the fact that the rain burned like acid, had served to keep casualties down.

Four residents, either caught flat-footed in the open or who had panicked and dashed madly about as they melted alive—rather than having the presence of mind to seek something, *anything* to shelter under—had been killed outright, albeit horribly: their skins seared away, the flesh bubbled and melted away from acid-discolored bones. Fifteen others, including eight children, had been hurt to varying degrees of seriousness. Many others, of course, had suffered minor contact injuries and gone about their business having done little more than wash the spot where a caustic drop had hit, frequently with their own spit. People tended not to pay a lot of mind to wounds if there wasn't a lot of blood or bones sticking out or whatever.

The crack of a 5.56 mm longblaster from somewhere made

Mildred wince. Some of the injuries had been nasty, as you'd expect from a chem storm, and the sufferers weren't helped by their friends' and families' inexperience in treating the injuries such storms inflicted. The single M-16 shot meant that a victim, though conscious, had been judged terminal by Singh, who then nodded to a wooden-faced young sec man who'd drawn short straw. Unconscious no-hopers had their jugular veins opened by a quick precise slice of Singh's scalpel.

Mildred had already daubed her patient's body with a solution of baking powder from MAGOG's stores, neutralizing any pockets of acid that might have been trapped in skin folds or joints. Now she was rinsing the wounds as clean as possible, as gently as possible. Next she would dust the open sores with broad-spectrum antibiotic powder. Beyond that, and keeping them clean, and treating the wounds with whatever was available to soothe pain, there was little to do.

Whatever was available in this case consisted of a brew of local herbs applied in poultices, which the locals swore alleviated pain from burns. Singh, whose education had, of necessity, included substantial training in herbalism, could only shrug. She wasn't familiar with the local herbs, and could do no more than trust the locals' own lore, which she knew as well as anybody was just as likely to mask toxic agents that would do more harm than good behind flat-out myth.

Yet again, Mildred wished Krysty was with them. Not simply because she loved the woman as a sister, but because Krysty's knowledge of healing herbs was truly vast, and what she didn't know, her instinct and intuition could tell her. She could have judged the efficacy or otherwise of the local home remedy, and if it wasn't up to snuff could have improved it or whipped up something that would work.

A shadow fell across her. She looked up.

Captain Marc Helton was walking past. He wasn't wearing his metal breastplate today, just OD fatigues. He carried the blistered lifeless body of a four-year-old girl in his arms. His eyes didn't see Mildred. Tears leaked silently from them.

She stared in frank amazement. He walked on out of sight around to the back of the adobe church in front of which the MAGOG crew had set up their aid station. The deaders were being laid out there in the shade of a *remuda,* a sort of awning made with wood uprights and frame and roofed over with branches and brush.

"I never will understand this damn outfit, little one," she said to her patient, who regarded her from eyes which, while the lids were blistered nearly shut, had thankfully not been damaged themselves. She straightened. "Come on, let's get you back to your mama."

KRYSTY'S PICKUP finally crapped in the desert around twenty-five miles on the other side of Milan, well beyond the sand-drifted ruins of the larger ville called Grants. It just coughed twice, flat died, and coasted to a stop.

Krysty didn't waste breath on cursing the wag or her fate. Nor did she bother raising the hood. She had no idea of how to repair it.

She had been lucky, she knew, to get her hands on the wag in the first place, much less nurse it this far. She had still lost ground on her quarry. MAGOG traveled fast when it had intact rails, as apparently it had from the slave camp onward. While the road mostly still existed, especially once she'd reached what had been I-40, it was busted here and washed out there and drifted hopelessly over with dunes someplace else. She hadn't been able to get the wag above forty miles per hour in the best of stretches, not without the thing setting up a nasty shuddering and chattering that she didn't have to be a mech to know couldn't possibly bode well. What with the stretches of even worse road, which were most of them, frequent detours and the odd false start, she knew she'd been unable to average better than twenty, twenty-five miles an hour.

Which was still immeasurably better than traveling by shank's mare.

She had reached Milan just before dark the previous day. The little ville, which consisted of a handful of predark ruins and a number of squat adobe structures built afterward ended, was surrounded by a living hedge of some kind of mutant maguey or yucca plants. These sprouted long slim spines, all the way up to twelve or fifteen feet in length, arching away from the plant's core. These stirred and shifted to point to her as Krysty's wag approached on the dirt track that led from the old blacktop.

The guards who pulled aside a barrier made from an old wag chassis and waved her inside looked tense and drawn. She wondered if they feared attack, but soon learned they had been hit with a freak chem storm that morning. MAGOG had pulled into town shortly after.

The train's personnel had provided emergency medical service to the stricken townsfolk. Several lives had been saved, the wounded succored. Supplies of antibiotics and analgesics had been left for them. In exchange, all they had asked was to top their tank cars with fresh water, which the ville had in abundance.

The townies, in short, thought the General and all his people walked on water.

By nature an outgoing person, Krysty had learned as a

child how to play things close to her chest. She merely grunted and nodded. She kept her own opinion of the General, and her experience at the hands of his sec men, strictly to herself. The people wouldn't have believed her anyway. People believe what they see. She was just a redheaded stranger from the West, well-armed but polite. Who was she to go running down their benefactors?

All she could do was attract ill will. She didn't need that. She understood a body's need for sleep as a healer did, and understood that she had to take care of herself to do what she had to do. If possible, she needed to sleep the night in the relative security of the ville.

She traded some of the tools she'd brought from the travelers' caravan for a night on a cot in the back room of Sawtelle's Possibles, a sort of general store. The room stank from the carcasses of numerous small animals and game birds, some of which Krysty was sure were mutants and not natural creatures at all, which had been hung to soften up and lose some of the edge from their gamy taste. She ignored it.

Information, meager enough, she got simply by listening to locals sitting over mugs of rank-smelling local beer, once or twice interjecting a brief, pointed question. No, the locals had no idea where MAGOG was headed, other than east. They reckoned likely it was somewhere beyond Burque on the Big River, past the Sandia Mountains that rose just to the east of there.

That meant the armored train was headed into the Great Plains. Into the belly of the Deathlands.

Krysty did learn that one of the two healers who had done most of the work was a heavyset black woman who could only be Mildred Wyeth. That filled her with a sense of relief so vibrant and foolish she almost smiled. At least one of her friends was alive. It boded well for the others.

That night she slept without dreaming.

In the morning she ate a breakfast of bacon and fresh hen's eggs paid for with three cartridges. Outside, the sky was clear and the sun warm. She noticed a wizened old woman shaking what she took to be a rattle, made from an old can on the end of a short stick, at a small child with scabbing-over burns on arms and face, and a whiteface heifer. The child then guided the cow toward the thorn wall by switching at its haunches with the long central stalk of a yucca. Krysty loaded her pack into the truck and paused to watch as beast and boy came up to the hedge of thorns.

The thorns began to stir, as they had when Krysty neared them in her truck. But instead of rotating their needle tips toward the child and the cow, as they had for her, the plants turned the spines away. The two were able to pass through without harm, simply brushing past the shanks of the spines.

Interesting. Krysty looked around for the old woman, who had vanished into one of the buildings of the settlement. Rather than a rattle, the object she had shaken over the boy and his charge had to have been a dispenser, containing some substance that gave them safe passage through the wicked thorns. Krysty suspected it was the pollen of the mutie thorn plant itself.

Shaking her head, Krysty got into her wag and drove on. She'd never know, and she felt a pang of regret at that.

The eastern gate was another truckbed weighted down with lava boulders and chunks of concrete, which the sentries obligingly rolled out of her path. Two hours later the wag engine choked and croaked.

She was on her feet again.

From the Divide, the declining land had run from mountains forested in pine and fir, to undulating hills dotted with scrubby trees, and then back to plain Upper Sonoran cactus and bunch grass desert, with wind-cut mesas rising above and arroyos like gashes of a giant knife below. The pavement here was clear and relatively intact. By bitter irony, which she did no more than allow her mind to brush over, she could have made the best speed so far had her wag survived.

Ryan's mentor and long-time employer Trader used to say that a man who cried over spilt milk was blinded by his tears. And women too; but Krysty hadn't needed Trader to teach her that.

She drew a deep breath. At the moment, the breeze was from the mountains behind her, as cool and fresh as a drink of water from a mountain stream, flavored with a hint of pine. She drank it in, drew sustenance from Gaia's sweet breath.

Then she shouldered her pack and marched east, not knowing where her quarry was, nor if it was even remotely possible she could catch it.

Her quest was all.

Vengeance was all.

Chapter Eleven

Real coffee. Mildred shook her head and drank down the aroma from her mug with the Mobile Anti-Guerrilla Operations Group logo on the side as if it were as substantial and stimulating as the bitter black brew itself. It probably wasn't near fresh. Likely it had been irradiated and sealed away in nitrogen-filled containers while she was still walking around in the twentieth century, oblivious to the impending end of the world, and even of the ovarian cyst that would cause her own functional death and rebirth into a world she never would have imagined even if she could. But it was still coffee, and delicious.

She shook her head again, enjoyed the sound and feel of the wooden beads strung on her thin dreadlocks rattling together. She'd had a hot shower that afternoon before the rail wag pulled out of Milan. The wonders of the fusion power cells in the lead and trail engines. A shy healer named Alisha had helped her plait and bead her hair when it was dry.

Life on this train was a lot like civilization.

And that's the pure bitch of it, girlfriend. She remembered how she came to be here. She *made* herself remember. It would be sheer betrayal of her martyred father's memory to make peace with the men who had enslaved her.

No reason she couldn't enjoy the truce, though.

She felt the presence, just at the border of her personal

space. She knew who it was without looking. He seemed to radiate some kind of energy. Or maybe it was just a cloud of male pheromones, affecting a healthy human female in her sexual prime.

Reluctant to give too much away, she made herself raise her head and look him in the eye before saying, "Is there something I can help you with, Captain?"

"Mildred," he said in that rich voice of his, like the amber of his eyes made liquid and poured, "may I join you?" She couldn't help but shiver. Damn it!

Damn him.

She shrugged. "I'm hardly in a position to refuse, now, am I?"

His brow furrowed. He looked like a little boy puzzled by an adult's response. Puzzled...and hurt.

"Of course you are. I'd never presume to intrude."

She goggled at him. She couldn't help it. She wanted to blurt out, "Are you for real?" She kept it down. She was a woman who prided herself on never bending the knee. But survival instinct imposed some constraint on her behavior. Or else she'd never have lived this long since Ryan and the rest had awakened her from her cryosleep tube.

She nodded. He pulled out a chair and sat.

Outside the night rushed past. Even though the lights were dim in the officers' mess car, reflection blanked out the stars, or even whether they were obscured or not by overcast. Alisha had mentioned that the rail wag wasn't rolling at anywhere near its top cruising speed of seventy miles per hour. It wouldn't until it crossed the mountains east of the Grandee and hit the giant, gently tilted tabletop of the Plains.

"I wanted to commend you for the excellent work you did,

both after the bandit attack and at the ville today," Helton said. "Healer Singh speaks very highly of you."

"That was nice of her."

"My name's Helton, by the way. Marc Helton."

"I know who you are, Captain."

Again that schoolboy frown of consternation. To her he looked about sixteen, maybe eighteen tops, although she knew that was mainly just her early-middle-aged perspective. In another ten years, everyone under thirty would look fourteen to her. Still, he probably wasn't much older than that. Kids matured quick in the Deathlands, if at all. And she realized that for all of that, for all his responsibility and the heroic status he enjoyed among MAGOG's personnel, he was, in ways, very young indeed.

Danger, Will Robinson! Danger! She could *not* let this man, her enslaver, murderer of innocents including her beloved friend and benefactor, become too much of a person in her mind. She understood in a way she never had why combatants throughout history had traditionally dehumanized their foes. Suddenly it didn't seem as despicable to her as it always had.

"You seem…reserved with me, Mildred," he said.

"Do I?" She stood up. "Maybe I'm unduly influenced by the circumstances of our first meeting, Captain. Now, if you'll kindly excuse me, it's been a long day."

She held her breath the whole way out of the car.

THE SUN WAS DIPPING TOWARD the Continental Divide when Krysty saw a most remarkable sight.

Keeping off the road and the railway tracks for security's sake, and at the same time trying to stay on heights in sight of both, she was walking along the rim of a cut blasted through a low mesa by the railroad's long-dead builders. As she walked, she swiveled her head left and right, constantly scoping the surroundings.

Movement caught the hem of her peripheral vision. She stopped, shucked the pack and dropped to the ground.

A single man was riding east along the railroad on an incredible machine. It consisted of a small platform with four struts extending from it spiderleg-style, to big spoked wheels rolling on the rails themselves. The man himself sat in a kind of chair, with his legs out before him, pedaling merrily. He wore goggles, a pale cap with a puffy top and a long bill pulled low over his eyes, and a dark coat which streamed out behind him along with a substantial brown ponytail. If he had noticed her up there on the skyline—not the best concealed of positions either, but far less risky than the right-of-way— he gave no sign. He merely continued on to meet the night.

Seizing her remaining M-16, Krysty raced down the slope. This time she stayed conscious of the penalties for putting a foot wrong and crippling her ankle, or tripping and rolling down the steep slope out of control, at risk of breaking an arm or leg.

Skidding, hopping over a cluster of prickly pear, scaring little brown birds into the air, Krysty reached the bottom. The track here was still laid along a raised embankment. She had to run to it, then slog up that steep slope.

The man and his strange machine were already a good three hundred yards beyond. "Hey!" Krysty shouted at his back, waving her arms as if that would do any good. "Hey, wait!"

The wind took her words away. Or he ignored her. He kept pedaling, making surprisingly good time.

Snarling, Krysty wound the longblaster's sling once

around her left forearm, then snugged the black plastic butt to her shoulder and lined the battle sights up on that distant dark back. She drew in a deep breath, let half of it go, caught it, took up slack on the trigger.

No. She eased off the blaster's trigger, let the weapon fall away. The shot was too long. The wind made it too uncertain. She didn't want to spook her quarry. The landscape here seemed to consist mainly of gently angled planes, but Krysty knew the desert offered a startling amount of cover; she didn't want him disappearing into the scrub, then setting up to ambush her when she approached the fantastic machine.

And she was unable to bring herself to shoot in the back a man who had done her no harm.

She sighed explosively and slung the M-16. Unlike MAGOG, the lone pedaler had to sleep sometime. And he was tied to the steel tracks as firmly as the monster rail wag was. She would follow him, relentlessly, and overtake him wherever he picked to rest. If she didn't catch him up until the middle of the night—when he was likely to be sound asleep—so much the better.

She scrambled down the embankment, then began trotting back toward the top of the cut to collect her backpack.

SHIFTING UNCOMFORTABLY, clearing their throats, and scratching their balls when they figured no officer eyes were on them, almost fifty of MAGOG's off-duty complement had packed themselves into the briefing car, a couple back from the General's personal carriages. The forty dusty-blue seats were full, and a number of sec men stood at the rear of the darkened car. The car rocked gently. The sliding armor shutters on the windows were closed to discourage snipers. This was the General's latest attempt at Cultural Uplift. Attendance wasn't mandatory. Just strongly encouraged.

At the front of the car Dr. Theophilus Tanner stood behind a podium, dressed in his cleaned-up, old-timey clothes, smooth-shaven, his long graying hair parted neatly in the middle. His eyes blinked rapidly, nervously. His manner suggested he was a butterfly and the single spot slanting its beam down upon him from the ceiling was a pin.

Front and center sat the great man himself, with Captain Marc Helton at his side. Around them were clustered various aides, who were generally not much more thrilled about being here than the sec men, and terrified the General might sniff out the fact. To a man, and the one or two women, they would rather have been in the bar car pounding down shooters.

Doc swept a last, hunted look around the room. It came to rest on the General, who nodded.

Doc cleared his throat and recited:

"'In Xanadu did Kubla Khan
"'A stately elm tree newly decree
"'Where Alph, the bastard river ran
"'Through fields of flowers pleasant to man.
"'And filled it with bare titty.'"

He said the last word tit-*tee*, emphasis on the second syllable.

There was a moment of utter silence.

Marc goggled. "What?" he asked the General sotto voce. "Where did that come from? What elms? What flowers and tits? There aren't any tits in 'Kubla Khan'!"

The General held a finger to his lips. "Easy, Marc, easy. The professor is having a flashback. It will pass."

The sec men began to hoot and whistle and stamp their feet. Hot damn, mebbe this was gonna be entertaining after all!

"Stand easy, there!" bellowed a familiar roar from the rear of the carriage. Sergeant Banner didn't add that they had better shut their pie-holes *right fucking now* or he'd put his boot so far up their asses they'd taste shit and shoe leather. He didn't need to.

Silence fell.

"A flashback?" Marc asked.

"When he was held captive by a man named Teague, baron of a place called Mocsin, up north," the General said, uncharacteristically quietly. "They made him recite poetry. Unfortunately his captors didn't have very refined tastes. They insisted that he spice up his recitations. If he failed to meet their standards, they did something to him involving putting him in a pen with some sows. He's vague on the details, but they seem to've been pretty sordid."

Up behind the podium Doc was well and truly lost. The audience's uproarious response had put him deep in fear mode.

He blinked past the awful spotlight at the General. "Did I make a mistake, sir?"

"You're fine, Theophilus. Just fine. Keep going."

His lower lip was starting to hang. It quivered. "You—you aren't going to put me in with the sows, are you? Please, not the sows!"

"There, there. There are no sows. This is a train, Theophilus. There are no sows on a train. Would you like to sit down for a few minutes, drink some nice ice water?"

Doc nodded spasmodically. He sat in the chair behind the lectern, grabbed at the pitcher on the table beside it, brought it to his lips and tried to drink directly from it. Water and ice cubes cascaded down his shirtfront, over his crotch and onto the floor.

At the back of the car somebody tittered. The General cleared his throat. The repressed laughter got repressed the rest of the way.

"Why do you indulge the old fool?" Hubertus whispered from behind the General's chair.

"Perhaps because I like having someone to talk who isn't constantly plotting," the General said.

His intel chief sank back in his own chair and hugged himself tightly. His mouth was a compressed line. *Things* moved around under his stiff tunic like nobody's business.

"Don't sulk, Hubertus," the General said without turning. "I didn't mean to hurt your feelings. I like the way you plot. I *pay* you to plot. But I confess yours is not my notion of convivial fucking conversation."

"Fine," Hubertus said, and hugged himself the tighter. "Just fine."

The General sighed. He was a man of wide vision and iron will. But sometimes even he had to acknowledge, if not defeat, a temporary setback. Sometimes he felt that the task of trying to reunite a shattered continent was trivial in comparison to bringing some measure of cultural awareness to the collection of ville rats, mud farmers, mutie bashers, loafabout-the-forts, second sons of mad dungheap barons, failed coldhearts, shitepokes, ne'er-do-wells and general spawn of the lowest nuke-raddled gutter sluts it was his pride and privilege to command.

He rose. "If you gentlemen will excuse me, I'm going to retire to my car. Loomis—" this last was directed to one of the ADCs "—please escort Professor Tanner to his compartment.

"Oh, and—" the General conspiratorially dropped his voice "—make sure the door's locked. He looks as if he might be inclined to wander, if you know what I mean."

"Yes, sir!" The aide moved to the front of the car to mother-hen the professor.

Marc Helton had risen, too. He excused himself and headed toward his quarters farther back in the train.

The General gestured to Banner. The NCO trotted forward. "We don't want to, ah, disappoint the troops too much. Why don't you let them pick out a video from the train library."

"Sir! Yes, sir!"

Doc had been ushered from the car, quietly and uncom-prehendingly, to his compartment. It was tiny and actually lo-cated in the General's personal car, connected to his quarters by a door that locked from the General's side. The General guessed it had been intended to house the mistress of the South American warlord for whom MAGOG had been in-tended. He had studied history of the building of the mighty armored rail wag in the records in its own database.

After he'd made someone teach him how to read.

As the General moved into the gangway between cars, it-self shielded by accordion-pleated armor, he heard Banner rumble behind him, "All right, let's take a vote. Our choices for this evening's vid are *Yentl* and *Anal Ski Adventure...*"

The door hissed discreetly shut behind him. But he wasn't alone as he pushed through into his own car.

"Yes, Hubertus?" he said over his shoulder. He was already loosening his collar.

His intel chief hovered behind his shoulder like a wasp. "The man is clearly utterly mad. What do you expect to get out of him?"

"Amusement," the General murmured. "Companionship. In his lucid moments he's actually quite delightful. A real gen-tleman. It's almost as if he comes from a whole different time. A gentler, more refined age."

He tugged off his tie and tossed it over the green plastic shade of a polished brass lamp. "If any such time existed, which I fucking doubt, myself."

He hoisted a decanter from behind the small bar. "Care for a nightcap?"

Hubertus shuddered and shook his head.

"Really, General, you should allow me to work on them. If they know anything that might lead you—us—to the Great Redoubt, I'd find out in a hurry, without any of this shilly-shallying."

"Relax, Hubertus. Relax. You catch more flies with honey than with vinegar. Although who the crap was ever triple-stupe enough to *try* catching flies with vinegar is way beyond me."

He poured two fingers of brownish fluid into a tumbler. He set down the decanter, picked up the tumbler and went to sit in his red plush chair.

"When the old guys bottled this stuff, they called it Ancient Age," he said, and laughed. "If they only knew."

He tossed it down. "Now that's smooth. Not Beam's Choice, but smooth. Of course, compared to what we serve in the bar car, kerosene is smooth."

He set down the empty glass. "Give it a chance, S-2," he said. "We just got started with them.

"And besides, if this lead we got in Kancity pans out, mebbe we won't need 'em."

He picked up the tumbler, turned it over and set it down again with a thunk. "And then…we'll just see."

IT WAS WELL PAST DARK when Krysty caught up with the man on the odd machine. A gibbous moon hung like a madman's swollen face over the mountains far to the east, with wisps of cloud blowing across it like lank black hair tossed by the wind. It illuminated another sorry straggle of blocky one-story buildings, these half-ruined, slumped in on themselves as if eviscerated by fire. Here the railroad tracks, gleaming like silver inlay in the moonlight, twinned themselves for a ways. A line headed off northeast, bent dead east, and paralleled the original tracks for a stretch, then curved back to flow like a river tributary back into the main line. She had no idea what that was about.

She was wary, nerves still jangled from adrenaline. As the day had drowned itself in a pool of scarlet fire in the west, she had sensed herself being watched.

Ryan and J.B. harped on how a body should pay heed to such sensations. They would argue endlessly whether it was a kind of doomie sense every person had a touch of that alerted you, or whether it was just perceiving, on a level below awareness, the fixed attention of a pair of eyes, mounted side-by-side for stereoscopic vision, that shouted "carnivore!" For the same reason, they both were big on not looking directly at somebody or thing you were spying on, lest it trigger the same instinctual alert in them.

As well as she knew both men, she never really knew who stacked up on which side of the arguments. Mebbe they switched. Anyway, it was nothing new to her; she *had* a doomie sense. She had learned to pay attention to it as a girl. She never forgot.

She was in the open, crossing the broad flat floor of a sandy wash. No sooner had her sentient hair begun to rise off her neck and swish around her shoulders like the tail of a nervous beast than she unslung the M-16, thumbed off the safety and raised it to her shoulder.

The blaster was an A-2 model, made with an inhibitor that

restricted full-auto fire to 3-round bursts. At some point in the weapon's lengthy history somebody has disabled that feature. Lining up the battle sights on a bush on the low bank thirty yards distant Krysty squeezed off a 6-round burst.

She saw a jet of yellow ichor arc out from behind the bush. Something began to thrash madly on the ground behind it, setting up a horrible agonized squealing that surely never came from the throat of a natural animal—or man. Krysty held down on the bush for a span, trying to keep breathing deeply and regularly, as the commotion diminished. Then she marched on. She didn't sling the blaster again.

It never occurred to her that whatever was subjecting her to covert scrutiny might not be a threat.

Of course it was a threat.

At length the sky and the land around her came again to mirror the darkness in Krysty's soul. She trudged on. She was convinced the man would stop to rest, somewhere she could catch up with him.

She was right. Watching from a low hill above the rail junction, she saw a fugitive little flicker of yellow inside the best-preserved of the ruins. A wisp of flame not quite cautiously enough concealed.

She stayed under cover, studying the assembly of sagging walls and rubble heaps. She saw no other sign of occupation. Her keen ears heard nothing at all but the never-ending hissing of the wind and the weird semiregular creaking of something, a door or a sign, being blown back and forth on thoroughly rusted hinges.

At last she decided the man was alone. She slipped back down her hill, circled around to a point where her approach to where she had glimpsed the flame light would be masked by the bulk of other ruins. Knowing all too well the sorts of things that stalked the night, she made herself take care not to focus too closely on the nearness of her prey, despite the eagerness singing in her veins so loud it actually roared in her ears.

She kept her confiscated M-16 at the ready in her hands. The only reason she left the safety on was to prevent an accidental discharge if she stumbled. The moonlight was bright, but deceptive. It was as likely to hide treacherous footing as reveal it, especially up among the ruins where all manner of dreck littered the ground.

Feeling naked, she crossed the open space and came in among the buildings. Slowly she worked her way between them. They were so old, had been derelict so long that they no longer stank of mold or decay or even char. They just smelled of the drifting desert dust, and here and there of the animals that had found convenient prefab dens among the black truncated walls.

Once she heard motion inside a building, a skittering scrape. Shortly afterward something bolted out of a pile of unidentifiable weed-sprouted refuse and darted off into the scrub. Both times she froze. Her fear wasn't so much for attack as some creature, disturbed, might make a commotion sufficient to alert the man with the ponytail. But whatever she startled into action was as interested in escaping attention as she was.

And then she heard…whistling. Thin, sporadic and not very skillful.

Willing her muscles to relax, knowing that tension-induced stiffness could betray her in a thousand ways, she moved toward the sound. It was more blowing half-melodically than actually whistling.

It stopped. She stopped, her heart feeling as if she'd just swallowed it.

The half-voiceless whistle started again. She moved, up to the wall of the building where she'd seen the light. There were no windows on this side.

The whistling stopped. After the space of a long breath, it recommenced. She realized the man was pausing now and again to listen. Probably not because he expected danger—unlikely he'd be whistling at all if he did—but no doubt from long habit. Few people, herself and her lost love and companions included, could remain at full red alert all the time. Or cared to.

She shed her heavy pack and made a cautious circuit of the building. It was long and narrow. Some of the eastern end had fallen down. But perhaps because it had been built of actual adobe, treated by some predark process to prevent the bricks being dissolved by the rains, the structure had mostly endured, showing far less damage than the cinder block buildings.

In the center of the rear, facing the track, there was a wide double door, hinged so that both halves swung outward. A breath-held touch, the slightest of pressure, told Krysty's taut senses that the doors were barred from within. She ascertained this making no more noise than the constant wind—this night her friend and shield.

She slipped down around the eastern end. The wall had collapsed enough to see within, but she couldn't see the man or his machine. Some kind of curtain had been hung to block light and sight from the occupied portion of the structure. Around the fringes, though, she could see the yellow glow of what she guessed for a lantern.

Around to the front, stopping frequently not just to listen for sign that the man had become aware of her but to scan the surrounding night with eyes, ears, nose and gut. Becoming too fixated on prey was a fine way to become it.

If anything was stalking her it was better at it than she was detecting it.

The front door was wood, intact, with the knob in place. It was locked. There was a round metal key inlet above, indicating a deadbolt. The door frame seemed solid, untouched by rot.

Krysty frowned, considering. While she carried little excess weight in the flushest times, and had been pared down further by the exertions of the past few days, she had some mass to her. It wasn't impossible she could slam the door with enough force to break the bolts out of the wood frame, or more likely, rip loose the screws that held the hinges. But she couldn't afford so much as one failed attempt. It was all or nothing, because the noise of her hitting the door would alert her prey, allow him to set up in ambush and just wait for her to come through.

She went back to the east end. The wall had slumped enough to see over, therefore far enough to scramble over, hopefully without making too much racket. Holding her longblaster by the flash suppressor she reached it over the wall, probed with the butt for major obstructions. Finding none, she let the blaster slide down to the floor, holding it by its sling. Then she flowed up and over with serpentine grace.

She got her blue cowboy boots onto what seemed to be a concrete floor, drifted with an inch or two of sand. Taking up the rifle she crouched, tried to soak in every detail of her immediate surroundings through the very pores of her skin. There didn't seem to be much except some heavy fallen-in roofbeams that had been burned through in the middle.

The whistling kept on. With something of a start she recognized the tune. Her mother had sung it to her as a child: "Whistle While You Work."

She stole forward, placing her bootheels deliberately and then rolling her weight onto the soles to minimize noise. The whistling stopped. She stopped.

The whistling began again. She reached out to touch the barrier. It was some sort of dark plastic, stiff and brittle from cross-linking, hung from a beam overhead. She brought the longblaster up in front of her, hooked the left edge with the muzzle, swept it aside as she stepped through.

The man inside had been whistling as he worked on his marvelous machine. It lay in the midst of the open floor, glinting like a metalloid spider in the light of a kerosene lamp.

Whistle congealed in his throat, the man looked up at her with brown eyes made huge by the lenses of his glasses.

Chapter Twelve

Ryan dreamed.

Across a vast dusty plain approached rank upon rank of men. Sunlight glittered yellow off their breastplates and funnel-shaped helmets. They carried bows. Before them trotted other men, half naked, bearing tall curved shields, brightly painted.

Ryan shifted his grip on the hilt of the bronze sword in his hand. The leather windings were wet with sweat. A round wooden shield was strapped to his other arm. To left and right of him stood ragged lines of men clutching spears and wearing heavy quilted cloth for armor.

It didn't seem fair, somehow.

The advancing ranks halted. The shield bearers scuttled out before the armored bowmen and planted the shields on the ground. Sling-launched rocks bounced futilely off them.

Knowing it was no less futile, Ryan felt himself shouting the order to charge. He and the men began to run forward, screaming hoarsely.

The screams turned shrill as arrows rose like smoke from the bearded men, then fell among Ryan's charging companions. Ryan felt one strike into his thigh, stinging like a serpent's bite. He ripped it out using two fingers of his sword hand and threw it aside. But he felt other impacts, other deep-biting stings.

He stumbled. His breath turned to jagged glass in his chest. He tried to force himself on but his muscles wouldn't respond.

Then he was running forward across what had been a broad field of grass. It was trampled flat, now, and huge patches were stained dark red with blood. The forms of men wearing uniforms in pale brown and gray lay in singles and in clumps. Some of them still moved and screamed. Thin sounds wisped past his head. He heard one terminate in a meaty thud, heard a moaning gasp from the man who ran behind him, sensed that he tumbled headlong in the blood-matted grass.

He had a longblaster in his hands, heavy and ungainly, with a big lock on the side with a heavy curving hammer drawn back above a percussion cap on its nipple, just like on Doc's LeMat revolver, but much larger. They were running toward a wall of ridge topped with an unbroken bank of thick dirty-white smoke, through which stabbed little daggers and great broad blades of flame. As they ran they voice high wild cries, like wolf-howls interspersed with shrill fierce yipping. From the rawness of his throat he knew that he was, too. But the thunder of the cannon and the rifles drowned all other sound.

Directly in front, a fire-flower unfolded, huge though it was hundreds of yards away. He saw the white cotton-ball puff of the bursting charge, and heard the sound of the cloud of musket-balls launched by the shrapnel shell even before they reached him and the men to either side, like the sighing of wild goose wings, like the arrows of the Assyrians—

Red searing pain. Krysty! Then black…

Peace, Ryan Cawdor.

This time he didn't fall into blackness. Instead he hung suspended in white brilliance. The soft voice was familiar.

Out of the dazzle a shape resolved. It was one of the little squat humanoid muties he had seen during his earlier bout of wakefulness. He was walking on his hind legs with an odd waddling gait. He seemed bent by more than his natural body structure, and the fur on his muzzled half-human face was largely silver. But the brown eyes seemed both warm and wise.

Somehow he didn't seem ridiculous at all.

You dream, the little mutie said.

Ryan already knew that.

We Little Ones have learned much of the ways of healing in all the snows and suns since Men made us. Some of us have learned as well to walk in the World Behind the World. I am one. I am called Far Walker.

So mebbe he hadn't been dreaming before. But it was hard to accept. Human-Ewok hybrids? Who talked American and called themselves Little Ones?

No way. Likely he had been dreaming, and dreamed still, and would too soon be awakened by the pain of a raven stabbing out his remaining eye with its beak.

No. Rest easy, Ryan Cawdor. You are as safe as you can be anywhere in the world. We who cannot fight have learned to hide quite well.

"What do you want?" Ryan was surprised that he could speak. He seemed to be just hovering there, naked but for the patch on his eye. It didn't bother him particularly. He'd never been real modest, and anyway, what was the point? What did Ewoks care?

That you help us. But first, that you heal. And to do that you must rest.

"I'm asleep, aren't I?"

You sleep. But you do not rest. You struggle constantly.

Krysty. The name tolled like a bell inside his soul. "It's the way I am. And there's someone I need to fight my way back to."

You fight only yourself.

The little stubby arm gestured. Ryan saw more clearly the enemies he had battled and died against in his dream. They all had long curly black hair and a single piercing blue eye each, staring at him from scarred, sun-bronzed faces.

With our assistance your body can heal you quickly and well. But your spirit must not fight against itself.

"How can I not fight?"

A wise and cunning man such as you should know the answer better than anybody. Did not your own mentor say, "There is a time to fight, but more important, was the time when you decided not to fight?"

Ryan sighed. Or dreamed he did. Who the hell knew? But if the Little One was going to quote Trader at him, he knew he was beat.

"But how do I do it?"

Let go. Free yourself and let yourself fall, not into blackness, but into light.

Ryan's eye narrowed suspiciously. "Is this one of those near-death things?"

It will be an experience of death considerably closer than "near" if you continue to fight yourself. We're at the crisis. You block your own body's attempts to heal.

"All right."

He shut his eye, exhaled, made the tension and resistance flow out of him.

Then he was the light, and the light was him, and consciousness went away.

"YOU GONNA SHOOT ME?" the man in the dark coat asked mildly. He laid his wrench on the floor and straightened slowly. "If you are, why don't you just get to it and save me the suspense, lady?"

"Not if you do what I tell you," she said. "Step back from the machine."

Hands held up before his shoulders, palms toward her, he obeyed. Watching him intently, lest he whip out some hold-out weapon and chill her, she moved forward for a closer look at the object he'd been working on.

Though she was no lover of tech, it was obvious this was a marvel. As she had seen from a distance, it was a platform six or seven feet long and about three wide. It had a seat at one end, made of plastic-looking mesh slung over a tubular metal frame. A square-section metal post jutted from the base of a platform at a forward angle, holding up a pedal set. A chain was looped around the crank and vanished into a slot in the base of the platform. There were various low housings that looked like compartments or built-in chests. Spindle limbs, actually tapering tubing frameworks, sprang from the corners and angled out to hubs. Beyond these were large narrow wheels that looked like metal, with wide spokes—really more like big disks that had been cut out, probably to save weight. Mounted outside these were simple spoked bicycle tires. She realized the cutout disks were spacers set to fit just inside the rails, and keep the actual tires rolling smoothly along the work-hardened and polished track.

There was no provision for steering the wag that she could see. Likely it didn't need such. This was a machine meant to go where the rails went.

She raised her head and looked at him. She had never allowed him to slip fully from her awareness, nor her peripheral vision, which was better at detecting slight movement than direct-vision anyway. He had to have made this thing. From the way his eyes flicked from it to her and back again ceaselessly, the way his grayish tongue kept slipping out to moisten his lips beneath the mustache that swept down either side of his mouth, she knew that to be so. It struck her as almost perverse that anyone would even think of doing so, much less lavish the time and effort—the love—required to craft such a mechanism. She couldn't help marveling.

"I'm taking this," she said. "I won't hurt you if you don't try to stop me."

"So you're just gonna rob me, just like that," he said. "You don't seem the type."

She frowned. She wasn't the type, but she didn't exactly welcome him reminding her of the fact. She jabbed air in his direction with her longblaster.

"Don't get in my way."

"Got no intention of doing that, let me assure you. But what exactly are you going to *do* with it?"

She looked at the machine. She looked at him, then looked back at the machine. It was as light as he could make it, she didn't doubt, but she could also tell it had to weigh several hundred pounds at least, especially with provisions packed on board. The man who stood across it from her was an inch or two shorter than she, and skinny. Even allowing for the greater efficiency of his masculine muscles, if he could manage it, so could she.

If she knew the same tricks he did.

"Go ahead," he said.

"What?"

"Go ahead." He nodded at the machine. "Try it. Try an' pedal it. See how far you get."

To her astonishment he sounded almost eager. Her first thought was naturally that the wag was booby-trapped. But none of her senses, none of her experience of human body language, could detect the least quiver of threat from him.

What she got, remarkably, was pride. He wanted to show off his marvelous toy.

"Don't try anything," she said. He shook his head. He was grinning openly now, his teeth a crooked jumble in the kerosene light.

Holding down on him with one hand she slipped into the seat. It was very comfortable. She put her feet on the pedals. They fit fine; apparently his legs were about the same length as hers. She pushed.

Nothing happened.

It was as if the crank was welded in place.

Scowling, she dropped her boots off the pedals and leaned forward. She took hold of a pedal and pulled. It rotated back at her as if mounted on glass bearings.

She pushed. Rock solid.

"See?" he told her. "You don't know how to make it go. What're you gonna do with it?"

"Are you triple stupe?" she snarled. She shouldered the blaster and aimed it at the bridge of his nose, right where a dirty piece of tape held the heavy frame together. "You jack me around, I'll chill you."

To her fury he laughed at her. "Ice me down. I'll sure teach you a whole lot about how to run my Yawl," he said.

"Oh." Her muscles spasmed with fury.

She dropped the point of her aim to just south of the buckle of his belt. She felt a dirty thrill to see his eyes widen slightly.

"I can shoot you without killing you. I can make you want to tell me."

"Mebbe you can and mebbe you can't," he said. He looked her in the eye, calm and straight. "I'm no fighter, furthest thing there is from a coldheart. But I might be a tougher nut to crack than you think, missy.

"And besides, even if I did tell you how to make my Yawl go, then what? You know how to fix it when it breaks? You know what kind of traps the muties or even the norms will lay to catch you? You know how to live through a chem storm, riding out there right under the sky of the Deathlands?"

Her eyes answered him. He nodded. "Anyway, if you won't drop the hammer on me for saying so, you don't rightly look the type."

Slowly she lowered the blaster and backed up off the machine. She *wasn't* the type. His pointing it out made her mad enough to wish she were.

She thought her heart had gone cold as the heart of a burnt-out star. Cold as chilled titanium. She saw now it wasn't so— not all the way through, anyhow.

She'd drilled the deserters Ben and Matt without a thought or a single regret. She'd do it again and have dinner if she were hungry. If they were hunting her or hers, she would chill them from cover without giving them a chance to defend themselves and her sentient scarlet hair wouldn't so much as stir. And what she would do if she caught the General, or his fine young captain, or any of his sergeants and merry men...

But she couldn't put this man down in cold blood. Much less torture him.

Ryan could have. Mebbe. If it was what he had to do to save himself and his companions. He could be as stone a chiller as the coldest coldheart. She had loved him for that, too, along with so many other things.

But even now, a woman bent only on revenge, she couldn't.

"And anyhow," her captive said, shaking his shaggy head, "why do you want to go and steal what might just be on offer for free, Krysty Wroth?"

Chapter Thirteen

"You know my name?"

"Appears I do, since you answer to it."

"How?"

He shrugged. "I been around. Kinda like you and your friends. Can I put my hands down now? Not like you'd need a blaster to kick my skinny butt, anyway. Like I said, I ain't no fighter."

She sighed from the soles of her boots. Then she clicked the safety back on and slung the M-16. He was right; she didn't need it to take him. But she knew that wouldn't be an issue.

She didn't fear him rabbiting on her, either. She doubted he would voluntarily be separated from his marvelous machine.

"You know my name," she said. "Would you mind telling me yours?"

He cackled. "Pretty lady with a longblaster can call me anything she likes except late for supper." He grabbed the left breast of his open shop coat and held it up. "See? My name's Paul. Just like it says here."

She leaned forward slightly and squinted. The name tag was filthy, but she could only just make out, embroidered in red on once-white, the name Paul. Right enough.

"That's as in Paul, the Rail Ghost." He paused. He seemed to be waiting. "Mebbe you heard of me?"

She shook her head. "Can't say as I have. But I guess I'm pleased to meet you anyway, Mr. Ghost."

He laughed, this time a nervous titter. "Just Paul is fine. They call me the Rail Ghost 'cuz I go everywheres the rail does, which is everywhere at all, and people scarcely ever see me. And never can catch me." He said the last a little wistfully.

"Until now."

He shrugged. "Hear you're better than most. You and your friends. Where are they, anyhow?"

Her brow furrowed suspiciously. Then it smoothed. She suspected the man could be as devious as anybody at need. She could not honestly suspect he was being so now. It just went against what all her senses told her.

"It's a long story," she said. "We…got separated."

Paul nodded judiciously. "So you're chasing after MAGOG to go and get 'em back, huh?"

"Y'THINK HE KIN DO IT?"

Corporal Brassard flicked the private a glance of pure contempt. The tow-headed youth was a newbie they'd picked up on the coast from a nest of inbred surf rats. They were bad as hillies, in the corporal's estimation. The kid was lucky to have a chin and only ten fingers. But he hadn't missed out on dumb.

"Course he can't, Mikkelz. Muties'll eat his lunch. Then we shag ass back to the rail wag and report we done our level best, too bad about the baron's daughter."

IT WAS A STRETCH to call the boss of the little ville of Tucumcari "baron." Miguel "Mike" Sanchez was a nervous fat man with sweeping white side-whiskers and watery blue eyes, one of which displayed a distracting tendency to look everywhere except where the other one was. He had a silver fob watch in the pocket of his sun-faded, sweat-stained vest, which didn't work, but did serve as a symbol of authority, such as it was. His handful of sec men weren't particularly sinister for the breed, lacking much of the usual vicious swagger, but likewise weren't real effectual.

His domain, which was just a little straggle of buildings, halfway reclaimed ruins or shanties scratch-built from materials scavvied out of the ruins of the old town, on whose erstwhile eastern outskirts it lay. He ran it with a sort of absentminded indulgence. Contrary to the current wisdom that held that the more ruthless the baron, the better off the ville, Tucumcari didn't seem to have suffered greatly from his slackness. As small as it was, the ville prospered, relatively, off scavvie grubbed out of the ruins of the old town, and off the game that thrived in the rolling plains and wooded hills surrounding. The inhabitants mostly grew up skilled trackers and dead shots, owing to the scarcity of ammo for modern cartridge blasters, and the slow reload rate of the black-powder longblasters they also used, both of which made it important to make every shot count. Their marksmanship probably accounted for the fact that neither coldhearts nor muties—animal or vaguely human—had taken much advantage of Baron Mike's laxity.

Until recently. In the past few months a band of about forty muties—with, rumor had it, a few norm renegades thrown in—had moved into the vicinity from the east, in hopes of easier pickings. They had successfully surprised the large Taitt family on its homestead in the woods a few miles northwest of town, overpowered them, and then killed, raped and, rumor again said, eaten them, in no particular order. The initial success, however, had proved hard to repeat once the countryside was aware of them. The locals seemed none too inclined to avenge the Taitts, who had been powerful enough almost to constitute a barony themselves and displayed some nasty tendencies toward their neighbors. And anyway, the Taitt stead was well-defensible for a sizable band. However they *were* inclined to come to one another's aid. They also liked to skulk and snipe.

Just like that the mutie leader, a hugely fat mustachioed scabbie called El Cabrón, found himself down to twenty-five assorted goons. So he decided to avail himself of the rule of law.

Now, the baron of Tucumcari had a daughter, Maria Elena, of legendary beauty, waist-length raven tresses, ivory skin and notable rack. She was largely thought to be a virgin, which lent her a certain novelty value.

So one night not long ago a picked band of muties had slipped into the ville and made off with the baron's daughter, leaving the head of her chaperone, an elderly lady cousin of impeccable respectability on the globe surmounting the end post of the banister in the foyer of the baron's splendid two-story frame mansion.

The raiders had also left a written message, which after it was painstakingly interpreted proved to contain an ultimatum: the baron would either compel his people to submit and pay tribute to El Cabrón and his band, or Maria would be guest of honor at an old-fashioned Deathlands mutie hoedown.

Enter MAGOG. The new ville happened to lie smack by a divide in the tracks, one line running southeast, the other northeast. The locals, like most people, had paid no heed to the old weed-grown rails until mighty rail wag had miraculously turned up along them a couple years past, gleaming and throbbing. Tucumcari was well up in the watershed of the mountains just to the west, and its denizens eager to trade fresh water and game to the General's posse for trifling quantities of ammo and meds. So amenable were the folk of the ville, from Baron Mike down, that the General hadn't bothered leaving any sort of garrison, a constant drain on his limited manpower.

But the General was about empire building, or rebuilding, and he understood the enormity of the task as maybe no one else then alive did. That was why he was so hipped on getting hand on the Great Redoubt, no matter how obdurately his intel chief failed to understand. So he jumped at the chance to bind the ville to him more closely through goodwill. It was also a chance to try to get some use out of another of the odd but highly capable band of captives—now quasi-recruits— Hubertus was always wanting to torture.

The albino youth, Jak Lauren, had been kept in a cell since the coldheart attack. It wasn't as punishment; the General had ordered him to be well treated, but considered him a feral rogue. Doc spoke glowingly of his combat prowess, though, so the General directed that the youth and a trio of MAGOG sec men be dispatched to rescue the baron's daughter.

MIKKELZ TITTERED. "Yeah. Too bad. Hear she got a rack."

"Besides," the corporal went on, ignoring the outburst, "he's a mutie. Who gives a rat's diseased dick about a low-life nukesuck mutie?"

"He ain't a mutie. Says he ain't."

"Shut up, stupe. 'Less you want me to reckon you for a taint, too. That what you are, a dirty mutie lover?"

"Both of you shut the fuck up," Karnes snarled. He had a hard thin stubbly face and mad eyes. The camou-stick face paint he like the other two wore in jags of brown and green and black made his eyes seem to stand right out of his head. He was junior to Brassard, just a scrubby private, but he came from a long line of woods-runners from the mountains up Taos way and put up with no man's shit.

They were all hunkered down behind an outbuilding near the woods in back of the former Taitt main house. Mikkelz, Karnes and the corporal carried M-16s. It was broad daylight. Despite that fact there was no sign of muties moving about the place. Just a few skinny horses browsing hopefully in the bare dirt of a corral. Along with Baron Mike's daughter, the raiders had made off with a startling percentage of his stock of scavvied predark liquor, which might have accounted for the lack of apparent activity.

"Corporal?"

"Shut up, Mikkelz."

"But that girl. You think—"

What Brassard thought they were being solicited about would remain a mystery, because just then a shirtless mutie scratching at one raw red edge of a fistula in his chest came around the rear of the shed in search of a place to take a leak and all but stepped on Karnes.

JAK WASN'T a lot of things, and squeamish was right up there.

All the same he was having trouble breathing in the ground floor of what had been the Taitt house. The miasma was made up of mildew, rancid human grease, dreck, piss so well fermented it seemed like the muties weren't to blame for it all, rotting food, burned bedding, farts, spilled alk, decomposing flesh and various vintages of puke. Squeamish Jak wasn't, but he did have a sensitive nose. And the nastiest stagnant black water bayou with an old swollen-up dead gator festering in it back home couldn't hold a candle to this majestic reek.

Also, somebody—the muties or the former occupants—had tacked up bedspreads and tablecloths and random scraps over the windows, casting the interior of the big old two-story structure into dismal gloom.

Slipping the hook-and-eye lock on the back door with the leaf blade of one of his throwing knives, Jak had come in through the kitchen, down a short corridor to the front room and the foot of the stairs. He had come upon three marauders, two sleeping muties and an apparently normal human passed out with his bearded face sideways in a pool of vomit. Three quick sure strokes of a throwing knife had insured that no ensuing ruction, no matter how frenetic, would disturb their rest. Nor anything else.

At the base of the stairs he paused. He heard voices from above, muffled as by a door. No hope existed of detecting any sentries or anybody abroad in the upstairs hall by body odor. However foul it might be, it just had too much competition. He put his hand to a wall and listened and felt, trying to sense footprints, breathing, even shifting of weight.

Nothing he could perceive.

He stole carefully up the stained hardwood stairs, as mindful not to slip in any pools of anything as to avoid making noise. Though his knives were tucked away in sundry convenient location, his hands were empty. His .357 Magnum Colt Python, returned to him by his captors for this mission, rode inside a shoulder holster in his left armpit. On the opposite side were pouches for three speed-loaders. A collapsible aluminum spear, provided for the raid, was stuck through his belt.

Sergeant Banner had been almost solicitous in making

sure he had everything he wanted or thought he needed for this snoop and poop. He had also been almost eager when making it clear that if the albino youth ran on them, his friends would suffer.

Halting at the top of the stairs, Jak stuck his head tentatively up above floor level. The window at the hall's end was swaddled in a big pale paisley comforter, stained with water or whatever, which allowed through a dim tobacco-spit colored light. Nobody was in the hall, and the only door closed was on his left. The voices came from behind it. Seemingly insubstantial as fog, he flowed up onto the second floor and up beside the closed door.

MARIA ELENA SANCHEZ hung naked by her wrists from the ceiling of the bedroom. Although bruised and contused here and there from rough handling and being tied, she was alive, unmutilated and even unraped. Her captors had even placed a flowered metal bowl beneath her feet in case she leaked from time to time. Despite not having slept for two days and nights she was wide awake. Because it was looking as if her intact condition was subject to change any moment now.

A huge hideous mutie ran the clipped back of the foot-long Bowie knife blade down a bare thigh. The curve of the metal seemed to fit by nature against the smooth creamy skin. The mutie made a sound in the center of him halfway between a purr and a gurgle.

The mutie wasn't El Cabrón. El Cabrón was huge, sure enough, a good 350 pounds of him propped on a brass bed, bare from the waist up. And he was unsightly enough, with scabs and seeping pustules all over his broad face and hairy body. But he was nowhere near so large nor so hideous as the mutie now caressing Maria Elena's shrinking face with fine forged steel.

"Hole says he's tired of waiting," said the mutie standing next to the one with the knife. This one wasn't near as huge, scarcely four feet tall. "Hole says he wants some fun, now."

El Cabrón glared with little bloodshot piggy eyes. His cheeks puffed out either side of the extravagant mustache that grew down the sides of his mouth to about his second chin. They were so fuzzed with coarse grizzled stubble they looked like blowfish bellies.

"*I* give the orders here, Skeeze," he said. "Remember that!"

Hole emitted a gargling outcry. The captive squeezed her eyes shut as the awful stench rolled up out of the depths of him and over her like a chem storm off the Plains.

He was *really* huge, maybe seven feet tall, maybe five hundred pounds. It was hard to tell for sure, since his vast body from the tops of his lumberjack boots to the collar was concealed in a black baggy garment that looked like an out-sized duffel bag and may have been. The fabric was so heavy and loose that it made it impossible even to guess details about what lay within. Which was no doubt for the best, since sprouting from the top of the sacklike outfit was a trunk-thick neck topped by, well, a hole. Topped in turn by a hank of dirty dark brown hair.

How he saw or smelled or heard, the terrified Maria Elena had no clue. He surely had no visible eyes, nose or ears. Just a huge reddish cavern in place of a face, fringed with scalloped yellow flesh that reminded the girl of toothless gums. But he didn't seem to miss much, and got around well enough to be El Cabrón's chief enforcer.

And he seemed to be on the brink of staging a palace coup.

"Hole says," Skeeze relayed, "that can change."

"We can't damage the merchandise." The mutie chief had changed his tone, wheedling now. "Just give it a day or two until her father caves. Then we get all the sweet thing we want."

"Hole," Skeeze said, "is not big on deferred gratification."

The door slammed open. So did Maria Elena's eyes.

The figure standing there seemed to fit right in with the others: a slim youth with a shockingly scarred face the color of a sheet of paper, and ruby eyes blazing above the sights of a gigantic silver revolver.

"Not move!" the intruder said. He seemed to be grinning with pleasure, but it might have been just the way a healed knife-cut pulled up the corner of his mouth.

"Back away from girl," the intruder said, gesturing at Hole with the blaster.

Outside a blaster yammered on full automatic.

Chapter Fourteen

At the sound of the mutie colliding with Karnes, Brassard spun and lit off half of a 30-round magazine from his M-16.

Right into Karnes's back.

Not all the rounds hit the private. None of them hit the mutie. He turned and fled, squalling at the top of his lungs.

Karnes went right down. He wasn't dead, though, even with a huge swatch of his blood sprayed all over the side of the shed and more squirting out of a dozen holes. He kicked and thrashed and made bubbling noises.

Shots cracked from somewhere. Brassard fired off the rest of his mag into the wooded slope behind the Taitt house, for no very good reason. Then he dropped it, slammed in a new one and grabbed Mikkelz by the sleeve.

"C'mon! We gotta get outta here!"

Muties came pouring out of the buildings. Some staggered. Some carried blasters, which they fired enthusiastically, as if they could compensate for a lack of visible targets that way.

Mikkelz stood as if he'd put down roots. Appropriately, he was getting a little green in the face.

"B-but Karnes!" he blubbered. Puke slopped out over his lower lip and down the front of his camou blouse.

Brassard tugged harder. "He's had it. If we don't get outta here, we'll join him."

"But the kid—"

"Fuck him. He's mutie meat now. If we can make it back to the wag we have a chance. But we got to move."

As if on cue, a mutie appeared around the end of a lump of weeds and rust that had once upon a time been a tractor, thirty yards away at the end of another outbuilding. He raised a longblaster and shot at them.

Mikkelz bolted right past his corporal and into the woods, heading for the wag parked on the far side of the hill to safety. Brassard followed, blazing off his new mag at the mutie for good measure as he ran.

More muties poured around the corner of the shed they'd just fled and began to kick the still-thrashing Karnes and beat him with farm implements and rocks as others fired after the fugitives.

THE SOUND OF BLASTERFIRE momentarily distracted Jak. The hunchback mutie Skeeze acted at once. With rattlesnake speed, he snatched up a wooden chair and hurled it at the youth.

Jak fired at the motion. The chair struck his hand at the instant the Python bellowed. The impact and recoil knocked the big revolver from his hand.

Hole held out his arms to either side, one gnarled hand brandishing the knife, which looked like a toy. The monstrous mutie bellowed a challenge. Standing silhouetted in the full force of morning sunlight blasting through what had to be the one uncovered window in the house, he seemed more a walking nightmare than a flesh-and-blood horror.

Jak was superstitious, but he wasn't easily awed. He also knew an opportunity when he saw one. He sprinted straight at the roaring mutie. Halfway across the floor he launched himself into the air, coiling his legs and then planting a perfect dropkick against Hole's chest right where his clavicle would be, in case he had one.

The impact of Jak's slight body was pitifully insufficient to damage the gigantic mutie. He'd have been hard-pressed to hurt him even if he was fired out of a blaster. But it was just enough to overbalance the mutie.

Hole bellowed again as he went over backward flailing his arms. He smashed the back of his hand against the wall and lost the Bowie. Then he fell right out the window, carrying most of the frame with him.

Jak rebounded off his chest and landed in a crouch in the center of the floor. Skeeze uttered a squeak of terror and scuttled for the fallen Bowie. As he reached for it, a throwing knife seemed to sprout from the back of his hand. He held up the wounded member in horror as blood ran down his arm. Then he dashed out of the room screeching in agony.

Ancient bedsprings creaked as El Cabrón leaped to his feet with surprising agility. His belly, covered in scabs and black hair, slogged ponderously back and forth and up and down with an almost tidal motion.

"You got balls, *jodido*," the scabbie chieftain said, "but mebbe not so much brains. I'm three times your size, and I ain't standing by no window."

As he spoke, he was reaching behind his enormous back to the waistband of his dungarees. Jak drew the short knurled aluminum rod from his belt.

"That little stick ain't gonna do you no good, Whitey," El Cabrón said.

He whipped his hand around. In it was a truly enormous pistol, a Taurus Raging Bull double-action revolver in .454 Casull caliber, chromed like a gaudy house witch-ball. A blaster truly worthy of the huge mutie chief.

Even as the revolver rose, Jak flicked his wrist. Four feet of aluminum tipped with a slim steel head snapped from the batonlike handle. El Cabrón's eyes widened. Jak pivoted toward him, getting a two-handed grip on the spear. The butt smashed the thumb of the mutie's gun hand. El Cabrón howled and dropped the piece.

Jak leaned back, ducking beneath the potent but clumsy swipe of the mutie chieftain's left arm. Then he thrust the spear hard between El Cabrón's flabby, scabby breasts.

The man sat down hard on the edge of the bed. Jak let go of the spear and danced back out of range. The mutie wrapped a huge hand around the haft of the spear and pulled. Pain made his eyes cross and his face turned blue beneath its pustules.

The spear came out with a sucking sound. El Cabrón's eyes blazed with triumph as he brandished it.

Jak shot him in the belly with his own Raging Bull. Fat and blood splashed away from the entrance wound. Jak had some experience with large-caliber handblasters and didn't try to fight the recoil or hold his arms rigid; that would have sprained both of his wrists. Instead he let the awesome recoil ride the big thick barrel straight up toward the ceiling, then let its weight carry it back down as the awful noise it made still ratcheted around between the walls. And fired again. And again.

"Enough!" Maria Elena cried. "I've survived a lot, but if you shoot that damn thing again, my head will implode."

Jak lowered the blaster, looking almost sheepish. He stuck it in his waistband, where it threatened to pull down his pants. He held his hands behind his legs in hopes she wouldn't see him shaking them to alleviate the stinging in his palms.

He went to the Bowie and picked it up. "Nice knife," he

said. Using the chair Skeeze had hurled at him, he stood on tiptoe and cut through the captive girl's bonds.

Unfortunately he lacked the strength to hold up her weight. They went down in a heap, chair and chamberpot spinning away.

"Thanks for rescuing me," Maria Elena said. "Now, will you please take your hand off my boob and cut my wrists free? I'll be lucky if my hands don't swell up."

Jak snatched his hand away as if her skin had turned red-hot. He still had hold of the Bowie, miraculously, and hadn't sliced either one of them in the fall. He quickly freed her.

She sat up and began massaging her legs vigorously. "Lord, it feels like my skin's full of red ants. I'll have to keep going on adrenaline and hope that's enough."

Jak had picked himself up and secured his Python. He moved swiftly to the door and peered out. There was no sign of activity inside the house, although there was a mighty commotion going on outside.

"There are horses," Maria Elena said. "If we can get to them we have a chance of getting clear."

She was a remarkably cool one, Jak had to admit. He went to her and helped her to her feet. She started to sag, gritted her teeth, and straightened up.

"Give me that fat bastard's pistol," she said.

"No way."

"I can shoot a blaster."

"Not that one." He frowned, then reversed the Python in his hand and proffered it to her. Volume of fire might just make a difference to their breakout chances.

"Don't drop."

She grinned. "I'll try to keep a better hold of it than you did. Now, let's get out of here."

He tested the Bowie's edge with his thumb. The hole-faced mutie had kept it well honed.

"Not yet," he said.

IN SCUTTLING OUT and leaving Jak in the lurch, the surviving MAGOG sec men had inadvertently provided him and the rescued hostage an excellent diversion. With all the general firing going on nobody paid any mind to shots coming from inside the house. Moreover, the muties still within the house, who had all been on the bottom floor, went racing out straightaway when Brassard opened fire without even noticing their three comrades weren't dead drunk, but merely dead. When Skeeze burst out of the bedroom a moment later, tumbled down the stairs, and ran out the back door still hollering and clutching his impaled hand, he had simply fled into the hills without alerting anybody that more foes were about.

Half the muties still functional went lurching into the forest behind the main house in pursuit, hungover or still drunk. The others stood peering outward in all directions, fearful the pesky locals had decided to mount a concerted attack, and firing off stray shots on general principle and to reassure themselves.

When an albino youth and a beautiful naked woman, who was a head taller than he was with black hair streaming behind her like a banner, burst out of the front door and raced madly for the corral, it took a few heartbeats for anyone to notice.

Someone finally did and shouted a warning. Shots began to crack. Dust spurted up from the yard, nowhere near the fugitives.

The youth carried a giant blaster in one hand and a heavy burden in the other. As he and the girl neared the corral and bullets began to hit closer, he paused, crouched and fired the handblaster. It boomed and knocked him on his ass.

The girl kept running. Despite the fact the circulation was still making its agonizing return to her limbs, Maria Elena vaulted the corral fence of peeled poles in a single bound. The horses reared and shied away from her. They all had on halters. She grabbed the lead-rope of one and swung onto its bare back.

Jak had picked himself and his burden up.

"Gate!" the girl screamed.

He ran around the fence as muties fired lustily at him, yanked up the rusty baling-wire loop that held the gate shut and swung it open. Maria Elena trotted the bay mare forward and reached a hand to help pull him up behind her as he stuffed the Raging Bull down his pants again. Still holding his parcel he put his free hand around her waist and pressed his face into her hair.

She kicked the horse's flanks with her bare heels and they went galloping into the scrub-clad hills in an ineffectual storm of lead.

THE BARON OF Tucumcari kept moaning, "Oh, my daughter!" Mildred kept expecting him to add, "Oh, my ducats!" but he never did.

"Tell me again," the General said sternly, "why you failed in your mission *and* left two of your comrades behind."

He stood, resplendent in a medal-bedecked OD jacket well-hung with medals, riding pants, spit-shined boots and chromed helmet, on the steps of his personal car looking grandly down upon the ville and its inhabitants.

Mikkelz opened his mouth to speak, and Corporal Brassard surreptitiously ground his heel on the arch of the private's foot.

"That wild albino boy musta alerted the muties somehow, sir," the corporal said. "All we know is we heard shooting and screams from the main house. Then they were all over us, firing up a storm. Poor Karnes caught a whole burst, never had a chance. Guess the kid never did neither. All we could do was shoot our way clear. We musta dropped eight, ten of 'em apiece, but they just kept coming. And your—sorry about your daughter, Baron Sanchez, sir. If anybody coulda saved her, we woulda, but there was just too many of 'em. Mutie scum!"

The baron wailed. Brassard spit expressively in the dirt. Then as if overcome by emotion he yelled, "Let me take 'em down, General! Let me take 'em! Just give me the men, the weps, the wags—I'll scour the filthy bastards off the face of the earth, I swear!"

He acted as if he was about to madly hurl himself somewhere not immediately apparent, so that buddies standing near him obligingly seized his arms to restrain him. The corporal duly began to struggle with them, not so vigorously as to risk breaking free, but raving, swearing and red in the face. For his part Mikkelz looked like he didn't know whether to laugh or puke.

Mildred turned and buried her face in J.B.'s shoulder. To their surprise they'd both been allowed out of the train at once. Of course, Doc was still securely inside—"temporarily indisposed," the General said. Although they seemed fully, and justly, trusted to do the jobs they'd been assigned within MAGOG, it seemed one thing hadn't changed: they were still hostages for one another.

"I can't believe Jak didn't make it," Mildred sobbed. "Sometimes he seems so vulnerable. But then other times he was like a force of nature. I never thought it could happen to him."

The Armorer had never thought of Jak as vulnerable, but for once, tact—or taciturnity anyway—got the better of him. He patted her reassuringly.

"Don't be too sure, Millie," he said quietly into her beaded plaits. "These rail wag heroes don't strike me as havin' the sense to pour piss out of a boot with the instructions printed on the heel. Mebbe Jak's gone, mebbe he isn't."

Mildred's shaking shoulders told him she wasn't convinced. "And there's always Krysty," he reminded her quietly.

"Four hundred miles away in Arizona! How will we ever find her again?"

"Dunno. But we will. We'll get shut of these yoohoos, and then—"

"I'm afraid I can't oblige you, son," the General was saying in a surprisingly gentle, but still carrying, voice. "We're on a mission, one bigger even than avenging two fallen comrades. We can't spare any more time. But I promise you this— once we've gotten...our objective...we shall return and hunt down these mutie scum like the filthy animals they are!"

Corporal Brassard at last tore free of his friends and threw himself on the bare tan ground, which he commenced to beat with his fists. "Vengeance, General! Let me have my revenge on those mutie bastards! I'm beggin' you, please!"

"Mebbe we can save you the trouble, Corporal," said Captain Marc Helton, who stood on the right of way just below and beside his General. He pointed over the heads of the crowd.

Trotting down the main drag of the little shanty ville came a bay horse, rolling its eyes and flaring its nostrils. On its back rode a beautiful black-haired woman, stark naked. Behind her rode Jak Lauren.

The crowd parted to let them through. The girl rode up to

her father, who was standing openmouthed, and hauled up on the lead rope to stop the horse. She flew off its back and almost knocked the baron on his duff, seizing him in a hug.

Corporal Brassard was on all fours like a dog. His face was about one shade darker than Jak's.

Private Mikkelz wasn't as dumb as he looked. He had already begun to back through the crowd of townspeople, hoping to slide away unnoticed. But two members of Hubertus's security police, in their white helmets, materialized on either side of him and laid hard arms upon him.

Jak swung off the horse and swaggered up to the General. He carried a pillowcase that had been pressed into service as a sack, heavy-laden, its closed end soaked through and dripping red.

White helmeted SPs leveled longblasters at him, and even Helton dropped a hand to the butt of his service blaster. Ignoring them, Jak grabbed the gore-sodden bottom of the pillowcase and upended it.

The huge severed head of El Cabrón fell out, bounced and rolled so close that the twin worms of blue-green snot that had emerged from the mutie's nostrils postmortem violated the sheen of the General's left boot toe.

"Got girl, got mutie," Jak announced in a loud voice. "Mission accomplish!"

MILDRED STARED out the window of the commissary car. For the first time she was really glad for the train's excellent soundproofing. She wished she could believe it would be the last.

She had been allowed one hearty loving hug of Jak, and J.B. one comradely clap on the youth's thin shoulder—gingerly, so as to avoid the razors Jak had sewn into his vest.

Then Jak had been disarmed at blasterpoint and led back to his cell: acclaimed, applauded, but treated like a wild animal, perhaps recaptured after a bold escape.

The baron's daughter, still naked, had thrown a fit. The General was unmoved. Hearts and minds or not, she was still just a civilian. If terms were given, if laws were laid down, they flowed from the armored train out, not the other way around. She had still broken through the youth's armed and edgy escort to hug him and plant a fervent kiss on his pale lips before being hustled none-too-gently away.

Jak hadn't seemed to mind that part.

"I can't believe you people," Mildred murmured.

In the double-paned glass she saw Marc Helton's brown Greek-god face furrow in puzzlement over her left shoulder.

Outside, a long pole was being raised to the vertical by having the butt end dropped into a hole, freshly dug while a gang of men pulled on ropes attached to the other end. Slowly the pole swung upward as its base fell into the hole. The task was complicated by the weight of a heavy square-section crossbeam, which had been nailed to the pole a few feet from its upper end—not to mention the still-writhing weight of Corporal Brassard, buck naked and nailed in place by huge spikes through the wrists and feet. Private Mikkelz hung from an identical crude cross, which had already been erected beside the railroad right-of-way at the ville's edge.

"Your own people, and you do that to them," Mildred said. She turned, not so much to look at Marc—although she had to admit, even here and now, that he was mighty easy on the eyes— but because she could no longer bear to watch the scene outside.

The young captain's expression was of pained incomprehension. It looked genuine to her.

"It's justice," he said, his very lack of emphasis indicating utter conviction. "They abandoned comrades in the face of danger. To us, that's a very grave crime."

He let his gaze slip past her, out the window, as if he were trying to marshal his thoughts.

"I have to admit I'm puzzled by your attitude as well, Mildred," he said at length. "It was your friend they left to the mercy of the muties."

She sighed explosively. "Yeah. And I guess by Deathlands standards I should be out there doing some kind of triumphant dance around the base of those poles."

She went to a table and sat. The officers' commissary was empty but for them. Everybody else was either on duty or outside watching the festivities.

After a few moments Marc joined her, bringing her a mug of steaming tea. She smiled thinly and thanked him in a small voice.

He sat down. He didn't feel the need to ask. Over the past few days he had repeatedly sought her out for conversation. Despite her rebuff of his initial attempt she had softened and guardedly opened to him. She was by nature a friendly and outgoing person, and desperately aware of being cut off from the friends with whom she'd lived in constant closeness for so many months. She didn't really have anyone to talk to; the aides were so reserved around her that she suspected they had been warned not to associate with her. Singh, although totally conscientious on duty, and extraordinarily skilled given the paltry educational resources that had been available for her training, was subdued almost to the point of invisibility except when discussing necessary medical or administrative matters. The comments she had made to Mildred on the day of the coldheart attack had been the only exceptions. Mildred suspected she spent her off-duty hours drinking or drugging herself into unconsciousness, or at least as much as she could without compromising her performance.

But it wasn't just loneliness that made her lose her unwillingness to talk to Marc.

Captain Marc Anthony Helton was an extraordinary young man, no getting around it. He was the son of the baron of Mobile no less. Though his childhood had been pleasant he had been rigorously trained, mentally and culturally as well as physically. He actually knew a good deal of history, from Mildred's time and before; and almost as rare, knew something about the history of the Lost Days of nuclear winter and the ensuing time since the big war—although his knowledge was of necessity sketchy, since few records had been kept and fewer still attempts had been made to gather and collate them into any kind of coherent account.

Even during the brief conversations they'd had, he had displayed an intelligence that seemed both broad and deep, and a quick and flexible understanding. If he had a noticeable fault it was a painful puppy earnestness. But he was never self-important, and although he seemed to try to hide it, he flashed signs of a keen sense of humor. He radiated an easy unselfconscious charm.

He also reputedly had the courage of a lion. The hardcases of MAGOG's sec force treated him with something like awe. She'd picked that up just from listening to the wounded soldiers talk about him. He had never been known to back down from a fight and never known to lose. He would have insisted on leading the expedition to free Maria Elena Sanchez had the General not personally ordered him to stand down.

He was simply a hero. Mildred knew what they looked like. Marc and her late beloved leader and friend Ryan Cawdor were miles apart in many ways, but they belonged to the same breed.

Of course it had been Marc who killed Ryan. His orders, anyway. That should have made him Mildred's sworn enemy for life. And maybe it did. Except that whole tragedy, the massacre and enslavement of the travelers' caravan, seemed totally at odds with everything she could see of the character of this dashing and dutiful young officer. She felt compelled to try to understand how the parts fit together.

And while maybe it was a too convenient a rationalization, she couldn't exactly try to trephine him with a fork. Not with her friends—J.B. in particular—held captive as well. She might as well be civil while she was compelled to associate with him. She might even learn something which could help them escape.

Besides, to be honest, she was flattered by the attention. Here was a man with movie-star looks and Harvard-professor brains. Women were in a minority aboard MAGOG, most in med or other support-tech roles, but from the way they looked at Marc, as had the women in the villes the train visited, he could have had his pick of any number of younger, thinner women. Yet here he was with her.

"Mildred, you've already made a sizable contribution to our endeavors—"

Don't remind me I'm an accomplice of murderers and slavers, she thought with a mental wince.

"—and there are people aboard this train who are alive only through your efforts. But I feel as if you have certain reservations about us, about what we're doing."

"You might say that."

"We—the General has a vision of rebuilding America. Not the way it was before the megacull—that's too big a project for our lifetimes. But of making a start. We can't end the squalor and suffering, but what we are doing is building toward a day when our descendants can. That's been the General's consuming vision since he found this train in an underground bunker twenty years ago. And for the past five years he's been traveling the surviving rail network, repairing as he went, working to seed little bits, oases you could call them, of civilization along the way."

"So you're saying the end justifies the means."

He winced. "I don't like where that leads any more than you seem to. It's the ready-made rationalization for any sadistic swine who gets to call himself a baron because he commands enough brutal sec men to beat a starved and captive population into obedience. But it's a large end we're talking about here, not the selfishness and greed of a dictator. And it's one that won't be achieved by pious hopes and warm words alone. It's a hard task. If we shrink from doing hard deeds, when we have to, it will never get done. And that's the simple fact."

She looked down into her cup. Not much enlightenment was to be found. The problem with trying to read tea leaves, she'd always found, was that in the end all it did was remind her she was drinking boiled weeds.

"You have a point. I can't deny that, and it's something to work for," she said.

"That's what I was hoping for," he said. He stood. "You have a lot to offer us, Mildred. I want you to be able to do so with a clear conscience."

"Well, you've given me a lot to think about, Marc," she said. "I can give you that much."

He smiled and left.

Chapter Fifteen

"Next stop, Tucumcari," the ponytailed Rail Ghost sang out. "Thanks for traveling by Paul Yawl."

Despite herself, Krysty smiled. Paul's eccentricities could be exasperating, or unnerving, but sometimes they were sweet and funny.

She turned her head and looked. So cheerful had Paul sounded that she was almost disappointed to see that Tucumcari was just another small town that had been burned out and fallen down ages ago. Paul said no bombs had fallen nearby, but somebody, mebbe even the inhabitants, had thoroughly trashed the ville in a more personal, one-on-one sort of way.

She had to look back again quickly because her stomach got queasy. She was unused to riding backward like this. Less still used to pedaling in that position.

For all its size, or lack thereof, the craft called the Paul Yawl contained many surprises. The first had come when they set forth from the half-ruined shed the morning after their first encounter. The wind was blowing briskly from the north-northeast. Paul had unstrapped objects from beneath the platform and assembled them into masts and a triangular sail. He had then unfolded from the platform a second seat at the front end, identical to his own, for her to sit in as they traveled.

That had been the point at which she had, mostly, accepted

that Paul had told the truth when he explained why he was willing to help her follow MAGOG: that he had been a hermit for years, and now badly wanted someone just to talk to. She sensed that there was more to it than that; but after even the briefest acquaintance, she just found it impossible to believe he harbored any sinister intent. It didn't mean she trusted him without restraint—few people had ever accused Krysty Wroth of being a fool, and not that big of one. She just doubted to the point of dismissal that he was actively planning to do her harm.

And anyway, as he himself pointed out, she could snap his neck without much effort.

The next surprise had come when the wind veered in early afternoon, as they were crossing a trestle bridge over a sandy wash that was too broad and flat to be called an arroyo. The sail emptied and they lost way. Paul had pedaled them to the far side, then got out, took down the sail, unstepped the mast, and stowed them back away. Then he unfolded a second set of pedals and gears mounted by Krysty's seat and rigged a drive chain to a complicated mechanism below the platform itself. That translated the motion of the passenger's pedaling into backward impetus.

It had also been a surprise to Krysty how sore her legs got so quickly. She assumed she was in rugged good shape from the fact she had walked thousands of miles and could run as long as necessary. It turned out that pedaling made use of a different set of muscles. Paul had veered erratically between sympathy and badly concealed amusement. He had been genuinely impressed when she whipped up a poultice of herbs she found when they sheltered for the night in an abandoned farmhouse near the tracks, that soothed the ache in her muscles enough to let her sleep.

The most recent surprise the Yawl had contained was when

approaching the mountains east of the Grandee. When the going got too much even for Paul's work-hardened muscles, he had produced a little two-stroke gasoline engine and attached that to the drive train. It had propelled them up and over the pass at a slow but steady speed. It was better than trying to make the journey by muscle power, but Krysty found herself having to fight impatience and the ever-looming dread that she would never catch the fleet, fusion-powered monstrosity of a train.

Today had been mostly pedaling against a mild head wind, and occasional coasting on downhill grades. Her muscles were still sore, but she was quickly getting in shape. Her own Gaia-given self-healing gifts were helping.

"It seems strange, somehow," she said as they began to pass the ruins of Old Tucumcari. "It's like it's part of another world." She had never felt the same detachment traveling the roads, even by wag.

Paul nodded. "It might as well be," he said. "It's a world that's forgotten the rails. It was already happening long ago, long before the big war."

"Don't people notice when they see you riding along them?"

He cackled. "Not so many do. It's not for nothing they call me the Rail Ghost."

It occurred to her to wonder, if nobody ever saw him, just who it was who called him that. It seemed unsporting to ask, so she didn't.

"And besides," he said, "once I'm gone, I'm gone, and it's as if I never was. Was I real or just a mirage? People aren't used to thinking about the rails, or noticing the rails, so when they see someone like me riding on the rails... Well, it just doesn't fit with what they've thought all their lives. So they put me out of their minds as soon as they can. Kinda like digging a goathead out of your foot. It's forgotten as soon as you can't feel it anymore. You just walk on."

"What if they see MAGOG? That's a little large to just put out of your head."

He got an odd look—then, faraway, pensive and sad at once. "Well, that's a question, there, missy. It is indeed."

They passed the ruins and approached the new ville. The two tall T-shapes that had been apparent at a distance resolved themselves into crosses carrying grisly, twisted burdens. Crows and ravens swarmed about the corpses.

"Is this a good idea, Paul?" Krysty asked. Since Tucumcari was a rail junction, their intention was to stop and ask the townsfolk which way MAGOG had gone, and if the occupants had let slip a hint as to final destination.

"Hard as it may be to believe, it's even possible to wrong a baron," Paul said. "And I reckon most folks will do all they can to pay back a slight. Just happens baron's got more wherewithal to do it."

He squinted up at the crucified shapes. "Got sec man boy haircuts. Baron Mike's pretty easygoing, baron or not, it wouldn't be easy to piss him off this much. Looks to me like this is on your pal, the General."

Krysty gritted her teeth at the characterization, even though she knew it was ironic. "Something else he has to answer for."

"Mebbe so. Just as like, they had it comin'. In these parts, missy, the wonder is how bad things manage to happen to them as *don't* deserve it, given the statistical unlikelihood of it an' all, if you catch my meaning."

Krysty started to fire back that neither Ryan nor the women, children and oldies slaughtered by the Big Ditch had remotely deserved any such fate. She bit it savagely down.

Arguing with Paul, she had learned already, was like trying to reason Doc out of one of his fugues. The kind of thing an old Latino rancher from outside Harmony, up in the high Rocks where she was born, compared to fighting a swarm of bees with your hat.

Paul took pressure off the pedals and began to spin down, backing off the intense exertion gradually so as to minimize the risk of cramps. "We're about to find out, one way or t'other. This here's our stop."

Following his example, slowing her own pedaling gradually so that she stayed just short of pushing, Krysty frowned at the ville. It was generally well kept, which argued for a relative measure of prosperity, which in turn argued for relative peace. At the same time, while the land surrounding was slightly greener and more thickly vegetated than the desert farther west, her experienced eye saw signs they were heading into the true Deathlands. For example, the way all the roofs in sight were kept studiously intact, even if they consisted mostly of ad hoc patching, and the way every window had some kind of covering, if not glass then a hinged shutter of gray-weathered plywood. They got chem storms here. Fortunately the sky showed no threat of one, and even the odd glimpse of blue here and there.

So it struck her as odd that there was nobody out and about and all the shutters were down. This was early spring in the high Plains, and midday heat not yet an issue.

"Where is everybody?" she asked.

Paul unfolded himself from his seat and stretched, then smoothed down his coat. He pulled off the goggles he wore to spare his eyes from windburn and bug strikes and stuffed them in a pocket. In their place, he put his heavy-framed

glasses with the taped bridge. "Dunno. Let's head on down
and find out."

The embankment here was low, just enough to allow for
drainage when it rained. He stepped down to level ground.
Krysty followed, longblaster unlimbered. She didn't like this
setup a bit. If carrying the M-16 openly made the locals nervous, too bad for them; if they didn't understand caution, they
were triple stupe.

But then, if they didn't understand caution, they'd be triple dead.

The new ville had been laid down without apparent regard
for the tracks, nor for their separation, which lay a couple hundred yards beyond the last hut of the settlement proper. It
seemed more to have nucleated around the baron's mansion
a few blocks away, with the tracks forming a southern bound-
ary of sorts, although a few structures lay outside it. They
made their way between the buildings, Krysty wary, Paul all
but skipping, giddy with the adventure or maybe the prospect
of additional human contact.

Just before reaching the mansion, Paul stopped to stoop
and peer intently at a patch of adobe wall. Krysty glanced over
his shoulder. She couldn't see anything but some scratches in
the mud coating that might have been fresh and might have
been some kind of symbol. Or just random scrapes. Paul
straightened again. Humming low in his throat, he covered
the open ground in front of the mansion in several swinging
strides, trotted up the porch steps and rapped on the door before Krysty could suggest he might hold off for a bit so she
could at least do a little reconnoitering.

It wasn't going to do to greet the baron blaster in hand. An-
grily, she slung the M-16.

The door opened. A stout woman in a flowered apron, her

gray hair piled in a bun, stood blinking through a pair of round-lensed spectacles at them. "May I help you?"

Though it was a cool day, and likely cooler inside, Krysty saw fine sweat beading around the woman's hairline. "Good morning, ma'am. We've come to see Baron Mike."

She glanced back over her shoulder. Then she looked back at them and smiled. "Of course. Come in. I'll take you to him."

"Baron Mike doesn't stand much on ceremony," Paul said over his shoulder as they stepped into the gloom of the foyer.

"What's that smell?" Krysty asked. Right ahead of them was the foot of the stairs. The polished-wood globe on the banister's end-pedestal was covered with a dark stain that suggested dried blood. That might account for the undertone of stench. What accounted for the dried blood was another question.

The woman led them to the left, back through a kind of parlor. In front of them a curtain that seemed to be made out of a comforter with incongruous marine life—angelfish, sea horses—printed on it in bright colors covered a round-topped doorway. The housekeeper stopped and waved them on with quick nervous gestures.

Paul cruised right on through. Krysty followed him tight. All her internal alarms were going off at once.

"Shit," she said, beginning to unsling her rifle.

Paul had stopped short on the other side. "That doesn't seem to half cover it," he said.

It had been a dining room. There was a huge sturdy oval table in the middle of it. On the table lay the nude body of a man. He was pretty portly and probably middle-aged. It was impossible to tell for sure because the parts of him that hadn't been cut off or opened were covered in blood. One blue eye stared out of red tracery at the chandelier hanging from the high ceiling above. Krysty realized her feet were sticking to the floor. Blood was congealing everywhere. The charnel-house stench was gagging.

She brought her rifle around. A hand covered in weeping sores grabbed its flash suppressor from her left and wrenched the weapon out of her hands.

She pivoted on her left leg, ramming her right up into the scabbie's balls. All the breath exploded out of his body. He folded like a bad poker hand, all the way to the floor.

Krysty was preparing to stomp him good and proper when strong stinking arms wrapped around her from behind. She shifted her hips left, then rammed her right elbow straight back, pushing hard with left hand folded over right fist for emphasis. It was the turn of the mutie who'd grabbed her to lose his lungful and double over. She whipped both arms up in front of her, completing her breakaway, and turned clockwise into him.

He had withered skin and a nose like a brown cancerous carrot, she saw before she smashed a forward elbow slam into the side of his face. That stood him up again, opening him for an uppercut into the stomach, delivered with a widdershins twist of the hips that lifted his sneakers out of the blood-muck with a sucking sound.

He fell. Even as she started to turn back to her first assailant, he came at her again from behind, dropping the M-16, held by buttstock and barrel, right over her head, pinning her arms to her sides. The mutie with the rotten-carrot nose wrapped her ankles in his arms and clung to her like a baby opossum. She was immobilized.

"Paul!" she screamed. "Help me!"

He just stood there between her and the table, shoulders hunched, staring at her with moist cow eyes.

"Don't hurt her!" commanded a thin voice that went into the eardrum like a drill. "Hole says he's been cheated once already. Hole says he wants woman unharmed."

Two figures had appeared through the kitchen door, on the far side of the table with its gory burden. The voice was coming from a weird round mutie who had to crane his head to see past the ex-baron's split-open paunch. He scarcely came to the waist of the monstrous figure with a fistula for a face that stood behind him.

Struggling against the grip of the scabbie who held her from behind, Krysty emitted a scream of pure fury.

Hole emitted a hissing gurgle. The weird little round mutie at his side emitted a lewd cackle. His eyes were grotesquely mismatched.

"You're so lucky," he said in his piercing hiss. "Hole like. You're better than black-hair cunny. Hole never had red-furred cooze before."

The little mutie rubbed clawlike hands. "Skeeze, neither."

The giant mutie bubbled excitedly through the hole in his face. Words could have been no clearer. A huge misshapen hand began to knead a growing stiffness below the sacklike black garment.

Krysty ground her teeth in frustration. She would soon have to summon the power of Gaia to enter her body and increase her strength to superhuman levels. It took a horrific toll on her, risked incapacitating her. But she wouldn't allow herself to be violated by this monster with the oozing gap for a face.

"Get ready—" Skeeze said.

Something thumped on the floor of the kitchen right behind Hole and rolled forward, almost between his boots. The giant and his rotund interpreter ignored it.

"Hole give you plenty of what a woman really want—"

Something went *crump*. A shimmer, like shock waves made visible, passed upward and outward over Hole and Skeeze, radiating in semicircles from the floor.

GET FREE BOOKS and a FREE GIFT WHEN YOU PLAY THE...

Lucky 7

SLOT MACHINE GAME!

Just scratch off the silver box with a coin. Then check below to see the gifts you get!

YES! I have scratched off the silver box. Please send me the 2 free Gold Eagle® books and gift for which I qualify. I understand I am under no obligation to purchase any books, as explained on the back of this card.

366 ADL D34F

166 ADL D34E

FIRST NAME	LAST NAME

ADDRESS

APT.#	CITY

STATE/PROV.	ZIP/POSTAL CODE

7	**7**	**7**	Worth **TWO FREE BOOKS** plus a **BONUS** Mystery Gift!
🍒	🍒	🍒	Worth **TWO FREE BOOKS!**
♣	♣	♣	Worth **ONE FREE BOOK!**
🔔	🔔	🍒	**TRY AGAIN!**

(MB-04-R)

DETACH AND MAIL CARD TODAY!

The Gold Eagle Reader Service™ — Here's how it works:

Accepting your 2 free books and mystery gift places you under no obligation to buy anything. You may keep the books and gift and return the shipping statement marked "cancel." If you do not cancel, about a month later we'll send you 6 additional books and bill you just $29.94* — that's a saving of over 10% off the cover price of all 6 books! And there's no extra charge for shipping! You may cancel at any time, but if you choose to continue, every other month we'll send you 6 more books, which you may either purchase at the discount price or return to us and cancel your subscription.

*Terms and prices subject to change without notice. Sales tax applicable in N.Y. Canadian residents will be charged applicable provincial taxes and GST. Credit or debit balances in a customer's account(s) may be offset by any other outstanding balance owed by or to the customer.

If offer card is missing write to: Gold Eagle Reader Service, 3010 Walden Ave., P.O. Box 1867, Buffalo, NY 14240-1867

BUSINESS REPLY MAIL
FIRST-CLASS MAIL   PERMIT NO. 717-003   BUFFALO, NY

POSTAGE WILL BE PAID BY ADDRESSEE

GOLD EAGLE READER SERVICE
3010 WALDEN AVE
PO BOX 1867
BUFFALO NY 14240-9952

NO POSTAGE
NECESSARY
IF MAILED
IN THE
UNITED STATES

Chapter Sixteen

Hole roared, a sound so horrible and huge it seemed as if it would crush Krysty's skull. His vast booted feet seemed to have shrunk to a cone point, as if he were being transformed into a giant blacktop. He raised his tree trunk arms over his head. His hands were great claws of intolerable agony. His bellow went on and on.

Skeeze's eyes bulged. As the distortion waves emanating from the floor seemed to intensify, as if the air itself were somehow becoming solid, his squat little body began to distort, to be drawn back and down toward the point from which the waves originated. Hole was half swallowed, arms flailing now, screaming as if he had no need to inhale.

"What—what's happening?" Skeeze's words soared in volume and velocity, as if played on a tape that suddenly speeded up. As they ended in a hideous shriek, his body seemed to shred and be sucked toward the point in rags of black and red. His larger eyeball stretched and distorted into a banana shape before it popped like a water balloon.

Implo gren! Krysty thought. They were as rare as their effects were horrible, but she'd seen them before. The comforter over the door whipped the legs of the scabbie, who held her pinned as air whistled toward the tiny singularity created by the gren. Watching his leader's unimaginable painful demise in horrified incomprehension, the scabbie had slackened his grip. Krysty managed to grab the M-16 with both hands and pull down hard as she whipped her upper body forward and down.

The scabbie went flying, leaving the longblaster in her hands, and cartwheeled over the late unzipped Baron Mike into the gren's distortion ripples, which were already subsiding. He shrieked fit to bust glass as his very atoms were stripped one from another and sucked in a maelstrom, right out of this world.

With a final pop of air rushing to replace vanished matter, the gren's implo effect died away.

The moldy mutie on the floor had also lost his grip on the redheaded woman. She kicked a boot backward to free it up, then snapped it forward as if to launch all the terror and fury that filled her right out of her silver-chased toe. The mutie's neck snapped with a sound like a broomstick breaking.

Paul rose slowly from the crouch he'd folded himself into at some point in the proceedings. He goggled at the doorway to the kitchen, which was now a rough semicircle. "What on earth did that?"

"Implo gren. Don't ask me how, because I don't know."

She was quickly working up a mighty head of anger toward the cowardly Rail Ghost. Before she could say anything more a tall figure strode through what had been the kitchen doorway, followed at once by a second.

Krysty had already shifted her right hand to the longblaster's pistol grip. Now she let her forefinger rest lightly on the trigger. She didn't aim the blaster at the interlopers. Somebody had bowled that gren between Hole's feet. These two were the obvious candidates.

The first and taller of the two new arrivals was a woman, as thin and taut as a wire sculpture, her face and hands tanned dark, her hair a blond scarcely darker than Jak's silver mane.

It was caught in a long ponytail at the crown of her skull. She wore a silver cord around her temples, form-fitting white trousers and shirt beneath a loose, many-pocketed khaki vest. A heavy-duty web belt cinched around her impossibly narrow waist carried many objects in pouches and holsters whose purpose was unknown to Krysty. Her face was of a beauty so finely chiseled and haughty as to seem scarcely human. Krysty was reminded of childhood tales of elves.

Her companion was a lean man with dark brown hair receding from a vulpine face, dressed in blue jeans and a T-shirt tie-dyed in a riot of color, with a white oval in the center printed with the visage of a rotund, richly bearded man. Krysty thought to recognize the image as the Blessed Jerry Garcia, but wasn't sure.

"What took you so long?" Paul asked.

The tall, ice woman gave him a blue-laser glare. "We have other things to do than redeem your poor judgment, Mark."

"Paul. The name's Paul." He held up the nametag stitched in his coat. "See?"

"Have it your way."

Outside blaster shots cracked in a sudden ragged volley. Wolf-howl war cries mingled with screams of fear and pain.

"What's happening?" Krysty asked. The newcomers ignored her.

"What's going on out there, Bryanna?" Paul asked.

"The baron's daughter escaped when the mutants came for her in the night," the tall woman explained. "She rallied homesteaders from the surrounding countryside. They're attacking now."

"Well, thanks for saving us, anyway," Krysty said stiffly, her hair swishing about her shoulders.

"You have much to answer for," Bryanna said past her to

Paul. "This mutant band is known to have interfered with the folk's free passage in the past. Acting against them is acceptable and does not constitute interference in the outside world. But you've come deadly close to dragging us into the affairs of the Mundanes...Paul."

He held up his hands. "Sorry, Bree. I didn't know. I just walked in here cold."

"'Flat-footed' is more like it. Try to exercise more caution in future." She regarded him a moment. Then her austere features seemed to soften ever so slightly. Or maybe it was a trick of the light, or maybe the room's closeness and the reek of death was getting to Krysty.

"You're still chasing the armored train?" Bryanna asked quietly.

Paul nodded. "It went northeast. According to the locals, members of the crew spoke of heading for Kancity."

Paul let his breath out in a long, "Hooo," and glanced sidewise at Krysty. "That's a rough one."

"Listen," Krysty said, wanting to grab the ice goddess, but thinking it wasn't a good idea. "You might not want to acknowledge my existence, here. But there's something I have to know, nuke-blast it—"

Bryanna finally turned her winter-sky eyes on the other woman. "The townsfolk saw three of your friends alive and well, Krysty Wroth. Only your Doc Tanner was missing."

She smiled thinly. "Perhaps he's having one of his spells, and was restrained to keep him from harm. And perhaps the General did not wish to risk allowing all four outside at once."

Breath hissed out of Krysty and her shoulders slumped. "Well, thanks. But how come everybody on the continent knows our names all of a sudden?" But she had phased out of existence for the gaunt blond woman again.

A black man with what appeared to be a polished steel headband clamped around his medium-length Afro appeared in the doorway. His eyes were covered by heavy goggles with dark lenses that seem to swim with muted colors like oil on water. He wore a camou blouse and OD cargo pants, and held a longblaster one-handed by a pistol grip. It appeared to be made from white plastic of some kind, and was a design unfamiliar to Krysty. Bryanna's mouth, none too generous to begin with, all but disappeared into a fine line. Krysty had the impression the woman disapproved of her seeing the wep.

"We got a way out open," the newcomer said. "Best we take it."

Bryanna nodded. "Ride free," she said to Paul with brisk formality.

"Live to ride," he replied. "Nationwide."

The trio left the way they had come.

The battle outside was rocking. Krysty heard the distinctive crash-tinkle-*whump* of a gasoline bomb going off not far away.

"Let's go before this death house burns down around us," she said tautly. Ashen behind his mustache, Paul nodded.

KRYSTY STRODE through bright sunlight and noise. Shots cracked. Men on horseback hunted muties through the narrow crooked streets of Tucumcari New Town. She ignored them. The only thing bubbling more furiously inside her than her anger was way too many questions.

"Who were those people?" was what got out her mouth first.

A mutie with three mouths spread across his face—all of

them open in cries of panic—pelted past them. Behind him, a man turned and reared his big palomino gelding and threw an ax after the fleeing mutie. Not a hatchet, a whole single bit ax, spinning through the dusty-impregnated air like a giant circular-saw blade. It smacked between the mutie's shoulder-blades and put him on his face into the dirt, so close to Krysty he almost struck her with a flailing arm. An outflung hand scrabbled hardpan dead in her path. She trod on it as if it were a tarantula without even looking and kept walking.

"Tech-nomads," Paul said.

A crash erupted as a heavy chunk of concrete was hurled through a thin plywood window shutter, then another molotail burst on the house they were approaching on their right.

A figure burst out of the door shrouded in flame and screaming wildly. It teetered and spun in front of them, arms waving flags of flame in a semaphore of intolerable pain. Krysty stopped to let the burning mutie pass. He staggered on, howling, to vanish between buildings. Her set expression never flickered.

Paul turned aside and puked.

When he straightened, Krysty had already marched a dozen steps toward the railroad tracks. Wiping his mustache on his sleeve, he trotted to catch up.

"What's the matter with you?" he demanded. "Are you triple crazy?"

As an answer, she grabbed a handful of hair on the side of his head, stepped back and yanked down hard. He doubled with a squawk of surprised outrage and pain.

A teenaged norm in a doorway five yards to their right touched off a replica Civil War Springfield. The black powder charge gave it up in a giant billow of dirty white smoke and a four-foot spear of orange flame. The .577-caliber Minie ball howled as it passed through the space occupied by Paul's scrawny neck half a heartbeat before, on the way to pulverizing the left shoulder joint of a mutie charging in from the left with a spear made out of a broomstick tipped and edged with shards of broken glass.

Krysty hauled him upright by the ponytail and towed him briefly after her like a Sippi tugboat with a barge, to make sure he got moving again, and in the proper direction.

"What are tech-nomads?" she demanded again. She didn't look at him.

"They're like a tribe," he sputtered, batting furiously at flecks of burning black powder thrown out by the longblaster that had landed on his coat sleeve and set it smoking. "A nation, more like. Bands of people who travel all the time. Some by road, some rail, some water, some…other ways."

They were at the southern edge of town, having left the massacre behind. Not all the erstwhile participants, however. A mutie was sitting in the driver's seat of the Paul Yawl, pressing frantically on the pedals with long two-toed feet.

Also futilely. On leaving the rail craft, Paul had repeated the trick that had frustrated Krysty's initial attempt to make it go: simply a matter of leaving it in the highest gear. No being of even approximately human strength could budge the several-hundred-pound wag a thousandth of an inch by pedaling, although it would roll as pretty as you please if you pushed. Caught in the grip of ultimate panic, the mutie didn't really notice he was having no effect. He just kept pushing harder until the quads threatened to pop out the black rubbery skin of his bare legs.

Krysty pointed the longblaster at him one-handed and squeezed off a single burst. Black flesh, skin strips and liquid spewed out the far side of the panicked mutie. He threw

up his hands, emitted a dismal croak and toppled over onto
the cinders.

"Look! Look there!" Paul sang out in outrage. "You got
blood on my Yawl!"

"Shut up," Krysty said. She planted her butt on her own
seat.

As Paul scrambled into his, forcing himself to ignore the
ooze and odd bit of tissue clinging to the mesh, three more
muties pelted desperately toward the Yawl. They were unarmed, stretching out various empty appendages in supplica-
tion. Krysty mowed them down with the rest of the rounds in
her 30-round mag.

Paul used the twist-grip mounted on his handhold to down-
shift, then began to pedal the Yawl. Krysty dropped the empty
box, reflexively tucked it into a pocket of her jumpsuit and
pushed a fresh mag home. Then, still cradling the M-16 in
case anybody else got notions of riding without a ticket, she
put her feet up on the pedals and added the power of her
strong shapely legs to Paul's wiry, skinny ones.

A shift of the wind blew a bloated worm of brownish
smoke across the track ahead. They drove through it without
slowing. They gathered speed.

When they were a hundred yards past the smoke, Krysty
saw a figure appear out of it beside the tracks. Paul saw her
eyes narrow and turned, fearful at what he'd see.

It wasn't anything he expected. That was sure.

A young woman with long hair streaming from her head like
a raven's outstretched wing had reined in a big bay horse. The
horse was bareback. So was she—aside from what looked at
this range like a pair of lumberjack boots she was neonate-
naked.

She reared the horse and waved, of all things, an FN-FAL

longblaster over her head. "Godspeed!' she cried. "And bring Jak Lauren back safe!"

"Lordy," Paul said. "Baron Mike's little daughter Maria Elena's done a mite of growing since last I laid eyes on her."

"She seems to know how to rally troops," Krysty admitted grudgingly.

The nude rider turned and vanished into the smoke again with a last Comanche whoop. Krysty found herself almost wishing she might make it back this way someday to see how the ville fared under its new baron. Life wouldn't be dull, she was sure.

That was triple-silly even to think, she chided herself savagely. Her path led right out of this life. Her itinerary left no room for doubling back, much less sightseeing.

She swung her eyes onto Paul like guns tracking in a mount. "You were a lot of help back in the baron's house."

He shrugged. "I told you at the outset. I'm no fighter. I avoid trouble when I can. When I can't—" Another shrug.

"I fight when I have to."

"And how much misery have you left in your wake, Krysty Wroth? Plenty more'n I have, I bet."

She scowled, said nothing.

"What I do," Paul explained earnestly, "is I try to move through life leaving as little of a mark as possible. Just go with the flow, like moving through water."

"No matter what marks you make in water," Krysty replied grimly, "they're instantly gone as if they'd never been."

"And is that how you see people, Krysty Wroth? Like drops of water merging facelessly into a stream, without individuality or meaning?"

"Guess I do," she said, "now. Except a few drops of water still hold meaning for me. And that's how it's going to be, until it's my turn to become one with the river."

Chapter Seventeen

"Just hold still," Mildred murmured, "and this'll all be over before you know it." She reflected, not for the first time, about what babies even the staunchest warriors could be when it came time to treating the wounds they feared so little to risk incurring.

Not that the baby-fist-sized crater in the troopie's leg was a combat trauma, exactly. They'd been stopped for yet another line repair a couple days back, a relatively minor one, fortunately—just a washout the train's own complement could fix expeditiously enough. Mildred dreaded the next labor roundup.

Her patient had taken a break from repair work to walk in among a field of head-high sunflowers, not yet in bloom, to take a leak. It wasn't the smartest thing a body ever did, given that they were now in the serious Deathlands—what had been western Kansas—with hotspots all around and attendant mutie menaces abounding. One had gotten him, in fact. Fortunately it hadn't been lethal—he wasn't sure what it was, even. Something had stung him. He'd screamed at the sudden white-hot pain and brushed something off his leg that vanished instantly among the tall green stalks. He'd run a dangerous fever for twenty-four hours, and the wound had swollen up in a huge blister that Mildred had lanced. She then had to debride necrotized flesh from the gaping hole it left behind, grateful once again they had actual anesthetics on board. Stupefying a patient on jolt and then tying him down and cutting him open was not her idea of a clean, efficient procedure.

But no anesthetic could be spared for just changing the dressing and disinfecting the wound. So the patient squirmed and sniveled and generally took on like a child. Of course, he was a child to Mildred's eyes. No more than seventeen, a dirt-farm boy who was drawn to swearing the General's oath by the lure of adventure or, more likely, the prospect of three hots and a cot each and every day.

As she was finishing up rebandaging the wound, the carriage vibrated. It wasn't the usual swaying of MAGOG underway. It felt like slow, heavy pounding.

It came again. The kid perked up.

"Ma Deuce," he said.

That meant one of the train's .50-caliber Browning machine guns corking off. Mildred knew the nickname from J.B, who come to think of it may've taught it to the sec men. He and that rasty old fart Leo were as thick as thieves, playing back in their gunsmith's wet dream armory car.

She snipped the last bandage with her broken nose scissors, then left the boy to pull his own BDU trousers back on and went to the window to look out.

The sky was all the colors of a really nasty bruise: bluish green, red, orange, yellow. It was going to take her a while to get used to that again, after the relatively clean skies of the desert southwest. It looked threatening, as in, more than the deep Deathlands sky always looked. At least I don't got to sweat the chem storms, she thought, or—

A dark mass slammed into the window with a thud muffled by two polycarbonate panes. Giant talons raked at the plastic, a horrific visage snapped at her with a long toothed beak as claw-tipped wings beat against the window. She screamed and jumped back, dropping her scissors.

"Screamwing," the kid soldier said.

The window held, as it would against anything short of a wag-chiller round, or maybe a kiss from Ma Deuce. The mutie vanished, whipped away by its wings or the wind of MAGOG's passage.

Maybe to prove to the kid—or herself—she wasn't faint-hearted, Mildred went right back to the window, pressed her face against it and looked up. A cloud of the winged horrors circled above the train, darting down now and again to attack it.

"There's millions of the things!" Mildred exclaimed, exaggerating slightly. "And they're a lot bigger than what I'm used to."

She was feeling all kinds of blaster-induced vibes now through the very fabric of the train: the .50s' deliberate mighty pounding, the quicker tempo of the lighter M-60s and MAG-58s, the ripping snarl of Minimis. As she watched, a burst caught a slow-flapping creature not thirty yards from the windows and ripped it apart in a spray of black.

"Yes!" whooped the kid, pumping his fist in triumph. He promptly fell over. Mildred helped him up, concerned he might've dislodged the fresh bandage or done some new hurt to himself. She kept a firm grip on his biceps to restrain any further displays of juvenile exuberance.

"That'll show the bastards!" he cried.

"Right. Now just calm down till you get your damn pants on."

He obeyed. Looking out again, Mildred saw something that made her heart feel as if someone had punched its Pause button.

From the train's crew Mildred had learned that with few exceptions only the steel-shelled carriages were part of MAGOG's original complement. The General had added cars as he'd come across intact ones that seemed to serve his need—with fusion-powered engines fore and aft, and some kind of special magnetic setup to increase the traction of the driving wheels on steel rails for stopping and starting, the engine could haul some improbable and unprecedented number of carriages. The armored carriages were almost all two-deckers, which accounted for the low ceilings, since the cars could be no more than fifteen and a half feet high overall to be sure of clearing existing U.S. tunnels and overpasses. The upper levels were usually the fighting decks. Some of the cars even carried pop-up heavy weapons turrets, that nestled within the armor shell—and the max height—until they were needed for action, then as the name indicated popped up to take care of business.

Some also sported casements that could open to the sky. These were intended to allow the crew to launch shoulder-fired SAMs at attacking aircraft. Mildred had been dubious about that—had the drug lords and guerrillas of South America been buying fleets of F-16s when the balloon went up?—until J.B., during one of their rare, fleeting encounters in the commissary, explained that lethal ordnance could be bolted onto just about any kind of airplane or helicopter, not just military jets.

One thing about the modern Deathlands: attack planes were as rare as good teaching hospitals. The General usually left the antiaircraft emplacements open to the sky, some reinforced with sandbags, to serve as additional firing points.

Just because there weren't many aircraft didn't mean death didn't fly, unfortunately.

One screamwing, especially bold or lucky, stooped like a falcon on the open-top emplacements. Its claws locked into the back muscles of an unwary sec man and plucked him right out of his armored nest.

Now, to Mildred's horror, she saw the man being borne kicking and presumably screaming away by the winged monstrosity.

His buddies saw it, too. They instantly sprang to do what they could to help him, which was to say that every blaster that would bear instantly poured fire at the mutie and its doomed prey.

Mildred saw the man's body jerk as bullet-sprays ripped into it: once, twice, three times. By the third, she was sure it wasn't moving under its own power anymore. The screamwing staggered from repeated strikes, but kept doggedly pounding the air until a burst literally sawed its left wing away at the root. Then it corkscrewed right down into the prairie, exactly like a stricken aircraft in an old days newsreel.

"What a world," Mildred said. She sighed.

The battle raged on outside. The screamwings could do nothing whatever to MAGOG itself, of course. The only question was what damage they could inflict on the exposed troops before they were all driven off or chilled.

"Gets worse from here," the boy said ingenuously. "They say Kancity's so hot we can't even go out without rad suits."

"Great. Just great." She made shooing gestures. "Go on. Get your skinny butt back to your station. Got a feeling I'm gonna get me some patients who need me a boatload worse than you do before too long."

NIGHT IN THE Deathlands.

As dusk settled, the best shelter Paul had been able to locate had been this long-abandoned line shack, whose frame sides and tarpaper roof had mostly survived the depredations of years and storms. The most conspicuous gaps they had covered over with scraps of planking they found lying around, or shards of petrified tarpaper broken off a roll left lying against one wall an unguessable time before. It would keep off the chem storms, well enough, and at least delay any night-stalking predators long enough for the pair to prepare a blaster-catered reception for them.

But quarters were close in there with the Paul Yawl, and would be closer still when they unrolled their bedrolls on either side of it. For ventilation, and maybe to stave off claustrophobia, they had left the door open. The sky was roiling brown and yellow clouds, twined with sinuous strands of self-luminous orange. Sometimes the seething cloud mass was lit from within by discharges, red, purple, blue-white. Your usual weather on the formerly great Plains.

The breeze was cool and didn't stink of toxins, anyway.

Paul and Krysty sat inside the doorway looking out and gnawing on their last haunches of the one-eyed pronghorn she had popped with her M-16 a few days back. A mutie herself, Krysty had no reflex revulsion against eating "tainted" flesh; for his part, Paul claimed he ate anything that didn't eat him first. To be on the safe side, because mutie meat could be poisonous, Krysty had tasted a bit of the kill's liver and heart, trusting her poison lore and her body's extraordinary recuperative powers to keep her from lasting harm. She experienced no adverse reaction, so they cleaned and cooked the little beast and ate him with appetite by installments.

"Guess I'd better finish this up tonight," Krysty said, sniffing briefly at the leg. She tore another chunk of roasted flesh out with her teeth and chewed. "Getting a little rank even for me."

True to his creed, the Rail Ghost just shrugged and gnawed manfully at his own chunk. The secret, Krysty knew, lay in letting the maggots have their way, only brushing them off right before you yourself were ready to chow down. That way they cleaned up the seriously nasty decay and prevented it from spoiling the surrounding flesh—just the way they did an open wound on a person.

"So tell me," Krysty said around a gamy but welcome mouthful, "how come you know so much about MAGOG?"

He chewed and thought, took a swig from a water bottle, swallowed. He had a great knack for finding safe water. Not always clean, exactly, but as with their food, neither was picky.

"Well," he said, drawing it out long, "as you probably worked out for yourself, being such a smart young lady, I have a thing for trains. I love trains. Only two things in this life I do love—I love to tinker. To make things, to fix things, to change things around so they work better, or do things they never did before. That, and trains. Loved them long as I remember.

"Only, as you also mighta noticed, there ain't none."

"Well, not many." In their travels the companions had come across a few working rail wags. But very few, and of so little apparent consequence that she'd put them so far out of mind, despite their novelty value, that when she'd first heard about MAGOG from the two deserters it had taken her a spell to work out what they were talking about.

Crickets struck up the band. They were unusually loud and strident. Krysty wondered if they were outsized mutie crickets. She checked to make sure her longblaster was ready to handle, to be on the safe side. Even normal little natural crickets were carnivorous, after all.

"No, not many at all," Paul went on. As he did tend to do.

"Just a few on milk runs here 'n' there, mostly back East. Biggest I know has a total working track run of sixty miles, belongs to the baron of Mobile. That's Caius Caligula Helton. Mighty forward-thinking baron, rich as Croesus and hardly cruel to speak of. His son Marc Anthony's an officer for the General on MAGOG its own bad self. Womenfolk who seen him reckon he's the most gorgeous man on legs. Light-skinned black kid, he is, kinda bronzy, curly hair."

The eyes Krysty turned on him were slits of green hellfire. He nodded. "Yeah, from your description of what happened at the wag caravan, I figgered he was the man in charge."

He held up his hands to ward the outburst he saw building rapidly on her lovely face. "Yes, I do know a lot about MAGOG. More'n mosta the people inside her, 'ceptin' the General and some of his techies. Mebbe young Marc. They say he's a studious sort.

"Don't ya see? I'm obsessed with her."

For a few moments they ate and listened to the mutie cricket choir and the shack creaking and groaning in the wind. Krysty stared at her companion, trying to assimilate what he was saying.

"I told you, I love trains. Well, MAGOG isn't just the greatest train around today, no sirree. She's the greatest train ever was built, or ever will be.

"See, one of these days somebody'll put this land back together. Mebbe the General, like he dreams of, mebbe someone else. And mebbe not back into one big piece like it was before. But see, the tech knowledge is still out there. There's folk right now…anyway. Once somebody gets his or her act together enough to really rebuild, they're not gonna mess around for long with trains like you 'n' I know 'em, even though they're the most efficient land transport currently going. Oh, no. They'll build magnetic levitation wags or some such, and then who knows? Mebbe antigravity. I heard some things, mebbe even seen one or two, tells me the old guys weren't far from latchin' on to the secret o' that. After all, it ain't hardly any less likely than them teleport booths you and your friends're used to usin'."

Krysty blinked almost as if struck. She *knew* Paul knew of them. Given how far and widely he had traveled, it wasn't at all surprising; come to think of it, despite her initial bemusement at what she thought was childlike egoism on her host's part, she was surprised they hadn't heard of him.

A thought hit her and chilled her right through—if Paul knew...

"Yep, missy," he said, reading her face like a page. Her hair was writhing around her shoulders like snakes on fire. "Old General, he knows who an' what your friends are, right enough. He's a crusty old bastard, and mad as a mudhen, but one thing—ain't no flies on him. No, none at all. He has his spies, people who ferret out bits of information from far and wide.

"But back off the trigger before you go blastin' off, Krysty Wroth. Bryanna told you folks back in Tucumcari saw at least three of 'em hale and hearty as you please. General hadn't iced 'em down by then, likely he reckons he's got reasons to keep 'em alive."

The lashing of her hair subsided. But her face was still deadly pale. "And is this General always rational?" she hissed. A spasm of angry fear knotted her gut. She threw the well-gnawed bone into the night.

Grass rustled as things rushed upon the prize.

"No. No, he ain't. But getting our bowels in an uproar ain't exactly gonna keep your friends alive, now is it? Our best bet's to keep a clear head and keep after 'em, ain't it?"

She made herself suck down a breath, deep into her belly until it almost felt as if her pelvis was expanding. Letting as much of the rage and fear and sorrow flow out of her on the exhale as she could, she nodded. "Yeah. It is."

After a moment, calm claimed her again. "So you've chased the train for years, Paul?"

His eyes glistened behind his goggles. "Yes," he said, hoarse, as if fighting tears. "Every night she drives through my dreams, shining like the sun. It's what I live for, to catch a glimpse of her. To run my hand down those shining steel sides."

"But you've never actually caught up to her, have you?"

Desolate, he shook his head.

"Then what makes you think you can catch her now?"

Amazingly, he grinned, that brown but brilliant child's grin of his.

"Why, because I never had the help of Krysty Wroth before."

Chapter Eighteen

The ville died hard.

Mildred wandered through streets of fire. The flames rolled out the doors and windows and fallen-in roofs of what long ago had been the center of a typical small Midwestern town, and later resettled by survivors who crept out beneath strange skies after skydark ended. They had a voice, those flames, a deep rushing roar, a crackle, a hiss. They gave light to the night sky overhead, reflecting off the restless low hanging clouds, bringing out the oranges and reds and yellows that already dwelt within them with hellish brilliance.

Off to the west, a line of crimson lay across the dead-flat horizon as another day died in fire.

An especially strong rush of burning-barbecue scent hit Mildred's nostrils. She heard a sizzling sound. Not wanting to, she looked to her right. The body of a man lay sprawled half out of the broken picture window of a building faced with some kind of shiny red stonelike sheets. He seemed middle-aged. A blue plaid shirt had fallen so that his head and shoulders were concealed. The stained white T-shirt he wore beneath had likewise slipped down, baring a wide soft pale back. Nostrils flaring, cheeks taut, she made herself look closer.

He showed no sign of stirring as the moaning flames devoured the lower half of his body. Since he was beyond help, she felt rushing relief that he was beyond feeling.

Some weren't so lucky. She heard screams from all directions. Also shots.

A hand grabbed her arm and spun her roughly. "Mildred. What are you doing here?"

"I don't know, Marc," she told him truthfully.

He was wearing his battledress and steel breastplate. His black USP was in his right hand. A burn glowed angry on his smooth right cheek.

"I guess the question is, what are you doing here?" she said. "Or maybe, why are you doing this?"

"Rebellion," he said shortly. "They killed some of our men left here to protect them. Something had to be done."

"That's always what they say, isn't it?" She folded her arms tightly beneath her breasts and turned to walk back toward the train, which was itself ablaze with searchlights, its steel flanks vivid with reflected flames.

He called something after her. A rush of flames from a storefront and the collapse of a weakened ceiling consumed the words.

THE GENERAL HELD his mesh-faced mask in the crook of his left arm. "Are you ready, Professor?"

Doc saluted him with his epee. "As ready as I shall ever be, sir."

Outside it was beginning to get dark. Putting on his own mask, Doc noticed red glints playing on the glass. He paused.

"I say, what are those flames outside, General?"

"Justice," the General said. *"En garde!"*

The General advanced. He came on with his upper torso held almost square to Doc, and his left hand above his shoulder. Doc adopted a more sideways stance, almost as it playing foils instead of epee.

With a stamp and a shout, the General thrust. It was a feint, too tight and short to be effective. Doc barely engaged it and then parried the actual thrust.

So they dueled as the ville outside burned. The General had the edge in vigor, strength and aggression; his was the stronger wrist. But Doc was subtler and more skillful.

The stiff blades rang and sang. The two were even in honors when the General called a halt to breathe and rinse mouths with water from sippy bottles. Doc was grateful; he'd been unwilling to call a halt, but was about to drop.

"Your skill is fine," the General told him. His face was red and he was breathing heavily, Doc was gratified to note. "I salute you."

"My thanks, kind sir. I studied at the *salle* of Adelmo Sicilio."

The General raised an eyebrow. "Indeed? And where was that?"

Doc moistened his lips. *Fool! You almost let slip too much.* "In—in a ville on the Lantic Coast. It was really quite some years ago."

"I see." The General nodded judiciously. "Well, whoever your master was, he taught you well. Shall we continue?"

Doc in fact was still weary, but he knew better than to thwart a baron. They faced each other again, faceless behind masks. The General's tunic had a stylized red heart appliquéd over his sternum to give his foe "Something to aim at," he'd explained.

They saluted each other and began to fence. This time they were more wary. Or just more tired.

"Sometimes you mystify me, Professor," the General said, rolling his wrist to deflect a rather weak thrust from Doc.

"How so?" he tried not to pant the words. He hated fencing people who thought they were Cyrano de Bergerac and wanted to talk. "I certainly do not try to."

"You're reticent about your past. But clearly you are a well-educated man, and a well-traveled one. Ha!" The last accompanied a touch on Doc's forearm. They stepped back and saluted each other.

"It almost seems you have some extraordinary means of moving about the country," the General said.

Doc smiled weakly behind his mask. "Semblances can be quite misleading. I see you have touched me again, sir."

"So I have. You seemed a bit distracted. Hardly sporting of me to take advantage. Forgive it."

He attacked again. Though his arms was beginning to feel like lead, Doc made himself mount a credible defense. The General had a tendency to telegraph everything, which helped.

"I am intent on reuniting the United States, as you may know, Professor," the General said.

"A most laudable ambition, sir."

"We're men of the world. At least I flatter myself I am. I know damned well it'd take about a century more than I'm likely to get to make much of an impression, even with an invincible armored train that can travel from one end of the continent to— Ha! Well parried! I'm searching for something."

"Are not we all?"

"A man who can fence with wits and steel at the same time! Brilliant, Professor. Bravo! But what I seek—" he bound Doc's blade, closed up to him breast to breast "—is the Great Redoubt. No point trying to hide the fact. Where the old U.S. government hid away all the means and plans to restore itself after the coming disaster. Continuity of Government, they called the concept—could anything be nobler?"

He pushed away. "It could be," he said, closing again behind leveled blade, "that a man as wise and observant as yourself might have learned something in his travels that might help lead to the Great Redoubt. It might even be he knew of some marvelous means of transportation, itself a treasure second only to the redoubt, that could greatly aid the search."

Doc noticed the General's parries were getting wider and wider as he worked himself up. He feinted, then lunged in a sloppy, floppy overextended attack that would have been inexcusable if it hadn't scored a hit on the General's tunic, at the shoulder of his sword arm. It forced another break, as Doc had prayed it might.

"Grah!" The General emitted an inarticulate sound of disgust. He came forward stamping, beating down Doc's blade. "I will not be denied, do you hear me?" he shouted.

But Doc had whipped his own blade around and up and, standing on tiptoe, launched a riposte on the high line. His stiff epee blade was bowed between the cup hilt and the little red symbol sewed to the center of the General's chest.

"Ah, sir, you strike me to the heart." He fell back and took off his mask. Sweat streamed down his craggy reddened face.

"That's enough for now," he said in a voice harsh with passion. "But think well on what I've said, my good Professor, for we shall talk again about it soon!"

"YOU'RE WAY TOO TENSE, hon," Mildred said, kneading Singh's shoulders with her powerful hands. "One thing you got to keep in mind, you don't do yourself or your patients any good tying yourself up in knots. It just makes it harder to work."

The healer smiled wanly back over her shoulder at Mildred, who breathed a short sigh. There was a sort of role reversal going on here. Singh seemed to be trying, maybe without realizing it, to abdicate her crushing burden to her new subordinate. She had a perfect rationalization in hand: the black woman was much more medically knowledgeable and neither could deny it.

Nor was Mildred constitutionally capable of doing anything less than what she could when her healing services were needful. This night they'd treated four men wounded during the deliberate devastation of a ville whose name no one ever knew. Despite feeling as if they'd had it coming, Mildred couldn't refuse to do her best for them. In the same way, while she wouldn't criticize her nominal superior—and couldn't criticize her dedication or effort—when she saw something that needed to be done, she did it.

But she didn't want the job. She liked, respected and tried not to pity Singh, who wasn't in the chain of command nor responsible for the atrocities MAGOG left in its wake. She didn't want to cut the ground from under her feet.

Neither did she want to get to like the job too much, even though she was acting more like a real physician for a more protracted period than at any time since Ryan and company had awakened her. And she especially didn't want to come to view herself as part of MAGOG. Not when it meant identifying with the people who had enslaved her.

"Singh?"

Mildred's heart performed some pretty odd aerobatics at the sound of the voice. Both women looked up at the door of Singh's tiny office cubicle, where Captain Marc Helton stood. "Would you mind giving me a few minutes with Mildred, please?"

"No, Captain," Singh said in an almost inaudible voice. Before Mildred could put her oar in, Singh jumped up and scuttled out.

Mildred made herself face the young officer. She had learned in the interim that when she encountered Helton in the burning ville he had been in the process of trying to rein in the men. Not supervising the destruction, as she had imagined.

So I wronged him. So what? It was only by degree. But standing there looking at his earnest, handsome, and at the moment painfully young-looking face, it was impossible for her to pretend that her only thoughts toward him were negative.

He was the most beautiful man she had ever seen.

"I don't really have anything to say to you right now, Marc." She marveled at how hard she sounded. She was a better actress than she gave herself credit for, if nothing else.

He shook his head. "Mildred, I'm sorry. Sorry you had to see that."

"Sorry I had to? Or sorry that I did?"

"We couldn't exactly keep it a secret. But I understand your scruples, your compassion. I honor you for them. I really do. But they're part of the distant past now. The things we do now...are what our reality demands of us.

"And we aren't doing this for ourselves. We're doing it for future generations. So they can live in a better world than we'll ever know. Someone's got to start building it. We've taken it on—the General has taken it on, and so have those of us who have chosen, who have *sworn*, to follow him. And if we find ourselves forced to do things that leave stains on our souls, in the name of a better tomorrow, then we're willing to pay that price. Or any other."

He really was a puppy. Maybe with the mind of a Nobel

laureate, but a puppy. She wanted to grab him and shake him and say, "Honey, honey, listen to yourself! You've got to know how trite and empty that all is!"

But he believed them.

"You're doing what you think is right, I know," she said. "But so were the men who blew up the world in the first place. Belief doesn't make everything right, Marc."

He frowned. Then he shut his eyes and shook his head. "I'm not explaining this well enough."

He half turned away, slumped in the doorway, hammer-fisted himself on the leg. "Nuke blast! If only I knew what to say to make you see—"

She smiled feebly. "I feel just the same way."

"Mebbe if you spoke to the General himself—"

"Don't even go there. All I'd say is to ask him to let my people go."

"Is that how you think of yourself and your friends? As prisoners?"

"Aren't we? We were taken at gunpoint and rounded up like cattle—taken as slaves, Marc."

He looked at her as if he was waiting for her to come to the point. She wasn't getting through. He was a child of a world in which slavery was an everyday part of life, distasteful to some, accepted—at least its existence—by most. Just as he was of a world in which race prejudice was something that existed between man and mutie, where hardly anybody troubled themselves about a slight difference in melanin concentration, so long as you weren't a *taint*.

What he had done to her and J.B. and Jak and Doc was like what he had done to the immigrants judged unfit to work on the track: unpleasant, regrettable, but duty. Part of the burden he'd taken on in pursuit of his dream, or the General's anyway. What it wasn't and couldn't be was the obscene defilement, the literal denigration, that it was to her. To him, to almost everyone today, slavery had little or nothing to do with skin color. What it mainly had to do with was luck.

She shook her head and turned away as her eyes filled with tears. "Never mind."

She felt his hand on her arm and whirled. He lifted it quickly. He looked as if she had slapped him.

"I'm sorry, Marc. But...please don't."

"But why, Mildred? I...like you. What's wrong with expressing that?"

"Damn you, don't play with me! In your eyes I'm just— just a fat old lady! Don't you *dare* patronize me. Don't play games."

His eyes were big and round. "But you're not. You're an incredible person. Your warmth and wisdom, your knowledge, your dedication, your bravery. I admire you. You have greatness inside. And I—"

He shook his head. "I enjoy being with you."

He reached for her face with his hands. She caught his wrists in grips of iron. "If you're not playing with me, Marc, then a thousand times don't keep this up. Please."

She slowly moved his hands back toward his chest and released them. "I like you, too, Marc. But for right now, I think you'd better go."

He left.

"ARE YOU GETTING anywhere, Captain?"

Marc stopped and spun in the narrow passageway. Out here you could really feel the train's motion as it hurtled along the tracks, beneath a tormented sky. It felt like riding within a great living organism.

"What are you talking about, Hubertus?"

The intel chief smiled. As always, it made him look as if he were a tailor who'd forgotten he had a mouthful of pins. "With Mildred, of course."

The young captain's eyes narrowed and his hands knotted into fists. "You were instructed to probe her, Captain. For certain information. Have you made any progress whatever?"

"I didn't ask her just now, if that's what you mean."

"That's a pity. The General has been most indulgent with those four. Scandalously so, I might say. But his patience won't last forever. Our intelligence analysis indicates very persuasively that they have knowledge that could prove crucial to the realization of our grand program."

"The Great Redoubt."

"Among other things. Although the location of the redoubt itself might pale into insignifance beside…*other* things they know. The General's forbearance won't last forever. If gentler means fail to produce result, then we will be forced to subject Mildred and her friends to stiffer measures."

"Lay a hand on her," Marc said, "and I'll shoot you myself."

"Me? I who am nothing but an instrument of our General's will, Captain? What of the grand design? What of your idealistic dreams?"

"I believe you heard me. Good night!"

Chapter Nineteen

The desert sky was cloudy, yet the morning was warm.

So was the rattler. And getting warmer by the second.

The dark lozenges running down its back, contrasting strongly with the dust-colored scales of its sides, identified it to Ryan as a Western diamondback. He knew the breed. They weren't as aggressive and prone to attack for the pure pleasure of feeling their fangs sink into flesh as their darker, eastern cousins were. During snake season, his father's barony of Front Royal in the Shens lost an average of one person per week to diamondback bites.

But the westerners were cranky enough. This one, pissed off anyway at being disturbed while sucking down solar energy on a nice flat piece of sandstone, was molting, and the sacs behind the obsidian-bead eyes were swollen huge with a winter's accretion of venom. Their pressure, and the itch of shedding dead skin, made the six-foot rattler double savage.

It had him scoped, too. It was reared back and flicking its tongue at him. It wasn't rattling yet. From Ryan's experience it might not. Crouching, dressed in just his jeans and boots and shirt with rolled up sleeves, Ryan tried to stay light on his feet, ready to dodge left or right if it struck.

He began to circle the snake to his left. His left arm was immobilized in a canvas sling. He actually could move it meaningfully, wiggle his fingers and everything, but without strength and not without pain. Still, he reckoned he had to only have cracked his collarbone in the fall, instead of busting it outright, for him to have this much use of it so soon after getting wounded. That, or the Little Ones possessed healing skills beyond even Mildred's.

Which was entirely possible. The Ewoks were some eerie little bastards, for all their almost comical friendliness.

Trying to track the persistently annoying heat source, the diamondback came out of the neat, powerful coil in which Ryan had discovered it. This was the serpent equivalent of being off balance, and what Ryan had been counting on. It could no longer strike to maximum range.

He darted suddenly back to his right, lunged in, grabbed. He caught the snake's tail just beneath its impressively long rattle. He yanked it off the ground with a smooth motion.

The rattler tried to double back to plant its spearlike fangs in his flesh. It was bastard mad. He could feel the muscles quivering violently beneath his hand as it tried to shake its tail to rattle its rage. They were like pulsing liquid steel.

The snake turned its arrow head left and right. Ryan turned his wrist deftly in the opposite direction to the snake's every move. It couldn't reach him. Quite.

So his reflexes and sure-handedness, and the depth perception he'd trained himself to have since losing an eye to his brother as a youth, were all back firmly in place. One more test remaining…

He swung the furious snake up in the air and let it go. As it came down writhing and rattling, he quick-drew his panga from his belt and struck. The head flew free in a gush of dark blood. The body landed in the middle of a clump of bunch grass, still doubling spastically left and right.

"Bravo," a voice behind him piped. "Very impressive, Ryan Cawdor."

He turned. The Little Ones' shaman Far Walker sat on his haunches ten feet away, gazing at the human with wide, wise eyes.

"Thanks." Ryan knelt, plucked a handful of dry grass, wiped snake blood from the heavy blade. He scrubbed it with sand to make sure it was all the way clean before returning it to his scabbard. Then he rose and picked up the decapitated body. It doubled as if still trying to bite him with phantom fangs.

"Good eating," he observed. "Tastes just like chicken."

"The protein will do your healing processes good," agreed the tubby little creature. "Regretfully we cannot provide a sufficiency to you."

No. The food his hosts had provided Ryan had been usable by his omnivore body, quite nourishing by the evidence, and even tasty. For various types of grain, grass, herbs and just plain weeds, spiced with occasional piñon nuts. Naturally—or as close to natural as anything about the friendly muties was—the Little Ones were strict vegetarians. But more than that, they were absolute pacifists. It was hard-wired into their genes by their creators, Far Walker had explained.

"Far Walker," Ryan said, "there's one thing I've been wondering about."

"Ask, friend Ryan."

"How in the name of glowing nuke shit did your people ever get the name Little Ones?"

"Ah." The mutie nodded sagely. Which was only appropriate; he was a sage, after all. Eldest among his people, although Ryan declined to ask how old that was, exactly, for fear the answer would be something like, "Four."

"We worship your people as our creators. We try to keep it low-key around you, to avoid embarrassing a beloved guest." His old eyes laughed as he said this. He laughed a lot. He was that kind of sage, Ryan reckoned. "Our racial memory stretches back far, and far. Beyond even the time our ancestors were captured and taken to the labs so that your people could work upon us the magic they called genetic engineering—from these very cliffs were we taken, and to here, in time, forever changed, were we returned."

Ryan nodded. He surmised that the predark whitecoats, with time and unaccountable black budgets weighing heavy on their hands, had tried to breed a rad-resistant race of servants. Even Mildred shook her head at the wilder excesses of certain scientists of her time, like blowing up the planet. Doc's accounts of his experiences in the bowels of the Totality Concept and its Operation Chronos, the most supersecret whitecoat projects of all, were fragmentary and hallucinatory; but they always brought to Ryan's mind the phrase power without responsibility. Like mad children possessed of near-infinite power, the whitecoats from before the Nuke were capable of damned near anything, and seemed to have done most of it.

"When it came time to name ourselves, for we were a new thing upon the Earth, and our forebears, lacking the power and knowledge of words, had never before possessed a name, we searched that racial memory. And from that collective unconscious, or perhaps preconscious, bubbled up one phrase—a single sentence we had heard repeated by your ancestors so many times that, without or even understanding it, it had imprinted itself, as it were, upon our very DNA."

"And that was?"

"'Those little ones sure are cute.'"

"You're laughing at me."

"Certainly." Far Walker clutched his fat buff belly and laughed out loud, to prove it was true. "But it is also the truth."

Ryan shook his head.

"You're healing up nicely, One Eye Chills," Far Walker said.

It was the name the Apaches had given him. Ryan didn't know if they'd come up with it on their own; their sense of humor, for whatever reason, was a lot like that he'd encountered among Indians who had trusted him enough to open up in his presence. Their perceptions were Indianlike in a lot of other ways, as well.

But then again he might have babbled it in his delirium. Or the shaman might have skimmed it out of his mind while inhabiting his dreams. Ryan never doubted for a moment, after his wits returned, that the Little Ones' shaman had done so. Had it been almost anybody else Ryan would have been at the least creeped out—and maybe made chilling-mad—by the notion of somebody wandering around inside his skull with him. But he trusted Far Walker not to intrude upon his mind and soul.

"Thanks to you and your people," Ryan said.

They began to walk back toward the Little Ones' ville, which consisted of burrows dug right next to the Big Ditch. Some actually opened onto the canyon. Evidently Ewoks weren't much given to sleepwalking. Ryan still carried his dead snake. He was serious about eating it. Just the feel of meat made his stomach rumble.

"You are most welcome, friend Ryan, as you are always welcome as our honored guest. Understand, please, that we are not—how would you say?—altruists. But we feel a great debt to your kind. They took much from us, it is true, but it is in our hearts that the gifts they gave us, of mind and speech, far outweighed our loss. We know you didn't, personally, have anything to do with it. We also know many of your people are to be feared, and never trusted."

"You hit the eye and not the brow, there," Ryan said, quoting a Russkie saying he'd picked up during the time he and his companions spent in that land.

"Yet we have come to like you, in person, as we admire your true heart and strong spirit."

"You're soaping me now."

Far Walker nodded. "Trying to. But I speak straight from the heart. We count you our friend, and hope you reckon us likewise."

"You did save my life."

"Indeed. And please understand, you owe us nothing for that. But still…when you are finished healing—not yet!—we would ask a favor of you."

"Well, why don't you go ahead and get to the trigger of the blaster, not keep stepping all around the muzzle?"

"We want you to slay a monster."

Ryan stopped. "A monster?"

"A monster. Perhaps not a terribly big monster, by your standards. No more than two thousand pounds' mass, and surely less than nine feet in height. But immense by our standards."

"So, a ton and less than ten feet. What kind of monster?"

"A bear. A most voracious bear. We lose many folk to its appetite—young and adults alike."

Ryan jutted out his chin and bobbed his head slowly, thoughtfully. "A bear. No bigger than a big griz or a polo bear. My Steyr longblaster's a little light for a bear that size, but I know how to place my shots to make 'em count."

"Not so fast, friend Ryan. I have no wish to mislead you. This isn't just any bear."

"It's not, huh?"

"It is an armored bear."

"What does that mean, exactly?"

"Its body is covered with scales. Some as large as your hand. We do not know whether they are made of bone, or just horny hide. But they are very hard and tough. Such, I fear, that even bullets from your mighty firestick, in caliber 7.62 mm, NATO, would bounce harmlessly off them."

"Now, isn't that just ace?" Ryan rubbed his chin. As usual, stubble rasped beneath his fingers, just a half-day past shaving himself clean. "What if I say no?"

Far Walker spread his three-fingered hands. "As I have said, you are our beloved and honored guest. We will shelter and heal you as long as you wish to remain among us. Of course, in so doing you run the same risk as all of us, that the armored bear will invade your burrow and eat your head."

"Makes sense."

"But as I said, we are not altruists, nor do we ask this great deed of you without offering something in return."

"Which is?"

"If you slay the monster—and, well, live—I shall guide you on a spirit walk, reveal to you the fate and whereabouts of your friends. I can even show you possible paths into the future for you and they—although such ways are perilous, and quickly obscured by fog."

"That's a powerful inducement," Ryan admitted. "Now, to do this, I take it I have to ingest mind-altering substances."

"That is customarily required, yes. Unless you care to undergo years of meditation and training, as I have done. Which, I'm afraid, still entails taking the mind-altering substances. Sorry."

The fuzzy shaman blinked around the sky. "Would you mind terribly if we started walking again? I feel uneasy remaining in the open too long."

"The bear?"

"Screamwings."

Chapter Twenty

MAGOG encountered its first chem storm. The only reason the captive companions were even aware of it was that a Klaxon sounded throughout the train, and the loudspeaker system announced an alert. All access ports to the outside from cargo bays to firing slits were to be sealed and left that way until the all-clear sounded.

Doc, in the special apartment he had been given, continued to sit, sip sherry and read *The Odyssey* on the screen in his room. He rather enjoyed the sensation of being totally insulated from the evil and madness without.

Of course, he was all too aware of the incipient madness and evil *inside* the armored train. For all his image of being rock-steady and straightforward as a brick, the General was mercurial, as Doc had learned from close at hand. Doc, who had long since acquired the trick of playing at having one of his spells when he was in fact perfectly lucid, knew Hubertus was pressing the General to submit them to what the intel chief termed interrogation. Of course, Doc knew a euphemism for torture when he heard one. The General wasn't so much likely to be swayed by his intel chief's rather whiny importuning as he was to dig in his heels and resist. But he also might decide at literally any moment to give his captives over to the question on his own whim, ignited by the obsessive lust burning within him to locate the Great Redoubt, and the key to continental conquest he believed it contained, as quickly as possible.

What could he do about it? Personally, aside from hoping for an opportunity he understood was unlikely to present itself, nothing. Therefore he had resolved to await his fate and meanwhile enjoy the comforts of his captivity as long as possible. He, of all the companions, had spent the most time in durance, and was least bothered by it.

But bother him it did. It always had. He longed for the day his comrades would rescue themselves, because he knew that when that time came, he would be delivered as well.

He did wonder, though, whether the death of his great friend Ryan Cawdor might just have fatally undermined the morale of the group. It had partially deranged poor Jak, as manifested by his continued insistence that their leader wasn't in fact dead, a phenomenon Mildred termed "denial." Individually, they were all quite remarkable in their abilities—he modestly, and not altogether correctly, excluded himself from such characterization—but had they become so reliant upon the example, courage and resourcefulness of Ryan that they could no longer act effectively?

He couldn't know. All he could do was bide, and read, and pour himself another bit of sherry.

THE TRAIN CONTINUED ON for another hour and then stopped—a surprisingly smooth and quiet process compared to the trains Mildred had heard in her previous life. It halted on a bridge over a running stream. A team in full chemical protective equipment suits from train's stores went out to test the water for pH and presence of toxic chems. When they radioed that the water was acceptably pure, the General ordered MAGOG unsealed. Pumps were deployed, and a platoon of men clambered on top of the train to hose it down. All the wags, even the soft-shelled ones, had metal skins and thus a certain resistance to the chems. But even the special alloy armor could be degraded by too much exposure. So despite the General's growing impatience a halt had to be made.

Nonessential personnel were allowed to stretch their legs. J.B. and Mildred met on a dirt road that ran parallel to the tracks. They hugged, kissed—a lot less fervently than they wanted, since they had an audience—and then, fingers linked, began to saunter along the road.

Mildred was balancing on a rut like a schoolgirl and giggling when she fell over. "Thought you'd wanna run through the flowers," J.B. said. To the left and right of the tracks the land was covered by fields of wildflowers that stretched clear to the horizons, a scene of wildly incongruous beauty despite the overcast.

But she shook her head, making her beaded dreads swing. "I don't trust flowers," she declared, "that can open up again so soon after a chem storm."

"Makes sense."

When there was no one close by she halted, faced him and took his hands.

"J.B., they're on to us."

"How do you mean?"

"Listen to me. This train has been all over the continent over the past few years. Everywhere they go, they suck up all the information the way they're pumping water out of that stream. As if their lives depended on it, which they do.

"And what do you think they keep hearing? These wild-ass tales about a bunch of traveling troublemakers consisting of a redheaded beauty, a feral albino teen, a doddering old fart, a blaster freak, a black woman and a one-eyed killer. And this traveling circus gets around even more places than they do.

"Now, you can be sure our boy Captain Marc had counted the buttons on that big old coat of Ryan's before he fell into the Grand Canyon. And if he didn't, that crusty old rhino Banner sure did. Five hits out of a possible six. Do the math. You can bet the General or his intelligence gnomes did."

"But Krysty—?"

"They got to reckon either something happened to her lately, or they just plain missed her." She took his hand across the table. "John, they've *got* to know."

"What can we do about it?"

She sighed. "I was hoping you'd know. Better yet, I was hoping you'd worked out a plan of escape."

He let go her hands, turned away, took off his glasses and polished them. "Been tryin'," he acknowledged. "But they're doin' an ace in the line job of keeping us separated. I could spring Jak easy, I reckon. But the General's keeping Doc tucked in his coat pocket, and the one's no easier to get at than the other."

He shook his head. "I oughta know how to take care of myself. Been doin' it since I was a kid. But I surely do miss Ryan. I can't stop thinking, if he was here, he would have worked out a way to spring us all before we cross the Grandee."

She touched his arm. "Don't berate yourself, John. There are circumstances nobody can prepare for. We're in some now."

"You're right. As usual. I ought to know better than to argue with a woman so much older than me."

She laughed and lightly punched his arm.

"But I think you're right about something else. They know who we are, which means we're living on borrowed time till they decide to really start digging into what we might know."

He cocked his head at her. "That pretty boy Marc been pumping you?"

Her face turned the color of wood ash.

"Dark night, Millie! I didn't mean it like that! Shit, I'm no good with words. Sometimes it seems I do more damage with my mouth than with my blasters. I meant to ask if he'd been trying to get information out of you, nothin' more."

"Consciously, that's all you meant. But it's okay, John. I understand. I know how you must wonder. I'd wonder the same if some foxy young thing was slinking around you."

"She'd have to get by old Leo, first."

She took his hands again. "I know you don't like dealing with this kind of thing. But listen to me. You're my man, John. I'm not shopping for any replacements. And I'm not straying."

She flew to him, wrapped him in her arms and squeezed him tightly. "I won't betray you. I won't betray myself."

She pulled her head back to gaze tearfully into his face. "Don't you see? Even if I'd never met you, I couldn't give in to Marc. Because it would mean accepting I was a slave. And I'll die first. Do you hear me? I'll die."

"All right, Millie, I heard you," he croaked. "And I will, too, unless you ease off on the bear hug and let me breathe."

Instead she kissed him passionately. He returned it. They broke apart.

"Whoo," he said. "Now if I can just find somebody to put my spine back in place—"

Wild screams interrupted him.

"STORM COMIN'," Paul said conversationally.

They were fighting a head wind today. For all her determination, Krysty was endlessly tempted to ask her companion to power up his little two-stroke mill. But she knew their fuel supply couldn't be large. One more mile, she promised herself.

As she had for the last twenty.

She could smell rain in the air. That was a reassuring sign; she wasn't smelling toxic chems. When she turned in her seat to look ahead, though, the clouds looked anything but re-assuring. They were clotted and yellow, shading into brown.

That might mean tornadoes, which weren't a big improve-ment on chem storms.

Paul's been this way before, she reminded herself. Chem storms and twisters alike were common out here. If he hadn't learned to spot them well in advance, as well as what to do when he did, he'd have left his bones bleaching along the tracks long since.

"Tell me more about the tech-nomads," she said. For once she would welcome his usually unceasing patter. Anything was better than waiting to see if a chem storm would catch them out here in this featureless flat land with nothing resem-bling shelter in view for miles.

"What do you want to know?" he asked, brusquely for him.

"Who are they? How do they live? Why are they called tech-nomads?" Actually, there was a question she'd been burning to ask him. But she felt she needed to get him well-primed and flowing freely before she did. Otherwise he might clam and never answer it.

To her relief he chuckled. "That's a lot of questions, missy. Too many to fit in my poor old head at once, much less an-swer. But I'll do what I can. Like I told you, they're free-rov-ing tribes. They travel all over the continent."

"So have I. But I've never run into them before. Or even

heard of them." But maybe she had: childhood tales of vagabonds with fantastic powers, sometimes malevolent, most often totally indifferent to the doings of others. Details in the stories were few and fantastic, but common themes of awe and dread skeined through them all.

"They keep kind of a low profile. They learned that the hard way."

He shook his head. "Got their start back before the big war. Good ten, twenty years. People started getting dissatisfied with the way society was going. So they dropped out. Actually, all kinds of folk were doing that. But a certain breed combined that dissatisfaction with wanderlust. They decided the way to stay beneath the system's scopes was to keep moving. So they hit the road and just kept rollin'. Perpetual Travelers was one thing they called themselves, or Permanent Tourist. But generally they came to call themselves tech-nomads."

"I guess I've got the 'nomad' part nailed down," she said. They were passing now through fields of early-spring wildflowers, vast patches of color, blue and white, although muted in the poor light filtering through the clouds. She wondered how the flowers survived the acid rains. "But I'm still not too clear on the 'tech.'"

"Well, I've been told the one thing that served as a kind of bond for 'em was a fascination with technology, the latest and greatest. Not the big-scale stuff. Really gadgets, you'd call 'em. For a lot of them it was a love-hate relationship with technology. They had a general distrust of it, but they loved those parts of it that made their lifestyle possible.

"Some of it was keepin' in touch with one another. Stuff like satellite phones, the Internet—they were among the first people outside government to use those things. Heck, some of 'em had *been* government techies before droppin' out. And a big part of it was transportation.

"See, a lot of them disliked the internal combustion engine—the automobile. Even those who didn't had a tendency to try alternate modes of transport, just out of sheer cussedness or love of novelty if nothing else. So they loved to experiment, with wind power, or muscle power—HPVs, human-powered vehicles, were big favorites—alternate fuels. Actually, it made some sense, what with oil prices going up and down so unpredictably, and the supplies always being vulnerable. They and the survivalist movement had a lot in common. A certain amount of plain old overlap."

A drop hit Krysty on the cheek.

It tingled. For a moment she thought it was just the impact. But as it lingered on her skin, she began to feel a slight but distinct burn.

She wiped it off convulsively. "Paul—"

He nodded. "I'm on it. Got a good five, ten minutes before it gets serious. All it'll do till then is spit, and that mostly water."

She gripped the handholds on either side of the seat until her knuckles threatened to burst through the skin, and pedaled harder.

"So, anyway, a lot of 'em took off on their bikes or trikes or land-yachts. Some took to sailing on boats. Some of 'em even took to the rails, like yours truly, the Rail Ghost—not sayin' I was one of 'em, this was all way before my time, o' course—"

"Paul!" It started to sprinkle. The rain wasn't painful, but as it lay on her skin it gave her a prickly sensation like the beginnings of a sunburn.

"Then the big war hit. Tech-nomads had a greater survival rate than the general run of the population. One, they were mostly dispersed out of the urban centers. Two, they tended to be into self-sufficiency, things like carrying along stocks of water-purifier tabs and nonperishable foods, even when they didn't know how to live off the land. And while many of them were loners, and they were split into a whole buncha groups and factions, they had a certain sense of kinship. They looked out for each other—helped when they could. Still did a lot of dying, just like everybody else. Or at least this is what I've been told."

It was raining quite briskly now. She only wished she trusted Paul's assurance they'd be out of it before it started to sluice the flesh from their bones.

"It wasn't until after the skydark that things got real bad for the tech-nomads. See, lot of folks blamed everybody identified with technology—scientists, engineers, plain old techs—for the megacull. So they started to hunt them down and lynch them. Not everybody joined in, but plenty did. Lot of tech-nomads died, and died hard.

"It was plenty ironic, if you go in for that sorta thing. Lot of people who were antitech in most ways died for being tech-lovers. The survivors drew in tight after that. No matter what they felt before, they dedicated themselves to preserving all the old tech lore they could, and even adding new. And they swore to keep themselves as far removed from the rest of the world—from the humans, anyway—as possible. It started off as sheer survival. But after all these years, it's tradition."

Krysty's hand burned. She saw the skin go red where a drop had hit. "Paul! We've got to do something. *Now!*"

"Right." He applied the brakes. She dropped her feet off the pedals, jumped off the platform, then ran alongside the Paul as he slowed the Yawl.

She didn't know where else to go.

Paul hopped off to the left. "Help me get her off the track," he called. Paul had a screw-jack system he could use for getting the Yawl on and off the rails with minimal exertion. No time for that now. They both grabbed handholds at either end of the platform and heaved it bodily up and off.

Then Paul was trotting down the embankment, hauling on the Yawl, and Krysty was following, trying mainly to keep it from overrunning him. At the bottom, he turned and began pulling the craft into a yawning circular opening.

A culvert! If she hadn't been riding backward, she'd have spotted it as well, she thought.

As she ducked into shelter, she heard sizzling as re-agents worked on her skin, smelled a burn stink from her hair, which was whipping in agitation. The corrugated metal passageway was big, enough to pass a wag. Stagnant water was pooled along the bottom. Paul set the brake on the Yawl, then used his hat to scoop up water to rinse first Krysty's skin and hair, then his own.

"Guess I cut it a little close, there."

"You might say that," Krysty said stiffly. But she was already unbending. He had found them shelter in time, if only just. "But what if enough comes down to raise the water level?"

"Don't reckon we'll get that much downpour," he said. "If it does, we can move higher."

"And if the culvert fills?"

He grinned beneath his mustache. "I got a few tricks up my sleeve, never you doubt. Old chem storms ain't made a real ghost of the Rail Ghost yet."

Outside the tainted rain was pelting down. Krysty's nose wrinkled at the astringent smell and she moved back from the mouth. They weren't the only creatures who had sensed the storm's onset and sought shelter, she saw. Dozens of frogs sat on the lower curve of the culvert or hopped around. Paul stalked one briefly and caught it up by the hips. He held it up toward Krysty.

"Hungry?"

She shook her head. She wasn't famished enough yet to eat raw frog. She still had self-heats in her pack, and Paul had snared a rabbit the night before. For somebody who couldn't bring himself to fight, he was a pretty redoubtable hunter, of very small game anyway. But Paul was Paul, and the only terms he could be taken on were his own. It would do her no more good to bother herself about his inconsistencies or even his cowardice than about his biting the head off the frog and munching contentedly away.

"Are you a tech-nomad, Paul?"

"Me?" He took another bite of frog. "Told ya, I'm a solitary. A perpetual floating hermit. Even though I decided to take a little sabbatical from hermitdom. Take me on a traveling companion. Mighty comely one, too."

Despite the occasional compliments, he had never evinced the slightest interest in her as anything but a traveling companion.

"But you have some means of communicating with them?"

He took the frog out of his open mouth and looked at her. Then he laughed. "Ah, but you're a sly one, aren't you? Just been waiting to pop that one on me, all the way from Tucumcari."

"The arrival of Bryanna the ice bitch and her pals was a little timely, you have to admit. Then there was the fact you said, 'What took you so long?', or words to that effect."

"Shoot. Here I was hoping you'd pass that off as ironic repartee. All righty, then. I knew they were in town. I saw the signs they left."

"Signs?"

"Hobo sign. Some of them fellers were the first tech-no-mads in ways, long time back before the Nuke, although they din't have that much to do with the technology, mostly just used it in furtherance of their nomadic ways. Rail riders like me. With real trains to ride on… Oh, well. To a Mundane—to a normal person—their marks just look like graffiti or even random scratches. But if you know the code, ah! Amazing what you can learn."

"You sure you don't have some other means to get in touch with them? You didn't exactly seem to be surprised to find them in Tucumcari, even when you were looking at that wall."

He was down to just the little froggy drumsticks now. He took a last bite, chomping them off at the knees. He threw away the flippered feet.

"I hate that part. Too much like eating a miniature scuba diver."

"Well?"

"You gotta allow a Rail Ghost a few mysteries, missy. Let's just leave it at that."

She glared at him. He gave her a placatory smile, then hunkered down to rest his butt on the curving tin wall of the culvert.

After a moment Krysty made herself ease up. She remained dependent on him. She had no practical pressure she could apply. If she applied threats or actual physical force, he might tell her what she wanted to know. He also might not. He had an awful lot of fortitude for a self-proclaimed coward, even without any stomach for fighting. But he would almost certainly look to escape her after that, and might well be willing to lead her into a trap to do so. He knew this environment, this odd in-between world of the rails. She didn't.

She went and stood in the mouth of the culvert, staring out into the chem storm. Black despair seemed to open like an abyss inside her.

"Don't worry, missy," Paul said gently. "We'll catch that old train. You'll see."

If only she could believe him! But they had come so far, risked so much. And they seemed no closer to MAGOG than ever.

She made herself draw a deep breath, forced her mind blank.

The chase would continue.

It wasn't like she had a choice.

MOST OF MAGOG's troops were young men not long out of their teens if at all. As such, and with each other overwhelmingly for company, they were prone to fits of sheer adolescent exuberance that were purely inexplicable to the rest of the population.

So there wasn't any point in looking for a good reason Private Jasper MacComb, formerly of the Zarks, should take it into his mind to race into the field of wildflowers extending north of the tracks, tearing off his utilities as he ran, to the wild cheers and applause of twenty or so of his buddies. He did it because they dared him to. It was spring, after all, even if it was spring in the Deathlands right on the heels of a chem storm. Spring makes wild animals do strange things. Adolescent human males definitely fell into that category.

Besides, they were backed up by what was likely the most potent killing engine extent in all the Earth. What could possibly harm them? What would be stupe enough to try?

Forty yards out and down to his skivvies, MacComb turned and waved his white undershirt over his head. "I did it!" he hollered back at his buddies. "Told you I would!"

"All they way!" they screamed back. "Take it all off!"

It wasn't that they actually cared to see his skinny white ass. They were wild young animals, too, and mainly wanted to see if he was triple stupe enough to do it.

Naturally, he was.

He skinned the shorts down his pale shanks. He had somehow been able to shed his baggy trousers on the run without great difficulty. But the underpants hung up on his boots. He started hopping around, cussing wildly, while his friends whistled and catcalled.

Standing down by the stream in the cut it had made, supervising repair of a balky pump, Sergeant Banner heard the ruckus. His jaw set. He knew that when the troops sounded like they were having that much fun, they were doing something prejudicial to discipline. He marched up the bank to tell them to stop.

He was way too late.

MacComb had come to a little clear spot in the field of flowers, which was why he stopped there to begin with. Now he hopped right over to the edge of it. And one of the flowers moved extending on its stalk—so it appeared to the watchers—to give him a kiss right on the left butt cheek.

They went loco at that. Their uproar drowned out MacComb's exclamation of annoyance and pain as he jumped and slapped the blossom away. They didn't see the red mark it left behind.

MacComb's jump took him in among the flowers. Another darted at his leg. He yelped again, recoiled, tripped on his skivvies and fell down.

The boys loved that. They hollered and punched one another and threw their hats in the air.

"What in the name of thermonuclear devastation is going on here!" a familiar voice roared.

The commotion instantly ceased. "Aw, shit, Sarge. We weren't doin' nothing. Just having us a little fun."

That was when the screaming started.

MacComb JUMPED to his feet and began racing madly back to the train, taking spraddling, high-kicking steps. He looked like all the sluts in the biggest gaudy in the Deathlands had painted their lips with crimson lipstick and just smooched him all over his bony fish-white body.

Except gutter-whore lip paint didn't tend to run like that.

He screamed in a shrill high voice like a wounded horse. He got no more than a dozen steps before he tripped again and fell. There was a wild commotion out among those lovely innocent blue blossoms. The screaming rose and rose until it sounded like it had to be tearing apart the body that produced it.

MacComb reared up once more. The blossoms were planted all over him, faces stuck to him like sucking mouths. Which they seemed to be. He looked as if he had been showering in gore.

His own.

A couple of his buddies plunged right in after him. Others began to follow. "You men, halt!" Banner shouted. "Stand firm there!"

The mass of would-be rescuers stopped. The blood-flowers, roused by MacComb's headlong passage, had been ready and waiting for the first two. They were already thrashing and screaming and batting at the blossoms that struck like rattlesnakes and clung like napalm.

Their baggy fatigues saved them, more or less. They came stumbling out of the flowers, one supporting his buddy, with their uniforms in tatters and blood steaming from dozens of punctures, each rimmed with a red circle like a tentacle's sucker mark. The one doing the helping lived. The other, his femoral artery opened by a particularly well-aimed bloom, bled out and died within fifteen seconds of Mildred's reaching his side at a dead run. Not even MAGOG's treasure of meds could save him.

The General ordered no effort be made to recover Mac-Comb's body. No one kicked about it.

MAGOG drove on remorselessly toward the ruins of Kancity.

Unknown parties sniped.

A gaggle of wags drove alongside the train as heavily armed coldhearts tried to clamber aboard. Though they appeared too close for MAGOG's emplaced heavy weapons to bear her crew drove them off with handheld blasters and grens. Before that happened several raiders managed to get inside the shell by blasting open the armored passage between cars with a shaped-charge warhead salvaged from an M-72 LAW wag chiller. Doc himself killed one in the sitting room of the General's personal car, using his sword cane, which the General had ordered returned to him.

MAGOG never slowed.

The great train was halted for three days by a major washout of a bridge across a river swollen by spring runoff. Despite being in a near-constant frenzy of impatience to get to Kancity, the General decided to repair the bridge rather than risk backing up and trying to look for another route.

After six men were washed away to their deaths when a wall of water came howling down from upstream, the General himself literally waded in to help with the operation. When a tribe of stickies attacked the repair party, the train's commander himself was wading waist-deep in water near midstream.

A stickie got an acid-oozing fingertip sucker affixed to the General's left cheek. The General blew the mutie's head apart with the .45 blaster he carried in a shoulder holster. When it fell back into the torrent the stickie tore open his face.

Streaming blood, the General continued to work until his men begged him to get attention. He headed in to the med wag long enough for a silent Mildred to neutralize and clean away the acid and bandage the wound. Then he went back in the river.

The bridge was patched enough to pass the armored train's weight. MAGOG rolled on.

And finally it approached its destination.

Chapter Twenty-One

Kancity was anticlimax.

Thanks to its proximity to the Whiteman ICBM launch complex, it had gotten plastered during the big war. The silos had attracted swarms of megaton-range warheads set for groundburst, which meant fallout and lots of it. It remained one of the hottest hot spots on the North American continent.

So much attention had been paid to the missile silos that little had been spared for the rails, in spite of the fact that the town had been a major rail junction. The Russians in charge of drafting the targeting-priority plan had probably figured that between the fallout and the near misses, not a lot of traffic was going to be flowing along the lines for a few thousand years anyway.

But as the General himself had gleefully pointed out, in a loudspeaker address to the troops as they approached the giant hot spot, rails are one of the very hardest things to damage with nukes, or any kind of area-effect weapons. They're steel, they're hard—extraordinarily so, from the work-hardening of having millions of tons pass over them—they're low to the ground. Anything in a nuke's radius of total destruction, well, they called it that for a reason. The thermal effect of an airburst could melt or warp rails, but for a surprisingly limited range. Blast effects were tricky, but most cases the dynamic overpressure from a blast—of any kind—simply rolled over the rails.

"Any fool with a cutting torch and a wag can cut a train line in a matter of hours," the General rasped. "But the highest tech, most powerful weapons ever devised practically had to score direct hits to target them at all."

He had chuckled as if it were a swell joke. Whether most of the crew found it funny or just incomprehensible was another issue. J.B. and Leo, in the armory car prepping for the final expedition—on which J.B. had been ordered to go—thought it was a hoot. But then they were that way.

Nonetheless the most direct lines for MAGOG, coming in from the west and southwest, had been cut—how the General knew that nobody was sure. Leo told J.B., though, that the General had spent years in preparation after finding the great train, and may have reconnoitered then.

After crossing the river the train circled north and east and came in from almost due north. They left the soft-shelled cars in a siding north of the ruins of the metropolis with most of the troop complement. Only the crews necessary to man the hardpoint-mounted heavy weapons and the train itself accompanied the armored engines and carriages into the city—and a recovery team of twelve men picked especially to fill the twelve rad suits the General had scavvied somewhere.

One of these was a not entirely thrilled J.B.

"I checked the suits myself," Leo told him as MAGOG picked its way through what had been the northern suburbs. The crew had rigged a specially designed dozer blade to clear obstructions from the line. It could deal with a lot of rubble, up to a collapsed building; but anything the blade couldn't handle, the rad suit boys would have to go out to play with. "They're good suits. Perfect condition."

"Still triple stupe to go into a place where the rads'll just knock a man right down dead without even bothering with convulsions and the bloody shits," J.B. observed.

Leo laughed his gravel-road laugh. "Welcome to the army, son."

J.B. grinned at him. "So how do I get outta this chicken-shit outfit?"

Leo's grin faded. "Die."

J.B. was also less than enchanted with the weapon he'd been assigned. His friends would've been amazed.

"Never used a flamethrower before," he groused. "Never wanted to. One thing I know about them—everybody on the whole battlefield shoots at them. Oh, and one more thing—they explode on impact."

"And just who in the name of glowing night shit is gonna be shooting at you, J.B.? Wasn't you just fifteen seconds ago bitching and moaning that it's too hot to live without lead long johns?"

J.B. was turning the nozzles in his hand. "Muties," he said shortly. "This thing hasn't got milspec markings on it. It's got a GE logo. Dark night, what'd General Electric be making a flameblaster for?"

"Did a lot of contract work for the gummint. U.S. didn't actually have no flamethrowers as such in their arsenal by the time the big Nuke rolled around. Used flame rockets and shit." He nodded to the twin tanks. "This here was prob'ly built for some gummint group."

Coarse and loud and obnoxious as he was, Leo was a consummate craftsman. As part of his job keeping MAGOG's weapon systems firing on all barrels, he had studied the train's data libraries almost as extensively as the General had, including the history and purpose for which MAGOG was built.

For the chief armorer and J.B. it had been love at first sight.

Like many master craftsmen, Leo was deliberately rude to outsiders so he wouldn't have to deal with them peering over his shoulder, jogging his elbow and asking triple-stupe questions. In person he was still vulgar, cranky and obnoxious, but less aggressively so. And of course the slightest hint of incompetence brought instant thermonuclear retribution down upon the perpetrator's ass.

Small chance of that with J.B. For one of the few times in his life the Armorer had encountered somebody who was as obsessed with weapons as he was. Each man internally paid the other the highest compliment each could imagine: Leo and J.B. each knew things the other didn't. J.B., of the four captive friends, was as happy as a pig in shit.

But J.B. never forgot that he and his companions were prisoners. Slaves, if honored, valued and well-treated ones.

But Leo wasn't the one responsible for J.B.'s plight. For the rest, he would relax and enjoy it as long as it was inevitable. When it wasn't, well, he'd be the first to act, and trusted himself to see the opening smart-quick.

"Were they any good at making flameblasters?" he wanted to know.

"Works," Leo said. "Test fired it myself. Don't forget, GE made miniguns."

J.B.'s whole face lit up in a smile. "Yeah. I did forget that. Double stupe of me."

"Yep." Leo grinned. "Tell you what." He went to a keyboard and brought up a display of what armored train's sensor suite was reading. "Rad count outside's nothing much. A body could go an hour or two unprotected and not even have his hair fall out. Why'n't we pop a door and let you try the thing out. It's a good idea, anyhoo. You gotta be prepared for the kick these babies have. Remember, what blasters launch is measured per grain, but these—" he relieved J.B. of the flamer's business end "—are measured in gallons per minute. You let this muzzle kick up vertical on you, boy, that'll ruin ever'body's day."

"Somebody'll notice from the telltales if we open a door. Hubertus's sec men, if nobody else."

Leo chuckled deep in his vast chest and vaster belly. "So? What're they gonna do, fire us? One thing to learn about life in this man's army, John Barrymore—it's easier to get forgiveness than permission."

MAGOG'S ELECTRIC BRAKES finally brought it to a stop in a railyard, mostly intact per the General's prediction, next to a river, with the rusted skeletal remains of what looked like an old hotel close on the left and a private airstrip, its runways heaved and cracked by an explosion of exotic mutie foliage, on the far bank. The river itself ran with a weird iridescent green fluid that put J.B. in mind of radiator coolant. It bubbled.

Three wags, a Hummer and two pickups were driven out of an armored transport car. It was a measure of how seriously the General took whatever it was they were after that he would sacrifice a prized Hummer. They couldn't spare the decontamination fluid to cleanse the wags, which would be abandoned after the mission.

They rolled a few blocks, up a hill and east. This part of Kancity, getting on toward what J.B. reckoned was downtown, looked as if it had been picked up whole to maybe a thousand feet and then dropped. The streets were surprisingly clear, though. There hadn't been many buildings in this part of town multistoried enough to rubble-out seriously. Most of the wags on the street had been burned-out early, and then worked on by years of chem storms and the real enemy of wags, rain. What they mainly encountered was vaguely wag-shaped mounds of rust and corrosion so fragile they fell away to red powder at a nudge from the Hummer's reinforced front bumper.

They came to what could only be called a compound, surrounded by fences topped with razor tape. Chain link was another thing that survived explosions, even nukeblasts, well. Whatever the fence had been treated with, it kept off water and acid better than the wags had.

The gate, however, was open. Inside lay several low but massive-looking concrete buildings. They had apparently been designed to survive a nuke near miss, and had. They were overgrown with lush green-black growth with obscenely fleshy leaves similar to what had busted up the old airstrip's runway.

J.B. did not like the looks of that in spades. An ambush here might be way unlikely, but the Armorer had come across rad-immune muties in his time. The Hummer provided nominal armor protection to its crew, the pick-'em-up wags none at all. To drive in close to the bunkers and bushes was just asking for something the Deathlands was only too eager to provide. Despite his lowly status as the grunt with the flamethrower, he opened his mouth to comment.

"Pull inside the gate and park," the mission commander's voice came over the talkie built into J.B.'s rad-suit helmet. "We'll go the rest of the way on foot."

It was a considerable irony for the Armorer to find himself in a squad commanded by the very man who had gunned down his best friend, marooned another, and taken him and his friends captive. Had J.B. been minded to risk tossing away not just his life, but Jak's, Doc's and Mildred's, this little pleasure trip would no doubt provide ample opportunities to arrange an accident to avenge Ryan.

But J.B. was the where-there's-life-there's-hope type. Otherwise he'd've just gone postal in the first heartbeats of the attack and gotten chilled wasting train sec men. The time would come to act. It had to.

In the meantime, if Captain Marc was the boy wonder everybody said he was, he might just be J.B.'s best shot of getting back to the rail wag alive.

"Dix," the voice said as the men climbed warily from the vehicles, clumsy in the suits and slow to avoid snagging them on anything and risking a tear. That'd be a sweet death. Here we fuckin' go, J.B. thought.

"Go forward and burn back some of that growth. The building we want is twenty yards in from the first one."

"Right."

"Woolf, go with him and cover him. And be careful."

"Yes, sir." The sec man's sullen response struck J.B. as less respectful than his own nonreg reply.

J.B. trudged manfully forward. The flamethrower was heavier than he'd guessed it would be and made him feel clumsy and conspicuous. The captain deployed the remaining men in a firing line. Having eight or nine blasters pointed at his back made J.B. feel special, too, but he had to admit the MAGOG bunch displayed decent fire discipline. Still, much as he hated to admit it, he wished Sergeant Banner was along. Nobody would dare imagine a negligent discharge with that blood-drinking old bastard on the line.

Woolf was a tall lanky black guy with a rolling gait. He carried an M-16 with an M-203 40 mm gren launcher slung beneath the barrel. It was loaded with a multiple projectile, which in effect made it a giant shotgun. He was a kid from

Seattle with an attitude. He wasn't much impressed by killer weeds, despite the little incident with the bloodflowers. He strolled out in front of J.B.

The Armorer opened his mouth to warn him how triple stupe it was to wander in front of the muzzle of a flamethrower.

One of the plants stirred. A big pod, dark green with yellow stripes running to its underside lifted up. Its tip exploded.

Hundreds of tiny pellets blasted out. Woolf took most of the charge. J.B. was in his blast shadow. The other projectiles spit harmlessly across what had been the parking lot.

Woolf dropped his blaster and staggered back. He turned. The front of his rad suit was peppered with holes, black but quickly going red. J.B. marveled he was still on his feet.

The sec man went to his knees, then he screamed and stood.

Tendrils were sprouting from Woolf's chest, nasty pale things that became veined with red as they grew, writhing, spreading red leaves. Woolf screamed again, his voice piercing even through his helmet and J.B.'s, though their talkie system had some kind of filter system that cut him out of the circuit when he got loud. He seemed to be trying to bat at his punctured chest, but wasn't in control of his arms. His body began to vibrate.

He took a slow step toward J.B. Another.

That was enough. J.B. aimed the flame nozzle at him and prepared to light him off.

A blast from the side almost took off J.B.'s head with overpressure and noise. Captain Marc stood at the Armorer's side. At his shoulder was the stubby blunderbuss shape of an M-79 gren launcher. That was another reason the Armorer had to hate him: he craved that weapon, instead of his triple-stupe squirt blaster. It was a treasure, far superior to the M-203 even though it had been dropped from U.S. service in the hybrid gren blaster's favor.

The triple-aught buck loaded in Helton's MP round shattered the visor of Woolf's helmet preparatory to ripping it—and his head—clean off its shoulders.

The headless body reeled back a step, then it advanced again.

"Do it, Dix," Helton said tersely.

J.B. hadn't actually been waiting. Already well-braced he gave the headless thing a quick pulse of flame.

A scream like a tortured child's burst straight out of the neck stump. Engulfed in orange fire and black smoke, Woolf kept walking forward, swinging his hips rather than his legs. The captain and J.B. moved to either side. Woolf passed blindly, walked half a dozen blazing steps toward the line of increasingly nervous squaddies, then collapsed.

Helton had broken open his gren launcher. It really was just a supersized break-action shotgun. He stuffed in a fat HE round and popped it into the vegetation. Green chunks and black ooze went flying.

"Roger that," the captain said. "That's how it wants to play, that's how we play it."

From then it was a cakewalk. A cakewalk where a single misstep or bad break could fry your nuts, true, but that didn't happen. Helton and a couple privates with M-203s shattered the foliage in their path from a safe distance with launched high-explosive grens. Then J.B. torched the rudely pruned shrubbery. He was especially gratified when several of the blaster-pod plants writhed in something like animal agony as they burned. Woolf had been a cocky prick, and too stupe to live, but when it came to a fellow human versus militant mutie topiary, J.B. was clear which side he stood on.

Once the weeds were well and truly whacked, Helton had the wags driven right up next to the bunkers. Then the team cautiously, but without further incident, penetrated the bunkers. It was difficult: their doors had been left swinging, too. The insides, as revealed by the beams of their helmet lamps, were well-covered in mold of myriad colors. Unlike the plants outside, the mold displayed no kung fu fighting skills. At least it didn't resist as the rad-suited men went in and out toting old computer CPUs as pointed out by Hubertus, the intel chief himself, who was MAGOG's resident living-steel expert and had been sent to supervise this phase of the op.

They piled a couple dozen boxes into the wags, then they drove back to MAGOG without incident, unloaded them into a special sealed compartment to be examined by techies, and stripped them and wrung them for their own decontam procedures. The rail wag was rolling as they unsealed their suits.

And that was Kancity.

Chapter Twenty-Two

The dark on the plains was so deep that only the polychromatic discharges within the seething, low-slung clouds provided any illumination to navigate by. Fortunately, steering wasn't much of an issue for the Yawl. The tracks did twist and turn occasionally to pass low hills or ridges, the countryside having at last begun to show some relief again. Except when running fair before a favorable wind, which they didn't have now, they never went fast enough to worry about curves.

As time ground on and they penetrated deeper into the Deathlands, Krysty became almost feverish with anxiety to catch up with MAGOG. Fear beset her that whatever its crew might find in Kancity might send it off in some random direction. Not even Paul's resourceful cunning and inexhaustible store of survival lore would enable the unprotected pair to follow the armored rail wag through the heart of the dead city and live. If they lost MAGOG here, they might never catch her up at all.

And so they were rolling on through the night, and crickets and creatures less identifiable sang to them as they passed. Night was the tech-nomads' natural domain. That's what Paul told Krysty. So she insisted they put it to the test, pushing on as long as they could stand to, each taking turns pedaling solo while the other slept, eating on the fly, stopping only to answer the call of nature, stretch-aching legs, replenish their water tanks.

She was half-drowsing. She hadn't slackened in her pedaling; she was almost able to do it in her sleep. At the moment, she could hardly feel her legs. She was surprised she didn't have thighs as big as barrels by now.

Paul was as always indefatigable in two areas: pedaling and talking. He was happily running his head on his favorite target, the history and lore of the rails. And how he fit into them, in however small a way.

"Travel out on the rail line at night often enough, you'll see ghost trains," he declared. "Mark my words."

"What?" she asked sleepily. It was almost outrageous enough to awaken her interest.

"Ghost trains I said, and ghost trains I meant. These tracks are haunted. Haunted by the ghosts of trains that plied them centuries ago."

"That sounds unlikely."

"Unlikely? Unlikely? So you're now the expert on railroads, I suppose, missy?" He shook his head. "Some people. Teach 'em a little and they think they know all. Why, I'll have you know I've seen them my very own self!"

"Oh, come on."

"It's true. I seen 'em myself. Great hurtling black masses of shadow, complete with phantom air-horns! You see 'em in the distance, maybe even feel the vibration on the tracks. And suddenly they loom up over you like some kinda giant black sea wave, and your heart goes right up your throat and you get ready to kiss you're a— You reckon it's all over for you. And then, *whoosh!* It rolls right over you, doin' no more than rufflin' your hair. And then it's gone, leaving no trace but maybe the dwindling ghostly red glow of a lantern swinging at the rear of the caboose."

She laughed. Even after having talked incessantly for what

seemed like months Paul still had the capacity to be wonderfully entertaining. "This happened to you, did it?"

"Many's the time," he said. "Oh, all right. Not but a few times. But I remember 'em well, you bet I do—I'll carry those mem'ries to my grave."

He cocked his head to the side. "In fact, hear that?"

"What?"

"Don't you hear it? I think it's one now."

"Don't be ridiculous." She'd listened to—and told her share of—campfire ghost stories as a girl. She wasn't about to fall for whatever trick he had up his sleeve.

Then she felt a tingling in her palms.

"Paul, what's going on?"

"Shh!"

She could hear it now: low and deep, like far-off thunder. But regular. Almost metronomic.

"It's coming!" He was hopping around in his seat as if he needed to pee immediately. "A ghost train's coming!"

Her first suspicion had been that they were coming within earshot of a natural, or maybe nuke-caused, phenomenon whose existence Paul was aware of and which he had decided to weave into a nifty little guerrilla folklore session. He had a mighty histrionic gift; she'd worked that out long ago. But she didn't think he was nearly a good enough actor to fake his excitement.

She could hear it now, a rushing sound like a wind whirling up. She turned in her seat, craned her head around to see a beam of white light stab out across the terrain from behind a hill less than half a mile away. In a moment the source appeared, inundating both of them with actinic glare.

"The ghost train!" Paul sang in ecstasy.

"Ghost train my ass!" she began backpedaling furiously, although it did no good. "Stop the Yawl, Paul. Stop it now!"

He blinked at her. "Stop us? Why?"

"That's no ghost, you rad-addled crazy! That's MAGOG!"

He did a comical take from her to the train and back. Then he reached down and yanked the emergency brake. Krysty thumped against the back of her seat. He was almost pitched out of his.

At once, Krysty was up and off the platform. The mighty train's approach was like an earthquake now. Paul had definitely been right about one thing: having that thing rushing down on you, looming higher and higher in the night, was exactly like being on the business end of a tidal wave.

Paul had snapped out of his religious trance. He caught the handhold at his end and together they heaved the several hundred pounds of the Yawl up and off the track.

MAGOG blasted by. The wind of its passage tumbled them down the embankment into a swamp. Fortunately the water wasn't toxic and only ankle-deep. Unfortunately it was pretty stagnant.

Feet sloshing in her boots, Krysty slogged back up the bank. The train flashed by, car upon car. Almost mindless with urgency, she looked for some handhold, something she could grab on to and try to haul herself aboard.

"Best not try it," Paul shouted from beside her. "She's goin' seventy at least. Lord, ain't she a beauty?"

Krysty lowered her arms to her side. They were rigid as bars of steel.

When the last wag, the armored blaster car, had clattered past, she lurched onto the tracks and dropped to her knees.

She felt Paul's hand gentle on her biceps. "Come on. Let's get the Yawl and out of sight and find us a place to catch some z's."

She shook him off. "No. Let's get the Yawl turned around and follow that son of a bitch!"

"NUKE SUCK!" the driver yelled.

The duty engineer jumped. "What?" He'd been slouched down peering sleepily at the readouts. All systems looked nominal—not that he would have been able to do anything but alert the brass if they hadn't been. There were some techs aboard who had studied the specs and manuals enough to have some clue what was wrong and maybe even what to do about it. He wasn't one of them. He was just a watch-stander who, it was hoped, would someday learn enough to be of some actual use himself.

MAGOG's control compartment was blacked-out, lit only by a few red lights and the glows of the monitors themselves, to preserve the crews' night vision in case the sensor systems caught the last train to the coast, so to speak, and they had to slide back some armored shutters and actually look outside. It had never really happened, so far as any of the crew knew. But it was the Book: it didn't have to make sense. You just did it. That was what being in the army was all about.

"We missed 'em," the driver said.

"Missed who?"

The driver gestured at the big central screen showing the view from straight ahead. The main windscreen shutters were up, and they could see out; but the front-mounted cameras had light-enhancement capabilities, and even with the giant multimillion candlepower headlight lit they could see better on the monitor. So the blackout still didn't make much sense.

"I don't see anybody," the engineer said.

"Of course not. We're past 'em now." The engineer glared at him. "Some of that rail trash. Buncha crazies ride around the tracks on little wags, use sails, all kinda crazy shit."

"People do that?"

"Yeah. Just rail rats, is what I call 'em."

"You ever actually run any down?" The engineer moistened his lips.

The driver nodded. "Oh, yeah." He gestured at a whiteboard pad hung next to his station. It showed sixteen hatch marks. "We even keep score."

The engineer sat up. "Think mebbe we might catch some more?" he asked.

THE GENERAL WAS LOSING at chess to Doc when Hubertus appeared down his spiral metal stairs and cleared his throat. He looked even more funereal than usual with his pinched face underlit by a single dim green-shaded lamp.

"Theophilus, would you do me a favor here, please?" the General asked.

Doc rose and bowed. "It's past time that I retired in any event. I bid you good evening, gentlemen."

He withdrew.

"This better be good, Hubertus," the General said. "Do we have the location?"

He and his techs had extracted and decontaminated the hard drives from the computers they'd scavvied out of the Kancity bunkers. The drives were of a special top-secret design that protected the contents from being flash-erased by thermonuclear warheads' electromagnetic pulses. The intervening decades hadn't done them any good, but MAGOG, constructed to carry on the War on Drugs, had good facilities for recovering data from damaged or even deliberately erased disks.

"We do not, General."

The General scowled. "I know I have a policy about not

shooting the messenger, Hubertus. But I have to admit I'm just a little pissed off here."

"I didn't say we had failed. I merely don't know the actual location of the Great Redoubt."

"And that differs from failure how?" But he sat up straighter in his plush red chair.

"Our analysis indicates that the information you desire is to be obtained at the Denver Federal Center."

The General made a constricted sound deep in his thick throat. "This is like one of those damned Russkie puzzle dolls. You just keep opening 'em and finding yet another one inside. I'm not getting any younger, here. I'm getting nuke-blasted tired of chasing leads."

He slammed the flat of his hand down on his chair arm. "But damn! If this is the last one…" He squinted up at his intel chief. "You wouldn't want to wind up crucified on the cow-catcher, now, would you, Hubertus?"

"In Denver, we will discover the final piece of the puzzle. Our analysis is conclusive."

He paused. "And the prisoners, sir?"

"Just keep the hammer lifted, there, Hubertus," the General growled. "If they don't spill by Denver and it doesn't pan out, I'll let you take them apart. If I don't decide to crucify you on the cow-catcher and give your job to the simp who cleans the heads."

"I am ever at Your Excellency's disposal," Hubertus said, and bowed behind steepled fingers.

KRYSTY WOKE to find Paul straddling her, with his hands clutching for her throat.

She pushed up with her own hands, pushing his arms up—those hands, so disproportionately large and powerful-looking—away from her windpipe. He straightened in surprise. She threw her legs up, locked her ankles around his neck and heaved him off her to her left.

She was on her bare feet with her S&W blaster out before he finished bouncing off the wall and landing on the dust-drifted floor. Then she was sitting astride him, holding his shoulders off the floor by the front of his coat with her left hand, pressing the snub barrel of her .38 beneath his ear into the juncture of neck and jaw with the other.

It was an abandoned farmhouse not a quarter mile from the track that they had fortuitously spotted when fatigue, and maybe emotional overload, had forced them to lay up for the night. He had offered to stand the first two-hour lookout and let her sleep. As utterly drained as she had ever been in her life, she had gratefully agreed, and been dead to the world before she had lain all the way down.

It was the same way it had worked since that very first night. Each had trusted the other enough to sleep in his or her presence. Forget about relying on each other to stand watch—being able to rely on waking up under those circumstances was rare. But Paul had never given her reason to doubt.

Until he tried to strangle her.

Even before she demanded "Why?", he was begging her to shoot him.

"Just kill me. Just go ahead and ice me down. I don't deserve to live."

Of all the things he could conceivably have said, that was about the one thing that would have calmed her down. She let loose her pressure on the long, heavy trigger, but kept the blaster where it was.

"Why did you do it, Paul?" she asked.

He was shaking his head as much as he could with the

blaster's muzzle stuck up under his ear. "Don't you know? I *saw* her! I never seen her from so close—near enough to touch, almost—only glimpsed her from afar. The most perfect thing that could ever be in my world. I watched her thunder by like a chariot of the gods and I was filled with love and wonder."

"And I'm going to destroy her."

"You're gonna destroy her. You have that power, Krysty Wroth, as big and fearful as the train herself. And the thought of that maddened me. Of you destroying the thing I love."

"But you knew all along that was what I meant to do."

"But it never really hit me. Not till…not till I saw her. Not till I bathed in the air that flowed off her smooth steel sides. She's what I told you, the greatest train that ever was and ever will be. And I'm a man who lives for trains."

He drew in a shuddering breath. "And that made me, a man of peace, that made me try to kill you. Who never did me any harm, whose cause is just. Who I promised to help as best I could. I got myself caught in a cleft stick, missy. You'd be doin' yourself, the world, and me a favor if you went ahead and took up all the slack in that there trigger!"

Instead she let go his coat and took the gun away from his head.

"I can't," she said. "I told myself when I set out on my vengeance trail that I would stop at nothing to put an end to the men who killed Ryan. That I'd chill anyone who got in my way, sacrifice anybody no matter how innocent if it would serve my goal.

"I'd sacrifice your life if it meant I could take down the General and, yes, his train. I would, Paul, just like I'm prepared to lay down my own."

She stood up. "But I can't do you like this. And besides—I still need your help."

He lay there looking at her. "What if I try to kill you again?"

"Will you?"

He sat up rubbing the back of his head where he'd banged a hole in the plasterboard with it. "No. I'm a peaceful man. Or mebbe just a coward. But one way or another, there's no way I could work myself up to it again.

"Besides, you got no call to believe this, and I surely don't expect you to. But I couldn't do it. I was all in a fever to put an end to you and save the train. But then when I got ready, when I was reaching out for your neck, I looked down and saw how helpless and pretty and…innocent you were. Like a little girl. And I couldn't help remembering how nice you always treated me, how you let me run on and on and never complained, and how you was always kind and gentle, and how you…trusted me. And I knew I could never hurt you. No matter what."

Krysty sat down heavily on the wooden bed frame that occupied the center of the room. There was no mattress, only a tangle of really nasty-looking rusted springs that were far more suitable for torture than rest. They had stretched their bedrolls to either side of it.

"Kind. Gentle. I'm a real ace in the line heartless avenger, aren't I?"

"I meant it in a good way! Don't go getting down on yourself, now."

"Don't worry. I've come this far—with your help. I'll still do what I have to. I guess it's just strike that it hasn't cost me my humanity yet."

He looked at her. "So what now?"

She stood up, tucked the gun away and stretched. "Would you mind taking watch again? I really need more sleep."

Chapter Twenty-Three

When the wind backed a few degrees and a hint of rankness came to Ryan's nostrils that lifted the hairs on his nape, he realized the armored bear was stalking *him*.

He wheeled. The beast stood atop a humpbacked sandstone boulder not twenty yards away. As advertised, his body was covered all over with broad triangular scales, glinting a dull ivory in the light filtering through the high, thin afternoon overcast sky. The head looked to be skull-like, skinless and hairless but extraordinarily thick; the muzzle was shielded with finer plates. To Ryan it looked as if he were being menaced by an angry bus, so the Far Walker's estimate of size was probably pretty much dead in the crosshairs.

The only part of the bear Ryan could see that wasn't armored was the eyes. He hadn't taken for granted it would have eyes, but had checked with Far Walker, who confirmed it did. They were glaring at him right now with what he hoped was only an eerie semblance of intelligence.

He had the Steyr in his hands, and was bringing it to his shoulder even as he turned. He tried to sight on the left eye. But the beast knew a longblaster, or at least a threat. It was already wheeling itself, to jump off its perch down out of sight behind a tangle of orange rock and brown scrub.

Ryan fired anyway. He heard the copper-jacketed 180-

grain boattailed bullet glance off the bony skull, then the bear was gone.

He didn't waste time reproaching himself for the miss. It happened.

From his belt he snatched a torch he had prepared: a limb of brushwood with dry grass tied around its head and smeared with the flammable pine resin the Little Ones used for glue. The hope was the pitch would give a little staying power to the easily ignited but quick-burning grass. He jammed the torch's butt into soft sand at his feet, whipped out a lighter and lit it, then snatched it up again, keeping the longblaster in his right hand the whole time.

If the bear gave him a shot, he could always drop the torch. On the cusp of the instant he had guessed the bear wouldn't, and he was right. It was charging at him from a clump of brush ten feet to his left that a person wouldn't think would hide a jackrabbit.

He swung the flaming torch right into the bear's face. Force-fed air, it roared and flared enthusiastically. The bear put its haunches down and skidded to a stop. That was the edge Ryan had been counting on the torch to give him: an animal's instinctive dread of fire.

The armored beast reared up and smacked the torch out of Ryan's hand with a swipe of its saber-taloned paw.

It cartwheeled over a scrub oak to his right and vanished from sight. Ryan threw himself the other way, hit the ground and rolled.

On his back he saw the bear gather and leap at him, aiming to pin him. If it landed on him, that would likely end the fight right there. He rolled frantically back to his right. The bear's ton of weight slammed the ground right next to him so hard he was bounced six inches in the air.

He reared up himself, got a boot under him. The bear came off the ground sweeping outward with its left arm. It actually encountered Ryan before it had gathered enough speed to be a bone-shattering blow. Instead it simply tossed him twenty feet through the air, over the same bush it had knocked the torch.

He kept presence of mind and body control enough to tuck and roll on impact, without breaking anything of consequence or even getting the air knocked out of him. He also managed to keep a grip on the rifle.

He got to his feet, a lot more deliberately than he was happy with. But the monster hadn't followed his flight with another bull rush. It respected his longblaster. Maybe too much.

The torch lay nearby. It had gone out. That was a stroke of luck. As friendly as they were, the Little Ones would no doubt be able to restrain their gratitude if he burned off the land they depended upon for forage, to say nothing of how embarrassed he'd be if he burned himself up in his own accidental wildfire.

Instinctively he ran bent over toward the bush he had just flown above. The bear charged right through the spot where he'd landed. It had circled ninety degrees clockwise and attacked from the south.

A bear could outrun a man on the flat. The monster's huge size and the weight of its armor might have rendered it slower. Ryan didn't count on that. He was betting his life on his grasp of elementary physics: it wasn't going to snap off many right-angled turns with its mass. He sprinted flat out, ran through a side of the bush, crossed an expanse of sand and scrambled onto another pile of boulders.

There he halted and turned, crouching with the Steyr ready.

The rocks would at least break the monster's charge. But it didn't come. He could see well enough past the bush well enough to observe the bear had disappeared again.

A flash of yellowish-white to his left. He snapped a shot off. It was a good shot. He heard the whine of a ricochet as the bullet tumbled after bouncing off a scale. The monster was trying to get south of him again.

Then it hit him. The rad-blasted monster was trying to drive him into the Grand bastard Canyon.

That made him hotter than nuke red. That was *his* plan.

He had set out in daytime because the Little Ones reported the creature liked to hunt at night. They knew perfectly well where its burrow was. If his luck was better than he had frankly ever expected, he would have found it sound asleep, giving him ample scope to chill it without so much as interrupting its dreams of happy slaughter.

More realistically, he could recce the surrounding area, figure out the best way to either bushwhack it coming back to the den or wait, watch its return, give it time to fall asleep and then do the deed.

If things got seriously crosswise, he had planned to use flaming torches to drive it into the Big Ditch, not forty yards to the north.

Of course, the beast knew the ditch was there as well as he did. Better, since it had hunted right along its lip for years. Belatedly it occurred to him to wonder whether it might be able to tell where it was in relation to the lethal mile drop by the very smell of soil and vegetation.

Which was way more than he could do.

The thing could also use the slightest scrap of cover. He could hear grass rustling right at the southern end of the boulder clump he was perched on. Could the bastard belly-crawl around the rocks, get into range to nail him with a swipe before he could react?

He didn't care to chance it. He grabbed a vaguely triangular plate of sandstone ten inches long and whirled it overhand toward where he'd heard the sound.

It couldn't hurt the bear. But whether the stone hit or not it startled the monster. With a rumble like thunder it reared up.

Ryan fired. He saw blood spray away from the right eye socket. Triumph blasted through him.

Prematurely. The bullet hadn't found the brain. The bear emitted a squeal and charged.

He sprang off the rock to his left, hoping to get into the bear's blind spot. The bear landed, again with uncanny accuracy where he had just been. It lashed out at him as it did.

One claw hooked the Steyr's sling. Like an attack dog who'd just hit the end of his chain, Ryan pivoted and slammed into the ground on his back. He let the rifle go. Otherwise the beast would troll him right up like a happy angler.

But the armored bear was momentarily disoriented by pain and fury. It stood on its hind legs, pawed the air and roared with hysterical fury, sending the Steyr flying unheeded.

Forcing air back into his lungs by sheer desire, Ryan jumped up and sprinted after the longblaster. Unfortunately the monster still had one good eye and two good ears. It ran to intercept him.

Ryan stopped, crouching, panting. His SIG-Sauer P-226 was in his hand. For what good it would do. But if he'd kept chasing after the longblaster, the bear would have climbed right up his back.

It was south of him again. Some days it was better to be lucky than good, even if you were a mutie armored bear.

But Ryan was very good. And he had already formed a new plan.

If the bastard outwitted him again, it deserved to win.

He turned and powered south for twenty-five yards, half the distance to where the edge of the world lay. Then he spun down into a crouch, holding the SIG-Sauer in a two-handed combat grip.

Hearing him start to run straight away from it, the bear had launched itself in full-throttle pursuit. It smashed through a scrub oak, charging right at him.

He made himself stay calm, lined up his front sight with that bloodshot left eye. Ignoring the fear that yammered in his belly, he gave the bear two full strides to time its up-and-down movement, then he squeezed off a compressed surprised break.

The blaster coughed and rose.

The bear's left eye exploded.

The little 147-grain 9 mm bullet didn't tunnel through to the bear's brain. It screamed in agony but kept straight ahead. Expecting it, Ryan rolled right, escaped its rush.

He headed back toward the canyon. The bear was still tracking him, by smell and sound. And it was personal now— the monster wouldn't stop pursuing Ryan short of death.

That was what he was counting on.

Even blinded and filled with pain and rage, the bear kept its cunning. It also seemed to stay aware of where the cliff was. It still kept trying to circle to Ryan's left as he worked west and stampede him into the ditch with short savage charges. Or rend him with tooth and claw, if it got lucky.

Ahead, Ryan saw a place where a chunk of the rim had fallen in and the empty space it left widened by erosion, leaving a semicircle of comparatively gentle slope down to the sheer drop. He darted ahead, surprising the bear and reaching the head of the sloping depression. As he did, he tucked his blaster in his belt and took out his lighter.

The bear was loping after him, slower than he could run. It couldn't charge or run full out and keep track of him now, it seemed. He found a big dry tumbleweed and picked it up.

The bear rushed him. Holding the weed by its stem, he lit it. It burned furiously, giving off a cloud of choking smoke.

He thrust the weed at the bear. It stopped and reared. Unable to see, it was far more fearful of the fire.

Ryan ran to his left. Tracking him by the crackle of fire and smell of smoke, the bear spun to keep its snarling jaws toward him.

The weed burned down and singed his fingers. He stood it as long as he could, then dropped it. A dead scrub-oak sapling stood up from the ground nearby. He dived on it, ripped it from the ground, lit it and thrust it into the armored bear's face as the creature, slightly unsteady on its hind legs, lunged after him.

He began to circle again. Roaring, weeping tears of blood, the bear turned and turned with him, slashing savagely but ineffectually with its paws.

It began to wobble. It was dizzy.

Ryan shoved the burning scrub sapling right into its face. "Come on, you mutie bastard! Come get me now!"

He began to back down the incline toward the canyon. When the bear failed to follow instantly he stuck his firebrand in its face again.

It roared and charged.

He turned and ran straight away.

He had always been told a bear couldn't run downhill well, because its rear legs were longer than its front ones and it tended to lose balance and roll. His plan didn't count on it. He was counting on basic physics again—and the hope the monster had been thoroughly disoriented by playing whirligig.

The bear was following, grunting as it ran. Ryan had gotten an early lead, but it was rapidly catching up. He made himself run as close to the edge as he dared. Then he hurled the torch out into space and wheeled left out of the bear's path.

With horrible agility the vast creature spun its huge frame sideways in a spray of dirt and loose gravel. Its jaws opened toward Ryan.

And its incredible momentum carried it right over the edge.

Ryan sat down.

"This better have been bastard worth it," he said out loud.

NIGHT AND DAY Krysty and Paul chased MAGOG west. Krysty had lost so much weight from exertion and skipping meals that her jumpsuit hung loosely on her frame. Paul got so worn down he hardly even talked.

Whenever she started to get overcome by dread that it was impossible to catch up to the fusion-powered train, she told herself it had been impossible to catch it the first time. Surely the odds were no worse now.

But she almost packed it in when they overtook another party of tech-nomads in what had been western Kansas.

It was Krysty's turn to sleep. She roused herself when she felt the Yawl slowing. Twisting her head, she saw a red light, tiny but intense, blinking at them from some indefinable distance ahead.

She reached for her M-16, which lay on the platform beside her seat. "Easy," Paul said softly. "They're friends."

With the pistol grip in her hand she started to ask him how he knew that. Then she set the blaster down.

Moonlight as orange as fire filtered down through the clouds. It gave enough illumination for her to make out three tall-masted rail craft parked on a siding as they approached. They were each much larger than the Paul Yawl. She didn't bother asking how he knew he'd find them here.

The tech-nomads were friendlier than the ones they'd met in Tucumcari. They knew Paul, although under the name David this time. They seemed willing enough to accept Krysty as his companion, whatever name he traveled under.

It was Krysty's turn to be reserved, although she hoped she didn't approach Bryanna in haughtiness. She had half-consciously been putting together all kinds of wild stories she had heard in her youth, of bands of tinkers with fantastic gadgets and fantastic skills, which they often bartered for food and other supplies, who traveled by mysterious means, often at night. They tended to remain aloof from the affairs of the people they encountered, but they supposedly harbored a darker side as well: there were stories of missing children and midnight murders. Krysty had tended to dismiss such tales as legends. Now she suspected some of them had really concerned the tech-nomads.

As usual, she was willing to follow Paul's lead, though, which in this case was into a building between the siding and the main track where they had built a campfire at the end where the roof had fallen down, while Paul borrowed some of their tools to work on his Yawl at the other end by some kind of artificial light. They had hot food, and spearmint tea, which they shared with Krysty as they talked.

"You're after the great train MAGOG?" asked the senior of the group, a robust elderly woman named Matilda. She had merry red cheeks, and white hair hanging in a pageboy bob from beneath a knit cap into which had been worked little metallic-looking spangles or charms in the shapes of stars and crescent moons. "You've missed her, I'm afraid. She took the line due west about fifty miles back. She stopped for water at a ville a day back. Locals say she was making for Denver."

Denver. The food Krysty had already wolfed down turned to lead in her stomach. She slowly placed the plate between her feet. They had added miles to their chase, so many miles. If MAGOG had clear tracks, she might be in Denver already!

Pain hit her like a bullet in the gut.

She stood up, only to double over the pain. Her hair started to thrash. Matilda jumped to her feet. "Child! What's the matter?"

She tried to take Krysty's arm. The redheaded woman waved her off. The first thing to leap into Krysty's mind had been dark legends of poison. But she already knew that wasn't the case.

Paul appeared, wrench still in hand, looking concerned. She shook her head at him. He seemed to shimmer and fade, and her vision went somewhere else.

In a moment she was back to herself. The tech-nomads had sat her on a pack safely away from the little fire. She tentatively accepted a water bottle; her mouth was dry as a bone. The cool water soothed the pain in her belly, which was already fading. She drank the bottle dry and handed it back with thanks.

"I'm all right now, I think," she said.

Standing over her with arms folded, Matilda nodded. "You're a bit of a doomie, aren't you? I've seen such fits before."

Krysty looked up sharply. In her altered state she had committed the deadly sin of losing track of her longblaster. She still had the snubby tucked away, of course...

"Don't worry your head," the tech-nomad said. "We don't persecute espers. Any more than we do mutants. We don't hate anybody. Although anyone who tries to impose on us lives to think better of it."

She went back to her folding stool by the fire and sat. "Why, some of us might even *be* mutants, or espers, or even both. Imagine that, if you will."

Paul was hunkered anxiously at her side. She patted his shoulder.

"Taos," she said.

"Beg pardon?"

"Taos. I—the train is going to Taos. I can catch her there. And something about...flying. Me, or MAGOG, I don't know which. Or both."

Paul grinned his grin full of skewed stained teeth. "I don't know much, missy, but I do know trains, and I'm here to tell you, rail wags don't fly."

"Mebbe.... I can't explain what I saw. Not even clear what it was. Just—"

She shook her head. "Hungry," she said. "Anybody know where I put my food?"

THE BURROW WAS COOL. The smell of earth and juniper fronds filled Ryan's nostrils and took the edge off the smoke of whatever pungent herbs the Little Ones were burning in the fire. The burrow was low, just high enough for him to sit cross-legged. The smoke collecting at the top was starting to get thick enough that it was surrounding the top of his head. He suspected that was the idea. Eventually he'd breathe in a good dose of the fumes. The smoke itself wasn't psychoactive, though. Far Walker had explained it was meant to open and cleanse him, physically and spiritually.

He hoped that wasn't going to involve puking.

Far Walker's assistant, a young female, daubed paint from a tiny basket-covered pot on Ryan's belly. Despite himself he gasped. "That's bastard cold."

"We keep it buried in a deep burrow," the old shaman said. His old eyes danced in the firelight. "Helps keep it fresh."

The assistant was drawing symbols on Ryan's chest. He looked down at himself. Upside down they made no sense to him. He didn't think seeing them right side up would help.

"What do these mean?"

"Nothing," Far Walker told him cheerfully. "They're just mumbo jumbo to help get you in the properly mystical frame of mind. What you see in the World Behind the World will be real—real enough, anyway—but to see it you have to let go off all resistance to fantasy."

"That almost makes sense," Ryan said, "so I guess what you're doing is working. Is this where I eat a magic mushroom?"

Far Walker held up a pouch. It appeared to be made of coyote hide, with the silvery fur outside. Ryan wondered where the pacifist Little Ones got it. Well, dead coyotes weren't exactly rare.

"Naturally," Far Walker said.

Chapter Twenty-Four

Denver wasn't as bad as Kancity. Most of the damage had been done by airbursts, which produced little fallout. The city had gotten a good dose of it anyway, courtesy of the hellacious hot spot ninety miles to the south, where the NORAD command center had been buried beneath Cheyenne Mountain. As J.B. explained to Leo the story that had come down to him, the U.S. had tried to build a stronghold impervious to nukes. The Russians had tried to prove it couldn't be done.

That round, it seemed, had gone to the Russkies. But they'd had to work for it.

Overall Denver wasn't too hot. The main rad danger came from localized pools of gamma emitters—basically spots rad dust had fallen and accumulated.

This time the tracks had survived all the way to their destination, a spur that led into the federal center itself. With a little help from the dozer attachment, they were clear enough to traverse.

As they entered the huge sprawling compound, moving scarcely faster than a man could walk, the General sat in his chair of command in his command center. Hubertus hovered behind his left shoulder. To the intel chief's immense but unvoiced disgust, Doc stood behind the General's right.

All around were monitors, with techies monitoring what

was to be seen on them. Doc looked here and there and overall didn't derive much information from it all. Until—

"Movement, sir!" a tech on the port side sang out. "Got
somebody flitting around in the rubble."

It was straight-up noon and fairly bright. They had the armored window shutters down and were relying totally on the
cameras and other sensors. The General was taking a risk
barging straight in with his train without sending scouts
ahead. But he believed in hedging his bets.

"Stay sharp, everybody!" he commanded. He twisted his
neck to grin at Doc and Hubertus.

"Action this day!" he declared. "I could welcome a good
fight. Anything's better than this damned waiting."

"I would venture to say, General," Doc said, "that a fight
is precisely the sort of guest to wear out its welcome rather
quickly."

"Ridiculous," Hubertus hissed.

"Be quiet, Hubertus."

As if to validate Doc's warning, something thunked against
the left-hand side of the command car. "Here!" called another
tech, swinging his pickup so that the screen was centered on
a puff of white smoke from a vertical V-shaped gap in a wall.
It dissipated quickly in the stiff breeze.

The tech fiddled with his controls. A pale figure began to
resolve out of the shadows beyond the thinning smoke.

"Tell Turret Bravo-One he's free to neutralize that nuke
suck when he gets a target. All other stations, hold your fire
unless you perceive an immediate threat to the train. And I
don't mean a kid with a rock!"

The image gained clarity. It showed a figure in a hooded
white jacket of some kind, possibly a rainslick, frantically
pushing a ramrod down an upturned longblaster barrel with a

black-gloved hand. Its features were indistinguishable shadows within the hood, but when it glanced nervously at the rail wag, Doc saw glints as from a pair of goggles or dark glasses.

"MAGOG-One, Bravo-One," said a voice from the arm of the General's chair. "Target acquired."

"Bravo-One, MAGOG-Six," the General said. "You are cleared to fire."

Evidently Bravo-One was armed with what J.B. so quaintly termed a Ma Deuce. Doc felt the familiar slow-paced pounding vibrating up through the floor as the turret gunner squeezed off a three-round burst.

The figure onscreen simply went away.

The techies began to cheer and stamp and pump their fists and exchange high fives. A somewhat uncalled-for display, Doc thought, for an armored train that had just vanquished a primitive with a musket.

"What in the hell was that?" asked Lieutenant Nguyen, an aide to the General.

"Long as it dies when you shoot it," the General said, "who cares? And if a front-stuffing charcoal burner's the best they got to offer, this'll be a breeze. Step it up, driver, we're almost there."

The buildings fell away to either side. What Doc took for the center of the compound seemed to be an open space several hundred yards wide. Most of it appeared to have been paved at one time, although between years of frost heave and vegetation pushing up from below, it was impossible to be sure. The sight lines were still clear all the way across, though.

Doc leaned toward the central screen at the front of the compartment, the largest display in the room. "I say, General, but is that not—"

"Driver," the General shouted, "reverse, reverse, reverse!"

"—a tank?"

A wag-sized tongue of flame stabbed out of the long cannon barrel of the low, dark war wag squatting across the open space several hundred yards away. Black bars shot across the main screen and it went black.

Doc felt more than heard the *crump* of the shell exploding against the engine's nose. He swayed forward, staggered, caught himself as the driver hit the electromagnetic brake. It gave the impression the shell had stopped the train dead.

That was absurdly wrong; even if it shattered the engine a mere shell couldn't stop MAGOG's thousands of tons. In fact, slow as it was already going, it moved ahead a further fifty yards before it stopped all the way and began to reverse.

In the meantime, the General was ordering the train's weapon emplacements to fire at any target that presented itself, and those on the front cars to concentrate on the tank. Finally he ordered, "Alpha-One, MAGOG-Six. Blast that bastard!"

"It will take them time to deploy the pop-up turret, sir." Alpha-One carried very special ordnance not usually called upon in a fight, and so was customarily kept retracted, out of harm's way.

"I know that, Nguyen, I'm not a stupe," the General said. Nguyen's face paled slightly between his natty white cravat and black beret.

By this time, another camera's imaging had come on the main screen, from slightly higher up than before. "Damage control reports negative damage to engine," a tech said from the front of the compartment. "Damage negative, sir. Uh, except for the camera, sir."

"They can't hurt us!" Hubertus exulted.

"Until they figure out to load armor-piercing rounds," the General said. "Can't you back this thing up any faster?"

No. As he of all people knew. But it was apparently enough to throw off the tank gunner. His next shot missed MAGOG clean and exploded inside the shell of a building to the left. A slumping second-story floor promptly caved in, pumping out big clouds of dust. Another building cut off view of the tank as MG backed deliberately out of the line of fire.

"They shoot like they got their heads in a bucket," the General murmured. "That's something."

"Profile of the tank is consistent with a main battle tank, M-1 Abrams, General," reported a tech. "We're still trying to identify which mark."

"I don't know what nuke fire difference that makes," the General growled, "but carry on."

Several other techs began to talk at once, reporting that the train was starting to take fire from the sides. Doc fancied he could feel the vibrations, scarcely more than a tingle, as heavy weapons mounted on other cars cut loose. He could see the results on the monitors: machine-gun bursts knocking craters in walls, explosions.

"A most civilized way to watch a war," he said half to himself, "if any such can be said to exist."

"All that's missing is the popcorn, Theophilus," the General said. "Driver, stop us with the front of the engine two hundred yards back from the corner. We don't want to have that beast right on top of us when it comes hauling around the corner."

Turret Alpha-One reported itself fully deployed and ready to fire. "Ace," the General said. "Now we wait."

They waited. More hooded, shadow-faced figures popped up in the rubble to either side to shoot at the rail wag. They didn't all have muzzle-loaders, but they didn't have anything

larger than small arms, either. They could do little damage to
the train, and every shot they fired was met with an enthusiastic cascade of return fire from the train. Doc wasn't sure
how much damage it was doing them, either; but it made an
impressive display.

"Well?" the General demanded. "Where's that god-
damned tank?"

The seconds ticked by. The war wag failed to appear. The
asymmetric firefight thumped and boomed along outside.

"That's enough!" the General burst out. "Send some men
out to take a look, see what the holdup is."

"We're still taking fire, sir," Nguyen said.

"I can see that. I'm not a chowderhead. Are you a chowderhead, Nguyen?"

"Sir! Yes, sir!"

"Well, at least you're decisive. You can stay. We will provide them covering fire, and they can take their chances like
the rest of us." He rolled his head back and rolled a pale blue
eye up at Doc, who for some reason was reminded of a vulture.

"Send the new recruits, Dix and Jak Lawrence, or whatever his name is."

"Lauren," Doc corrected automatically. His lips were
very dry.

"Him. The albino. Let 'em earn their keep. And send a laser
designator with them."

J.B. AND JAK BROKE from the side of MAGOG like startled
quail and scuttled for the building fronts on the right-hand
side of the train. Bullets cracked and ricochets zinged around
them, and little dirt fountains spurted as they ran. Behind them
MAGOG's awesome firepower boomed a hearty reply.

They slammed their backs right up against a blank concrete

wall of a building. J.B. clutched his fedora to his head—they had both refused helmets—as a burst of launched 40 mm grens from an MK19 raked the second story over their heads and brought dust and fist-sized chunks of concrete cascading down on them.

"Dark night!" he exclaimed. "We're in more danger from our own rad-blasted side!"

Scarred lips twisted in a snarl, Jak nodded toward the train. "Not on their side."

"What's that? A pronoun? You must be serious." He ducked as a shot from the buildings on the far side of the train pinged off the wall above their heads. "Right now I'm more on the side of the people inside the train shooting out than I am of the people outside the train shooting at us. Let's move!"

They ran along the building fronts, dodging around piles of slumped rubble too big to jump over. The train provided excellent cover on their left. That was, until they passed the end of the train and had to dash on another two hundred yards in the clear.

J.B. let Jak take the lead. The youth was toting a Franchi SPAS-12 riot shotgun while J.B. carried his own beloved Uzi. It didn't have great range, but if somebody too far away seriously needed to die, the boys back in the rail wag turrets would do their enthusiastic best to oblige.

For just a moment he wondered how the friends would ever get around the MAGOG bastards. A few hundred men had the firepower of a pre-war regiment. Then a white-hooded figure stepped out of a building ahead of them and raised a bolt-action longblaster, returning J.B. to the present in a hell of a hurry. Jak splashed the being with two rounds from the SPAS in semiauto mode.

They ran on.

"GREAT BIG RAIL WAG," a voice crackled from the arm of the General's chair. "This is your boys with their ass in the grass. We have the war wag in sight."

Hubertus and Nguyen both started to carp about proper radio procedure—the shocking lack thereof. The General held up a hand.

"Ass in the Grass, this is the General. I read you loud and clear. What's the status of the tank?"

"Looks to be shy a track on the left-hand side, General. Can't tell about the right. Don't guess it matters."

The General smiled. "No. Don't guess it does. You boys sit tight. Daddy's coming. And make sure you keep it down in the grass so it doesn't end up in a sling."

"EVERYBODY'S A COMEDIAN," J.B. said to his talkie. He wasn't thumbing the Send button. "Still, it's too bad the old bastard's such a bastard. Different circumstances, I could get to like him."

Just past the corner a long-dead wag lay on its side with its nose up against a squat concrete planter. It provided a nice convenient observation post for J.B. and Jak, both covered and concealed from the immobile but still lethal tank.

"Look here," Jak said.

He was hunkered over the body of a white-hood who had caught a couple rounds from an M-60. The hood had fallen askew, revealing a head concealed by a midnight blue ski mask. A busted pair of shades lay slaunchways across the masked face.

Jak had run the mask's lower edge up the side of the chill's face, using the tip of the former Hole's former Bowie knife, which he had kept as a trophy of his Tucumcari adventure.

Actually, the armory more kept it in trust for him, and issued it back to him when he was let out to fight.

What was being revealed was a chin and cheek and nose that looked entirely normal, except for being the same chalk-white as Jak's. "Relative of yours?" J.B. joked.

Jak slipped the mask up farther to reveal a blue eye staring intently at nothing in particular. "Not so good-looking," he said.

Behind them came the squeal of metal on metal under the pressure of enormous weight, loud even over the gun battle still going on. "Here comes train," Jak commented.

"Time to do the deed," J.B. said. He lay flat on his belly and slithered to peer around the edge of the planter. He brought the little laser pointer up by his face, aimed it at the tank and pressed the button.

DOC COULD FEEL the tension mount as the train crept back toward the corner. As near as he understood it, the General needed to knock out the tank before it landed a penetrating hit on the engine. The fusion power plant wouldn't explode even if it took a direct hit, he gathered. But it couldn't be repaired. Not even MAGOG's library held sufficient data for that, and probably no one alive had the skill to fix it anyway.

They were themselves at risk, should the gunners get a shot at the command car. That didn't concern him. Neither did the fate of the General's engine. He was worried about Jak and John Barrymore.

At least the great train's umbrella of fire had kept them safe so far. And when MAGOG hove into view, it was highly unlikely the tankers would spare much thought for the pair even if they somehow became aware of them.

The empty plaza approached. "'For what we are about to

receive,'" Doc quoted a Royal Navy prayer ancient in his own time, "'dear Lord, make us thankful.'"

"MAGOG-Six, Alpha-One. We have acquisition, we have a tone!" Doc could hear a buzzing in the background of the talkie call.

"Fire, dammit!" the General barked. Alpha-One already had.

So did the Abrams. Its 120 mm main blaster roared and ejaculated flame, rocking the sixty-ton monster back on its suspension. The shell struck with almost mathematical precision.

In the center of the rubble-clearing blade.

The shaped-charge warhead went off, turning the copper lining the inverted cone molded into the front of the charge into a jet of high-velocity plasma. It burned a hole the size of an old fifty-cent piece right through the heavy steel blade. In the interval of open air between blade and MAGOG's armored prow, as brief as it was, the incandescent stream lost heat and velocity with dramatic swiftness. Such that when it actually reached MAGOG's hull, all it did was spray-paint a pretty, shiny copper circle on the metal.

The Hellfire missile launched from Alpha-One's rack, however, homing on the tiny laser spot J.B. was shining on the tank, struck the turret ring and blew the Abrams's turret right off.

THE DATA RECOVERY TEAM had a brisk time of it going into the building to which Hubertus's analysis directed them. The sunlight-hating defenders, whatever they were—humans with some shared skin disease, muties, health cultists who worried way too much about melanoma—fought with wildly assorted weapons and not much skill, but tenaciously. The MAGOG sec men picked were expert at their craft, which was chilling, and they had the blasters, the bullets and the grens to do it. They left eight men cooling to ambient temperature, and brought back nine wounded, three of whom would die later. But they also brought back a Zip disk in a special lead-lined, Faraday-cage case.

Before the train had fully backed out of the DFC, the General had his heart's desire. Not the Great Redoubt itself, yet, but the key, the ultimate key: the redoubt's exact location, and how to get inside.

Only the General himself and Hubertus were permitted in the General's sitting room when the disk was read on a laptop not connected to the train's local network. But before the train had rolled out of Denver south, word had flashed the length of the train.

The Great Redoubt was in south Cali. Somewhere that hadn't fallen into the Cific.

From prior exploration, MAGOG's crew knew the rail lines through Vada were too badly cut up to fix or find a way through. The quickest route west lay south.

Through Taos, in what had been New Mexico.

Chapter Twenty-Five

His sawed-off Izhmash 12-gauge double-aught gun snugged in its holster beneath his unwashed left armpit, his Mini-14 riding in a sheath strapped to his Fat Bob gas tank, Hogan, late of Noo Berdoo and Chato's nameless army, made his break for it.

It was a leisurely break, at least here in its earliest stages. He rode at a walking pace down a knife-blade canyon, actually a cleft split out from the side of a mesa, so narrow he could stretch out his long arms and almost touch the striated sandstone walls with his fingertips. In case he wanted to fall over. His big sled wasn't really made for cross-country work, and was none too stable at this pace, but he didn't dare crowd it any faster.

Since making good his escape from the goat-screw the attack on the armored train had turned into, he had been hiding out on top of a mesa twenty miles to the northeast. It was getting warm up there, and he was getting low on water.

It was in his mind to split back for the Coast. Odds were his erstwhile bros had cooled down a bit in his absence. Or with any luck they were all dead—whatever. He'd had a bellyful of the desert and the weird-ass crazies a man encountered therein.

At last he reached the bottom. He hit the accelerator. The big bike responded with a characteristic farty roar. Soft sand sprayed in a roostertail as his back tire spun and launched him toward the mouth of the cleft twenty feet away. The open road beckoned. He let out a wolf howl of triumph.

As he charged out of the cleft, a black-leather-clad arm chopped down over his ape-hanger bars from the side and clotheslined him neatly, busting his nose and somersaulting over his seat to the pale sand.

THE BIG BIKE ROLLED a few more feet and toppled over. Ryan watched it dispassionately.

Thanks again, Far Walker, he thought. The Little One and the rest of his tribe were miles away, but Ryan reckoned the little shaman could hear him right enough. Despite his refusal to guarantee accuracy of any of the prophetic visions Ryan had received on their shared spirit journey, this one had panned out just right.

With a grunt of effort, Ryan hauled the bike upright again. He had to be careful; his clavicle was still sore, and the banging he'd gotten from the armored bear hadn't done it any good, even though nothing had gotten broken or rebroken. He forked the tiny saddle and rolled back to the fallen rider, wheels crunching in the sand.

Moaning, the biker raised his shaved head. Ryan kicked him in the temple, but not hard enough to break his neck. Probably. The coldheart subsided.

Ryan dropped the kickstand, dismounted and walked to where his own traps waited behind a bush. He pulled the biker's panniers off the rack over the rear tire, dropped them to the ground, then lashed his own pack in their place. The one-eyed man drew the Mini-14 from its sheath and threw it onto the half-conscious biker's chest. He slipped his own Steyr SSG into its place.

Finally he took an extra water jug—a clay pot with a basket woven around it that could be soaked with water to keep it cool by evaporation—he'd brought from the Little Ones' settlement and tossed it to the sand beside the prostrate biker.

"Sorry," he said. He swung a long, lean leg over the bike again, gunned the engine and was gone in a swirl of dust.

"TAOS," PAUL EXPLAINED as they coasted, gratefully resting their weary legs, down the last grade toward the ville, "is one of your bigger villes between the coasts. It's a rendezvous for pilgrims off the Plains as well as the mountain men, woods runners, coldhearts, and all the other curious two-legged fauna that range the Rocks. Ol' baron's notorious for welcoming anyone, man or mutie, so long as they got jack or goods to pay for their stay."

They had pushed hard to make the prophesied rendezvous, Paul seeming as driven as she. Unlike the earlier stages of their journey, in which they had been following MAGOG directly, they had encountered frequent breaks in the track. Strangely, these worked to their advantage. While MAGOG had to stop at every break and wait for repairs to be made, it was easy enough for Krysty and Paul to portage the Paul Yawl to intact line. If necessary, they could even take off the baffles that held the little craft to the rails and pedal to the next good section on its bicycle tires, which had solid cores themselves, and never went flat. Mad and obsessed he might be, but Paul was a certifiable genius as designer and builder.

They rolled around a hip of mountain cloaked in tall Ponderosa pines and saw the ville then. The usual straggle of shacks and reclaimed ruins dominated a sprawling multiple-storied adobe structure like a combination fortress and apartment block. Krysty's heart gave a quick pulse.

MAGOG was here.

Paul made a strange, soft sound. "Looks like you done it, missy."

She smiled at him through sudden tears. "We did it."

He shook his head. "Don't remind me."

They stashed the Yawl in the ruins of an old motel outside the current limits of the ville. Krysty twisted her hair into a knot and covered it with the cap she'd taken from the dead deserter. Then she shouldered her pack and M-16, and she and Paul walked the rest of the way along the track.

On their approach she had noticed strange platforms dotted along what seemed to be paths into the ville. Although no one appeared to be watching the tracks, and from the way weeds grew up alongside and between the tracks, obscuring them from view, she judged that here as elsewhere people paid them little mind. But beside it stood a tall pole with an outsized wagon wheel nailed to the top of it like a piss-poor attempt at a windmill. With a start, Krysty realized there was a twisted half-mummified corpse attached to the wheel. On the other side of the track stood a more conventional gallows pole, with a partial skeleton, still clad in the faded and tattered remnants of a frock coat, dangling from a rope. As they approached, a raven perched atop the gibbet uttered a dismal cry and flapped off.

Krysty turned a questioning look to Paul. He shrugged.

"I should mention he welcomes anybody as obeys his laws, as well as can pay," he said. "Brutal but fair, the baron of Taos."

NUMB, WITH A SENSE of almost floating unreality, Krysty pushed her way through the throng of gawkers and sec men toward the great gleaming train. The bracing mountain air was freighted with the smells of unwashed bodies and piñon smoke. And worse, apparently the baron focused his mania on law and order at the expense of considerations such as a working sewer system. Paul trotted at her elbow, pale and drawn.

"How do you think the baron feels about this General and his rail wag?" she asked.

"Baron's a realist," Paul said. He was double glum because even from a distance it was obvious the General had set sentries on the ground and atop the cars to discourage the curious from getting close enough to touch MAGOG. They hadn't had to shoot while Paul and Krysty were watching. Largely because no one doubted they would in the first place. "Guess he reckons an armored train with the firepower to level his whole ville, ice down all him and all his sec men, all their relatives, and ever'body in the whole wide world so much as *looks* like 'em, all without working up a sweat, can pay its way sorta by definition."

"There's something I still don't understand," she said. "I've been wondering more and more why more people don't use the rails. The fact the lines are mostly forgotten doesn't quite seem to explain it."

"Well, it's one thing to travel light, like we been doin' and the tech-nomads do, with vehicles and goods that you can portage past breaks. It's another to carry enough goods to make trade pay. That's why the tech-nomads deal in services and little gadgets. The General, now, he has unique advantages."

They had almost reached the juncture of the line they had arrived on and the one which MAGOG had followed down the Grandee valley from Denver. The great lead engine gleamed in the morning sun. Paul paused and wiped a tear from his eye, overwhelmed.

"He's got fusion power and carloads of pre-war supplies,

plus plenty of manpower and the means to get more, and he spends half his time stopped to fix the line. Which, after all, is why we…why we caught him."

She stopped and touched his arm. "Better we split here," she said in a throaty voice. "Won't do you any good to be seen with me."

"You sure you know what you're doin'?"

"No. Only what I have to do."

"Wait." He flicked furtive glances up and down the narrow mucky lane, then stepped back into a noisome narrow alley. She followed him warily.

His hand fished in the pocket of his coat and came up with a heart-shaped locket on a silver chain. "Take this."

"Why Paul, how sweet." She opened it. It contained a portrait of a handsome woman in a high-collared blouse, painstakingly hand-painted in miniature. It looked as if it were decades old, not centuries—not a survival from predark days.

"Thank you. Who is it?"

"Nobody. Just never mind. What's important is this."

He reached out, tapped a tiny stud barely visible on the lefthand lobe of the heart-shaped case. "This'll call any tech-nomads within a twenty-mile radius."

He shut the locket, then pressed another button on the right lobe. A tiny red light began to blink from the top. "That means there's tech-nomads within twenty miles of here. Friendly ones, at least to me. Gotta be cautious with strangers, though. Not all those tales you hear are false."

He shut off the light. She paused, staring down at the locket.

"I can't take this and leave you no way to contact your friends."

He laughed. "Why, missy, whatever makes you think that's the only way I got to reach 'em? I told you, I'm a gadget kinda guy. Just naturally tend to collect 'em. Even when they don't got anything to do with trains."

She smiled and slipped the chain around her neck. Then she leaned forward and kissed his cheek. "Thank you, Paul. For everything."

She started to turn away. He caught her by the arm. She swung back, surprised. It was the first time since they had met that he had laid a hand on her.

"Chill him," he said in a voice clotted with emotion. "Bastard defiled the most beautiful thing I've ever seen or ever will see. Spreadin' slavery, death and misery, all in the name of doin' good. Chill him."

"Yes," she said. "I will."

She walked away without looking back.

THE GUARDS EYED HER appreciatively, but warily, as she approached a car several wags back of the engine that had a door open. "That's close enough," one called. "What do you want?"

"Looking to sign on," she said.

"Shee-it," said the other guard. "I was hoping the local gaudy made outcalls."

"Don't pay him no mind," said the first guard, who was older and harder-looking. "His momma dropped him on his head. He ain't right. Why you want to enlist, anyway?"

"Tired of scavvin' and scufflin'. Three hots and a cot a day sound pretty good, and bein' a train trooper can't be no more dangerous than the way I been living." Which, she reflected, was if anything an understatement.

"You wanna be, like, a comfort-gal, mebbe?" the second soldier asked hopefully.

She glared at him until he wilted. "I can fight. Better'n most."

"You can, huh?" the older sec man said. He nodded with his chin. "Know how to use that longblaster?"

"I'd be triple stupe to lug it around if I didn't, now, wouldn't I?"

"Well, you got the sand in your craw for the life, anyway. And bringing your own weps... But it ain't my say-so."

He stood up off the step. "C'mon aboard and talk to the sarge."

As she put one of her blue cowboy boots up on the brief metal stairs, he leaned forward. She recoiled, dropping a hand toward her concealed handblaster.

"Keep it lifted, girl. You ain't local, are you?"

"Do I look like a nuke-sucking ville rat?"

He smirked. "You get signed on, come by some evening after duty and I'll tell you what you look like. No, it's just that we got orders not to let no local yokels onboard without we hose 'em down. They all smell like last week's dreck. You pass the sniff test. So move it along, sweetcheeks."

HOPING AGAINST HOPE that Sergeant Banner's falcon-sharp eyes wouldn't catch the gesture, Mildred put out a hand to support herself against the stainless-steel top of an examination table.

"Come on in, recruit." Fortunately a doctor learned to mask her emotions with brisk professionalism long before leaving med school. "What'd you say your name was?"

"Marcy, ma'am," Krysty Wroth said.

The redhead was playing ingenue country girl to the hilt. Ingenue by Deathlands standards, anyway. It didn't stop her exuding that don't-fuck-with-me menace that was baseline for anybody who ventured out into the devastated and des-

perate world on their own, except for full-metal-jacket coldhearts and a few dedicated pacifists.

With her clear skin and fresh face she did a fair job of passing as a woman in her early twenties or even late teens. She
was aided by the shocking amount of weight she had lost in
the weeks since Mildred had seen her. Never remotely plump,
Krysty was so pared down it gave her limbs an appearance
of near-adolescent coltishness.

"If you'd excuse us, Sergeant," Mildred told Banner.

He shook his head. "You know better."

Mildred grimaced. But she knew it was standard operating procedure that a new recruit be supervised constantly by
someone in authority until the powers-that-be were satisfied
he—or occasionally she—wasn't some kind of coldheart in-
filtrator or vengeance-bent survivor of one of their casual
atrocities in the name of "progress."

Since the latter description fit Krysty like a chamber fit a
round, Mildred could only hope the redhaired woman had a
good plan. There was a light in those green eyes Mildred
didn't like. Especially since it was exactly what she'd expect
to see in Krysty's eyes, once she came among Ryan's murderers.

"Okay, Marcy," Mildred said. "I need you to strip down to
your skivvies."

Without blinking, Krysty complied. It was the little things
that still blindsided Mildred with occasional culture shock
even after the time she'd been awake: lack of body modesty,
in this instance. There were assistants moving in and out of
the infirmary as well as the sergeant lounging in the doorway.
And that would mean little to the average new recruit, and
probably meant less to Krysty.

Banner was professional enough not to leer, at least. Although he didn't look away as Krysty shucked down to a pair of oft-washed cotton panties.

Krysty rolled up her jumpsuit and placed it on the floor with what struck Mildred as unusual care. As if maybe she didn't want anything heavy, metallic and concealed going thump.

Straightening, Krysty firmly adjusted the ball cap on her wound-up hair. Mildred had to smile at that. The sergeant would undoubtedly take it as a last typical defiant gesture from a free-range loner who had decided to swap independence for whatever security the behemoth train could give.

Her friend was, Mildred noted with an ever-so-slight pang of envy, one of those rare women who lost body fat from the breasts last. Otherwise, aside from being shockingly gaunt in comparison to the way Mildred had last seen her, Krysty's milky-skinned body was utterly perfect. Only to be expected, since any wound that failed to kill her would heal in days without leaving a mark.

She went through the ritual of examining her, and ached to say something to her long-lost friend. But not a breath nor a syllable of condolence for their shared loss or the fierce joy of reunion—tempered by stone dread for Krysty's safety, here in the beast's steel belly—did she dare utter in the presence of Banner, nor even the ubiquitous assistants.

All she could manage was a reassuring squeeze of Krysty's shoulder. The redhead responded with a slight nod and smile, as if incidental.

"Everything's in tiptop shape, as far as I can see," she said brightly, as Krysty put her clothes back on. "Only wish more of the newbies we get through here were in half as good a shape as this one, Sergeant."

Banner grunted.

Mildred stuck out her hand. Krysty's grip was strong, and spoke volumes.

"Welcome to MAGOG, recruit," Mildred said. "I only hope you know what you're doing."

BANNER STOOD in the armored gangway between cars, his square close-cropped head inclined toward the open door. The plating to her left seemed to have been patched. The burn marks left by the weld job were still visible on the plating. Beyond the sergeant, Krysty saw an oddly plush interior, more like a wealthy and pretentious baron's sitting room than anything she'd expect to see on a giant mobile killing machine such as MAGOG.

Inside thoughts and emotions whirled in a fierce maelstrom that threatened to overwhelm her self-control. She was within steps of confronting the General himself. From what Banner had said there was nothing unusual to that. The General interviewed all new recruits personally once they'd passed initial screening and med inspection, especially when there weren't large numbers of them. She was only the second today. She got the impression that was more applicants than they usually saw in a day, even in a sizable ville.

So a trip to see the big man didn't automatically mean she'd been burned. The inner turmoil was engendered by the fact that she hadn't really planned further than simply worming her way inside MAGOG's impenetrable alloy shell. What would she do when at last face-to-face with the man behind the murder?

She wasn't unarmed. She had been relieved of the long-blaster and had surrendered her lockback folding knife. She had been counting on the soldiers being bored and lazy and just plain not thinking she might be carrying a holdout. The gamble paid off. The quartermaster corporal even assured her the M-16 would be reissued to her once she was sworn in.

But she couldn't just walk in and blast the General. Because she didn't want just him. She wanted the handsome, callous young officer who so blandly oversaw mass murder. She wanted the sergeant. She wanted the man who had actually pulled the trigger on Ryan.

She wanted the *train*. Perhaps in part because of poor Paul's worship of it, it had come to symbolize for her the evil that had destroyed Ryan and the travelers' caravan. She knew it was just an inert mass of metal, ultimately, just a blaster. Probably the largest and most powerful blaster remaining in the Deathlands, and maybe anywhere on Earth. But just a thing—inanimate.

And yet it wasn't. As long as it existed, its very presence would summon men to it to put it to use as the General did—or even worse. It wasn't just a tool of defense or survival like a hand- or longblaster, which might, like any other tool, be put to evil purpose by a bad man. It was an instrument of raw force, of coercion, of aggression.

MAGOG was her enemy. As much as any being that rode within it.

The thoughts spun through her head in dizzying succession. And then she stepped into the doorway, and found herself looking into the eyes of Doc Tanner.

The sad pale eyes widened slightly. Then narrowed again, slumping at the corners, into an expression of weary befuddlement. Doc was as accomplished a survivor as any of them, and a masterful actor.

The second thing she saw was a man sitting in, of all things, a plushly upholstered red chair, just in front of Doc.

She didn't need the stars on his collar nor the medals on his chest to know him for the General. He radiated force and presence, as if his sheer will had resurrected MAGOG and given the train new life, which, from what Paul had told her, wasn't far from the truth.

To his left stood a peculiar-looking man with a hairless head, dark glasses, a stiff white tunic and riding pants. At a glance Krysty knew him for a mutie. She wondered if the General, or his subordinates anyway, knew as well.

To the right, wearing BDUs but not his steel breastplate, stood the young captain who had commanded the raiding party. Marc Helton, Paul said his name was. He was even more beautiful at close range than she had observed on that terrible day that seemed so long ago, and yet burned in her mind as if it had just been doused with gas and lit.

"Here's the new fish, General," Banner said in that harsh ruined voice of his.

"Thank you, Sergeant Banner," the General said. His voice had many of the same qualities the sergeant's did, although it didn't sound as if he'd taken near as many punches to the throat. "That will be all. Come on in, recruit. Let's have a look at you."

Krysty felt her fingers turning into claws as she stepped into the compartment. Three of the men she had sworn to kill stood within easy range of her handblaster. But the General and Helton both wore side arms, and neither seemed to be doing it just for show. As well, the sergeant was behind her, and she also sensed the presence of a pair of guards flanking the door on the inside.

She wasn't concerned about the impossibility of her own survival if she made her move now. She took it for granted that she would die exacting her vengeance. But she doubted she could get all three. Certainly not and stay in any condition to complete her revenge. And Doc was in the line of fire, and she couldn't count on him for help….

The door slid shut behind her. Banner was gone. One of her primary targets beyond reach, without shifting the odds anywhere near enough in her favor. She made herself breathe deep. Take it as it comes, she cautioned herself. You didn't come this far to fail.

"Theophilus," the General said without looking back, "will you please excuse us? Duty calls."

Doc's head snapped up as if he'd been dozing. "What? Oh, to be sure, ahh… General. General Grant? No, no, that can't be right. Lee? Quarters?"

He wandered from the compartment muttering to himself. The General watched him go. Then he swung his own ice-blue eyes back to bear on the newcomer like a heavy-weapons turret.

"Well, recruit. You certainly seem to possess all the qualities we're looking for, and more. Much more," he said in a fulsome tone.

"Believe me when I tell you how bitterly I regret that we won't be able to put those qualities to use, Krysty Wroth."

Chapter Twenty-Six

The guards stepped forward and grabbed her by the arms. Young husky men they were. She could feel their warmth, sense their size and strength even before they clamped their hands on, smell their masculine avidity.

Caught. The word tolled like a bell in her brain. Now was the time to make a play, the only one she was likely to get....

But did she have one? She could take one guard, possibly both, since they almost certainly underestimated her own formidability. But there were the General, Helton and the General's mutie shadow to factor in as well.

The General seemed to read her thoughts. "Don't take this one for granted, boys. She's as deadly as any man you're ever likely to meet."

She didn't bother to deny it. "Everybody seems to know who I am. How did you know?"

He smiled. "The boots."

Her gaze followed her heart: right down to the silver tips on the toes of her blue boots.

"Combine that with the striking scarlet hair, and the green eyes, and the quite remarkable beauty. And with the fact that of the party of mysterious adventurers my intelligence service has been gathering reports of for years, now, only one member failed to be accounted for."

He smiled. "We presumed, quite reasonably, that you were

dead. I am unsurprised to see that we were mistaken. And given that, it was inevitable that you would somehow, against all odds, find your way here."

"General," the man in the tunic said in a pinched, nervous voice, "really, I—my people—did all that could be expected under really very trying circumstances—"

"Shut up, Hubertus. Didn't I just exonerate you again?" He didn't glance at his intel chief. "Be thankful you provided me a comprehensive enough portrait that I was able to identify her right away. Otherwise we might just have clasped a red-haired viper to our collective bosom."

He stood up. He was shorter than Krysty, a fact she would never have known if she hadn't actually found herself looking down on him. The animal force of his character made him seem much larger.

He approached her, took off her cap and tossed it aside, reached behind her head and plucked out the pins that restrained her hair with surprising deftness. Her hair slid down over her shoulders like wary snakes.

"So this is the famous hair." He twined a strand around his blunt forefinger and lifted it. It flowed off.

"Wonderful," he said.

He began to walk around her, studying his prize appreciatively from every angle. Behind him, Krysty saw the youthful captain looking anxious.

"You can't imagine how disappointed I was," the General said, "to have to presume you dead. In this day and age where a few pitiful dregs of humanity live and die without leaving any more mark than a piss in a pond, you're different. Your bravery and resourcefulness have come to me through my reports as something almost superhuman—surpassed only by your beauty."

He stood before her again. She smelled soap and sweat from his body. "The fact that you're here before me attests amply that your abilities were not overrated. My eyes tell me the same of your beauty. Krysty Wroth, I salute you!"

She felt as if she'd swallowed twenty pounds of Number 4 buckshot. To have come so far, to have overcome so much…only to be trapped by a simple stupe oversight.

It can't happen this way! her mind screamed in denial. But of course it could. It happened that way to hundreds or thousands of men and women and children every day. Even as he gloated over her she knew he was wrong: she wasn't superhuman. She wasn't immune to the common human destiny, which, like a dog's, was to die in a ditch.

"What do you want from me?" she asked.

He raised his eyebrows. "Everything. You've haunted my sleep, Krysty. How I burned with frustration because I could not have the one thing I most wanted. The thing I most needed."

He started to pace in front of her. She kept her body awareness acute, alert for any sign of slackening in the grip the soldiers kept upon her. None came.

"I'm about to win. I have the secret I've sought for decades now—the location of the Great Redoubt. I don't expect you to know what that means, so hear this—it simply holds the key to rebuilding America.

"But dreamer though I am, I'm also a realist. Even with the information and resources contained within the redoubt it will take years to restore America. More years than are left to me, I'm afraid.

"And that's what's been stealing my sleep. Because what could be more perfect than to blend my genes, my intelligence and drive, with those of Krysty Wroth, the ultimate woman?"

"I'm not that special. Nothing special at all. I'm just a

woman who tried to avenge her mate and failed. And there's got to be something wrong with me, because I keep bringing out these fantasies in tin-pot tyrants. Why do you dregs always seem to think that big boobs and sentient hair mean you can sire some kind of master race on me?"

She thought he might hit her. She hoped he'd shoot her.

Instead he laughed.

"What makes me different from all those crazed shitheap barons who figured they'd possess you? I've got the goods. Even if they didn't underestimate you—and believe me, my dear, that's one trap I'm not going to fall into—they had to worry about Ryan Cawdor and your other friends coming along to spring you and destroy them. And I don't."

She stiffened at the sound of Ryan's name coming out of his mouth. "You bastard," she said. "Don't you ever speak that name again."

He stepped in close and pressed a finger to her lips to still her. "Enough. Don't let your emotions diminish you by causing you to make promises you'll never be able to keep. I don't have to worry about your man because I have destroyed him. I claim you by right of conquest. And besides—"

He put a hand behind her head and dropped his face to nuzzle her neck. "You're a woman who goes for the alpha wolf, Krysty. How can you help falling in love with the man who killed Ryan Cawdor?"

She kneed him in the balls.

She was a woman who knew how to knee a man's balls and make it count. And if she lacked some of the muscle mass she'd once possessed, she had built incredible wiry strength in her legs from pedaling the Paul Yawl back and forth across the mutie-haunted Plains. The impact lifted him clear up onto his toes and doubled him over with a long agonized *whoof.*

The violence of her attack startled the men who held her arms enough to relax their grip. But not long enough. As she tried to twist free, one of the guards stabbed a fist into her kidneys. Bright lights exploded behind her eyes as agony filled her body. She dropped to her knees gasping for breath.

The General wasn't doing any too well, either. He was on his own knees a few feet away with puke slopping down his chin as he tried to hold it back. Instead a convulsion racked him and he yacked all over his fine plushy carpet.

Marc Helton hovered over the General and got his boots barfed on. The covert mutie called Hubertus was dancing around with a little .25-caliber Beretta Minx blaster in hand, trying to get a clear shot at her without stepping in vomit.

"Put that away, you nitwit," the General gasped, and gagged. "She's not to be hurt! That goes for your men, too."

Her arms were twisted cruelly up and back. One guard kept a hand pressing on her shoulder to keep her on her knees and also to keep her elbow hyperextended, so that it could be easily snapped if she struggled. The other held the hard muzzle of a handblaster to the back of her skull.

The General got a boot planted on the floor and ratcheted himself to his feet, shaking off Helton's attempts to aid him. Hubertus, his tiny blaster vanished, came up to dab gingerly at his baron's lips with a napkin. The General snatched it away and wiped his mouth clean himself.

His grin was like a skull's. "You have spirit," he wheezed. "It'll be an enjoyable project to…break it." He was still having trouble fitting air into his body.

"General—" Helton said.

The General ignored him. He leaned toward her, eyes glinting like a raptor's. His breath stank of vomit.

"You are going to bear my heir, woman. And we're going to get started tonight, after I've...had a chance to recover. You don't have any choice in the matter."

"General," Helton said, "what you're talking about is unacceptable. Think of what we're working for. The ideals you stand for—"

"Shut up, Marc. I love you like a son, but if I have to listen to one more word of your sanctimonious prattle—"

The guard to Krysty's left, in response to the General's perceived command, moved to put his blaster away. His grip on Krysty's arm slacked again.

She wrenched it away with a counterclockwise heave of her hips, then spun back with an elbow that more by luck than by design nailed *him* in the nuts. As he folded around himself, her right hand freed, ducked into a pocket of her jumpsuit and came up with the snubnosed Smith, blasting.

Her first shot shattered a lamp's green plastic shade. The second hit Marc Helton in the shoulder as he lunged in front of the General. The third went into the low ceiling as the guard still upright let go of her left arm to wrestle up her blaster hand.

After a moment's wild struggle, his comrade came back to himself enough to punch Krysty in the kidneys again, more viciously than before. She stayed on her feet, but the first guard twisted the blaster from her hand. He started to slam it back into her face.

"Halt!" The General's shout froze him. He had his arm under Helton's now, supporting the younger man. "Don't damage the goods, damn you! Why haven't you got restraints on her? Hubertus, don't you teach your men anything?"

Her hands were quickly pulled behind her back and fastened with nylon restraints. The General, the breast of his own jacket sodden with gore, was holding a handkerchief to Helton's wound. The young captain was assuring his superior he was all right, although his ashen complexion belied him.

"Marc, Marc," the General murmured. "I don't know what I'd do without you. You saved my life."

He drew the captain's head down and kissed the side of his forehead. "Go to the infirmary and get yourself treated," he said.

"But, sir—"

"*Now.* That wasn't a suggestion, Captain. You, there. Quit cradling your gonads and help the captain to the med car. I got hit worse than you did, and I'm standing straight upright like a true man."

Reluctantly, Helton allowed himself to be led aft by the wobbly-legged guard, holding the napkin pressed to his wound. The General turned to his intel chief, who looked pretty poorly despite the fact he was one of only two people in the room not to have sustained some kind of injury.

"Hubertus," the General said with a ghastly smile, "why don't you start softening my future consort up a little as we finish taking on supplies? Keep in mind, if you break anything, or leave any marks that still show in the morning, I'll broil you in your own grease."

The intel chief stiffened and his mouth got even more pinched than before.

The General gave Krysty a look that froze her blood. "We got the secret of the redoubt in Denver," he said deliberately, "and this bitch has the secret of that matter-transfer network you're so hot for tucked away beneath those twitching red tresses. We have all the time in the world to get it from her, you and I, which means we no longer need her friends, doesn't it, Hubertus?"

Hubertus got a weird little triangle smile. "I believe that is correct, Your Excellency."

The General nodded brusquely. "All right. Have your men round them up and lock them down. Tonight after we get under way have them shot off the train."

"Tonight, Your Excellency?"

"No need to alarm the good people of the ville. Hearts and minds, Hubertus. Hearts and minds."

"MARC! MY GOD, what happened?"

He grinned weakly. "I seem to've gotten in the way of a stray bullet," he said.

He was leaning on one of Hubertus's nasty sec men. That man didn't look too chipper, either, but he wasn't bleeding anywhere Mildred could see. She got Marc onto a table and shooed the sec man out.

"You want to tell me how it happened?" she asked, cutting away Marc's blouse with a pair of broken-nosed medical scissors.

"No."

"What do you mean, 'no'?"

"I mean, no. I can't tell you how it happened."

She flicked her eyes sideways to his face. His expression was bleak in a way that she had never seen it before.

She got the blouse off, forcing herself to be professional about the buff lean upper torso thereby revealed. The bullet had punched through his deltoid just inboard of his left shoulder. It had evidently missed the joint; he was moving the arm on his own, wincing when he did.

"Stop fidgeting. Oldest medical advice on record—if it

hurts when you do it, don't do it. Now, can you at least tell me what you got nailed with? Or is that classified, too?"

"Handblaster. A .38 Special, I think."

She swabbed the entry wound with alcohol. There was no exit. Probing with the rapid ruthlessness required by trauma treatment, she quickly ascertained that the soft lead slug had struck a rib, cracked without breaking it, and traveled around to come to rest at the edge of his scapula, right beneath the skin.

Had she been back in her own time. she would've packed him off to the surgeons. Given where she was, and who her patient was...

She dabbed alcohol over the lump, picked up a steel kidney pan and a scalpel. "Marc, I'm going to do a little minor surgery. It won't take any time at all. Would you like a local anesthetic?"

"And spoil my tough-guy image?" This time his grin was as brilliant as ever. He looked as if he'd done no more than stripped off his shirt to catch a few rays of mountain sun.

"All right, Rambo." She made a quick deft cut.

The bullet popped into the pan with a clang. It was hardly deformed. The site bled barely at all.

Which was fortunate, because a sudden horrified insight had transfixed Mildred.

Krysty's hideout S&W was a .38.

She looked at him, feeling the blood drain away from her own face. He looked away.

Quickly she stitched the incision, cleaned it, covered it with a pressure pad and wrapped Marc's shoulder in a bandage. "We're going to put your wing in a sling, Captain," she said, nattering to keep from asking the questions that were churning her guts. "Need to discourage you from flapping it around."

The door to the infirmary opened. Four men stood there in full battle dress, including Fritz helmets and overgarment bulletproof vests that looked like something baseball umpires wore. Two had little MP-5 K machine pistols, one a Benelli autoloading shotgun, the fourth a holstered Beretta and a set of ready restraints. All wore the gorgets of Hubertus's sec force.

"What's going on?" Marc demanded, rising.

"We've come to arrest the healer," the sec man with the handblaster said. His eyes wouldn't meet Marc's. "General's orders, Captain Helton."

Chapter Twenty-Seven

The whip struck Krysty's naked buttock and curled around it in a slither of silk. It stung like a scorpion's sting.

She ground her teeth together and glared at her tormentor.

Hubertus tittered. "You are tough and resilient. Excellent, excellent. Challenge adds spice to the game."

The car in front of the detention wag was the interrogation car. It was very comprehensive. Much of it consisted of a single large open compartment, with stainless-steel walls and a floor that sloped downward gently to a drain. Brackets jutted from strategic points on the ceiling, floors and walls. Along one wall was an extra-wide sliding door, to facilitate discreet disposal of prisoners who were used up in the course of their questioning.

Krysty's wrists were suspended from two overhead brackets by special manacles padded to avoid so much as bruising her pale skin. Similar anklets on her legs held her ankles wide apart. She was naked.

The intel chief walked around to stand in front of her. There were strange stirrings beneath his tunic, as if agitated animals were in there with him.

He brandished the long-handled whip. "You imagine that you can hold out. You have endured torture before, yes?" He tittered again. "You have been anticipated. This device—and certain others—have been designed especially to break down the resistance of just such as yourself. All without leaving a lasting mark. On the outside, that is."

He flicked the end of the lash lightly against the exposed lips of her sex. She bit her lip. Holding the lash against the handle with his gloved hand he ran the end of the handle down the inside of her right thigh.

"A wonderful contrivance, this whip. Deceptively simple in appearance. Silk, specially weighted, thin enough to…stimulate the nerves without cutting your skin. Which is really quite remarkably tough and resilient itself. You might think this is an artifact of our own violent time. You would be wrong—such cunning work requires skill and resources quite unavailable today. This, like MAGOG itself, dates from the lost days before the big war. Indeed, like most of the rest of the appurtenances here in my thoroughly soundproofed playroom, the General found it along with the original train."

He stepped close. "The General is infatuated with you," he said, voice trembling with barely suppressed rage. "He's coddling you. But believe me—in time he'll grow tired of you. He'll give over this ridiculous notion of getting an heir to his empire-to-be on you. And when that day comes…you will be fully mine.

"In the meantime—" he reached up and caught a pink nipple with his fingers, pinched and twisted it so cruelly Krysty couldn't prevent a gasp escaping her lips "—I still can plumb the limits of what you can endure. And exceed them."

AN ENDLESS TIME LATER, after the sun had set, the intercom in the interrogation chamber chimed. Hubertus's face twitched in annoyance. "Yes?"

"This is the General. How's the reeducation of our recalcitrant guest coming?"

The intel chief scowled at the limp form hanging from the ceiling. "She's lapsed into unconsciousness." He didn't mention that she had done so without ever letting him hear her scream. "I was just on the point of reviving her to continue our session."

"Don't bother," the General said brusquely. "We're getting under way. Send her to the cells."

"The cells?"

A gravelly chuckle. "Let's let her feel the hope and joy of being reunited with her friends. Then let her see them being marched off to die. The way to break a wire is to keep bending it, back and forth."

Hubertus paused. Then he smiled. "And I thought *I* was the sadist. It shall be as you command, Your Excellency."

THE DETENTION CAR contained an administrative area, a guard ready room and six cells isolated from the other compartments. Since being brought aboard MAGOG, Jak had enjoyed the block pretty much to himself. For minor offenses, Banner and his NCOs preferred informal punishments, often as not administered by Banner's granite fists.

J.B., Mildred, and Doc now shared the block with their young albino friend.

"What now, my friends?" Doc inquired in a sonorous voice. "Pleased as I am at our reunion, I fear we shall not be vouchsafed long to savor it."

With a slight shock as slack was taken up in the coupling, the car began to move.

"Let's be a little cautious, here," Mildred said. "The block may be bugged. Probably is, given what the train was designed for in the first place."

"What bastards do," Jak asked, "chill us for talking? Gonna chill soon anyway."

"You're right," J.B. said. "But so's Millie. We don't want to tip our hand."

"Our options would appear extremely limited," Doc said, "unless we encompass abandoning our flame-haired friend."

"No way," Mildred said. "All or none."

"Reckon we all feel that way," J.B. said. "But just for the sake of argument, if we could get shut of here—not like we could or anything—what're the chances we could spring Krysty? Seems to me like lettin' ourselves get iced down without trying to help her is just another way of abandoning her."

"The General spoke often of our fair Miss Wroth during the times I was his kept companion," Doc said. "It seemed he developed rather an unhealthy obsession with her—perhaps the more so when he imagined her to be dead. She appears to have come to play a premiere role in his fantasy life."

"Which is to say he's gonna guard her like his own personal living sex toy," Mildred said grimly.

"Inelegantly put, Doctor. Yet true in all essentials."

Jak was lying on his bunk watching *Fist of the North Star* with the sound down. The animated original, not the lame live-action version, which MAGOG also offered. He'd watched the vid enough he'd memorized all the dialogue anyway.

"Stop yakking," he said, "guard coming."

An instant later the door slid open. Four of the sec men came in, two supporting a semiconscious Krysty. She was dressed in her usual clothing, which she'd worn aboard, minus the ball cap. They thrust her down on the bunk of the cell between the ones occupied by Doc and J.B., locked her down and left without a word.

"Krysty!" Mildred called. "Krysty, are you all right? Talk to me."

The woman lay on her face. Her hair hung limp to the floor, like normal hair. "Krysty!" Mildred shouted.

She stirred. Slowly she raised her head, as if it weighed a hundred pounds. "Mildred," she whispered. "I'm so glad to…see you again. All…of you."

"What on earth did they do to you, girl?"

"Tried to…make me scream," she said, laboring for every word. "They failed."

Painfully she sat up, ignoring Mildred's urging her to take it easy. She began to massage her wrists.

"Well," J.B. said, "on the bright side, that's one hurdle down."

He sat on his own bunk, crossed his leg and began to work on the heel of one boot.

"John Barrymore," Doc said, "I fear this latest development might not be a hopeful portent."

The Armorer looked at him from under his eyebrows. "Meaning what?"

"Since our arrival at this remarkable conveyance, we have been kept most scrupulously separated. And now we are united, including Krysty. Does that not strike you as ominous?"

J.B. shrugged. "Then I guess we best strike while the iron's hot." He twisted off the boot heel, which had been hollowed out. Inside was concealed a length of det cord. He shook it into the palm of his hand, stuck in the pocket of his leather jacket, then replaced the heel. He went to work on the other heel.

The forward door slid open again. Banner entered, followed by two sec men, one armed with a Remington pump shotgun, the other a Benelli. "Good," the sergeant said to Krysty. "You're awake."

She licked her lips. "Why is that good?" she croaked.

"So you can tell your pals goodbye. The rest of you, up on your feet. It's time to die."

J.B. crossed his arms. "Supposing we don't feel like cooperating?"

Banner held up a Taser. "I zap your ass. We carry you. Then you die. Your choice—easy or hard."

The far door into the compartment opened. A man stepped in.

Banner frowned. "Captain Helton. You shouldn't be here, sir. This is a special detail. General's orders."

Marc wore crisp fatigues and the spotless white sling Mildred had provided him with. "I know what the General ordered, Sergeant," he said. "But there's been a change."

"I wasn't informed, sir."

"*I* was. We're to take the new prisoner along."

Banner raised a dark eyebrow at the word "we." "Take her along?" he said.

"So she can watch, Sergeant. The General feels it will be highly…therapeutic."

"MARC, YOU BASTARD," Mildred said quietly. "I was so wrong about you. I never imagined you were capable of something like this."

Their hands bound behind them by nylon restraints, all five had been marched back to the interrogation chamber. It was dark except for blackout pin lights, appropriately blood-colored, gleaming like mutie rat eyes at the junctures of walls and floor. The two sec men had slid the oversized door open. Trees rushed past outside, black in the night. Chill mountain air blasted in.

J.B. tipped his head so that the brim of his fedora hid most of his face from his captors. He caught Jak's ruby eye and winked.

Jak smiled enough to just show his eyeteeth. Understanding was immediate and total. There was no plan—except that they wouldn't die without a fight.

"I never thought I was either, Mildred," the young captain said. "But I've always been one to do my duty, however distasteful. Sergeant Banner?"

The sergeant had taken up station by the open door, ready to usher the guests outside, one by one. He looked to Helton. "Sir?"

"I'm sorry."

Without haste Helton raised his hand. In it was his blocky black Heckler & Koch USP.

The flash filled the compartment with brilliant reflection. The sound was surprisingly flat, the edge seemingly taken off by the wind-blast eddying through the compartment.

A black hole appeared between Banner's black brows. He flung his arms out to his side as if to balance himself and toppled backward into the night.

Helton pivoted. The two sec men gaped, stunned by this incomprehensible spasm of events. He shot one once, through the sternum, shifted, shot the other twice in the chest, then snapped back and fired another shot into the center of mass of the first man.

Both collapsed. They had made no more noise than Banner.

Wind howled in from the void.

Helton holstered his blaster. He moved behind Mildred and freed her wrists. She went at once to the swaying Krysty, steadied her, helped her to sit down on the floor.

The captain liberated J.B. next. As Helton moved on to

Doc, J.B. quickly picked up the dead sec man's Remington and racked the slide. An intact shell dropped out the bottom. Not trusting a sec man's blaster handling, the Armorer had insured his blaster had a live one up the spout. He leveled it from the waist on Helton.

The captain looked at him, eyebrow raised. Then he finished releasing Doc and went to free Jak. Finally he knelt behind Krysty and undid her wrists.

Jak had the Benelli now and pointed it at the captain. J.B. had tipped his weapon up to point at the ceiling.

"Careful where you point that scattergun, son," J.B. said gently. Realizing he was covering both Mildred and Krysty as well as Helton, Jak hastily lowered the weapon.

Helton stood facing Mildred. "Perhaps you've corrupted me," he said. "I like to think not, though. I'd like to think I've always retained some standards of honorable—if not always decent—behavior. But thanks for your moral guidance, just the same."

He took her hand. J.B. moved to her side and put his arm around her waist.

"You're a very lucky man, Mr. Dix," Helton said. He kissed Mildred's hand and stepped back.

"You are free to go, obviously. I suggest that you do so as quickly as possible. I do have one favor to ask—do not try to harm the General. I don't feel in my heart that I've betrayed him—rather, that I've spared him from besmirching himself for no good reason. And I will not betray him."

"I'm still going to kill him," Krysty said. Her head was up, her voice clear. "You, too, for that matter."

"Now, Krysty—" J.B. said.

Helton smiled at her. "All I can say is, take your best shot and welcome, Krysty Wroth. But from *outside* MAGOG."

Her eyes locked his. He didn't flinch. She nodded.

"You have yourself a deal, Captain. And—thanks."

He nodded and left through the forward door.

"How you feelin', Doc?" J.B. asked.

"If I apprehend your question properly, John Barrymore— sane. Quite sane. This mountain breeze quite clears the head. It smells like freedom."

"Right answer. Jak, hand that piece to Mildred. You gals hold tight here. Jak and Doc, come with me."

LEO SAT at a worktable in the shop compartment. He was eating stew from a steel tray and reading a book on twentieth-century blasters.

The door slid open. Leo scowled. No one had better dare intrude upon his inner sanctum like this. Not even—

"Dix?"

The bulky chief armorer rose, then, holding his hands up. It was indeed his assistant who had entered—behind a leveled Benelli 12-gauge. The unlikeliest pair of human beings Leo had ever set his bulging blue eyes upon followed him: a tall, gaunt old man with lank graying hair, wearing a stand-up collar and a frock coat, and an albino kid with ruby eyes.

"What's the joke, Dix?" Leo demanded. "'Cause I'll let you know in advance I ain't laughing."

"The joke is," J.B. said, holding down on the blaster tech as Doc and Jak moved purposefully past him, "that you're gonna live. Provided you don't go making any false moves."

BECAUSE THE LINE TWISTED through the mountains, and even more because it was hard to pick up line breaks at night even with the headlight and low-light TV, MAGOG hadn't picked up her usual speed. She wasn't going that much faster than a fast run.

So J.B. told himself as he put the sole of his boot against the baggy rump of Leo's coveralls and pushed him out the door of the interrogation chamber.

"See?" he said. "Nothing to it. Who's next?"

They had recovered their belongings—especially their blasters—from the armory car. They had also toted along a few extra items J.B. thought might come in handy. He'd had to impose a crushingly strict discipline on himself, because he was just like the proverbial kid in a candy shop. He had made himself load them up with self-heats Leo kept stashed away so he could eat when he felt like it without interacting with other members of the human race. Primarily, anyway.

"J.B., have you flat lost your mind?" Mildred demanded.

Krysty shot her a sudden grin and leaped into the darkness.

"Where one so fair leads, I can but follow!" Doc declared. And did, trailing a cry of, "By the Three Kennedys!"

Jak was next, as silent as a white shadow.

Mildred stood staring at J.B. with giant eyes. "Ladies first," he told her with a grin.

"John, don't you *dare* not follow." And she was gone.

"Dark night," J.B. said to the dark night. He shook his head. "The things a poor boy got to do."

He jumped.

Hit.

Bounced.

Rolled.

TO EVERYBODY'S SURPRISE they all survived with only bruises and contusions that wouldn't leave any lasting marks to speak of. Even Leo, who'd been ejected with his wrists bound behind him.

When J.B. hurried forward to set him free, Leo was sitting beside the tracks staring after the train. To the smaller man's surprise, the look the erstwhile chief armorer turned on him was calm.

"I oughta hate your treacherous ass, Dix," he said. "It's like you just hauled me outta Paradise."

"Tell me about it," J.B. said with genuine feeling.

Leo nodded. "That's one reason I don't hate you. I know it chafes your bung as much as mine to leave that behind. Or be left behind by it, as the case may be."

With his former assistant's help he hauled his considerable bulk aloft. "The other thing is, I was starting to get the feeling everything was heading south in a hurry. Just didn't feel right."

He shook his head. "Buncha damn military assholes on that train, anyhow. Never did like 'em a damn."

J.B. had salvaged the Browning A-5 that Leo especially loved. It was returned to the big bearded man with a pocketful of shells, on condition he not load the weapon until he was at least a mile clear of the others. He agreed glumly and stumped off back along the tracks toward Taos, muttering to himself.

J.B. watched the bearlike shadow slowly dissolve into the darkness, then he turned to and walked back to the others.

They were clustered around Krysty, peering at something she held in her hand. Curiously, he walked up and stood on tiptoe to peer over her shoulder.

In the palm of her hand she held a heart-shaped locket. A tiny red light glowed at its top.

FIFTEEN MINUTES LATER the armory car blew up in a brilliant white flash.

The explosion cut the wag in two. The front coupling immediately snapped free of the carriage ahead, as it was designed to do.

The next fifteen cars followed the shattered wag off the tracks and down a fifteen-yard slope, into a little stream rushing to hurl itself into the mighty Grandee gorge.

Chapter Twenty-Eight

"We do not involve ourselves in the affairs of the outside world," the tech-nomad woman declared flatly. She called herself Rounda, in apparent ironic acknowledgment if not outright celebration of her shape. Though she was fat, it appeared to be the hard fat more often seen in men.

Flames jumped head-high from brushwood piled in a clearing masked by a low ridge from direct sight of the tracks. Krysty wasn't too worried about discovery by MAGOG's crew. J.B. had set his bomb to go off when the train was miles beyond where the friends had made good their escape. With no way of knowing exactly when the fugitives had baled—and plenty on their hands to keep them busy—it was vanishingly unlikely the General's makeshift army would mount a search back along the rail line. And less still an effective one.

And even if they did, Krysty thought, it might just force the arrogant bastards to face reality.

She stood next to the fire where every one of the twenty or so people gathered in the clearing could plainly see her. Her hair flowed out around her head in a sort of halation, like flame itself. Despite the protracted abuse she'd been subjected to short hours before, she felt as if charged with electricity. As if the energy of the living Earth was flowing up through the black soil and soft short grass and the soles of her feet.

A male tech-nomad, taller and narrower than Rounda and with thinning gray hair, tried to soften his comrade's blunt words. "The one you call Paul, and whom we knew as David or Mark among other names, appears to have done both you and us a disservice," he said gently. "We are sorry to disappoint you."

"Speak for yourself, Cedric," a younger man said. He was one of the few tech-nomads to show a weapon, a crossbow slung across his back that seemed primarily made of neither wood nor metal. What exactly it was crafted from was unclear in the wavering light.

"Paul knew what he was doing," Krysty declared. "He was one of you, wasn't he?"

Cedric frowned thoughtfully. "There are ways in which he is. He tends to walk his own path."

"Like the rest of us don't," scoffed another young male from outside the bonfire's light-circle.

"We have our traditions," Rounda snapped. "The Rail Ghost ignores them when he sees fit—as this ill-conceived gathering shows."

The young man in the shadows emitted a sound that was half-laugh, half-snort.

"You people got your ways," J.B. said, "like everybody. This General does, too. Guess which set he plans to make everybody follow?"

"We don't help Mundanes," Rounda stated.

"But you do help yourselves, don't you?" Krysty said. "J.B.'s right. The General is set on conquering the whole continent. He thinks he's about to get his hands on the means to do so. What do you think is going to happen to this secretive free-roving lifestyle you're all so protective of?"

The tech-nomads made scoffing sounds. "Others have tried

to bring us to heel before, Krysty," Cedric said, not unkindly. "But our history is long."

"Could be it's about to have run its course," the Armorer said.

"Has anybody with the General's means tried before?" Krysty challenged, her hair waving. "There's nothing in the world to compare to that monster rail wag of his. Paul told me that, and I believe him."

She swept them with a fierce gaze. "And you do, too," she said in a voice so quiet the others had to lean toward her to hear.

"What do you mean by that?" Rounda demanded.

"You follow it, don't you? You keep close track of where it travels and what it does. That's why you've kept turning up so conveniently since MAGOG first smashed its way into our lives. The Rail Ghost wasn't the only one chasing after the train."

"Don't push your nose where it doesn't belong," the bow-man said. His name was Robear. "Mundanes who pry too deeply into the tech-nomad world tend to vanish from their own. Without a trace."

Jak had been sitting on the grass with his knees up and his arms around them. Now he leaped to his feet, eyes blazing, hand on the hilt of the shortsword-sized Bowie. "Big talk cheap," he snarled. "Threaten Krysty, fight Jak."

The young tech-nomad spun to face him. The Armorer stepped between them, arms outstretched. "Hold on, now. Let's everybody leave the safety on for now. If we really want to go blasting somebody, we both got plenty enemies just a few miles down that steel road, as I don't reckon anybody'll deny."

As he spoke he raised his open palms, each to the level of the respective would-be combatant's eyes. The wise Armorer knew that as long as predators, especially hotblood young male ones, kept gazes locked on each other tensions would soar. Break that lethal lock of forward-mounted eyes—hunters' eyes—you might just break the spasm before hammers dropped and blood flowed.

So it happened. Robear and Jak each took a step back and then, as if to the same signal, crossed their arms and turned stony faces to the fire.

"That's better," J.B. said, dropping his arms. He stayed interposed.

"If what you say is true," Rounda said to Krysty, "so what?"

"First, it shows that no matter what you say to outsiders, you're all too well aware of the threat the General poses to your way of life. So you must know it's about to go up, far up. You know of the Great Redoubt, don't you."

Rounda dropped her eyes. "We have heard of it. Legends."

"You know better than that. The General knows more. He knows where to find it. It's where he's taking MAGOG, just as soon as he repairs the damage we did getting away. And when he gets his hands on what's inside— Tell me, you who worship your freedom and technology—what happens then?"

An uncomfortable stillness had settled upon the tech-nomads. "He will be supreme," Cedric said quietly.

"So will you simply give up and go extinct? Or will you stand up to be smashed down by MAGOG backed by all the might that brought about the big war?"

"But our traditions—" Rounda began.

The young man who had dissented before stepped into the light. He was tall and stiletto thin. To go with his inhumanly fine features he had green hair and pointed ears. For all her intuition Krysty couldn't tell whether he was an actual mutie, or whether it was a dye job and makeup.

"Blow this," he said. "Let's not delude ourselves. We all pay lip service to the traditions, but it's not as if we don't break them where and whenever it's convenient. And even if we fool ourselves, Krysty, don't let us fool you. We're bound together by shared culture, sure, and bonds of kinship and friendship, too, some of us. But we're not any kind of monolithic."

It was his turn to glare around the circle. "And I for one have no intention of allowing this madman—whom everyone here knows sure as nuke death is every bit as much our enemy as these people's—to make himself omnipotent and then come hunting us down like rabbits. We're people of technology. That's our link and life. But if that means more to us than just another superstition handed down from before skydark, then it imposes on us a cultural obligation to at least make an effort to think rationally. Not slam our minds shut like the bigoted mud-ignorant Mundanes we're all so proud of despising."

He looked to Krysty. "You have a plan to stop the General getting his claws on the Great Redoubt?" He grinned wickedly. "You might say I'm all ears."

No one dissented. "All right," she said, nodding. "First, understand I'm not asking you for any major interference in what you call my world. I don't ask for you to involve yourselves directly at all. All I ask for is transportation, which I hope and believe you can provide. And maybe a little extra muscle power."

"Say we provide these things," Rounda said, now sullen rather than confrontational, "how do you plan to stop the General becoming all-powerful."

"I'm going to kill him," Krysty said. "Him and his giant armored train."

BLACK SHREDS OF CLOUD fled overhead against the stars. Between them and the ground, Krysty and her companions moved at a more sedate pace.

Flying! she thought, and had to fight hard to keep from bursting forth with exuberant laughter. As if sensing her mood, Corwin—the green-haired tech-nomad youth—looked back over his shoulder and grinned before returning his attention to piloting the bizarre and wonderful craft.

Three of them hummed quietly, five hundred feet above the pine-furred flanks of the mountains, with snow-clad peaks looming yet above them. Though each differed from the others in details of appearance, all of them were flyweight constructions of open tubular frames enclosing two seats, with a little internal-combustion engine that powered a fanlike blade at the rear. For lift each was slung by guys beneath a ribbed arch of synthetic fabric—parasails, the tech-nomads called them. They were strange shadows, ingenious wisps, worthy aerial cousins to the Yawl.

Corwin and two of his kindred were ferrying Krysty, J.B. and Doc to a place Paul had told her of. Once the three friends were dropped off, the odd craft would fly back for Mildred and Jak, and to shuttle in the handful of nomads who had volunteered to assist them. There was hard work to do and scarce hours of darkness to do it before the day—and soon thereafter MAGOG—arrived.

Their route was quite short. The flight should take no more than twenty minutes, Corwin assured her, cutting a chord across a loop of many miles in the track MAGOG had to travel. A good thing, too, she realized. Even the fires of her lust for revenge could only sustain her so long before the mountain wind chilled her through.

She understood, now, part of the doomie premonition that

had come upon her at the tech-nomad camp back on the Plains: the sensation, more than a vision, of herself in flight.

She understood the rest of that presentiment, too, and even how to make it come true.

The only question remaining—and it was a coldheart, a stone chiller—was whether she could pull it off.

But now she was flying! She let herself laugh out loud for joy, and her pilot joined his laughter to hers.

And so they fled through the night, toward their rendezvous with destiny, and a thousand tons of fire, steel and malice.

IN THE CURDLED-MILK light that flowed across the land before the sun's first bright arc appeared above the mountains, the Rail Ghost stirred. He climbed out of the bedroll laid beside his beloved Yawl—stood, stretched, yawned. He walked outside to pee.

As he stepped out the door of what once long ago had been a gas station, a strong hand seized him, whirled him back up against the rough peeling stucco of the wall. A strong arm pinned him with a bar across the throat.

"My gawd," he gasped, "it's One Eye Chills himself!"

Chapter Twenty-Nine

"Honored, sir," the Rail Ghost gasped as a pinprick of intolerable brightness above a mountain to the east announced the sun's arrival. "But I thought you were dead."

"I got better," Ryan said.

"You can let me down, you know," Paul said. "I ain't no fighter. Besides, I'm on your side."

Ryan put away the SIG-Sauer he'd been holding to his captive's head and eased back away from him. "I know."

"You do?" Paul eyed him suspiciously, rubbing his throat. "How do you know that? And how'd you know how to find me, anyway? How'd you even know to look for me?"

"I had a dream."

Paul waited for the explanation. But that was all the one-eyed man would say. The morning breeze blew a curly lock of jet-black hair across his rugged face.

"Well, then. Ryan Cawdor, what can I do ya for?"

"Where can I find Krysty?"

"Didn't your dream tell you that?"

"It didn't go quite that far."

BURNING WITH THE FEVER to get back underway on the final quest for the Great Redoubt—not to mention his rage at being cheated out of a ravishing if unwilling mate—the General ordered the rear engine to simply bull the cars aft of the break off the track into the stream. A dozen barons' ransoms in tools, weapons, supplies, even good salvageable metal, all to be abandoned without a backward glance. Only the fusion-powered engine itself was too valuable to lose.

The interrogation wag, and the cell car, had been close behind the armory carriage and been wrecked in the initial derailment. The General ordered Hubertus not to waste time sending men to investigate. There were no clues to be found beyond a few pools of congealed blood anyway, as it happened.

Hubertus's suspicions had come to rest firmly on the sloped shoulders of the missing Leo. "He was secretive as a mole, that one," the intel chief said to the General in the command center, where the great man himself was waving off yet another attempt by a steward to serve him scrambled eggs from a chafing dish. "He had a bad attitude. No respect for authority at all. Small wonder that Dix was able to suborn him."

"If that's what happened."

"Of course it's what happened. What else could have happened? It's obvious. Somehow the traitor smuggled arms to our captives in the cells. They used them to murder poor Sergeant Banner and my men. Our chief armorer planted a bomb in his own workshop—his own shop, which I remind you he let hardly anyone else so much as set a toe inside—to cover their escape. It was all that simple."

The General grunted. "Spilled blood doesn't go back in the body," he pointed out. "Go and remind our damage-control crews of that fact, while we're at it, in case we're not ready to roll in—" he checked his wrist chron "—fifteen minutes."

THE DIRT ROAD THAT RAN along the rail embankment was a poor surface for the outlaw motorcycle, which wasn't exactly a cross-country bike to begin with. Every rut and bump transmitted itself like an iron-shod kick right up through Ryan's butt and jolting up his spine. The big bike Ryan had borrowed from the coldheart was running on fumes. Regardless, he crowded it as hard as he could, gambling on speed.

The brutal jouncing the road gave him was actually a help. It helped him keep himself in the moment. He had clamped his mind down as tight as his prodigious will could force it. He dared not think about the future.

The past, as always, was just a spent shell case.

He had plenty to worry about, had he let himself. Paul told him Krysty had determined to get herself aboard the armored train. To Ryan that meant she had, even though the dreams Far Walker had guided him through faded into impenetrable fog right around Taos. He took for granted she was capable of anything. The fact she'd caught the rad-blasted train, notwithstanding the fortuitous aid of a mad genius and Rail Ghost, proved that. Not that she hadn't already proved it to Ryan many times over.

But even as good and smart and tough and fearless as she was, his mind could shape no image of how she might wind up any way but caught or dead, or both, once inside the monster's metal gut. It was no different than letting yourself be swallowed by a giant beast. So he didn't try to imagine what was happening. Instead he tried not to.

Of one thing he was locked-down sure: time was blood.

Then he rounded a bend to see the great train a quarter mile ahead. Its trail engine was just passing the remnants of the derailment and its aftermath. Shortly beyond that point the stream ducked under the tracks from right to left. Right after that, the line curved right—west—around a forest-crowned promontory. The lead engine was already out of sight.

Ryan leaned into the high handlebars and twisted the throttle higher. He hadn't dared give the bike more than about two-thirds for fear of the machine shaking itself, not to mention him, to pieces. But he reckoned it and he could hold together long enough from here.

Nearly a thousand feet of wags lay in the stream, damming it, with the water swelling up around: a tumble, senseless and forlorn, as if a giant child had fetched his toy train a cosmic kick. A thousand feet of wealth, beyond a baron's dreams of avarice, had been discarded without thought, as if to prove its former owner was, even without it, in many ways still the most powerful man on Earth.

Bouncing a yard in the air with what seemed like every bump in the track, Ryan raced in pursuit of MAGOG. Some of the wrecked wags zigzagged along the embankment with one end in the stream. Before he reached them Ryan stopped, turned to face the bank directly and charged right up it. The bike made heavy going. He had to push with his legs for all he was worth to get it the last few feet up and over.

There was just space between the ends of the ties and the edge of the embankment for him to herd the bike along. He went full-out across the trestle over the stream. At least the ride was smoother up here.

The rear of the train was being sucked toward the bend. Ryan faced a snap decision as tough as green wood: how to get inside. The cars would be locked tight as a matter of course. He had, however, noticed what looked like little metal boxes on top of some of the armored carriages, with heads—and heavy weapons—sticking out of them. Since even a man as ruthless and profligate as the General would hardly be willing to combat the loss of his sec men, not to mention the big blasters that happened to be topside when a chem storm hit, it stood to reason those emplacements had to be connected to the interior.

He slanted the bike down the flank of the embankment and charged up the jut of mountain around the base of which the tracks flowed. The slope was gentler than the railway bank, but he had some bad moments toward the top when his rear tire started to spin out on a bed of fallen pine-needle tripods, long, slender and slick. Sheer brutal acceleration dug the tire through the needle layer and propelled him forward by plowing at the brown earth beneath.

At the top he saw he was in luck. The jut he had just ridden up formed the base of a huge backward L. The leg stretched off west, almost paralleling the track for several hundred yards.

One thing Ryan knew as if he'd watched it all: however Krysty managed to get herself in, she hadn't hesitated. He could do no less.

Leaning forward as flat to the tank as the bars would let him get, he charged down the leg of the L. His engine whined protest as he ran up the gears.

Cars began whipping past to his left. Men in open emplacements, hearing the mad mosquito whine of his engine, shouted and pointed at him. He heard shots.

The promontory ran right up almost to the tracks before dropping steeply to the valley floor. Ryan and the bike went straight off the end.

Hanging there with nothing but fifty feet of air between him and spectacular demise, Ryan had for the first time the leisure to wonder if this was a good idea.

The answer was probably no. But he couldn't exactly turn back. All he could do was rely on his one-eyed aim, steel muscles and tungsten nerves. And luck.

Luck almost finished him then—that and a trick of aerodynamics. His aim was dead-on. He saw the flattened shiny-metal top of an armored carriage rushing up at his front tire. But inevitably he wasn't traveling fully parallel to the track. Rather he was crossing at a very shallow angle. After the fact he wasn't sure if a semiconscious attempt to correct his course caused it, but as the bike descended it suddenly started to go crosswise to its line of flight.

And one more thing: the guy standing flatfooted on top of the wag shooting at him with his longblaster set to full-auto.

Ryan managed to bring both tires down simultaneously, square on the flat top of the wag. That took up most of the shock of impact. Then he laid the ride down and let her go.

Inertia had its way with things, as it always did. Screeching and sending up a tail of sparks, the bike slid on its side diagonally across the roof. Its hurtling mass took the sec man in the shins, snapped the bones like a child's fingers and carried him right off the edge and out of sight.

Inertia also urged Ryan strongly to follow him and the bike. He managed to catch hold of an armored vent and arrest his progress as his bootheels shot out over open space, at the cost of the Steyr's butt fetching him a whack in the kidneys.

He hung there a moment, taking rapid stock of his situation while his body tried to remember how to breathe. Two cars ahead, a man's head stared back at him immobile, like a startled gopher. Three cars back, however, two alert sec men were bodily picking up a tripod-mounted M-2 machine gun and turning it to bear on the intruder. It was no easy task even for two.

Ryan hauled himself to a kneeling position. Without time to sling up properly he braced, laid the crosshairs on a camou-clad chest and squeezed off.

Some irregularity in the track made the wag sway slightly as the firing pin popped the cap on the cartridge. It threw the blaster's long barrel up a few seconds of arc.

The bullet missed the target, but not the man. He had turned his head to say something to his buddy, and the boat-tailed slug hit right on the side of his chin, tearing his lower jaw straight out of his face. Screaming a fountain of blood, he toppled from the emplacement and rolled across the roof, leaving a wide scarlet smear.

By that time Ryan had jacked the bolt and gotten the rifle on line again. The second sec man had gone into hero mode and just sat down spraddle-legged behind the .50-caliber weapon. His thumbs were reaching for the butterfly trigger when a 180-grain bullet punched through the seam of his blouse half an inch above the second button, passed between two ribs, drilled a neat hole through his heart and, as an added bonus, knocked a chunk of vertebra right out the back of him, snipping the spinal cord. He just sort of slumped down with his head dropping to his chest as if he'd just fallen asleep. Which he had—forever.

Ryan spun one-eighty and whipped off a shot without bothering with a sight picture. It was intended to make the guy or guys in the emplacement two cars up duck if they were up to anything sneaky. It did.

He heard the bullet whack the emplacement's armor wall and whine away. He saw neither head nor blaster barrel.

He jumped up and ran, hunched forward to streamline himself so the slipstream wouldn't pitch him off the train. As he did, he slung the Steyr and drew his SIG-Sauer. It was far better suited for close-quarters work than the long scoped rifle.

He leaped the gap between cars. It wasn't that far, not

even hard for a man in his shape. It was still something better not to think about.

Shouts and shots came from behind him. He didn't hear the supersonic crack of any near-misses. It might have occurred to somebody that blasting right along the long axis of a train strung with open-top emplacements with your buddies' heads sticking out of them is not the wisest course of action. Still, they inspired Ryan to pick up his speed. The last thing he wanted to stake his life on was some trigger-happy soldier-wannabe's blaster handling skills.

He jumped the next gap, to the next car with an open emplacement. As he did, a head poked up. The eyes in it got very wide.

Ryan snapped off two quick shots, sort of looking over the front sight as he did. The head snapped back, and a spray of blood and what he hoped was a chunk of skull shot out behind it. The head went away, to be replaced at once by a hand holding a longblaster. And spraying the roof blindly with bullets.

Ryan launched himself in a flat dive, slid forward alongside the steel-alloy box without picking up any new orifices along the way. He grabbed the top of the wall, hauled himself up and pumped two shots into the back of the guy crouched down firing over the parapet.

Movement caught the corner of his eye. He jerked back. Something spread out and massive clanged against the edge of the raised emplacement where his head had just been.

A sec man had just tried to brain him with the tripod of an M-2. The MG itself lay at the bottom of the pop-up turret where its crew had dropped it while trying to get it swung around to shoot along the train instead of away from it.

Ryan swiveled his hip and kicked the third sec man in the

close-cropped head as the man struggled to chamber the tripod for another whack. The man fell back against the far wall, dropping the metal stand. Unfortunately it missed him on the way down.

Dropping in after it, Ryan didn't. He punched the man in the face with his left fist, knocking his head back against the armor plate. Then he shot the sec man in the left temple with the muzzle so close the flash instantly scorched away the short hair and quick-cooked the skin around the entrance wound.

Ryan rooted quickly through the turret. If this were his rail wag, and enterprising coldhearts could escape the traverse of his heavy blasters by getting in really close and swarming up the sides of the cars, he'd have...

Yep. Grens. A crate with a dozen or so stashed inside for easy dropping on coldheart heads. Little steel baseballs whose explosive hearts were wound round and round with yards of wire, meant to shatter into hundreds of nasty little high-speed projectiles on detonation. He tumbled a half dozen or so into his pockets, then pulled the pin on another and yanked open the hatch in the floor.

A startled face was peering right up after him. "Surprise," Ryan said, and dropped the gren on the bridge of the sec man's nose. Man and gren dropped to the bottom of the compartment.

Ryan leaned away. As usual with grens there wasn't much visual display, especially from outside. But there was lots and lots of noise, both during and after the explosion.

SIG-Sauer in hand, Ryan dropped to the compartment floor. It wasn't that far a drop; evidently this was a double-deck wag. He almost landed on the headless guy.

The other occupant of the wag, at least the upper story, was thrashing around in his own entrails. It looked as if he'd unaccountably tried to wrap himself in a twenty-foot string of greasy purple sausages. And doused himself in blood.

It sounded like a man rolling around in his own guts.

Ryan quieted him with a hammer: two fast shots to the head. A 9 mm CAR-4 lay on the rubber runner that covered the metal decking. It only had a little blood on the stock and receiver. Short and handy and fully automatic, it was even better suited for face-to-face interpersonal transactions than the SIG-Sauer. Always sensitive to such nuances, Ryan tucked away the SIG-Sauer where it would be handy on the off-chance the occasion for a little quiet murder presented itself, and picked up the carbine. He worked the charging handle. A cartridge spun away; he caught the yellow gleam of a fresh one going in. Golden.

With no time for a serious search he pulled a spare magazine from the pocket of the man he'd just chilled. Pulling a gren from his pocket, he moved toward the front of the wag. He had some high-speed house cleaning to do.

Chapter Thirty

The little two-stroke motor snarling and sputtering like an angry badger, the Yawl rocketed along the rails at a speed Krysty never imagined it could attain. Paul had his conductor's cap crammed far down on his head to keep his wind of passage from plucking it away. His goggles saved his eyes from being dried by the arid breeze, and from the impacts of grit and bugs that bounced off like hail. His ponytail streamed behind him like a brown pennant worked through with gray threads. He hadn't known that his creation could attain such speeds—not for sure.

Ryan Cawdor wasn't the only man in desperate pursuit of MAGOG that day.

Paul had lied to Krysty about his Yawl's capabilities, by omission at least. But he did so, he told himself, to keep faith with her, with his promise to aid her as best he could, rather than to break it. Her intelligence was as remarkable as her beauty, but he had known from the instant of their meeting that her intelligence was far from in total control of her being. She had said as much, often enough. She was bent utterly on her revenge. It tinged her judgment.

Had she known that Paul could really crank the engine, well past the fifteen miles per hour or so he ran it at on the flats, not to mention the ten or less that he pushed the Yawl up grades, she would have insisted that he wind the throttle as far it would go and dog it down. Which would, of course, have burned the engine out in a matter of miles, stranding them when wind, muscle and downgrades all failed them. The time they would have lost on the brutal climb out of the Plains toward Taos in her bed of high mountains alone would have lost them any time they had made up on the Plains themselves, and then some. MAGOG would have been long gone, across the sheer, thousand-foot deep Grandee gorge and away to Cali to the fabled Great Redoubt.

And at that point, he knew, far more than just Krysty's quest would be doomed.

He hadn't heard the arguments Krysty made to his kinfolk by the bonfire the night before. Beyond telling her sorrowful tale, she hadn't spoken of her motivations to him, considering them plain enough—saving the land from the tyranny of the General was for her a far secondary consideration, abstract at best, pallid and small beside her need to chill him and the train that obsessed her as cruelly as it did Paul. If in taking her revenge she could spare the continent the risk that the mad, capricious General *might* conquer it—and certainly spread death and misery on a scale unprecedented since the megacull itself, even if he failed—that was fine. Whatever the future might be like, she had no great desire to be part of it. Without Ryan she would just coast along, deal with life as it was presented to her.

But Paul understood perfectly well the threat the General and MAGOG posed. That was why the mad act of attempted murder he had been driven to by the ecstasy induced by his first vision of the great train in the steel hadn't been repeated. He was torn by his love for the wondrous locomotive on the one hand, and on the other his love of the freedom of the open roads and skies and most of all the rails—and his love for Krysty, inevitable as it was platonic.

But choosing to defy his adoration of MAGOG didn't mean it had ended. Nor even abated the least little bit. The vision of that perfect hurtling mass of metal drove him now, faster than he had ever been driven before.

He would burn out the little engine, already crying out in its torment in a voice that tore his heart. He would sacrifice his beloved Yawl. He would catch MAGOG.

He had no illusions about somehow aiding Ryan and Krysty. He hoped they succeeded, hoped—against hope and logic—they might somehow be united this side of the last train for the coast. But as he had said and proved time and again, he was no fighter. They would win or lose their hearts' desire by their extraordinary skill and will. If he tried to help, he'd only be in the way.

It was his own destiny that drew him through the bright morning as a giant magnet drew a tiny wisp of iron.

STARTLED FACES looked at Ryan. Hands reached for blasters. At least one alert sec man ducked beside the huge cylinder that dominated the center of the wag, to use its impenetrable metal mass as cover from which to shoot at the intruder.

Ryan chucked the gren he held ready in his hand and slammed the door again. So perfect was the wag's soundproofing that he heard nothing of the blast, only felt it as a rattle transmitted through the fabric of the train itself as he ducked back into the open hatchway of the car he'd cleared.

Some instinct made him shut the door. A heartbeat later he felt the slam of a gren exploding on the other side.

He yanked the door open, the CAR-4 in his right hand blasting. He saw a young face open in a look of total astonishment a handbreadth from his own, underlit by flickering muzzle flare in the dim passageway. The sec man wore no armor. A handful of the pointy copperjacket 9 mm slugs punched through him to lance into the chest and belly of the man behind and drop him as well.

Ryan had another gren in his left hand. He threw it over the heads of the two mortally wounded sec men as they fell, toward the flame-flowers unfolding toward him from the man behind the pop-up turret root. He ducked back as needlelike 5.56 mm bullets glanced off the metal doorframe and howled past, spinning like tiny circular saws.

He dropped the mag from the CAR and stuffed in the spare he'd scavvied. The gren cracked off. Screams sounded. He drew his SIG-Sauer with his left hand and whirled around the door.

No one stood in the passageway. Crossing his arms, he lunged through into the next carriage. As he passed the doorway, he squeezed each trigger once.

The shot coughed from the extended barrel of his SIG-Sauer, ricocheted off the steel bulkhead and fortunately missed him. The CAR's bullet hit a waiting sec man in the belly. Hearing the grunt of pain even as the noise of that shot echoed around him, he squeezed off a quick 3-round burst.

Blood sprayed the left side of his face.

A wounded man raised himself on the elbow of the arm that was trying to hold in his guts, aimed an M-9 Beretta at Ryan with the other. The one-eyed man thrust out his left hand and fired twice. A miss bounced screaming off the wall, then an eye exploded in a splash of aqueous humor. The man's head slammed against the bulkhead, leaving a red smear, then slumped.

He heard sounds from the other side of the turret root. Purposeful sounds, not the agony-maddened thrashings of a wounded man. Moving slowly, as quietly as possible, he slung the CAR, went to the gleaming steel cylinder and flattened his back against it. As he did so, he drew a gren from his pocket and prepped it. Then he leaned sideways and backhanded the gren, banking it off the bulkhead now to his right to the cylinder's far side.

At the same moment, a gren came rolling along the runner by his left boot.

He faced away from it and dived forward. The bomb cracked off at once. Had he tried to kick it back it would have torn his foot off. His gren went off, too.

The blast propagated up and out in an inverse cone, the direct force missing him. Tiny fragments of blast-shattered wire zinged through the air. Some bounced off the wall now behind him and struck him. As small as they were, they didn't hold momentum long; most were absorbed by the tail of his long heavy coat. A few stung the backs of his calves through his faded jeans.

Things were still clattering and creaking when he jumped to his feet. His right hand ripped his panga from its scabbard as he dashed clockwise around the turret root. He struck down to his right as he passed it.

His unseen opponent had displayed the same presence of mind and quick reflexes he had in diving beneath the destructive fan of Ryan's gren. He was a hair slower on the rise. The heavy panga struck him on the crown of the skull and split it open.

No sec men remained functional on this upper deck. One sat with his back against the bulkhead watching the blood pulsing out of the stub of his arm, which had been severed at midbiceps, as if he didn't find it particularly interesting.

It was working, Ryan thought. He wasn't exactly thinking his clearest. He was seasoned enough to recognize the fact.

All he really knew was that he had to find Krysty again, even if only to die in each other's arms. To do that he had to get to the train's head as quickly as possible. That was where he would find Krysty. Or people who knew where she was. And then he'd tear all the parts off or out of whoever he had to to find her.

But it would be triple stupe to wade straight through the heaviest opposition. Individually the train sec men he'd encountered so far hadn't shown him that much, except maybe for the blaster whose brainpan he'd let air into with his big panga. But in the bad old real world, he knew, it took one lucky bullet or unlucky ricochet and it didn't matter a spent casing how good you were. You were staring at the ceiling without seeing it.

He wiped the brains off the panga on the back of the dead man's camou blouse. He sheathed the machete and doubled back toward the rear of the carriage. Time to get off this level.

DOWNSTAIRS WAS BARRACKS. He blew in with the CAR-4 ready in one hand and a gren in the other. But the rows of bunks down either side of the passageway were empty.

Something somewhat like a plan hit him.

He began ripping OD blankets off the bunks, throwing them in heaps on the deck. He tore loose sheets and strewed them everywhere. For good measure he dumped a few thin mattresses. Then he pulled a scavvied butane lighter from his pocket and started setting everything on fire.

It wasn't much of a fire. He seriously doubted it was going to do any damage to the armored wag's structure. But there was a lot of it, and it made a lot of smoke.

Fire was hard to ignore.

He decided to share some with the next carriage forward.

It proved to be an infirmary. Several green smocked assistants looked up from unknowable chores with faces that were just big ovals of fearful surprise.

He waved the wadded-up flaming blanket he clutched in his left hand. "Fire! Fire!" he shouted. He had to struggle not to cough from the smoke pouring from the makeshift torch. "Everybody off the train! Fire!"

The med techies just stared at him. Steel hard and on a mission as he was, he wasn't quite up to slaughtering helpless healers unless they really pushed him to it. He wanted to trigger off a burst from the CAR-4 to get them headed in the right direction, but this car was armored, too. It would be triple stupe of him to chill himself with his own ricochet.

"What's the matter with you people?" he shouted. "The train's on fire!"

They still just gaped. He hurled the smoldering blanket at the nearest tech. She sidestepped.

Two things happened at once. A slight, small woman in a white jacket emerged from a little cubicle office at the left front of the compartment, and a sec man came rushing in the far door with an M-16 longblaster held at port-arms.

Ryan pushed the CAR out to arm's length and lit up the newcomer. The sec man screamed, dropped his black longblaster and held up his arms in a futile attempt to ward off the bullets that were tearing through his belly and chest. It just cost him holes in his arms.

The CAR ran dry. In the sudden echoing silence, the riddled sec man sank down the door with the light going out of his eyes as the blood drained from his body.

The healers began to scream and stampeded away from Ryan. One of them seized the woman in white, who stood blinking with an expression more of sadness than terror, by the arm and dragged her out of the carriage past the body. The other two healers yanked open a door to the outside and in blind panic hurled themselves right off the train.

Alarms started going off. About fucking time, Ryan thought.

Forty-five seconds later a gaggle of sec men thundered into the med wag waving longblasters. Finding the door still open and no one in the car, they charged ahead. Someone shouted *"Fire!"* and they all crowded toward the burning barracks car, coughing and stumbling and grabbing fire extinguishers from brackets on the wall.

A moment later Ryan stepped back into the open doorway to the outside. He had been clinging to the door itself like a baby opossum, with his panga in his teeth. Everybody was looking in the other direction. He sheathed the panga again, drew his handblaster and raced for the front of the giant rail wag.

THE GENERAL WAS STILL eating in his personal car when the alarms went off. His intel chief and Marc Helton, with his arm in a sling, were in the compartment with him.

"Now what?" the General demanded. "Hubertus, is it too much to ask for a man to be allowed to finish his breakfast in peace?"

The intel chief stepped to the intercom and spoke quickly to the command center. "Sensors report smoke in the infirmary car and the barracks carriage behind it. There are also confused reports about an intruder driving a motorcycle onto the train." He sniffed. "Those latter sound far-fetched to me. It's probably time to check the liquor stores and see if there's been another break-in."

"I'll check on it, General," the captain said, heading toward the rear of the car.

"That's my boy, Marc," the General called after him. "Always good to go."

Helton slid open the door and stepped into the sheltered gangway between cars.

As he let the door slide shut behind him, the door in front of him opened and a man stepped into the gently rocking passage.

Chapter Thirty-One

The man was a tall, wild, desperate figure. His face was lean and scarred beneath a half-mask of blood and a black eyepatch. His black shaggy hair reeked of smoke. A single eye blazed like a blue beacon from the relatively clean side of his face.

He raised a strange-looking handblaster to within an inch of the tip of Helton's nose and pulled the trigger.

Click.

"FIREBLAST," RYAN SAID without heat. Even though the fire he set had cleared a lot of obstacles out of his way, it hadn't been an easy journey. And he'd taken it at a dead run—no time to count rounds.

The young officer knocked away Ryan's empty SIG-Sauer with his good forearm and rammed a side-kick straight into Ryan's sternum. The one-eyed man flew back into the door, which had slid shut behind him.

The uniformed man bullrushed him. Ryan brought up a knee. Panther-quick, his assailant turned his hips and took the knee on the quadriceps. The impact still stopped him, lifted his body of the walkway shifting beneath their boots.

Ryan raised his right arm to shoulder height and slammed the elbow forward into the officer's face. As the man's head snapped back, Ryan followed with an overhand left. It was the officer's turn to reel back against a steel door.

Ryan struck at his head with the butt of the SIG-Sauer. His opponent blocked with his left forearm, tearing free of the sling. At the same time he drove a right uppercut into Ryan's solar plexus.

Air fled the one-eyed man's body in a rush. He bent over and was head-butted in the face. Blinking at the sparks that seemed to float in his vision, Ryan staggered back. His adversary lunged at him, trying to jam his left forearm into Ryan's trachea. Ryan got his chin down in time and grabbed the arm. Pressing him into the door behind him, the officer tried to punch him in the face with his right fist. Ryan caught his wrist with his left hand.

For a moment the men struggled in deadly silence. The officer was as tall as Ryan and had the same build. He was fresher than Ryan and years younger, which made up for some of the disadvantage of his injury—which clearly wasn't enough to render his left arm useless anyway.

But the officer's exertions weren't without cost. The camou cloth at the front of his left shoulder began to darken with a spreading stain.

Ryan quit trying to pull the arm away from his neck. He clamped his hand on the man's injured left shoulder and began to probe for a wound with a thumb like a steel talon.

He found what he sought, and dug.

The man's face paled and sweat began to stream from his hairline. "Bastard!" he gritted.

"Bastard back!" Ryan snarled. "Where's Krysty?"

The amber eyes widened. "Krysty Wroth?"

The door opened behind him. Hands grabbed him. Something cracked hard against the back of his skull, and white flame stabbed through his brain.

The world spun around him.

HE DIDN'T QUITE lose consciousness.

The young officer backed into the next car ahead of them. At least two sec men holding Ryan's arms behind him frog-marched him forward into what looked like a gaudyhouse parlor with a red carpet and dark-stained paneling on the walls.

A man in a uniform with a chestful of medals sat in a red plush-upholstered chair. Next to him stood a tall, thin, bloodless and hairless specimen.

"And you must be Ryan Cawdor," said the man in the chair. He had a harsh voice, well suited to the snap of command.

Ryan glared at him. "And you're the nuke-sucking crazie who calls himself the General. Where's Krysty?"

The General rose. "Sadly, she's unable to be with us to witness the resolution of this little melodrama. Marc, Marc, you disappoint me. You told me you killed this man."

The captain looked up from examining Ryan's SIG-Sauer with the built-in suppressor. His expression was calm and slightly haughty. He wasn't a man to lower himself to making excuses.

The General drew a Model 1911 .45 ACP handblaster from a holster at his waist. "So it looks as if I'm going to have set things right myself," he said.

He aimed the big blaster at the middle of Ryan's forehead.

AT LAST HE SAW HER, his silver dream, shining in the mountain sun.

His Yawl was shaking herself apart beneath him. Something had gotten loose and begun to clatter but hadn't made any perceptible difference in his headlong speed. His engine was starting to smoke.

Somebody on the train noticed him as well. A heavy machine gun opened up from the last car. There were tracer rounds mixed in with the regular loads. They threw red fire-balls at him that looked to be the size of baseballs, seeming to float lazily toward him, then suddenly rushing by with a thundercrack sound.

The shots were going wide overhead. The gunner didn't seem to know quite what to do and was spraying the land-scape instead of chopping the stream down into his target. Paul hunched lower in his lawn-chair-style seat. He wasn't afraid for himself, not really. He was now as Krysty had been on her quest preoccupied with the dread he might not reach his objective. It was all that mattered.

"Hold together, baby," he begged his machine. "Just a lit-tle while longer, that's all I'll ever ask of you again."

THE GENERAL'S ARM SWUNG. The big 1911 bucked in his hand.

Captain Marc Helton's eyes widened and he swayed. He looked down at himself.

There was a small, neat hole in the front of his camou blouse. He touched it with his fingers. The tips came away wet with red. He looked wonderingly at his commander.

"Captain Helton helped your woman and your friends es-cape last night," the General said, still pointing the blaster at his protégé. "I made some inquiries and discovered he'd been seen leaving his quarters not long before it had to take place. He'd already been showing signs of lacking the stomach for the real hard work we're about to begin."

Ryan had seen men shot or stabbed through the heart be-fore and not go down right away. Still he had to admire the captain's determination to stay on his feet. Even though it was a lost cause.

"Mercy is weakness in the world we're forced to live in," the General said.

Helton dropped to his knees.

"Weakness led, as it will, to betrayal. It hurts me to have to do this to you, Marc. But you can take this last thought with you—I would have done the same if you really were my son."

The captain slumped down, buttocks on calves, chin on chest. By some chance he was balanced so well that his torso stayed upright even without muscular tension to keep him that way.

"We'll tell your father you died after heroic single combat," the General told the corpse. "Which is only the truth, after all."

Hubertus sneered. He took a step forward, planted his boot in the center of the young captain's chest and pushed him onto his back.

Holstering his .45, his superior shook his head disapprovingly. "That was gratuitous, Hubertus. There was just no fucking call for that at all."

He turned to Ryan. "And as for you, Cawdor, you'll do just fine as a replacement for your woman, when it comes to telling us what we want to know about the mat-trans network. Even if I can't put you to the same use I was going to put her to. Although it is damned tempting to run you through the preliminaries, just on general principles."

The intercom spoke. "MAGOG Six, Command Center One. We have a situation, sir."

THE BLASTERWAG that brought up the rear of the train loomed above Paul like a cliff. He finished tying the little engine's throttle in the wide-open position and stood up.

The .50-caliber blaster was booming overhead. Paul had long since gotten under the umbrella of safety below where the big machine gun couldn't shoot. It didn't matter much for his Yawl. The little craft was shaking now as if suffering some kind of seizure. Its skinny tires began to bounce on the rails.

There were hand- and footholds welded to the end of the blasterwag. The Yawl raised toward a collision with the car. Paul walked the few steps to the front of the platform, holding his arms out for balance. He braced himself.

The Yawl struck the rear of MAGOG. Paul jumped, caught handholds, swung a dizzy moment above the fast-moving ground, then got his toes into the foothold.

He looked back. His Yawl was bouncing like a bucking Brahma bull. It got transverse to the tracks, flipped, cartwheeled down the embankment, its path angling away from the train.

"Goodbye, baby," Paul called. "I'm sorry."

He pressed his cheek against MAGOG. The armor plate was cool.

He couldn't hold on very long before his arm strength gave out, even though he was shielded from the buffeting wind of the rail wag's passage.

But he believed he wouldn't have to.

"Now, WHAT?" the General demanded irritably.

Apparently there was a voice-actuated pickup for the intercom, because the voice responded, "We're approaching the Grandee gorge rail bridge, sir."

The General flicked a glance at his wrist chron. "So? At least we're here on schedule."

"There's someone on the bridge, General."

"What? Now what?"

Hubertus moved to the table next to the General's chair, picked up a remote control and pressed a button. A panel slid up on the front bulkhead, revealing a large screen monitor.

It showed a single figure standing perhaps fifty yards out onto the bridge over the sheer-walled canyon. Ryan felt his whole body tingle.

"Increase magnification!" the General barked.

The image grew larger.

It was Krysty.

She had an AT-4 wag-chiller rocket launcher shouldered but not yet aimed at the onrushing train.

"That bitch!" The words seemed nearly to strangle the General. "Full speed ahead! Run her down! It'll take more than a shoulder-fired rocket to stop my train."

The guards who held Ryan's arms were watching in amazement and growing apprehension. They were apprehensive about the wrong thing.

With a powerful twist of his hips, Ryan yanked his left arm free. The guard on that side had let his grip go slacker than his buddy's. Ryan instantly reversed the rotation of his hips and came back with a savage knife-hand strike that collapsed the guard's windpipe.

Strangling on his own cartilage, the guard clutched his throat. The other guard leaped on Ryan's back. He wrapped his arms around the one-eyed man's head, clawing for his eye.

Ryan backed up hard against an oak-paneled wall, trying to dislodge the guard, who bit at the top of his head and began pummeling him with one hand.

Ryan staggered from the wall. He was punching back over his shoulder with one hand and trying to haul the man off with the other.

Hubertus appeared before him. The sides of the man's tunic bulged and worked as if some creature trapped inside with him was trying desperately to escape. Then a side seam parted and a greenish jointed crustacean-claw unfolded, tipped with a sting like a scorpion's tail. It lashed out at Ryan.

Ryan ducked and leaned forward. The sting sank into the sec man's trapezius muscle just behind his left shoulder.

The man almost blew out Ryan's eardrum with a bone-chilling shriek. Ryan threw him off, then dodged to his right to avoid a darting thrust as a second claw snapped as if spring-loaded from the intel chief's other side. The poison tip struck the wall and stuck momentarily in the paneling.

The injured guard was howling as if he were on fire, spin-ning around the room, grabbing at the place where the stinger had gone home. Already his neck and shoulder were swell-ing with great purple-green buboes as the hematotoxin in-jected by the sting made the blood cells in his veins literally explode. His wild gyrations took him right into the General and knocked the .45-caliber handblaster the commander had just drawn spinning from his hand.

Hubertus's glasses had fallen away. His eyes, rimmed in red and yellow, stood out on short fleshy stalks. The pupils were hooded slits in golden irises. The intel chief wrenched his claw free from the wood.

Ryan circled clockwise as he backed away from the mon-ster. Something bumped the back of his leg.

The stricken guard's screaming reached a crescendo as the whole left side of his neck ruptured. Blood already shot through with the black of corruption erupted and painted the low ceiling with arterial spray.

Ryan's hand reached reflexively behind him. Heat seared his skin.

He grabbed the chafing dish by one brass leg and hurled it at Hubertus. Liquid fire soaked the front of his tunic.

The cloth blazed up as if it had been drenched in gasoline. Hubertus screamed. The skin and flesh of his face began to melt.

The intel chief burned with an acrid chemical stink. Ryan wondered in a flash whether it was flesh over the weird carapace or some clever plastic mask. Hubertus turned and ran blazing to the outer door. He yanked it open and flung himself from the train.

The General hit Ryan on the blind side, slamming him into the wall. The wood veneer split where Ryan's head smashed into it. His vision wavered.

The General's weight bore him down to the luxuriant carpet. The man was twenty years older than he, but powerfully muscled and fit.

"I am so fucking sick of you and all your fucking friends." Every time he said "fucking" he hit Ryan with a brass lamp. Blood obscured Ryan's eye. He grappled blindly for the hand that held the lamp.

"General," the intercom yelped. "The track!"

The General paused with the lamp cocked and ready for another whack. "What about the fucking track?"

"It's broken!"

Chapter Thirty-Two

With a convulsive shake of his head, Ryan cleared blood from his good eye and joined the General in staring at the big monitor.

The view field had shifted to show the bridge. At this magnification it was glaringly obvious how the tracks had been pried up and bent to run to the right of the bridge.

Straight off the sheer cliff above a thousand-foot drop.

The sight was enough to distract anyone. Even the General. And then the car lurched forward as the driver hit the brakes in a frenzied futile attempt to slow the monster engine.

Ryan dug his heels into the carpet and gave a mighty upward pelvic thrust. It didn't dislodge the older man, but it did get him off balance and into position for Ryan to slam his right boot into the side of his head and knock him sprawling.

Ryan was up on all fours and scrambling wildly for the open door. The howl of the wind was like mocking laughter. Lying a few feet aside on the carpet was his SIG-Sauer. He veered aside just far enough to snag it in passing and then followed Hubertus out into the morning.

The General laboriously picked himself up. Locked steel wheels screamed like banshees. Krysty was back in frame on the monitor. She wasn't even pretending to aim the wag-chiller anymore. It had only been a prop, an added distraction to keep MAGOG's crew from noticing the diversion of the track before it was too late. Although by the time the train had come around the final bend before the gorge, given its enormous mass and length, it had almost certainly been too late already.

As the General stood, the tall redheaded woman looked up straight into the camera. It was as if their eyes met.

He came to attention and snapped off a perfect salute. And held it as MAGOG rushed off the edge and into space at forty miles an hour.

THE BRAKES WERE SINGING their last useless song. People were dropping off the train like ripe fruit in an orchard. Nonetheless, Krysty's companions, including their tech-nomad helpers, stood up from the rocks where they had been hiding near the track to watch. It wasn't the sort of thing you *couldn't* watch.

The people baling off of MAGOG had other things on their minds anyway.

"There was good tech on that train," Robear said. He had piloted one of the parasails.

"There were good people on that train," Mildred added.

"Mebbe," Jak said. "But helping do bad things."

"Gone's gone," Corwin said. "I make it a habit never to miss what I never had, myself."

J.B. removed his fedora. He couldn't have said why.

"One thing I believe we may safely say, my friends," Doc announced. "*That* is something one does not see every day."

ON THE FAR SIDE of the train Ryan made himself go limp as he hit. He bounced, rolled, bounced, rolled. He felt an odd sense of detachment, as if this were happening to somebody else. He certainly had no control of the situation, or any hope of gaining any. He just went along and hoped he wouldn't hit anything too big.

And that he'd stop rolling shy of the canyon.

AS THE ENGINE LAUNCHED itself on its final journey, Krysty began walking forward, heedless of the proximity of the linear avalanche of steel. Her safety didn't matter now.

She wasn't exultant. She felt a certain sense of completion. Mostly she felt a floating numbness, as if her feet had gone to sleep and could no more sense the track-bed beneath them.

The train was a waterfall of metal and noise. The noise of a mighty crash floated up from below, distance-softened but still loud, as the engine struck the valley floor. With a squealing, crunching, rending cacophony the train began to telescope and bend as more and more cars piled on.

She approached the end of the bridge. Still the cars swept by to their doom. People were flinging themselves off, heedless of the speed.

The last car passed. She saw a figure clinging to the rear. A familiar figure.

Waving.

Grinning like a boy with a brand-new toy, Paul the Rail Ghost shouted something to her. She would live out the rest of her life believing she had somehow heard him say, "Lookit, Krysty! I really did catch the last train for the coast!"

And then they were dropping away, he and his beloved behemoth. With the roar of its motion gone, the crunching and grinding from the bottom of the gorge sounded almost subdued.

Another figure was rolling along the ground toward her. A man who had possessed enough sense to relax and just let himself roll, rather than stiffen his limbs so they'd shatter on impact. Her friends were approaching from her left, calling out to her.

The man stopped almost at the toes of her boots. A blue eye looked up at her.

A single blue eye.

"Morning, lover," Ryan said to her. "Nice day for a little spin."

She sagged. The strength went out of her knees. She folded down beside him. He sat up and caught her.

Their lips joined in a kiss that lasted a lifetime.

Standing nearby beside his gaping friends, Jak nodded in quiet satisfaction.

"See?" he said. "Said Ryan not dead!"

FULL
BLAST

The President's fail-safe option when America is threatened is an elite group of cybernetics specialists and battle-hardened commandos who operate off the books and under governmental radar. This ultra-clandestine force called Stony Man has defeated terror on many fronts. Now, they're dealing with an escalating crisis from outside the country—and a far bigger one from within....

From within the ranks of America's protectors and defenders, a conspiracy to overthrow the U.S. government appears unstoppable.

STONY MAN®

*Available
June 2005
at your favorite
retailer!*